Guardians of the Gate

Guardians of the Gate

VINCENT N. PARRILLO

iUniverse, Inc.
Bloomington

Guardians of the Gate

iUniverse books may be ordered through booksellers or by contacting:

iUniverse
1663 Liberty Drive
Bloomington, IN 47403
www.iuniverse.com
1-800-Authors (1-800-288-4677)

ISBN: 978-1-4620-2931-0 (sc)
ISBN: 978-1-4620-2930-3 (hc)
ISBN: 978-1-4620-2929-7 (e)

Library of Congress Control Number: 2011910174

Printed in the United States of America

iUniverse rev. date: 07/18/2011

April 1893

Slow, steady rain fell, dimpling the otherwise smooth, dark river waters. Visibility was so poor that the pilot of the motor launch strained his eyes through the rain and mist to detect his still-unseen island destination.

Standing next to the pilot, a stocky, scholarly-looking man—with gray hair and a stubby gray brush mustache—also peered intently ahead. Unfamiliar with his surroundings, he even more eagerly searched ahead for some sign of safe harbor. Though no wind stirred, he shivered in the dampness. Ignoring his own discomfort, forty-six-year-old Joseph Henry Senner, a German Austrian by birth, kept gazing ahead, searching for a glimpse of anything but the damp curtain before him.

The pilot confidently steered his boat to where he knew the island would be. He knew every inch of this river in all of its manifestations. To him, it was a liquid mirror, always revealing nature's moods. Its blue waters reflected the brightness of sunny days, giving a rich border to the adjoining land, while its dark waters suggested the somber mood of an overcast sky. Even blacker were its waters on a moonless night. When moonlight danced upon its surface, however, the shimmering beauty was a perfect companion to the romantic orb above. Today, though, under a cheerless, early morning sky, the river suggested a dismal, dreary world.

He remembered other times when turbulent spring storms thrashed, forcing soil into the swollen streams and tributaries emptying into the river, making its muddied and agitated waters flow more quickly. Severe winters brought ice floes and a ragged appearance to the river, making crossings hazardous, if not impossible. Winds would occasionally churn the waters, creating whitecaps that challenged any navigator venturing forth. Mostly though, as today, the river was calm and gently flowed to the waiting sea.

He knew that once, long before he was born, the waters of this river harbor teemed with salmon, mullet, and a variety of other fish. Large beds of oysters, clams, and mussels abounded just a few yards away from the small river islands. The shoreline then contained only marshland, woodlands, and small rocky cliffs. Slightly upstream on the western shore, magnificent palisades arose, their cliffs stretching forty miles northward along the riverbank.

Except for the palisades, all was now gone. The encroachment of civilization had eliminated most of nature's abundance. Landfill development altered the shoreline. Raw-sewage dumping polluted the water, making it unfit for most marine life. Although enshrouded today in mist and rain, the shoreline was now dotted with buildings, warehouses, piers, and docks, with only an occasional tree as an inadequate reminder of what once was a common sight.

His silent reverie ended because at last, just as he knew he would, he had piloted the boat close enough to the island to reveal vague building shapes, which became more distinct with each passing second.

"Here we come, sir," he said, satisfied with the accuracy of his approach.

"*Ja*, I zee," replied his passenger in relief, even though the buildings appeared somber and uninviting.

One large building loomed prominently among the island's structures. Although it was only two stories high, its four gables thrust the building upward yet another story, creating a cross-shaped cathedral ceiling on the second level. On each side of the two roof arches, standing at midpoint along the length of the building, stood small square towers, their sharp-peaked, four-sided roofs extending above the main roof of the building. At each corner of the building itself, other picturesque towers—twice the height and size of the middle towers—rose majestically.

On a sunny day, the rows of windows of this large building gleamed. Today they were dark, offering their solemn contribution to the dreary harbor scene. Even so, the building—built of Georgia pine and covered with a thin coating of galvanized iron, topped with a blue slate roof—was an impressive sight. Its elegance suggested a Victorian seaside resort, but no vacationer had ever booked a reservation here.

After partially circling the island, the pilot steered the motor launch into the channel to the landing dock, and Joseph could see people moving. Although the damp morning chill

Ellis Island main building, 1893–97

3

continued its onslaught, it could not dash his spirits. Behind his gold-rimmed spectacles, Joseph's blue eyes excitedly watched the scene unfolding before him, his face reflecting his anticipation of stepping onto his island domain as the new commissioner of immigration for the Port of New York.

His arrival was expected, and from the entrance of the main building, twenty-nine-year-old Ed McSweeney intently watched the approach of the motor launch. Hands stuffed into his overcoat pockets, his black hair complemented his dark clothes and derby. Adjusting the round, wire-framed glasses resting on his nose, he waited under the shed roof running the length and width of the building. As the launch reached the landing dock, this Irish American—one of many working at the immigrant station—opened his umbrella and walked into the mist and drizzle to greet his new boss.

"Welcome to Ellis Island, Dr. Senner. I'm Assistant Commissioner Edward McSweeney. I'm delighted to meet you."

As McSweeney spoke, Joseph searched the man's eyes for any clue about him and noted that McSweeney's eyes looked away a bit too quickly.

"Tank you, Mr. McSveeney. Dis zertainly is not day to be on boat, is it?"

McSweeney maintained his outward composure as he inwardly cringed at the heavy German accent that he would now have to endure. With a pleasantry that belied his thoughts, he replied, "No, it's not, sir. You'll find it much more pleasant inside though, I'm sure of that."

Under their umbrellas the two men strode up to the entrance of the main building, Ed's taller, lanky frame contrasting with Joseph's thickset body. When he closed his umbrella and removed his derby, Ed's slightly receding hairline also set him apart from Joseph and his full head of hair.

"This level contains the baggage rooms," Ed explained. "The immigrants check their belongings here and then go

4

upstairs to the Registry Hall. Our offices are upstairs also, so if you'll follow me?"

Joseph nodded and followed his assistant up the broad stairway and into the large hall.

"Impressive, isn't it?" smiled Ed, noticing the look on his superior's face. "Most of the immigrants come here from small towns and villages. They're overwhelmed by this grandeur."

Joseph nodded. The impact of this grand hall was striking. The hall was virtually the full size of the building itself. Its vastness was enhanced by the cathedral ceiling and the light—even on this overcast day—that filtered through the tall, eave-high windows. A wide-planked pine floor, resembling a sailing ship's deck so familiar to the arriving ocean voyagers, set off the woodwork. The place even seemed to have the scent of a ship. Ten parallel aisles, framed by railings, marked where the immigrants began the screening process. Potted plants, American flags, and red, white, and blue bunting festooned the hall.

As Senner gazed about the hall, Ed studied his face, trying to assess his new boss. Ed was already scheming. Senner was as much a greenhorn as the new immigrants and knew nothing of how Ellis Island functioned. If he could keep Senner a figurehead, or busy in public relations activities, the real power in the day-to-day operations would still be his.

"Your office is in this corner, Dr. Senner. Let me show you."

With false cheerfulness, Ed guided the commissioner to his office. The room was pleasant but not richly appointed, with a large mahogany desk and chair, two other wingback upholstered chairs in front of the desk, a large bookcase behind it, and an empty table off to the side. On better days the windows offered a delightful view of the river and New York City skyline.

"Cigar, sir?"

"*Ja*, tank you," said Joseph, taking a cigar from the humidor Ed held before him, who then lit both their cigars.

After savoring the first puff of the mild, aromatic tobacco, Joseph said in his heavy accent, "I must say dot I am very much impressed by dis building."

"It's handsome, indeed it is. And, think about it, it was designed by the lowest-bid architect!"

Joseph chuckled. He drew on his cigar again, simultaneously studying his assistant. McSweeney was certainly a likeable fellow, but Joseph was wary, wondering if McSweeney was trustworthy, someone on whom he could depend. The man's shifting eyes troubled him.

"Did you know this building is almost as large as the original size of this island?"

"No. Really?"

"It's a fact. The original island was little more than a mud flat. Back in the seventeenth century, there were large oyster beds just offshore, and the Dutch settlers came here on Sundays and had oyster roasts. A century later the English executed pirates here, leaving their bodies hanging from the gibbet as a warning to other would-be pirates. To make this place suitable for an immigrant station, the government spent half a million dollars. They doubled the area with landfill, dredged a channel, and constructed new docks so that the ferryboats could approach and unload passengers. Of course, they also built this and the other buildings on the island."

"You know many tings about dis place, Mr. McSveeney."

"I like to know the history of a place. The shadows of the past often linger in the present."

"It zounds like you are philosopher too."

"Ha! Perhaps so. You know, the reason we're on this island is that no one wanted the immigration station elsewhere. Joseph Pulitzer led a fierce campaign against us locating at Bedloe's Island where that French statue is."

"*Ja*, I know, Mr. McSveeney. You forget dot I am journalist also."

"Yes, of course. As you know then, Pulitzer was very effective. He had raised the money for the statue's pedestal, so he succeeded in getting its sculptor, Bartholdi, to speak against our using that site for the processing center. Then the army opposed our using Governor's Island. So, here we are, an unwanted immigrant station at a place no one else wanted, admitting foreigners many Americans don't want here in the first place. It's a thankless job."

"Den vy do you do it, Mr. McSveeney?"

Startled by the question, Ed looked back at Senner, his mind racing to find the motive for the question; was it simply asked out of curiosity or was there more to it?

"Why—I suppose—I guess I like the challenge and the opportunity."

"Opportunity?"

"Yes, opportunity," replied Ed, now recovering from his initial loss for words. "There's an opportunity here to help people get a new start in life. This place is their first experience in America. It shouldn't be unpleasant, and I think I can help make the necessary processing a less stressful one."

"Noble zentiments, Mr. McSveeney. I agree mit dem. Now, may I zee de rest of de facilities?"

"Of course," replied Ed, smiling, as he opened the office door, gesturing to Dr. Senner. Instead Joseph held out his arm to indicate Ed should leave first. Together the two men visited the hospital, doctors' quarters, bath house, laundry, electric power plant, kitchens, and dining hall.

"These are dormitories for detained immigrants," Ed next pointed out, showing some old brick-and-stone buildings.

"Dey are much older dan de other buildings. Vaht ver dey before?"

"This island was once Fort Gibson, set up just before the

7

War of 1812 to defend the harbor against the British. The fort had a battery of twenty cannons aimed in a circular pattern out across the harbor, but they never fired a shot. The British never sailed in here. The army dismantled the fort in the 1860s, leaving these buildings. We've remodeled them inside."

Joseph found the dormitories clean and neat. Their wooden floors, glass windows, and slate roofs were no doubt much better than the living quarters that many of the immigrants had left behind in their old countries. Outside again, Ed brought Joseph to some other old buildings, constructed of even heavier masonry.

"These were magazines for the navy's munitions," he explained. "The navy once shared the island with the army, keeping just a small squad on guard here. They're our buildings now. Because they're the most secure, we use them to store all our records. We even have the records from Castle Garden, the old immigration station that New York ran for decades over at the Battery."

"De records may be secure, but are de people?"

"What do you mean?"

"Mein God, man! Most of dese buildings are made of vood! If un fire comes, dere vood be no stopping it! Vere is de firefighting equipment? How vood ve fight fire here?"

"I'm—I'm not certain of that."

"You mean dere is no plan for evacuation? No vater pumps? No alarms or fire hoses?"

"N-no."

Shaking his head, Joseph continued. "I cannot believe dot no vun realized de enormous fire dangers! Just tink of de possible property damage und—und loss of life!"

Joseph did not see the brief, resentful frown before Ed turned around and, in an outwardly calm and deferential manner, replied, "You're right, sir. We need to take precautions. We do have the fireboats though. They can come to our assistance if needed."

Joseph instinctively sensed the real impact of his words on McSweeney. He liked that effect, for he wanted to assert his power early over his more experienced assistant. With his authoritarian leadership style, he preferred to maintain efficiency through intimidation. Besides, he felt keenly about what he was saying.

"Dey vill not be of much help if de fire is on un side of de island avay from de dredged channel. My boat had to circle half de island to approach de dock. De vater all around de rest of de island is too shallow for de fireboats to get close to shore."

"That's true, sir."

"Someting vill have to be done about dis und quickly. I vill make my recommendations to de Treasury Department."

Returning by boat to the Battery at the end of his first day, Joseph cast a worried look back at his new realm. Unlike the morning, this time the shiver that coursed through him betrayed his mood. His mind kept returning to the horrible image of flames shooting out through one of the buildings as screams pierced the air.

That day he began an involuntary ritual he would repeat each evening as his boat left Ellis Island. He looked back at the buildings, mentally bidding them farewell, for he fully expected to find them in ashes the next day.

*   *   *

A few hours later, in an uptown brownstone, Margaret Stafford sat on the bed, coughing slightly, and watching her husband lather the soap in his shaving mug onto the soft-bristled brush. Then he applied it to his face, repeating the process several times until his day's beard was covered with the white lather. Next, he sharpened the unfolded straight razor against the leather strop and began to shave.

She never tired of watching him. It didn't matter what he was doing. Even an everyday ritual like shaving fascinated her. Sometimes when he lay asleep beside her, she would prop her head on one hand and contently gaze at his handsome face.

Matt's good looks turned many a woman's head, and she delighted in that. His hazel eyes, more green than brown, had an intensity that riveted your attention. He had thick and slightly wavy dark brown hair. In an age when most men were shorter, his well-proportioned, six-foot frame only added to his physical appeal.

She watched him place the razor above his lips and, with short, swift strokes, cut away the hair stubbles. He didn't follow the fashion and have a mustache. Although that was his own preference, his wife's telling him that he looked so much better without one reinforced his inclination.

On his last stroke of the razor by his right ear, Matt's peripheral vision caught Margaret watching him. Only partly dressed, her long brunette hair seemed to flow and lay nestled on her ivory-colored chemise. Her breasts moved slightly to the rhythm of her breathing. Her delicate features, creamy flesh, and partly opened mouth gave her an enticing, seductive appearance.

"Have you been watching me the whole time?"

"Of course."

Smiling, he fully turned toward her as he wiped his face with the towel. "Did you like what you saw?"

"I always do, my darling."

Matt came to her, pulled her to her feet, kissed her lips, and embraced her.

"That's good, because I certainly like what I see."

"Matt, would you mind terribly if we didn't go out tonight?"

Surprised, he looked at her. She was not a very passionate woman, so he knew their fleeting embrace probably had not stirred her to thoughts about a different kind of evening. Yet she so relished going out that her question was highly irregular.

"Peg, are you feeling all right?'

"I'm just tired, that's all. Maybe this darn cold I've had has just worn me out."

Matt felt her forehead. "You've no fever, but that cough is hanging on for a long time. Let me get my stethoscope."

"Oh, Matt, I'm fine, really."

"Hush, you," he said, returning with the instrument. He listened for a few moments, ordered deep breaths, and moved the chest piece several times.

"Well, darling, you've got healthy lungs, but I've known that for a long time," he said with a smile, enjoying his double entendre.

His wife's scent and cleavage inspired him. He lowered her chemise to expose her breasts and caressed them with both of his hands, gently squeezing them and rubbing the side tips of his index fingers against her nipples. Moving his hands from her breasts to both sides of her face, he kissed her lips and held her again. He could feel his desire growing.

Peg enjoyed his touch but felt no similar yearnings.

"I told you. I'm fine. Just a little fatigued, that's all. I'm sure I'll feel better after I lie down for a while."

She slowly pulled away from him a little, smiled faintly, and readjusted the chemise to cover her breasts. Peg's health, always fragile, concerned Matt, and he accepted her need to conserve her strength. Compassion replaced his fading passion.

"All right, Peg. You get some rest. Now that we have a telephone, I'll call the Jacobsens to tell them that we're not coming."

"Don't just say I'm too tired to go, Matt."

"Don't worry, Peg. I know what to say."

May 1893

Commissioner Senner took his customary morning stroll through the Registry Hall. He noted the bright red fire buckets strategically placed throughout the building. Soon the sprinklers would be installed in the main building. Installation of the hydrants was underway, as was the placement of fire hoses and water pumps in crucial locations.

As an added precaution, he had instructed that the ferryboat docked overnight at Ellis Island keep its boiler going in instant readiness for rescue operations, if needed. He also designed an evacuation plan and required all island personnel to learn their responsibilities in case of fire. Further, he intended to install an electric alarm system connecting the main building with the boat.

Satisfied with the progress thus far in fire protection, Joseph studied the lines of immigrants and the smoothness of operations at each of the processing stations. He stopped by the registry desk of thirty-nine-year-old John Mueller. The man had a warm, effusive personality that eased the immigrants' anxieties, an excellent quality to have at Ellis Island. Many arriving immigrants, fleeing brutal repression in their homelands, feared those in authority. John, however, put them at ease with his charm, talkative nature, and compliments. He kept a box of rag dolls and spinning tops by his desk, freely giving them away at his own expense to each child he encountered. Joseph saw how he effectively made the processing such a positive experience for the immigrants.

"That's a beautiful baby you have," John said in German to the nervous young couple before him.

"Thank you, sir."

"I see here that she is called Gretchen."

"Yes, sir."

"Well, she looks as beautiful as her mother."

"Thank you, sir," beamed the man as his wife sheepishly smiled.

"We have a few questions to ask you before admitting you. They're nothing to worry about, just information we need for our records. It will only take a few minutes, and you'll be on your way. All right, sir?"

"Yes, yes, of course," answered the man, relieved.

Joseph nodded his head approvingly and moved on.

Watching from behind a nearby column, Ed glared as he watched Senner. A school dropout, Ed had worked in a shoe factory, and at age twenty-one became president of the Lasters' Progressive Union that he helped found two years earlier. Like Senner, he was the beneficiary of a presidential appointment to Ellis Island, a reward for energizing labor support for Cleveland's successful election.

Previously, as an inspector, Ed had been able to work well with Gen. James R. O'Beirne, his own predecessor. In typical military fashion, O'Beirne had delegated many responsibilities to Ed. Effectively in control, Ed enjoyed his power base and its potential to fill his pockets with additional income under the table. Now O'Beirne and his boss, Col. John B. Weber, were gone, and Ed had no desire to yield the power and influence he had gained.

Senner's authoritarianism and bombastic personality grated on him, as did the man's accent. Senner was a hands-on administrator and had sharply curtailed Ed's role, and he did not appreciate his relegation to a more subservient position. So Ed grew more resentful daily.

He waited until the commissioner reached the end of the Registry Hall. When Senner stood at the far side of the row of ten desks, Ed approached him.

"How does everything look today, Commissioner?"

"Hello, Mr. McSveeney. Everyting is going vell. I tink de new system ve have implemented is vorking out."

"It seems so, sir. You're to be complimented on the new procedures."

Flattered, Joseph grinned his appreciation. "Tank you, Mr. McSveeney."

Before Senner's appointment, the inspection of immigrants had simply been census taking and identifying nationality. Now tighter legal controls were in place, with mandated inspection restrictions to keep out "undesirables."

Senner had created procedures to meet the new government screening specifications. He still had the immigrants check their baggage on the first level and walk upstairs. At that point the medical examination began. If they cleared their health inspection, the immigrants moved in lines to the other side of the building for their legal inspections. Upon clearance, they were issued landing cards. Then they went downstairs to reclaim their baggage and to go by boat to New York or New Jersey.

Glancing at his assistant, Joseph decided the timing was right for a conversation.

"Mr. McSveeney, yesterday I spent zum time looking at last year's immigration records. I zee dot de very first immigrant to arrive here vas of your nationality."

Oh, yes, sir," said Ed, smiling. "She was Annie Moore, a fifteen-year-old from County Cork. You should have seen her.

She was a rosy-cheeked lass traveling with her two brothers to join their parents here in New York, parents they had not seen in several years. Their ship had a difficult crossing, and they had been very seasick. Even so, when the barge crew lowered the gangplank, this lovely young girl hurried down first."

"You zaw her?"

"Yes, sir, General O'Beirne escorted her inside to that registry desk over there, the first one. As an inspector back then, I asked her some identification questions, nothing as detailed as now. A brief ceremony followed, and Colonel Weber gave her a ten-dollar gold coin as a special memento, more money than the lass had ever seen. They asked her to say something. This young country colleen, bewildered by all that was happening and nervous in front of a crowd of dignitaries and reporters, spoke to us, her voice choked with emotion. All she said was a few sentences about the gold coin, and that she would keep it forever as a reminder of the day, and how thankful she was to us all and to this country."

His eyes misting, Ed's emotions were apparent. "She touched me deeply, Dr. Senner. Seeing that sweet colleen and hearing her lilting Irish brogue, it was then that I realized that I was part of something special. I'm one of the guardians of this gateway to opportunity. Annie Moore spoke for all who have since passed through this hall or have yet to come. I felt something stir within my heart that day. I feel it now. There's a great satisfaction in being a part of this place."

"Dot is quite a story, Mr. McSveeney," commented Joseph, genuinely touched. "I like dot expression you used, de 'gateway to opportunity.' Dot is vaht dis place is, is it not?"

"I like to think so," replied Ed, smiling yet aware of the wetness in his eyes.

"It zounds like a moment I vood have treasured myself. Nowadays, dough, ve seem to be getting less Irish coming here and more from de other parts of Europe."

"That's true, sir. It used to be different. More than three million Irish have come here since the potato famine in the 1840s. More than four million Germans too."

"You do know your facts, Mr. McSveeney."

"As I said, Commissioner, I like to know the history of a place, but you're right. The tide is changing. This year we're getting so many more from southern and eastern Europe. How different they are! Their clothes are strange. They're darker and dirtier. And did you ever get close enough to smell some of them? I tell you, once is enough! I really don't know how they're going to fit in."

"Neither do I, Mr. McSveeney. Perhaps dey vill not und den go back."

"I hope you're right, sir. Otherwise the likes of you and me will one day be outnumbered by the likes of them. May I never live to see that day!"

"Vell, let us not get too gloomy, Mr. McSveeney. Dere are many fine Irish and Germans to help de other Americans keep dis country going."

"Right you are, sir," replied his assistant as he walked away smiling.

*   *   *

The work day proceeded uneventfully at Ellis Island and at most other places throughout New York City. At Presbyterian Hospital, it also turned out to be a fairly routine day, although Matt's return home had been delayed by an emergency appendectomy.

His unexpected task completed, Matt washed and dried his hands, rolled down and buttoned his shirtsleeves. Putting on his jacket and hat, he hurried outside and hailed a hansom cab.

Rushing into his brownstone home, he called out, "Peg, I'm home."

"In here, Matt," she replied from the bedroom. As he

entered, he saw her seated before the mirror of the vanity table. As she put on an earring, she said, "I was afraid you wouldn't get here in time. You've got to hurry and change clothes. We've less than a half hour to get there."

"I know, but as I told you on the telephone, no one else was available for the surgery."

"I understand, Matt. Just hurry."

She watched in the mirror as Matt put away his medical bag. He had been her childhood sweetheart back in Massachusetts, where their parents had known one another. Four years ago they had married in their hometown Lutheran church after he graduated from college. Then came medical school and Matt's internship. They had been challenging years, but the only real hardship had been her miscarriage. Her tubal pregnancy had nearly cost Peg her life.

Those terrible days were behind them. They were now living a happy, promising life in New York City where Matt had accepted an offer to join the staff at Presbyterian Hospital. Not only was he doing well professionally, but their social life also thrived. Although they were certainly not in the top tier among the city's elite, Matt's background, education, and career gained them entry into an enviable social circle, one that sometimes intermingled with the so-called "first families" at larger social gatherings. He was, after all, a surgeon at the hospital of choice for many affluent families—families who felt that personally knowing a skilled surgeon might be a valuable connection for them one day.

The city teemed with activities with all its theaters, concerts, lectures, shops, museums, and restaurants. Their widening network of friends and acquaintances brought them numerous invitations to garden and dinner parties, other formal affairs, high teas, beefsteak dinners, and private gatherings. In fact, they often had more invitations than they could accept. Although he was less enthusiastic about it, Matt also liked their frequent excursions into the New York social scene. So, when the mirror revealed an unhappy look on his face, she looked at him questionably.

Matt paused for a moment and looked at Peg before speaking. "Couldn't we just skip tonight?"

"Don't be silly, Matt. The spring gala only comes once a year. Everyone who is anyone will be there."

"Then they will hardly miss us."

"Matt!" she said in astonishment.

He moved behind her, put his hands on her shoulders and his cheek alongside hers, and asked softly, "How about a quiet, romantic evening at home? Just the two of us nestled all cozy by the fire."

She looked at him in the mirror.

"Matt, tell me you're joking. This is an important occasion."

Matt wasn't joking. He really wanted to stay home. Lately he found their whirlwind social calendar tiresome, especially since he was working such long hours. He missed their tender, intimate moments, now few and far between. He tried to tell her, sitting beside her on the small bench, his back to the vanity table and mirror.

"Sometimes I just think we're so busy doing things and going places that we don't have time for each other."

"Why, Matt, we do everything together," Peg answered, not understanding. "We go to a lot of places, and we share the good times together."

"Yes, but we're not alone much, except to dress, eat, undress, and sleep."

He placed his hand on her upper arm, slowly moving it upward to the side of her face. Matt was a person often given to touching. Of course, his dexterous hands served him well in performing surgery, but he also enjoyed experiencing the sense of touch and did so frequently. Whenever he kissed Peg, even lightly, such as in saying hello or goodbye, he liked to touch the side of her face—temple, cheekbone and cheek, either all at once or tracing his fingers downward and holding them on her cheek for the length of the kiss.

Stroking her hair, he continued, "I want other times when just the two of us are together. We don't even make love very often."

"Oh, Matt, now that is unfair," she said, taking his hand in hers. "I'm sure most married couples ease off on that after a few years. And you know that I've been sick off and on. Come on now, hurry up, and get dressed. I promise you we'll nestle by the fire another night. And tonight we'll make love when we get back."

"I'll hold you to that," he replied, hopefully.

Matt opened his armoire to pick out his clothes for the evening. As he picked out his formal attire, he glanced at his other suits, hung according to when last worn, as were his shirts and ties. Shoes, always shined the night before, presented no delay in getting ready. His hair, regularly cut every three weeks, further ensured a good first impression from top to bottom.

Their evening out was very enjoyable, even Matt admitted. The night's dancing and merriment exhausted Peg, however, and their lovemaking did not happen.

A few nights later, after a wearying day at the hospital that included two operations, he was welcomed home by Peg, wearing only a robe. His.

"It's such a damp evening," she said, handing him a glass of champagne. "Come in by the fire."

Matt took off his tie and jacket and followed her. Standing in front of the fire and facing him, with the dancing flames from the crackling fire sending rhythms of light throughout the darkened room, she said in a sultry voice, "I suppose you would like your robe back."

With that, she undid the robe, removed it, and held it out to him with her left hand, the flickering glow from the fire behind her warmly illuminating her naked body. Matt could not remember a more sensuous moment. He put down the glass and embraced her, his hands roaming up and down her back. Peg dropped the robe and held him. Removing herself from his embrace, she lay down the floor.

"Aren't you rather overdressed?"

Matt swiftly stripped and lay between her opened legs, kissing and caressing her once again.

Within moments, Peg said, "Matt, I want you inside me."

Eagerly, he granted her request. The wonderful physical sensations that followed, combined with the seductive buildup and long interval since they were last intimate, had their effect. It was over much too quickly. Peg had a small orgasm that immediately triggered his. They lay quietly in each other's arms for a minute or two before Peg got up and put on her own nearby robe.

"Where are you going?"

"Your dinner is almost ready, Matt. Stay here and relax. I'll call you in a few minutes."

Matt lay there, experiencing mixed feelings. He was delighted by what had happened. At the same time, however, he did not feel fully satisfied.

April 1894

"Good morning, Mr. McSweeney."

Walking into the Registry Hall, Ed turned and saw the beaming face of registry clerk John Mueller.

One of Senner's privileged staff of German Americans, Mueller had emerged as a particular favorite of the commissioner, who often praised the clerk's competency and attitude. Ed also thought the man's job performance was exemplary and wished the rest of the staff were like him. If so, then perhaps the newspapers would stop their frequent accusations that island employees were exploiting the immigrants.

Ed himself profited in free travel passes from railroad and steamship companies and in kickbacks from the island concessionaires. However, he did not exploit the immigrants as some of his staff apparently did. It was one thing to profit from commercial interests, but he drew the line at taking advantage of the helpless. If he found such predators, Ed publicly vowed, he would rid the island of them.

"The top of the morning to you, John," he replied, "and how are you on this fine day?"

"I'm quite content, but I doubt the commissioner will be when he learns of this newspaper exposé about him."

"What's it say?"

"First of all, did you know he was Jewish?"

"Really?" McSweeney replied, shocked at this news. He now knew another reason to dislike Senner.

"Yeah. He changed his name when he came here after deserting his wife and squandering his entire fortune on some wild speculation over in Germany."

"You don't say?"

Mueller nodded, saying, "I wonder how the commissioner will react to this?"

"Mad as a hornet, you can be sure of that. It's certainly news he wanted to keep hidden. Can I borrow that paper?"

"I thought you might want a copy. Bought one for ya. Keep it."

"Thank you, John. I do appreciate your kindness."

Whistling happily, Ed headed to his office, the newspaper tucked under his arm. A smile of anticipation played at the corners of his mouth.

Mueller watched him leave, allowing himself a brief smirk of satisfaction.

*   *   *

A short time later, Commissioner Senner took his daily stroll through the Registry Hall. An immigrant now in charge of the processing of other immigrants, he had no previous experience in government or in running such a large operation. A modestly successful lawyer in Austria for thirteen years, he had tired of his chosen career and gladly accepted an invitation from an old friend to become the foreign editor of the *Staats-Zeitung*, a major German-language newspaper in the United States. Quickly emerging as an influential journalist, he became politically active and an enthusiastic campaigner for Grover Cleveland, speaking to German American voters throughout New York, Wisconsin, Illinois, and Indiana. That effort led to

President Cleveland rewarding him for his ardent support by appointing him to this position.

Walking through the hall, Joseph studied the faces of the new arrivals. He paid particular attention to the dark-haired, dark-complexioned men standing on line together in several large groups. Shaking his head at the unpleasant thought of their steadily increasing numbers, he watched his staff inspect the immigrants. These inspections were actually a double check against ones conducted by the shipping companies. The new immigration law held ship owners responsible for screening and rejecting unacceptable immigrants—the physically unfit, anarchists, criminals, and others of disreputable or immoral background.

To meet federal requirements, the company's doctors examined the aliens before departure. On board, each alien answered specific questions under oath about age, health, nationality, resources, occupation, and employment prospects. The shipping companies prepared and numbered manifest lists of the passengers' answers. Once in New York harbor, ship officials gave each immigrant a tag to wear matching the manifest sheet number and grouped the immigrants accordingly. At Ellis Island the inspectors used the manifest as a guide to confirm the responses and the immigrant's eligibility to land.

This system should have worked well, but it did not. Numerous discrepancies occurred between the answers on the manifest sheets and those obtained by the inspectors. When this happened, the immigrant was detained for further investigation by a fact-finding Board of Special Inquiry. The board either allowed the immigrants into the country or deported them, depending on the information uncovered in its interview. Joseph was tired of the time-consuming discrepancies.

"I vant to zee Mr. McSveeney," he instructed his secretary as he strode into his office. He then sat at his desk, impatiently tapping his fingers while awaiting his assistant.

Ed looked up from the newspaper when he heard the knock at his door.

"Excuse me, Mr. McSweeney, the commissioner wants to see you. He's not in a very good mood."

"Thank you, Mr. Kohns."

Ed got up and put on his jacket. With a smile in anticipation of Senner's discomfort for a change, he folded up the paper, tucked it under his arm, walked to his superior's office, knocked, and entered. Senner's stern face telegraphed the brewing storm within him, suggesting to Ed that the man was a seething volcano, one who put the Irish to shame in displaying a fierce temper.

"Good morning, sir."

"Gudt morning, Mr. McSveeney," Joseph curtly responded, reinforcing Ed's thoughts. "I am tired of de greed of dese shipping companies. Dey are costing us too much time und money."

"Sir?"

Puzzled, Ed sat in a chair facing Senner.

"Gudt grief, man! You know vaht I am talking about! Ve are detaining and deporting more aliens dan ever before, especially Italians. Dere is no excuse for it! De numbers for immigrants are down dis year, but de number of undesirables is higher! Ve are feeding und housing more detainees dan ever before! De vorkload of our boards is soaring!"

"Perhaps, Dr. Senner, our inspections are better than in past years so we're now catching more undesirables."

"Nonsense!" roared Senner, his German accent even more noticeable in his excitement. "If de shipping companies ver screening properly, dese aliens vood not be here in de first place. Dey vant big profits so dey bring in as many immigrants as dey can. As long as dey can zell tickets, dey do not care! Dey hide de truth on de manifest sheets to escape blame."

"The companies pay a fine of twenty dollars for each immigrant we deport," countered McSweeney. "That's more than the ticket price, and they have to return the deportees at the company's expense."

"Dot is just de deportees!" Joseph shouted, rising and pacing about. "And de ship is going back dere anyvay! Vaht about de ones ve just detain because of de discrepancies? Ve conduct inquiry hearings und dese have doubled. De backlog obliges us to feed und house dem until ve can clear dem or deport dem. Ve must put a stop to dis! Ve must get de shipping companies vere it hurts—in dere vallets."

"How can we do that? Twenty dollars is the maximum fine."

"I have idea. Ve vill make dem pay for de cost of food und lodging of any detained immigrant, even dose ve later clear for entry. Let us zee how quickly dey change dere tune!"

"They'll fight you on this, Dr. Senner. They have powerful allies."

"If it is a fight dey vant, it is a fight dey vill get!" Joseph said, pounding his fist on the desk. "Und, I assure you, Mr. McSveeney, dey vill know dey have been in vun before it is over."

"Yes, sir. Oh, by the way, have you seen this newspaper article?"

Ed handed over the newspaper and watched with amusement as Senner sat down again and read the article.

"So, dey are at it again, are dey?" He steamed. "Vell, ve vill put quick end to dis. Mr. Kohns!" he called out loudly.

"Yes, Dr. Senner?" replied his secretary at the office door.

"Call de editors of all de New York newspapers. Tell dem I have something to tell dem dis afternoon at two o'clock."

"Yes, Dr. Senner."

As the man left, Ed asked, "What are you going to tell them?"

"De truth, Mr. McSveeney. De truth."

*   *   *

25

At two o'clock, reporters from the city's daily and weekly newspapers crowded into the commissioner's office.

"Gudt afternoon, gentlemen," smiled the commissioner, seated behind his desk. Standing next to him, also facing the reporters, was Ed, who had no idea what his boss was going to say. Although curious, Ed did not like his relegation to that of an uninformed onlooker.

"I tink you are all avare of de charges made against me in de *American Israelite*. I invited you here to set de record straight. First, I am not at all disturbed by dis alleged exposé. Instead, I am veary of it. It is old story. It appeared first in de columns of *Truth* tree years ago. Dis makes de fourth time it has been printed. Now dot I am Commissioner of Immigration, de matter has revived interest."

"Are the charges true, Dr. Senner?" interrupted one reporter. "Did you desert your wife?"

"No, I did not. My vife accompanied me ven I come to dis country. She is still living mit me, and ve are very happy."

"Did you lose your fortune in some wild speculation?"

"Everyone acquainted mit my history," said Joseph, his voice choked with emotion, "knows dot I sacrificed my entire fortune to save de life of my fadder."

"How's that?"

"Dere ver medical expenses—doctors, nurses, zurgery, hospitals—for months. It is all here in de records for you to zee.

"Gentlemen, de Liederkranz Society, of vich I vas member, appointed un committee of five to investigate de story ven it first appeared tree years ago. Villiam Steinvay, un highly respected man in dis country, vas chairman. Dey found de charges absolutely mitout foundation und reported dis.

"Last year it vas again given publicity in de columns of dot labor newspaper. De publisher, John Feierabend, vas indicted for libel. Feierabend signed affidavit admitting de story vas printed mitout investigation. Zubsequent inquiry has shown dot dere vas no truth in de charges. So I mitdrew my complaint. Here is copy of affidavit."

"Will you file libel charges this time?"

"I have not decided."

"Why do you think the *Israelite* printed this story?"

"It is probably because I changed my name ven I decided to renounce my Jewish faith. De editor of de *Israelite*, vich is published in Cincinnati, is Rabbi Isaac Vise. I believe de man seeks to discredit me for my decision."

"You changed your name?"

"*Ja*, I changed it from Samuely to Senner. I come to dis country to start new life, so I choose new name."

"Why did you change your name?"

"I decided I needed more American name. Dot's all. As proof dot I have notting to be ashamed of, I have here numerous letters of congratulations from people in my native town after news of my appointment reached dem."

Persisting, a reporter asked, "Weren't you really trying to hide the fact that you are Jewish?"

"Dot, sir," he replied with seething anger, "is foolish question. I hide notting! I give you my reason und dot is de end of it."

Joseph had no desire to explain that he had long ago lost whatever faith he had. Also, he had seen too much anti-Semitism in Europe to risk experiencing it in his new life in a Protestant country. He was far from alone in the number of Jews in America who changed their names for this reason. Moreover, like many other Jews of longer residence in America, he was alarmed at the growing influx of Orthodox Jewish peasants from Eastern Europe, whose visibility was triggering a rising anti-Semitism. So, like other more assimilated Jewish Americans, he tried to dissociate himself from them and play down his ethnicity. Despite his bravado, he was concerned as to what this newspaper story would do to his social standing among the *goyim* with whom he associated.

"Is there anything else you wish to say, Dr. Senner?" asked another reporter.

"*Ja.* I have served de public for tirteen years now. In all dot time I have vorked hard to make my contribution to dis country. Because my enemies cannot find anyting negative to say, dey tink dey can dig up someting from my past in Europe und damage my career. Dey shall fail. I have notting to hide. I invite you to investigate de matter yourselves. Good day, gentlemen. Tank you for coming."

"Vell, Mr. McSveeney," asked Joseph when the reporters had left, "do you tink dot vill close de matter?"

"I'm sure of it, Dr. Senner. You handled yourself well."

"Good. Den ve can channel our energies toward de real enemy.

"Sir?"

"De ship owners, Mr. McSveeney. De ship owners."

*   *   *

"Dr. Stafford, come quickly!"

"What is it?"

"We have an emergency!'

Matt ran down the hall, following the nurse into the admitting room where the unconscious boy lay on the examining table, his right foot wrapped in a blood-soaked towel. He had fainted from shock.

Standing nearby were two factory workers. It was evident from the blood on their clothing that they were the ones who had brought the boy to the hospital.

"What happened?" questioned Matt as he began checking the boy's pupils and pulse.

"Giovanni. He's-a my sister's boy," answered a distraught man. "He fall off-a the machine! His foot—it get-a caught in the gears."

"Why was he on a machine?"

Young boys working on spinning frame, circa 1890s

"Why? That's-a his job! He-a works with me."

"Was he working barefoot?" asked Matt, noting the boy's other shoeless foot.

"Si. All-a the kids no wear shoes."

"How old is he?"

"Thirteen. Can you fix his foot, doctor?"

"I'll let you know. Please wait outside."

As the men left the room, Matt unwrapped the bloody towel. He looked at the mangled flesh and crushed bones that were once a foot. A foot on which the boy had walked, jumped, and ran—but never would again. He knew instantly that all he could do was to amputate and protect the boy from gangrene and an even worse fate.

He went to the waiting room where a distraught woman had joined the men.

"*Mi scusi, come é il mio ragazzo?*"

"Doctor, this is-a my sister, the boy's mother. She is-a ask about her boy."

"Tell her that I am very sorry, but the boy's foot is crushed beyond repair. I must amputate it to save his life."

"No-o-o-o! No-o-o-o! *Non amputate!*" screamed the woman, now crying hysterically. She had only understood that one word, but it was enough. Whatever dream had brought this boy and his family to America had, in one brief moment, become a nightmare.

That evening when Matt came home to their brownstone apartment on West Seventy-Third Street, Peg had dinner ready as usual. He didn't have much of an appetite, and when he told her about the boy, she understood. They embraced, standing there silently, locked in each other's arms. His eyes misting, Matt forced a little smile, looked at Peg, and lightly kissed her lips.

"Thank you," he whispered.

As they unclasped, he kissed her hand and walked into the parlor. Peg watched him, her heart going out to the boy she did not know and to the man she knew all too well.

Later, sitting in his comfortable parlor chair, Matt looked over the top of his evening newspaper at Peg sitting opposite him. Intent on her needlework, she took no notice.

Melancholy filled him. As he thought back to the unfortunate boy, he realized that he would always remember his name: *Giovanni Ciarleglio.* He had done his best to comfort the family and especially the boy, still groggy from the morphine, after he had regained consciousness. From the boy's address, Matt knew he lived in the squalor of a tenement district. Although he had never been in a tenement, Matt could easily imagine the dark, poorly ventilated, overcrowded, and disease-ridden hovel that Giovanni called home. Like a great many other Americans, Matt's conscience had been shocked a few years earlier by the photographs and articles of Jacob Riis in the *New York Tribune.* Those collected observations were also published in a book called *How the Other Half Lives.* Matt knew that Riis

New York's Lower East Side, circa 1890s

was a Danish immigrant who understood firsthand about the ragged underside of immigrant city life. Yet Riis had overcome his own destitution to become a respected journalist and social reformer.

Matt reflected on the lives of Giovanni Ciarleglio, Jacob Riis, and his own. The boy had never known anything but poverty, and his future prospects were most discouraging. Riis had risen out of poverty into fame and, as far as Matt knew, into a personally satisfying life of social commitment. Giovanni's life would likely never be as fulfilling.

And what about Matt Stafford? he wondered. He had nothing in common with either of them. He had never known poverty. He would probably never be as famous as Riis, but as a surgeon, he would live a more comfortable lifestyle. Here he was, a success at age twenty-seven. *So, why am I not content? Why do I feel so empty?* He was liked and respected at Presbyterian Hospital. It was a prestigious hospital, and the work environment was fine. Yet somehow he didn't feel fulfilled in what he was doing, at least not in the way he fancied Riis must be.

Matt looked again at Peg. They loved each other, so why did their relationship seem lacking? Ever since the miscarriage, their lovemaking had been less frequent and less passionate. Having known no other woman intimately, he assumed Peg was right about how such things change over time. Yet his cravings for sex had not diminished. Even after their infrequent couplings, he wasn't contented. *What's wrong with me?* he wondered.

They knew now that Peg would never be able to have a child, so their future would be just the two of them, unless they adopted. That was a big disappointment, dashing his plans about being a father and passing on his legacy to his own flesh and blood. Had that reality somehow affected their intimacy? *No,* thought Matt. They didn't love each other any less because they couldn't have a child. Still, he couldn't find a logical explanation in his mind for the vague discontent gnawing at him. He tried to dismiss these depressing thoughts, but they wouldn't go away, and they haunted him for several nights, making falling asleep difficult despite his fatigue.

May 1894

"Ed, what the hell is that bull-headed boss of yours doing?"

McSweeney, receiving the telephone call at home just before dinner, listened to Michael Stuerzel, shipping executive of the North German Lloyd line. Ed had a cozy relationship with him, especially since enactment of the tighter immigration restrictions. Besides free sailing privileges, Ed also received monthly bonuses and expensive Christmas gifts in return for helping the steamship company circumvent, when necessary, any of the mandated procedures.

He had expected this call and knew exactly what Stuerzel meant.

"Are you talking about the new billing procedures?"

"Procedures, hell! I'm talking about his charging us to feed and house the greenhorns your people detain! I've got a bill here for more than seven hundred dollars, with instructions to remit payment to Felix Livingston, the restaurant concessionaire."

"Mike, I warned you that he planned to do this."

"Yes, you warned me, and I told you to stop him."

"Mike, he's very pig-headed. You know that. You just said it yourself."

"We've had a good relationship these past few years,

33

Ed. You've been rewarded for it. Are you telling me that our confidence in you is misplaced?"

"No, not at all, Mike. Sometimes though, he takes a position and sticks to it, come hell or high water."

"There's no talking to him?"

"I've tried. God knows I've tried. Further talking won't accomplish anything."

"How strong is his position? Will Washington back him up on this?"

"I don't know."

"Well, I'm not going to pay this. None of us are. I've talked to some of the other shipping companies, and we're going to flex some muscle. Our people in Washington are working on this now. We're going to call that bastard's bluff. In the meantime, you keep working on him too. I want him to give this up."

"I'll do my best, Mike."

"There's an extra bonus for you if you succeed."

"Thanks, Mike. I'll do what I can. Goodbye."

Ed put the earpiece back in the telephone cradle and frowned. "Damn Senner!" he grumbled aloud. "He's making my life difficult. Why does he have to pick a fight with the shipping companies?"

*   *   *

A few days later, Senner received the shipping companies' challenge. Seething with rage, he burst into Ed's office, the letter crumpled in his fist.

"De steamship companies have banded togetter," he began. "Here is letter from attorneys for de—," and he read from the letter, "North German Lloyd line, Red Star line, Cunard line, Netterlands line, Vite Star line, French line, Allan line, und Fabre line. Dey say dot dey refuse to pay de costs for food und care of detainees. Dey say I do not have de authority to make dem pay."

"Maybe we should rethink our position, Dr. Senner. Perhaps we can find some other solution."

"Not on your life!" shouted Joseph, his face red with rage. "Dey vill pay de costs until dey eliminate de problem!"

"How can you force them to pay? This might be a battle you can't win."

"Are you suggesting dot I just give in to dem?"

"Are you certain that Washington will support you? If they don't, it might be wiser to back out gracefully and protect your reputation."

"Vaht makes you tink Vashington vill not support me?" Joseph demanded, his anger rising even more.

"You know the political realities. Those companies have a powerful lobby. They make big campaign contributions to congressmen. You're sticking your neck out. You're already under attack by Republican newspapers and politicians trying to discredit Cleveland's administration. They could use this issue to their advantage."

"How?" Joseph asked, raising one eyebrow and staring intently into Ed's face.

Ed pressed his argument further. "The papers could make you look bad by accusing you of grandstanding or of using your office to attack free enterprise."

"I vill take dot chance, Mr. McSveeney. I have Stump's support on dis. He is not vun to cave in to dese people."

Joseph wheeled about and stormed out of Ed's office. Later, he sent a letter to Washington to Superintendent of Immigration Herman Stump, informing him of the shipping companies' boycott. Despite his bluster with McSweeney, Joseph knew Stump's support could waver under pressure.

* * *

"Matt, Peg, how wonderful to see you!" greeted Sarah Klaessig, the sixtyish widow of Wall Street financier Kurt

Klaessig. Her upswept coiffure, diamond necklace and bracelet, and her elegant, embroidered blue gown suggested the woman of wealth and culture she was.

She was standing near the doorway into the Grand Ballroom of the luxurious Waldorf Astoria Hotel, site of the annual spring gala that Peg enjoyed so. Overhead in this large foyer hung one of the hotel's many gasoliers, those chandeliers lit by gas instead of candles. On either side of the main doorway stood marble statues of Zeus, king of the Olympian gods, and of Hera, queen of heaven, appropriate symbols for the city's elite. To the side was a large, gilt-edged mirror above a long mahogany table, enabling the guests to check their appearances one last time before their grand entrance into the ballroom. Elsewhere, red velvet couches lined the perimeter, in stark contrast to the dark blue, thick-piled carpeting. The pleasant sounds of the orchestra inside the ballroom playing a waltz nicely complemented the sensual richness of the scene.

The Waldorf Astoria Hotel at Fifth Avenue and Thirty-Third Street, late 1890s

"Good evening, Mrs. Klaessig," said Peg, wearing a stylish pink gown that flattered her small figure. She too wore full-length white gloves.

"Yes, indeed. It's nice to see you again," added Matt, whose tuxedo matched those of the other men in attendance.

"My dear, please call me Sarah. We're all friends here."

"Certainly, Sarah," Peg replied. "That is a beautiful gown you're wearing."

"Thank you, my dear, and the two of you are a stunning couple. Now go inside, you two, and have a good time."

Matt and Peg were among the three hundred people in attendance. In between the dancing and social conversations were the fleeting conversations with newly introduced people. Most would be forgotten quickly—except one.

Sarah Klaessig came to their table. "Peg, dear, may I borrow your husband for a moment? There's someone I would like him to meet. It's a man, don't worry."

Peg smiled. "I trust you with my husband, Sarah. Go right ahead."

Sarah escorted Matt over to the far side of the ballroom where two men were engaged in conversation.

"Dr. Matthew Stafford, I'd like you to meet Thomas Handley, vice president of the Bank of New York."

Shaking hands, Handley smiled and gave the perfunctory greeting he had offered countless times, but with the art of making it sound fresh and sincere.

"How do you do, Dr. Stafford?"

"I'm fine, sir. It's a pleasure to meet you."

"And this," said Sarah, continuing the introductions, "is Dr. Joseph Senner, Commissioner of Immigration for the Port of New York. Dr. Stafford is a surgeon at Presbyterian Hospital."

"Hello, doctor," said Senner, shaking hands. Last month's newspaper accounts of his Jewish origins had only partly impacted on his social standing. His high-status position still garnered him invitations to major social events such as this, while those to more private social gatherings had decidedly dropped. Sarah, as an old friend and fellow German speaker, maintained an easy friendship with him.

"Pleased to meet you, Commissioner."

"Come, Thomas, let's leave these two men to discuss doctor things. We'll go somewhere and talk about my favorite subject—money."

Everyone laughed, and they left, leaving Joseph and Matt facing one another. A waiter came by with a tray of drinks.

"Sherry, sir?"

"Yes, please," answered Matt, taking one of the glasses.

After Joseph placed his empty glass on the tray and took a filled one, Matt asked, "Does your position still allow you to practice medicine or is it purely administrative?"

"Oh, I am doctor of law, not medicine, young man. Und no, I do not practice law as Commissioner. In fact, I have not practiced law in dis country at all."

"I apologize, sir. I didn't understand."

"No offense vas taken, so no apology is necessary."

"*Sie sind sehr freundlich.*" [You are very kind.]

"Are you German?"

"My mother is. My father is English."

"I see. Yet you speak German?"

"Yes."

"Fluently?"

"Yes, sir. I also speak French and some Polish."

"Do you? Und how did you come to know zo many languages?"

"I learned German from my mother, of course. The French came easily, with so many French-speaking people living near me in Massachusetts, and some of my wife's family are Polish."

Impressed, Joseph offered, "We could use doctor mit your

language abilities at Ellis Island. Vood you consider vorking dere?"

"I don't know, sir. I'm now established at the hospital."

"Do you vant only vun job your whole life? How vill you know vaht you are missing?"

"You have a point, sir, but aren't your doctors all in the Marine Hospital Service?"

"*Ja*, but mit your language skills und experience, I could get you placed on special assignment to be mit us."

"That's a generous offer, sir."

"You vill never zee de variety of people und dere physical conditions at your hospital, as you vill on our island. People come every day from all over de world. Und you vood vork more regular hours mit us."

"Yes, I know, sir, but—"

"Look, do not say anyting now. You tink about it. Here is my card. Call me next week, next month, even next year, venever you are interested in knowing more. I vill introduce you to my chief medical officer. You can talk to him, learn all about us, und den make up your mind."

"Thank you, sir."

"Gudt. I hope to hear from you zumtime."

They shook hands, and Matt returned to Peg, slipping the card in his pocket. He smiled at the thought of working at Ellis Island. The thought of meeting such a wide variety of people was tempting, but not at the cost of giving up his important position. Besides, Peg would never approve.

June 1894

The sky above Washington, DC, on this mild, sunny day was bright blue, with traces of thin, fleecy cirrus clouds high in the stratosphere, creating a marble-like effect.

Joseph's carriage clattered southwest on New York Avenue. As it turned left onto Fifteenth Street, reaching the east front

US Treasury Building east colonnade, circa 1890s

side of the Treasury Building, he could see the White House straight ahead. His driver stopped at the entrance by F Street. After paying, he looked up at the grand structure before him.

Joseph marveled again at the magnificent granite structure in the Greek Revival style. Especially impressive was the colonnade running the length of the building. Each of the thirty columns, standing thirty-six feet tall, was carved out of a single piece of granite. One of the largest office buildings in the world, its interior design was classically austere.

Joseph had received a telegram from the Superintendent of Immigration summoning him to the capital. He knew, of course, the reason. What he did not know was how steadfast Stump, or his superior—John G. Carlisle, Secretary of the Treasury— would remain against the pressures exerted by the shipping companies. Before his initial action against the steamship lines, Joseph had cleared it with Stump. However, he knew from experience that his boss's support always hinged on political expediency.

With some apprehension, he entered Stump's office. "

"Gudt afternoon," he said to the fortyish, stoop-shouldered man seated before him. "I am Joseph Senner."

"Good afternoon, sir," replied Stump's secretary. "Mr. Stump is expecting you. Please go right in."

"Tank you," said Senner, nodding his head, knocking on the door, and entering.

Herman Stump was seated at his desk. A delightful, gray-haired gentleman, Stump was a master at delegating responsibilities. More content to let others handle the details of administration, he instead preferred to serve as arbiter between warring factions. At this he was successful, for his pleasant blend of personal charm and social grace endeared him to many. Right now, though, Stump, troubled by the controversy with the shipping companies, was uncertain about what to do.

As Joseph entered his office, Herman looked up from his

papers and stood up. With a welcoming smile, he extended his hand across the desk and shook hands.

"Hello, Dr. Senner. It's good to see you again."

"Tank you, Mr. Stump. It is good to zee you too."

"Sit down, please,' said Stump, as he himself did so. "It looks like we've got a real rhubarb on our hands."

"I am not zurprised, are you?" tested Joseph, peering intently and attempting, as usual, to learn from the speaker's eyes what he could.

"No, I guess not. The question is how do we handle it? That's why I asked you to come down here. I want to ensure that we are in full agreement and that we understand each other."

"Of course."

After a moment's silence, Joseph prompted, "Vere exactly do matters presently stand?"

"You always come directly to the point, Joseph," said Herman with faint amusement. "Very well, let me bring you up to date. A few days ago Secretary Carlisle received a letter from the law firm of Lord, Day, and Lord, representing several of the steamship companies. It's similar to the letter you received. The lawyers claim we have no legal basis to charge the shipping companies for the food and care costs of the detainees. Their contention is that we have created arbitrary rules, and they have advised their clients to refuse to honor any bills for such maintenance."

"Dey have been zinging dot tune for un month," Joseph commented. "Only now dey have gone over our heads."

"They have another attorney, Dr. Geoffrey O. Glavis, who is based here in Washington. He's seen Secretary Carlisle. The secretary has also received numerous calls from senators and congressmen who support the steamship lines."

"Und vaht is Carlisle's position?" Joseph asked, knowing full well that without Carlisle's support, Stump would cave in to the shipping companies.

"Carlisle has asked me to reply to the letter. He doesn't want to set the precedent of Treasury getting directly involved in immigration implementation issues. We are to handle the problem ourselves. He said he'll support us, no matter what our decision."

"So vere do we go from here?"

Stump studied Joseph's face for a few seconds and then answered, "I've had my staff research the issue. I have here several documents supporting our position. Here are two letters from Windom when he was Secretary of the Treasury. Both address the issue of the companies paying for detained immigrants. Then there's my circular from last November, spelling out the rules and regulations regarding maintenance of the immigrants."

Joseph perused the documents with the trained eyes of a lawyer. After several minutes, Joseph's eyes locked on the superintendent's. "Dese are helpful, sir, but dey do not legally oblige dem to pay."

"Perhaps not, but they do give us some precedent. We need a starting point, and these documents don't exclude paying costs for detainees later admitted."

"Dot is true."

"This can go either way, Joseph. If we take a stand, we've got to be strong enough to hold our ground." He hesitated and then added, "If we're not, we should stop now before we both get bloodied."

"Mr. Stump," Joseph interrupted, struggling to keep his rising anger under control, "if ve allow de steamship lines to vin, de situation vill only get worse. Dey vill have even less reason to screen dere passengers. Ellis Island vill become so overcrowded mit detainees dot ve vill have no place to put dem! Ve vill need more staff! Ve vill need more dormitories, bathing, and laundry facilities! Dere is no room on de island to expand! Dere is very little room to increase our operations much further.

Our budget vill be blown sky high from de volume of detainees! De steamship companies must be penalized zo dey vill stop dumping on us any alien mit de money for passage! Dey cannot continue to make profits at our expense!"

"Calm down, Joseph."

Senner remained silent for a moment before continuing and then softly added, "It is just dot ve cannot allow dem to set our policy."

"I'm inclined to agree with you. I must confess that I am more than a little annoyed myself. Those bastards went over my head, as you said, to force my hand."

"Den you are villing to fight dem?"

"I want to, Joseph, and I will fight them if you can give me the answer to one question."

"Vaht is dot?" he asked, wondering what the pivotal question would be.

Stump paused briefly, clasped his hands together on the desk, leaned forward, and asked, "What if the steamship companies still refuse to pay? This thing could drag on in the courts for months and there's still no guarantee that we'll win. Meanwhile our costs pile up and so do the number of detainees."

"I have tought about dis. I suggest ve zend boarding parties to de ships and examine de immigrants dere. Ve vill not let de immigrants dot fail inspection zet foot on de island or be admitted into de country. Dot vay de companies vill be stuck mit dem."

"That's a bold idea, Joseph. Will the companies allow it?"

"Vaht choice do dey have? De law requires us to examine de immigrants. It does not specify vere. It does not have to be on Ellis Island. Ve have de authority to conduct our examinations on dere ships if ve so choose. Ve hold all de cards."

"You're certain of this?"

"*Ja.*"

Stump laughed and exclaimed, "Ingenious! I think it will

work. I'll run it by our people here first though, just to play it safe."

Senner nodded his head in agreement. Then, in an afterthought, he added, "You know, Mr. Stump, dere is extra ace ve can play to exert even more pressure."

"What's that?" asked Stump, intrigued.

"If ve conduct our onboard examinations very metodically, de time ve spend could coincidentally delay de steamships' planned departures out of New York. Dey just might miss de tide, or even un few days if ve are backlogged in processing all dere passengers. It vood upset dere schedules und prove costly to dem."

"Joseph, that's a master stroke," complimented Stump. "All right, I will check everything out. If our legal staff confirms the strength of our position, we will proceed with your plan."

"Yes, zir."

"We'll take it one step at a time. I will send a reply, reaffirming our position and documenting its historical basis. Let's keep your plan to ourselves for the moment."

"I understand, zir. No zence tipping our hand early."

"One more thing, Joseph. The companies are after your scalp. They want you out. They're trying hard to make this a personality issue. I want to avoid that."

"Zir?"

"When are you going on vacation?"

"At de beginning of next month."

"Fine. I'll delay my response until you go away. I don't want reporters near you. I want this to be a matter between Washington and the steamship companies. If anyone questions you, you are to say that you only follow instructions you receive from Washington. That way, no matter how events turn out, you'll be protected."

"Tank you, sir. I appreciate vaht you are doing."

45

"It's the least I can do for you, Joseph. You've got a tough job up there, and you need all the support we can give you."

Joseph left Washington satisfied and now confident of Stump's support. He would no longer be the target over this issue. Smiling to himself, he secretly hoped the companies did not back down, for he would love to send boarding parties onto their vessels. It would be a decisive display of power.

"*Ja*," he said aloud to himself, "dey vill learn, vunce und for all, who has de real power."

July 1894

On the morning of July twelfth, Joseph returned to work after a nine-day vacation, disturbed to learn of the escape of four detained stowaways. Still at large, their story was in every newspaper. Known for demanding efficiency in his island's operations at all times, his staff fully expected him to be outraged at the public attention over this lapse.

Summoning his assistant, he angrily asked, "Mr. McSveeney, how in de vorld did dis happen?"

Ed had been stewing for days. He did not like the notoriety the escape had brought to Ellis Island. He had been in charge. It had happened on his watch. Now he had to face this devil of a boss whose personality and management style were becoming even more unbearable. Ed prided himself on his administrative skills and his warm communicative style with staff and colleagues. Senner, on the other hand, was brusque, and Ed didn't like his sarcasm at all. And now, here he was, on the carpet before a decidedly unsympathetic boss.

"We still don't know, Commissioner," he replied quietly, hoping his conciliatory tone might soothe his superior. "We know they had been allowed to leave their quarters to eat in the dining room, but no one knows what became of them after that."

"How did dey get off de island? No vun can swim dot far to shore in dese currents! Und dey need landing card to take de ferry out of here!"

"Yes, sir, I know. Right now it's a mystery."

Joseph mimicked Ed. "Right now it's a mystery." He paused in an apparent attempt to control his anger and then exploded, "Vell, I do not vant a mystery! I vant full investigation. Start mit de staff. I vant to zee detailed report on dis by Monday morning. I vant answers!"

"Yes, sir, I knew you would. I already have a full inquiry under way."

"Gudt."

Mr. Kohns' knock on the door interrupted them.

"Excuse me, Dr. Senner," his secretary said, opening the door. "Some reporters are outside."

"Here ve go. Mr. Kohns, have dem come in."

As Ed stood next to his seated boss, the reporters barraged Senner with questions on the stowaways. As the questions turned to the battle between immigration officials and the steamship companies, Ed listened with particular interest. The exchange covered familiar ground: Stump's pointed letter to the companies, their attorneys' defiant refusal of Stump's decision, and other events leading up to the present stalemate.

"Commissioner," asked the *New York Times* reporter, "what will happen next?"

"I only follow instructions zent to me from Vashington," he answered.

"Sir, you must have an opinion about what will happen next. What is it?" pressed the reporter.

"If de steamship men continue to defy de government, it is possible I shall receive orders to examine all immigrants aboard de ship."

It took all of Ed's energy to stop himself from bolting to the nearest telephone. He couldn't believe what he had just heard! "Can you do that?" asked the incredulous reporter.

"De immigrants are aboard de ship in de eyes of de law until de Immigration Bureau allows dem to leave. Ve bring de immigrants here to Ellis Island to accommodate de steamship people. Ve could just as easily conduct de inspections on board de vessels."

Ed stared at his boss, hardly concealing his surprise. The remaining questions and replies were inconsequential to the bombshell his boss had dropped. After the reporters left to file their stories, he leaned forward, placing his outstretched arms on Joseph's desk, facing him. Joseph wore a smug look.

"Will we actually board their ships? Is this a bluff or do you actually plan to do it?"

"Dot vill be Vashington's decision, Mr. McSveeney. I do not know vaht ve vill be told to do. Still, you must admit, boarding dere ships is interesting idea."

"It's provocative, that's for sure," Ed answered, as he sat in the chair behind him. He was still uncertain whether Senner knew something or was playing some kind of game. "Has Washington suggested we would board their ships?"

"It is vun of several options being explored," Joseph replied, staring at Ed. "Ve vill just have to vait and zee. Vy are you so interested?"

Joseph stared. Ed shifted and twisted in his chair. He wanted to get out of there, get off the island, and get to a telephone. To deflect Joseph's question, he answered, "I am the assistant commissioner. I have a right to know. Anything involving Ellis Island involves me, Dr. Senner.'

"Ven I know anyting, I vill tell you. Right now I suggest dot you concentrate on finding out how dose stowaways managed to escape."

"Yes, sir," Ed said and left. He hated it when Senner

dismissed him like that, but he had to alert Michael Stuerzel at North German Lloyd.

By the end of the week, Ed had completed his investigation. To his dismay he could not find who had helped the stowaways escape. Mueller, who had engineered their escape for ten dollars from each man, knew how to escape detection. That included ensuring the men got far away from New York.

The escapees had not been apprehended, and with each passing day, the possibility of their capture diminished. Ed knew that Senner would not be pleased by his report, and he eagerly anticipated his own vacation the following week.

*   *   *

On Saturday, July 21, Joseph received his instructions from Washington. He was to examine aboard ship the immigrants of all steamship lines who refuse to pay for the maintenance of their detained passengers. He smiled with delight at the news and quickly leaked it to some reporters.

The Sunday newspapers carried the story. With McSweeney on vacation, Senner took charge of operations. He assembled a task force under the command of Capt. Otto Heinzmann, Superintendent of Landing. Heinzmann, part of Senner's inner circle, was a genial German with a cherubic face and prominent side whiskers.

The two men spent Sunday afternoon discussing the operations plan and their personnel needs. They selected the *Edam*, newly arrived from Rotterdam that afternoon. Anchored at the foot of Sixth Street, Hoboken, all its passengers would still be on board the next morning.

Early Monday morning Joseph stationed himself at the Barge Office. This two-story granite structure, located on the southeastern tip of lower Manhattan, was where steerage passengers—beginning in 1890 when the federal government took control of immigration from the states—had been processed

Barge Office looking south, circa 1890s

until Ellis Island opened in 1892. It was from here that the ferry traveled back and forth to Ellis Island, transporting employees, immigrants, and their relatives. From this locale he would be able to stay in touch with Washington if things got nasty, since the island still did not have telephone lines to the mainland.

Shortly after nine o'clock, Captain Heinzmann left with his squad in a motor launch. With him were registry clerks Mueller, Lee, and Hesselberg; gatemen Kumpf, Weppler, and Seedorf; inspectors Crater, Bock, and Converse; Doctors Geddings and MacDowell; and Mrs. Stucklen, the matron in charge of female passengers and children.

As their motor launch moved closer to the *Edam*, Mueller leaned forward. "So, doctor, how do you like this little adventure?"

William MacDowell was fifty-one, but his gray hair and heavily lined facial features made him look much older. His demeanor and slight build heightened that impression. Over the years of working together, he and John had often shared conversations, although their relationship was limited to only those occasional exchanges.

"Don't like it one bit," he grumbled, "not one bit."

"C'mon now. At least it's a break in the routine, and it's a pleasant morning for a boat ride."

John's smile and amiable manner softened MacDowell a little. Like a successful salesman, John had that knack for weakening people's resistance.

"You've got a point there, John, but I still don't like traveling out to a ship to inspect greenhorns."

"I thought all doctors made house calls," John teased.

"Ha! Most do, but I haven't made one in years, and you know something? I like it that way. I hope this is a short-term 'adventure,' as you call it."

"Well, here we go," said John as their launch reached the Sixth Street pier.

Captain Heinzmann, wearing a naval cap and a double-breasted coat with brass buttons, led his squad on board the *Edam*. The ship's captain offered no resistance but immediately ordered his communications officer to inform his company's New York office about the boarding by immigration officials. At Captain Heinzmann's request, he produced the passenger manifest list.

"You have only sixty passengers, Captain?"

"Yes, that's all on this trip."

"I see. Please have them all brought up on the main deck."

"I'll see to it immediately."

Heinzmann set up the workstations, and the processing began. The passengers walked aft in line and halted just outside the main deck saloon. Inside the two doctors and matron waited. After passing their medical examinations, the passengers walked through the saloon and out to the other side of the deck where the registry clerks and inspectors waited. At strategic points the three gatemen controlled the traffic flow.

When all sixty had been processed, Captain Heinzmann informed the ship's captain, "All but six of your passengers are cleared for landing. These six must be detained for special processing. They are to remain aboard ship until we can schedule their inquiry hearings."

"Can't you just detain them on Ellis Island, as you've always done?"

"Normally we would do so, Captain," said Heinzmann. "However, your company refuses to pay for their maintenance there. So I'm afraid they must stay here on your ship unless, of course, your company pays for their stay at Ellis Island."

"How soon can you schedule their hearings?"

"I'm not certain. I know we have a full schedule today. Probably within the next few days."

"Days! No, we must leave with the morning tide tomorrow!"

"I don't think so. These six will remain on your ship until we clear them. Commissioner Senner is at the Barge Office if your agents wish to speak to him. Good day, Captain."

Shortly after Otto Heinzmann returned to the Barge Office and made his report, the telephone rang.

"It's for you, Dr. Senner. It's the call you've been expecting."

Joseph smiled and went to the phone.

"Commissioner Senner here ... *Ja*, dot is correct. All immigration inspections vill now occur on board your ships ... No, ve vill no longer accept detainees from companies unvilling to pay for dere costs ... No, dot is straight from Vashington ... No, dere is notting to discuss ... Look, either you pay for dem und ve take dem to Ellis Island, or you do not pay for dem und you keep dem on your ship. It is your decision ... Oh, you vill pay for dem? You have made a vise decision. All right, ven I receive your commitment in writing to pay for de detainees, I vill transfer dem to Ellis Island immediately ... You vill have it here in tirty minutes? Den dey vill be off your ship in vun hour. Gudt day."

Joseph put the receiver back in the telephone cradle.

"Ha! Dis is a red-letter day, Otto. Mark my vords. Before dis day is out, all de steamship companies vill capitulate."

By late afternoon, Joseph learned he had been right.

February 1895

"Please, don't do this! I beg you! Please!"

John Mueller smiled at the nineteen-year-old woman sitting before him on the hotel bed. Now down to her chemise, she had reluctantly stripped as he had ordered.

She was looking down, unable to face him. He gazed on her long black hair, the creamy flesh of her arms and legs, and the white chemise he would soon make her remove. He knew she feared him, and he liked that. Her tears and pleading only heightened his lust. He grew harder with the realization of his total control over her. With increased anticipation, he relished the thought of forcing her to submit.

She was one of several dozen immigrant women he had lured to this same room, its corner location, thick walls, floor, ceiling, and door effectively keeping within any sounds.

At the island he kept an eye out for unescorted young women. Multilingual, he could converse with many nationalities and that widened his opportunities. Finding a likely candidate, he would question her to confirm her vulnerability. His cleverness in gauging reactions inevitably led to success in getting what he wanted. Using a pretext of the woman's ineligibility for entry, he would threaten to deport her unless she agreed to have sex with him. By no means crude in his approach, he entrapped his victim with a combination of finesse and threat.

Once he had ensnared a woman, he would give her a landing card, saying it was a "temporary" one, and send her in a prearranged carriage to his hotel room with the promise of a "permanent" entry card once she had submitted to him. He pretended she would be arrested and deported if she did not agree. Afterward, he would warn her that if she told anyone, no one would believe a foreigner against a government official and she would be deported for her accusations. Often coming from countries with repressive governments, these desperate women believed him.

Once inside the hotel room, he plied his victims with champagne. At the very least this weakened their defenses. Some women, unaccustomed to the bubbly alcohol, became light-headed while others became giddy and thus more fun to possess.

That was part of the pleasure for him. He never knew how they would respond. Some just lay there passively and let him use them. Others tried to resist. Then he enjoyed slapping them as he forced himself into their struggling bodies. Often he used drapery ropes to tie them spread-eagled across the four-poster bed to put them completely in his power.

He especially liked virgins; their faces contorted in terror when they saw his erection. He laughed at their shrieks. With the loud ones he used a gag to keep them from screaming, partly to offset the remote possibility of anyone hearing, but also to establish further their total helplessness. Their struggles and sobs always aroused him further.

Sometimes the women he had in this room were prostitutes, ones he detected at Ellis Island during his inspections. Immigration law gave him the power to deport them, but they could serve a better purpose. Typically, they unleashed his inner self, as he used crude language and groped them right at the immigration station. Then, using his temporary landing card ruse, he would oblige them to go to his hotel room for a tryst. Although he felt that these experienced women—doing their best to please him to get their promised permanent card if they did—were a good night's toss in bed, they did not give him as much satisfaction as when he could take the inexperienced ones. Like this woman. Her innocence and submissiveness exhilarated him. She would be special.

God, how he loved this! His nagging wife brought him misery at home, but these encounters thrilled him so. His wife no longer aroused his passions, but in this room he was a stallion and master of women.

He stared at the beautiful, forlorn creature. She was a Ukrainian Jew whose husband had died from typhoid during the ocean crossing. Eleven other passengers had died as well. On arrival in New York, the survivors were quarantined for four weeks. He had singled her out, for she had no relatives, no sponsor. It was fairly easy to isolate her from the others, and he conned her into going to the hotel instead of informing her about available help from an immigrant aid society.

Mueller had learned of her brutal experiences in her homeland, including pogroms that had killed the rest of her family. There was nothing left for her back there. She had been totally dependent on her deceased husband. He had no family in this country to take responsibility for her. Completely alone and powerless, she was a perfect target.

"Stand up and remove your chemise," he demanded.

"No, please."

"Do as I tell you, woman. You don't want to be deported, do you?"

The woman slowly shook her head.

"Then do as I say."

She stood before him and raised the garment up over her head. His eyes followed its upward movement, delighting in the fine shape of her thighs, the tantalizing sight of her pubic hair, shapely hips, narrow waist and firm, upright breasts. *She was perfect!*

As she stood, looking down, with her left arm across her breasts and her right hand demurely on her mound, Mueller marveled at his good fortune. He had a beautiful young woman standing naked before him, and he had total power over her.

"Turn around."

The woman complied. He looked at her shapely form and wet his lips.

"You have a lovely ass, my dear," he said, and she blushed with shame. Hurriedly, he stripped while her back was turned.

"Turn around and face me," he said as he walked to her.

She turned, and her downcast eyes fell on his erection. Unable to bear the sight, she quickly shut them.

"Kneel."

She did not move at first, so he grabbed her shoulders and pressed down until she knelt. He then grabbed the back of her hair and yanked it hard. As she opened her mouth to cry out, he thrust himself into it, still holding her head, rocking back and forth. The young woman gagged, but he didn't relent, delighting in the sensations. Powerless, her mouth unwillingly providing his pleasure, she struggled to breathe and endure.

As his pleasure increased, he withdrew, lifted her up, and pushed her, face down, over the sidearm of the sofa. Holding her head down with one hand, he caressed her upraised buttocks with the other, allowing his hand to slip into the crevice. She gasped. When his movements elicited an involuntary moan, he boasted, "Want me, do you?"

Without further warning, he thrust himself into her from behind, and she screamed.

"Shut up, you bitch, or I'll wallop the daylights out of you," he barked as he slapped her backside and relentlessly pounded his body into hers.

Silent now, the woman felt both the ravishing of her body and the tears running down her face.

After he came, he released her. She dropped to the floor, sobbing. He poured himself another glass of champagne, his eyes never leaving her.

Finally, she weakly asked, "May I go now?"

"Go? When we haven't even used the bed yet? Oh no, my dear, we have a long evening ahead of us. America is a very rich country, and your entry fee isn't yet fully paid."

July 1895

Matt and Peg laughed at the sight of the man who had just fallen into the lake while attempting to step off the dock into a rowboat as it drifted away from him. Now standing knee-deep in water in his drenched clothes, he smiled a sheepish grin at them as they pedaled by him.

It was a pleasant afternoon, and hundreds of people were taking advantage of the weather to enjoy the popular pastime

Bridge at Fifty-Ninth Street in Central Park, 1895

of a Sunday outing in Central Park. As they rode along the pathways, passing fountains, playgrounds, and decorative flower gardens, Matt and Peg saw many families, sweethearts, or groups of friends picnicking, strolling, bicycling, horseback riding, or playing—all enjoying themselves in dozens of ways. The two of them rode on their tandem bicycle over bridges, under arches, and along pathways, all offering interesting vistas as the park's terrain and vegetation changed from flat grassy fields to gentle slopes to rocky ravines.

At last they reached the band shell, where a uniformed band played a John Philip Sousa march. Finding a quiet spot away from the other picnickers where they could still hear the music, they stopped by an old hickory tree near the edge of a large expanse of grass.

"Didn't I tell you I'd find the perfect spot?"

"Yes, you did, Matt, and so you have. This is lovely."

Matt untied the blanket and picnic basket from their bicycle. Together they spread the blanket and sat upon it. Peg opened the picnic basket.

"Well, darling, what splendid repast have you made?"

"I thought we'd try some new foods. Pigs' knuckles, calves' liver, and tripe."

"Oh, my God! I hope you're joking."

"I hear they're very good for you. You'll like them."

"Peg, is that really what you brought?" he asked in dismay.

Laughing, she answered, "Oh, Matt, you should see the look on your face. I'm just teasing."

"You little vixen," he said, relieved and joining in her laughter. Impulsively, he grabbed her, pulled her down beside him, and kissed her. This blissful spontaneity quickly ended though, as she gently pushed him away and sat up again.

"Now, Matt, behave yourself. Look, I really brought some

of your favorites. Here's potato salad, coleslaw, pickles, ham and cheese sandwiches, buttermilk, and chocolate cake."

Masking his disappointment at the brevity of their physical tenderness, he smiled and said, "Excellent, darling. You made wonderful choices."

"I expect you to eat some of everything."

"Don't worry about that. I'm starving."

Nonchalantly, they ate, chatted about incidental matters, and enjoyed the music. Later, putting their picnic remains back in the basket, they engaged in more small talk until Peg asked, "Matt, what is it you want to tell me?"

"How do you know there's something I want to tell you?"

"I can tell, Matt. It's just the way you're acting. So what is it?"

Relieved that her intuition had opened the door, he broached the subject, saying, "Do you remember my telling you that at the gala Commissioner Senner spoke to me again about Ellis Island just as he did last year?"

"The gala! What a wonderful time I had there! Yes, I remember your telling me about him. What of it?"

"I called him yesterday."

"Why?"

"He invited me to call him if I wanted to learn more about a position on the island."

"Matt, why would you even consider it? They don't even have a hospital, do they?"

"Yes, they do, but I understand it is not fully equipped."

"And your work would not be as prestigious as being a surgeon at a leading hospital like Presbyterian. I don't see any sense in it."

"Actually, working at Ellis Island would offer several advantages."

"Like what, Matt?"

"First of all, I wasn't thinking of resigning my hospital

position. I thought I would take a leave of absence for a while and then return."

"Why would you do that?"

"I could broaden my experience with such a different assignment. It would bring me into contact with many kinds of people, ones with a greater variety of medical problems. That would give me a stronger background as a hospital physician."

"Have you spoken to Dr. Jensen about this?"

"I sounded him out before I placed the call. He also thinks I would benefit by the experience. He's willing to give me a leave if I want it."

"For how long?"

"Probably six months. Just long enough to have the experience in a meaningful way."

"Would you have to wear one of those terrible uniforms those doctors wear?

"I don't know. They're commissioned officers in the Marine Hospital Service. I would be on temporary assignment."

"Matt, if this is what you want, I'll support you. But doesn't a city hospital have enough variety of medical problems? Don't you have immigrant patients now?"

"It's not the same, Peg. The doctors at Ellis Island see some medical problems we never do, because those people are not allowed into the country. They are sent back before ever getting a chance to enter one of our hospitals."

"Then why is it so important to see cases you will never have to treat in a hospital?"

"Peg, I'm a doctor. I want to learn about such things firsthand. Who knows? Someday I may encounter one of these rare cases at Presbyterian. Besides, you know how I love meeting new people. Here's a marvelous opportunity to see so many different kinds of people."

He looked at her watching him intently as he tried to explain. Everything he said was true, but he kept back a key element.

He believed that Ellis Island would provide him with the least disruptive change of scene to alleviate the restless dissatisfaction continually eating away at his peace of mind. How could he explain that to Peg? She would ask more questions than he had answers for. Some things are better left unsaid and this was one of those times.

"You're certain this will in no way jeopardize your standing at the hospital, Matt?"

"On the contrary, Dr. Jensen says my experience on the island will enhance my credentials. So I'm going to look into it, unless you are strongly against it."

"All right, Matt. Do what you think is best."

"That's my girl. Now, let's head back. I want to row you around the lake."

"On one condition."

"What's that?"

"That you stay out of the water, unlike that man."

The two of them began laughing again as they mounted the bicycle and pedaled to the dock.

August 1895

Matt's anticipation grew as the ferry neared Ellis Island. Even though this was just an exploratory visit, his spirits were soaring.

He didn't quite understand his feelings. Perhaps they were fed by the novel experience of traveling by ferryboat in New York harbor, or perhaps it was his approach to an island filled with different peoples pursuing a dream as his grandparents once had done. Whatever it was, he enjoyed the refreshing summer breeze on this midafternoon day and eagerly watched the island's buildings grow larger as the boat approached the dock.

He had waited a few weeks before calling Senner, who was pleased to hear from him and made arrangements for the visit and a meeting with Dr. John H. White, the chief medical officer.

After disembarking, Matt entered the main building and approached one of the gatemen, a lanky, brown-haired person in his thirties.

"Excuse me," he said to the man. "Can you direct me to Commissioner Senner's office? He's expecting me."

"What is your name?" the man asked with a light German accent.

"I'm Dr. Matthew Stafford."

"Oh yes, Doctor. The commissioner told me you were coming. I am Guenter Langer and most happy to welcome you. Please go up these stairs and turn right. It is the first door. You cannot miss it."

"Thank you, Mr. Langer," Matt replied, gratified by the warm reception.

Senner's welcome was even heartier.

"Dr. Stafford," he began, enthusiastically pumping Matt's hand within his firm grip, "dis is *wunderbar.* I cannot tell you how delighted I am dot you are here. Come, let us vaste no time. I vill show you zum of our operations und den introduce you to Dr. Vite. You vill like him. He is very good doctor und fine fellow."

Matt followed Senner into the Registry Hall balcony where they looked down at the milling rows of immigrants.

"My heavens!" exclaimed Matt. "I expected to see many immigrants here, but I didn't imagine them in such a wide variety of colorful clothing."

"*Ja,* dis is normal. Dey vant to make gudt impression zo before dey arrive, many change out of dere traveling clothes, vitch are dirty, smelly, und zumtimes have lice, und throw dem overboard. Vhat you zee are dere folk costumes dot dey usually vear back home on special occasions. For dem, notting could be more special den dis day to come into America."

"That is most interesting."

"Dis is de last batch to process today for dere legal inspection. Dey have already passed medical inspection, vitch I will let Dr. Vite tell you about."

"I've never before seen so many women wearing kerchiefs on their heads."

"*Ja.* It is dere custom in central Europe, but not here or

in northvestern Europe. Dis place is vere ve ask questions to determine if dey qualify for entry. De law forbids polygamists, prostitutes, und criminals. Ve also try to prevent de exploitation of young, single girls as vell as de entry of dose likely to become public charges."

"How long does it take to process an immigrant?"

"At dis station de questions take only few minutes, but because dere are zo many in line, dey may vait one or two hours for dere turn. Und de same is true of de medical examination. On average, de whole ting takes about tree or four hours. Of course, if dere is a problem, den it could be much longer."

"What happens next if they pass?"

"Ve give landing card to each vun mit permission to leave de island. Dey go down dose stairs over dere und den, depending on dere situation, dey either vait for relative to claim dem, get ticketed for dere railroad journey, or go to de vaiting room for ferryboat. Downstairs dey can also exchange money, buy food, und send letters home telling everyvun dey have arrived safely."

"It sounds very well organized."

"Tank you. It zeems to vork. Come; let us go find Dr. Vite."

John White, a surgeon in the Marine Hospital Service now detailed for duty at Ellis Island, was waiting for them in his office. Matt guessed his age to be in his early fifties and noted that his rather short hair, which was turning gray, framed a ruddy-complexioned face with blue, sparkling eyes. His manner quickly revealed a delightful, energetic personality and a keen mind. After the introductory formalities, Joseph excused himself and left the men alone.

"I understand you're from Massachusetts," John began, "and a graduate of Dartmouth."

"That's correct, sir."

"Well, I'm a Harvard man myself," said John teasingly, "but

we'll overlook your Dartmouth training since you're a fellow New Englander. Tell me a little about yourself."

"I've been a surgeon at Presbyterian Hospital for three years."

"It's a fine hospital. You work under Dr. Jensen then?"

"Yes, sir."

"A good man. I know him well."

"I agree, sir. I've enjoyed working with him."

"This would be quite a change, Dr. Stafford. What attracts you to us?"

Matt explained that he wanted a leave of absence to work with immigrants, to sample the variety of people and medical problems, and to add a new dimension to his practice that might bring him satisfaction.

White smiled. "Ah, the idealism and romanticism of youth," he said gently. "I remember such feelings. I think you would thrive on an assignment here. Are you married?"

"Yes, I am. Peg is also from Massachusetts."

"Childhood sweetheart?"

"Yes, sir."

"How nice. Any children?"

"No."

"Well, they'll come along soon enough."

Matt's smile faded, but he said nothing.

"All right," White continued, "let me take you around and acquaint you with our duties here."

The two men walked out onto the floor of the Registry Hall, to the top of the stairs where the immigrants entered the hall from the baggage room below.

"We've completed our work here for today, but this is the first station," he said, pointing to the top of the stairs. "Two of our doctors stand here on either side, making initial observations. Those with obvious or suggested physical defects are immediately removed from general processing and sent to a medical examining room for closer scrutiny. The rest move, one at a time, along to the second duty station twenty-five feet away. This, in addition to your hospital duties, is where I would assign you.

"You watch their movements as they approach. Are they coordinated and walking without a limp? As they make the required two right turns to reach you, do they have a sense of balance, and can they easily adjust to a new field of vision? You then examine for any physical deformity, especially missing fingers; for eye diseases, especially trachoma; for heart or breathing irregularities, especially consumption; for skin rashes, especially scalp disease; or for any other medical problem you can detect. You also note their facial expressions and responses to questions for any possible mental defects. Again, if there are any problems or possible problems, you mark an appropriate code in chalk on their clothing, and they go to an examining room for a closer look."

"So what they get here is a fast general exam."

"Yes, and for many it's the first one in their lives. Many have no idea what a stethoscope is and look with anxiety as you place the chest piece on them."

"It all must seem so strange to them."

"Indeed. Well, let me show you our examining rooms and our hospital."

Matt continued on his personally guided tour. The examining rooms were much as he expected, but the hospital was, as he had thought, far less than Presbyterian, lacking the more extensive facilities and services of the hospital he knew. He soon learned there was not even a place to house those with contagious diseases. Those patients had to be transported into New York City for confinement.

After bidding farewell to Dr. White, Matt reflected on their time together. It had gone well, he thought, and he knew he would be offered the job. Even with the limitations of this hospital, Matt nonetheless felt that he could enjoy a short-term assignment at Ellis Island.

The position appealed to him. He had always been fascinated by the courage of those who came as strangers to start life anew, far from their homelands. He warmly recalled boyhood memories about his grandparents telling him stories of the overland journey to Hamburg, the difficult ocean voyage, and adjustment to life in America. He understood now why he had been so excited earlier. The romantic image of working with immigrants, of being one of the first Americans they encountered on their dramatic adventure, fired his imagination.

As he was leaving the main building, Matt realized that he did not know how to find his way back to the ferry. He followed the rest of the crowd, assuming that they knew. He didn't notice the departing officials turn and exit through another door on their way to the ferry. So he continued along with the hurrying, excited, jabbering throng. These were the newly processed immigrants, their relatives, and friends.

Very quickly, Matt learned the reason why the officials had taken another exit. Not only was he jostled, but he was also bruised by the immigrants' baggage. He noted the baggage came in all shapes and sizes. He saw bags, baskets, boxes, bundles, and valises made of canvas, leather, and wood. There seemed no end to the variety.

In the short walk, he learned that wicker baskets are the most agreeable kind of immigrant baggage, as one yielded gently when accidentally pushed into his ribs. Deceptively treacherous were the large, soft-looking, feather-bed bundles. A sturdy Slav girl carried one slung over her shoulder. Its misleading soft, fluffy wrapping hid an iron pot or kettle in its center and, when she turned, her pack gained considerable momentum, striking into his shoulder. His greatest pain, however, came from a small tin trunk carried by someone from the British Isles. Its ragged edge crashed into his shins, breaking the skin.

Upon reaching the landing, Matt stepped out of the line onto the open deck of the ferry and watched the people coming aboard. Behind him, the late afternoon sun cast a golden hue on the city skyline as he watched the scene around him. Homebound island employees came aboard singly and in small groups. A few stopped on the deck near him. One was Guenter Langer, the friendly gateman.

"Dr. Stafford, did you enjoy your visit?"

"Yes, I did. It is quite a place."

"Maybe I will see you again sometime."

"Yes, I think you will."

"Good. I would like that."

Guenter then turned back to his colleagues, and Matt resumed his people watching. Often guided by someone in American clothes, the immigrants clustered together. Some were with their relatives. Others gathered with their own ethnic groups. Noting their distinctive local costumes and physiological features, and listening to their accents, he attempted to identify their origins.

Four or five Swedish men appeared. A group of Irish girls followed. Behind them a French family boarded and then three Chinese men. *Where did they sail from?* he wondered. Next, a group of about thirty strong-looking men boarded, escorted by an employee of a transportation company. This was a mixed group of East European Slavs and Matt enjoyed the challenge of distinguishing their nationalities. Slovaks were conspicuously different from Hungarians in their clothing. More subtle dress differences existed among Croatians, Slovaks, Poles, and Lithuanians, but differences in the shape of the head, facial features, and body build all aided him in his identity game.

First he identified the Slovaks, each with a knife, fork, and spoon sticking out of their boot tops. The Poles behind them were a little taller and seemingly more agile in their movements. Mixed in with them were even taller men he realized were

Lithuanians. The one Magyar in the group was a darker, muscular man with a mustache. Behind him were a few fairly tall men with prominent cheekbones and less-rounded heads that he recognized as Croatians. Men from the district of Carniola, known as Krainers, followed; they resembled the Croatians but were heavier and had long-stemmed pipes sticking out of their boot-legs. Last came a man distinct from all the others. He was sunburned, swarthy, and bulky, with broad shoulders, easily recognizable as a Dalmatian.

Following these men were women, also from East Europe. They all appeared to be healthy and stocky young women, wearing top boots, kerchiefs over their heads, and skirts shorter than the full length in fashion in the United States. Revealing their particular district in Eastern Europe was the stylistic differences in their apparel. The kerchiefs on their heads varied in color, as did the style of their boots. Their skirts also differed in shape, in the cut of the waists, and in the embroidery.

East European immigrant women and children
on deck of S.S. Amsterdam, 1899

Several Jewish families came next. The men all wore untrimmed beards, and some of the males wore curled sidelocks by their ears. Matt recognized the married women by their wigs. None possessed the muscular development of the preceding East European groups, but their clothing was similar to the Christians of the same localities. He noted with interest the American relatives of these Jewish immigrants, for they were Americanized in their dress and general appearance. The men had their hair cut American style and were either clean shaven or wore trimmed Van Dyke beards. Their clothing was similar to any American businessman. The women wore no wigs and looked like other well-dressed American women.

Once all the immigrants had entered the boat, Matt listened to the hum of conversation, catching snatches in different languages. Most of the government officials and employees, as well as the immigrants, were speaking in foreign languages. He decided it might be interesting to hear the conversational topics of newly arrived immigrants, and so he listened to those coming aboard.

"Are those factories hiring?" he heard in French from a man speaking to someone who, judging by his clothes, was an American.

He next heard a snatch of dialogue in German between two families, " ... delayed because of our baggage."

A Jewish family with their American relatives next passed. The wife complained, "The ship sailed the day before we got to Hamburg, and we had to wait ten days for it to come back. They wouldn't let us use our tickets on another ship!"

Following them came a cheerful-appearing group of chattering Italian families and their relatives. From them Matt heard, "Cici Rossi is going to marry Giovanni Bianco's widow, Serafina."

"He has eight children?"

"No, nine."

"Serafina has seven?"

"Yes."

"Some family for Cici. *Don-na mi-i-a!*"

Behind this group were two Polish men in a heated discussion. Matt edged closer. One was insisting that honesty was the best policy, and so, he had answered truthfully all of the inspector's questions. The other countered that he had lied in all his answers. Since he too had been cleared without any problem, he insisted that it was more practical to lie first, because it might work, and if it did not, you could then tell the truth if you had to do so.

Shaking his head in amusement, Matt saw a uniformed government employee running to the ferry slip just as two deckhands were beginning to loosen the mooring ropes. "Holdt dot boat!" he shouted to someone on the upper deck.

"*Was ist los*, John?" came the reply.

"Der Commissioner vants you to vait," he answered.

"All right," said the voice on the upper deck, immediately supplemented by, "*Ja wohl.*"

"*Mach' schnell!*" someone on the lower deck called out emphatically.

Matt looked in the nearby direction of the German voice from the lower deck where someone had said "hurry up" in German. He saw those about him glancing with considerable amusement at a group of young men he had heard speaking English when coming aboard the ferry. While they waited, Matt eavesdropped on the conversation of two immigration officials who were smiling and discussing the matter in Hungarian. He understood only a little of that language, but he picked up enough to learn that those young men were employees of the railroad companies at Ellis Island.

Hurriedly, Commissioner Senner reached the boat and went aboard. He noticed Matt immediately.

"Dr. Stafford! Gudt to zee you! How vas your interview mit Dr. Vite?"

"Fine, sir."

"*Wunderbar*! I hope dot you vill zoon join us."

"Thank you, sir," replied Matt, "I believe I shall."

Joseph smiled, nodded his head, patted Matt's upper left arm, and said, "Gudt. It vill be gudt for you und for us too."

He then walked past Matt to a group of island employees, where he began conversing in German. Listening to part of their conversation, Matt discovered Senner's sense of humor and warm, affable personality. Gone was the aloof, restrained autocrat of the newspaper depictions.

Matt's thoughts were suddenly distracted by an itch on his right wrist. Slowly he lifted it and saw three or four little red points in a row, close to a vein. One of the nearby immigration officials standing next to him observed his movements and asked, "Flea?"

Realizing the marks did indeed indicate flea bites, Matt smiled slightly and replied, "Yes."

"It looks like you've got another bite trail on your neck. You probably picked them up from those Greeks going through the island. They had quite a few."

Since it was useless to hunt for a flea in the open air, Matt shrugged his shoulders, smiled, and extended his hand to the dark-complexioned man.

"Hello. I'm Matt Stafford."

"Frank Martiniello," he replied, shaking hands. "Glad to meet you, Matt."

Frank was about four inches shorter than Matt. He had a big smile that displayed his glistening white teeth. He appeared to be about Matt's age and his friendly manner easily made Matt feel comfortable speaking to him.

"What do you do on the island?"

"I'm an interpreter. Are you a doctor?"

"Yes. How did you know?"

"I heard the commissioner ask you about your interview with Dr. White. Are you joining us?"

"I haven't made a final decision yet, but I think so."

"I think you'd like it. It's a busy, interesting place. There's never a dull moment. I've only been here two months myself and I love it."

"Two months! Is it all you expected it to be? How are the people to work with? Do you find the work fulfilling?"

"Whoa, Doctor, one question at a time," said Frank, putting up both hands in front of his shoulders.

"Sorry. It's just that you seem the perfect one to ask these questions. I mean, you're new here and you have a fresh perspective."

"I do? Okay, I do. I'm not sure what I expected exactly, but I can tell you that I like what I'm doing. I work mostly in the Registry Hall, and that's a pretty noisy place, as you can imagine, with hundreds of people in there, all talking in different languages. Sometimes though, I'm at a Board of Inquiry hearing, and it's much quieter there."

"What do you do there?"

"Same thing. Interpreter. When someone is detained over an irregularity, we have this procedure to review the case and determine if it can be resolved or not. If not, they are deported."

"Are many deported?"

"Well, first let me say that only a small percentage of the immigrants require a hearing. For those who do, I'd say, from my experience, that maybe half of them are sent back."

"Tell me, how are the people to work with?"

"Oh, they're a fine bunch of fellas. Of course, a lot of them don't speak English well, so they kinda keep to themselves, especially the Germans. A lot of them work on the island, and they kinda have their own little club, you know what I mean?

76

And I'm one of the few Italians at the place, so the German and Irish workers aren't too friendly. Still, the job is a good one. Not too many of my people have a government job. I'm proud to be here."

Matt astutely picked up on the social isolation and prejudice Frank was experiencing at work. It was indicative of a more widespread societal reaction. In the newspapers and in his own social circle, increasing concerns were expressed about the changing character of immigration, now that the majority of newcomers were no longer from northern and western Europe.

Just as the ferry was drawing away from the slip, a blond, apparently Swedish, immigrant ran to make the boat. Hearing the railroad employees shouting, "Run, Yon, run," Matt and Frank turned to watch. Encouraged by the shouts, the running man used his carpetbag to deflect the efforts of the gateman trying to stop him. By the time the man reached the edge of the slip, the ferryboat was about six feet away. Spurring him on, the railroad employees laughingly shouted, "Yump, Yon, yump!"

As the Swede hesitated an instant before jumping, the gateman succeeded in grabbing him, causing the railroad employees to laugh even more.

Matt turned back to study the human diversity surrounding him on the boat. He had decided that Ellis Island would truly be a fascinating place to work. And the people he had met so far—Joseph Senner, John White, Guenter Langer, Frank Martiniello—had all impressed him. He looked forward to receiving an offer from the Immigration Bureau.

"Frank, I believe I will be working with you at Ellis Island, and I'm hoping you'll be my friend."

Frank smiled brightly. "I've never had a doctor as a friend before."

"You do now."

"Then I look forward to the day you start."

"So do I, Frank, so do I."

October 1895

Arriving at the main building for his first day of work at Ellis Island, Matt felt an even more intense nervous excitement than he did in August. He liked the feeling, knowing it came from anticipation.

He realized that his willingness to plunge into a new world, facing unknown challenges, was not as great as the risk taken by the arriving immigrants. They had taken a permanent step, courageously forsaking the traditions of their homelands to pursue a dream. His was a temporary move, and he had to make no sacrifice to achieve it.

Matt reflected further on the fact that immigrants left behind others who also suffered but lacked the resolution to make a change. Unlike those reluctant people in Europe or even those in America whose inaction trapped them in the more limited world of the familiar, he had acted to extend his horizons. Excited and eager, he was about to test himself, meet new people, and discover more of the world about him. *Come on, Ellis Island, let's see what you're all about*, he thought to himself.

With a determined step, Matt reached the corridor that connected the commissioner's office with the other principal offices of the building. Only those on official business were allowed into this part of the building, its access guarded by a gateman.

"Dr. Stafford, it's good to see you again."

Matt recognized him. "Hello, Guenter. It's good to see you too."

"Is this your first day with us?"

"Yes, I'm on my way to see Dr. White."

"Good. Welcome aboard, doctor," Guenter said, initiating a handshake. "Let me know if there's anything I can do for you. Anything at all."

"Thank you, Guenter. I may take you up on that."

"Any time, Dr. Stafford. Do you remember where Dr. White's office is?"

"Yes, I do."

"All right, then. I'll see you later."

As Matt walked down the busy corridor filled with clerks and messengers passing to and fro, he saw a poorly dressed, forlorn Syrian beggar wandering about, looking into the various offices. The man was walking up to each passerby, pointing to a piece of white pasteboard attached to his shirt. When he came up to him, Matt read the pencil-scrawled sign, "Please help a poor sick Arab."

The man had a scarf wrapped around his neck, masking the lower part of his face. Matt first thought the man had smallpox in the early pustular stage above his scarf until he noted the man was already badly marked from an old assault of the disease. Anxious to be on time for his meeting with the chief medical officer, Matt left him alone.

Dr. White wanted Matt to learn about a few of the hospital patients before beginning to conduct medical exams in the main building. As the two men walked over to the separate building, the older man gave Matt some insights into making cursory medical judgments.

"Remember, Matt, no one would even think of buying a

horse until first seeing how it stands, in order to judge its state of health. Human posture, especially at rest, gives us an even better chance to detect physical and mental problems. Some postures give us clues about abnormal pelvic or abdominal conditions. If a person doesn't have good muscle tone, the ligaments give way and stretch. A hernia, for example, may be an indicator of a larger problem—general muscular deficiency, defects in nervous organization, or other abdominal irregularities.

"If the immigrants are carrying baggage, they will have to stop and rest. That's when to look at them. You can get a quick sense of their blood pressure and breathing ability as they reach the top of the stairs. You'll also quickly learn that their carrying baggage or a coat on the arm will make obvious to you any deformity of the upper extremities or serious impairment of joints at the shoulder, elbow, or wrist.

"Another little trick we have is stamping the inspection card and handing it to the immigrants. They almost always look at the card to see what was marked, and the way they hold it tells us if their vision is defective."

"I'm impressed," replied Matt, "about how much you can learn just from observation."

"You'll pick it up in no time. It is no more difficult to detect poorly built, defective, or broken-down human beings than to recognize a broken machine."

"Interesting. How long have you been here at Ellis Island?"

"Since it opened in January of '92. Almost four years now."

"I take it you enjoy your work?"

"Very much, and I think you will too. Of course, I've got the advantage of living here as well. The government provides my family with a house and servant right here on the island."

"Really? That's convenient."

"Yes, it is, for the most part. We like it."

The chief medical officer led Matt to the entrance into a male ward. Matt gazed about at the twenty men lying in their beds.

"Some of these men are convalescing from a serious illness. The rest have slight injuries or ailments that prevent them from doing manual labor. An immigrant's real asset is his physical strength. That's what keeps him from becoming a public charge. So it is in everyone's best interests not to discharge any patient from the island until he is fully restored to health."

"Excuse me, Dr. White," said a soft feminine voice behind them.

The two men who were standing in the entrance turned around to see a nurse standing there.

"Hello, Miss Devereaux," said Dr. White. "Forgive us for blocking your way."

Matt was spellbound. Her oval face, framed by blonde hair, was exquisite, with exotic brown, almond eyes, delicate nose, sensuous lips, and flawless white skin. About five foot five, she had a shapely, petite figure.

"Miss Devereaux, I'd like you to meet our newest addition, Dr. Matthew Stafford. Dr. Stafford, this is Nurse Nicole Devereaux."

"How do you do, Miss Devereaux," said Matt, extending his hand and flashing his most charming smile.

"I'm pleased to meet you, Dr. Stafford," Nicole replied, looking at him directly and smiling. She held eye contact for a brief second after speaking and then withdrew her hand and turned to Dr. White. "Now, if you'll excuse me, I had better see to the patients."

"Of course," said Dr. White, stepping aside to let her pass. Noticing Matt's gaze following her, he chuckled. "She's a pretty one, isn't she?" he asked needlessly. "She charms everyone here, patients and staff alike, and she's an excellent nurse."

"I think she's the most beautiful woman I have ever seen."

"Don't let your wife hear you say that," said White, chuckling. "She's a real looker, though, that's for certain, but she's not very sociable."

"What do you mean?"

"She's friendly but distant. She does her job extremely well, but she doesn't mingle. She keeps to herself, doesn't have many conversations with her colleagues, and declines to come to the annual Christmas party my wife and I host for the staff."

"Is she spoken for?"

"She's not married, but beyond that, I have no idea about her personal life. She's a very private person. No one knows much about her. Well, let's move along."

Overcoming his distraction, Matt followed John into another ward.

"Twice a day," continued White, "morning and night, in each of the wards, patients not bedridden line up at the foot of their beds for us to check them. This also gives them an opportunity to bring any personal matters to the doctor's attention. They eat their meals three times a day in the dining room."

"How do you plan a menu?" asked Matt. "It must be difficult."

"Why do you say that?"

"Well, you've got so many races or nationalities here, all with varying food preferences and dietary habits. And you've got to offer some variety in the daily menu too, don't you?"

"I see what you mean. First, let me say that the menu is the product of considerable experience and study. What's important, really, is that we don't try to please the immigrants as much as we try not to waste good food. It's a waste of good oatmeal to serve it to Italians, but every race and nationality will eat Italian bread. And I don't know of anyone who has objected to good kosher roast beef. It all seems to work out. Let's go back outside now."

As they left the hospital, the two men heard the boisterous sounds of children playing.

"Come," smiled John, "you have yet to see some of our more rambunctious patients."

Near the hospital was a playground in which about fifteen boys, ranging in age from eight to fourteen, were playing soccer. Most were wearing stocking caps.

"This number of detained boys is normal. They represent about a half-dozen different nationalities. They are all being treated for ringworm. That usually requires their detention here for a year or more. I would think you've dealt with this problem at Presbyterian."

"Yes, indeed. I've treated several cases of this scalp disease. It's such a difficult disease to cure. After weeks of daily shampoos and ointment treatments, you think you've ended the problem and then a new lesion develops."

"I know what you mean. It's frustrating. You would think the application of antisepsis to the infected area would end the problem, but it does not. There's so much that we don't know about the human body."

Matt continued to watch the boys playing. "Look at them," he said, amused. "They're having a grand time. They seem to have no language barrier either."

"They have solved their language problem by all of them speaking Italian," John replied. "In less than a month, a new boy—whether Dutch, Jewish, Polish, or Irish—is heard here on the playground yelling in Italian as loudly as anyone."

"Why Italian?"

"We are getting more Italian immigrants than other groups nowadays, so their dominance exerts itself. Since more of the boys speak Italian than any other language, the rest quickly learn it."

Pulling out his pocket watch, John noted, "Well, time is passing quickly. We had better head back to the main building.

Another shipload of immigrants is due here momentarily and we'll be needed."

Matt followed him back to the large building dominating the island. His orientation completed, Matt's real learning was about to begin. However, the first lesson did not begin on the medical inspection line where he thought it would. He was pleasantly surprised, as John escorted Matt to Matt's duty station, to find Guenter Langer waiting there.

"Guenter, what are you doing here?"

"I asked to be assigned to you, Dr. Stafford. I hope you don't mind."

"Mind? Of course not, I'm delighted."

"Good," Guenter replied, smiling.

Until Matt arrived, Guenter had been ambivalent about his work as a gateman. Immigrating at age seventeen with his family, they had settled near other German immigrants on a farm in northwestern New Jersey. Ten years later, still single and dissatisfied, he had had enough of farming and ethnic isolation, and moved to New York City. Ironically, as he sought to distance himself from his ethnic background, he had used his German associations to get a job at Ellis Island and was surrounded by numerous German colleagues. Dr. Stafford, as a part-German, native-born American, offered him the role model of a person with a wider social world. Although Guenter had no interest in becoming a doctor, he found in Matt a means of broadening further his world, and so he sought this assignment at Matt's duty station.

Guenter's smiling countenance changed into a more serious expression, as he said, "Dr. Stafford, I need to ask you something. Did you see an Arab carrying a sign in the corridor when you first arrived?"

"Yes, I remember him."

"He didn't belong there. He walked right by me. He was right behind an official at the time, and I thought he was being escorted past me. Anyway, I later realized the situation and took him to a medical examination room. It turns out he's got smallpox. Since you came into contact with him, you'll have to be vaccinated."

"Smallpox! Well, I've been vaccinated recently, but I don't understand. That man already had smallpox once!"

"Some people can have a second attack," John offered.

"I didn't know that or I would have isolated him myself," replied Matt, embarrassed at his error.

"It is unusual, but it does happen."

"I can see that I still have much to learn."

"All of us always do, Doctor. Let's see what we can learn from this next batch of immigrants."

As the immigrants came to them one by one, John twice demonstrated the examining procedure and then stood back to observe Matt's work. Satisfied, he patted Matt's shoulder and left, saying, "You're doing fine," and headed to one of the small examining rooms.

Matt's first immigrant examinee and, in fact, most of his examinees that day, were Italian. Not able to converse with them, Matt could only repeat the greeting *"Buon giorno!"* and then proceed in silence. If they passed, he smiled and nodded his head to let the individual know the examination was successful. For the one-in-twenty unfortunate failure, or questionable entry, he would first mark a letter in chalk on their front left shoulder. Most times it was "E" for eyes, "H" for heart, or "P" for physical and lungs. Then he would gesture with upraised index finger to indicate "wait," then open his hand, palm up, and sweep it to his right to indicate that Guenter would escort the person to a private examining room.

At the end of the day, he encountered Frank Martiniello on their way to the ferryboat.

"How was your first day, Doctor?"

"It was fine except for one thing."

"What's that?"

"Most of the people I saw were Italian and I don't know the language. I couldn't talk to them."

"I could teach you Italian."

"Would you?"

"Certainly. You said we were friends, didn't you?"

"Yes, and I meant it."

"Well then, we could do a little each day during our lunch hours."

"Frank, you're a treasure. I really appreciate this."

"Doctor, it's no big thing. Besides, I have a hunch you're going to be a fast learner."

November 1895

Matt was making his morning rounds before heading to the main building to inspect the new arrivals. Near the male ward, he quickened his pace, smiling to himself. Nicole Devereaux was on duty there and he was anxious to see her again. In the past four weeks, he had seen her every workday, and each day further reinforced his attraction to her.

He still knew little about her, except that she seemed happy in her work. She was gracious to everyone and had an excellent bedside manner with her patients. Otherwise, she kept to herself, avoiding even the small talk so common among working colleagues. All he knew were the superficialities of contact with her and, most especially, her beautiful face with its enigmatic smile.

Matt reflected on that smile and then on Peg, who had left yesterday to visit her family in Massachusetts. Although their marriage lacked complete fulfillment, this in no way diminished his love for her or his sense of fidelity. So Nicole's attraction troubled him.

Often, thoughts of Nicole crept into his mind. They were just fragments—her face perhaps, or just her hypnotic eyes or sensuous lips, even the occasional wishing for her partly opened lips to press against his. Conflicted about having such thoughts, he would try to dismiss the images, but they would return. This morning he even had a waking dream about their lying naked together, making love. Aroused, awake, and alone, he had quickly taken a cold shower.

He and Peg were still active socially. Frequently invited to dinner parties and social gatherings, they had gone to many, but he still only partially enjoyed this whirlwind of activity. Although he yearned for a greater portion of quieter, more private times when he could just relax and read, Peg seemed to thrive on the social scene, so he yielded to her wishes.

He smiled at the recollection of Peg's bubbly presence in the midst of people. Then he recalled this morning's dream about making love to Nicole Devereaux.

And so, he smiled again, this time at the thought of seeing Nicole. He knew, of course, that his dream was a fantasy. He was married, and Nicole was simply a beautiful single woman some fortunate man would have. While he found Nicole captivating, he also found it difficult to have a conversation with her, not knowing how to handle himself in her presence.

As Matt drew near Nicole's ward, he heard a loud commotion. Dashing into the ward, he saw Pete, one of the male attendants, attempting to restrain a violent patient.

"What's going on here?" he cried out.

Nicole, standing near, quickly explained. "We were letting this man out of bed for the first time in a week. When Pete brought him a bathrobe to put on, he began acting crazy."

This was a side of Nicole he hadn't seen before. Wide-eyed, her eyebrows arched, she looked scared. *Even so*, he thought, *she still looks incredibly beautiful.*

Before Matt could respond, a patient in a nearby bed began laughing. "You people don't understand. That man is a Bulgarian. I know. I understand his language. He won't wear that bathrobe because it is red. Red is the Turkish color. He hates the Turks."

"Bring him a different-colored robe then, Pete," Matt instructed the attendant.

Slowly Pete released the Bulgarian and left with the red robe. The man just stood there, shifting wary eyes from Matt, to Nicole, and then back again. Pete returned with a green robe. The man put it on and smiled at them.

Matt asked Nicole, "Are you all right?"

"Oh yes, Dr. Stafford. I don't know how to thank you."

"Well, that's easy," said Matt, suddenly emboldened.

"Oh?"

"Yes. How about having dinner with me tonight?" Matt asked, amazing himself. He watched her eyes on him.

After a few seconds, a seemingly thousand heartbeats long, Nicole smiled and said, "Why, that would be lovely, Dr. Stafford."

Matt was elated.

"Wonderful!" he said, attempting to conceal his joyous relief. "After work we'll take the ferry back together, have dinner, and I'll see you home."

"That sounds nice. Thank you for asking me."

"The pleasure is mine, Miss Devereaux."

Matt got through the day, the endless day. His thoughts constantly returned to their morning encounter and then to the evening. He thought about a lovely restaurant in midtown that had booths, secluded by velvet draperies, subdued lighting, and an intimate ambiance. He knew he was playing with fire, but he wanted their time together to be perfect.

*   *   *

Their shifts over, they discreetly met at the ferry dock. As usual, Frank and Guenter were on the same boat, and Matt talked with them while Nicole pretended not to be with Matt, who was confident that the men detected nothing unusual. Once ashore, and certain the others were on their way, he rejoined Nicole, hailed a hansom cab, and instructed the driver on where to take them.

"I'm so pleased you accepted my invitation," he began after they were seated in their private setting at the restaurant.

"Well, I had heard about this handsome surgeon coming to work at Ellis Island on a short-term assignment. I was intrigued and wanted to know more about you. Our having dinner together gives me that opportunity."

"Thank you for the compliment, but you are most definitely the better looking of the two of us."

"I don't think so, but thank you."

"No, really."

"Tell me about yourself. Who is Dr. Matthew Stafford?"

Comfortably, Matt revealed accounts about himself that he rarely shared with anyone. Without further probing, he told Nicole stories about his boyhood, about his best friend Skip who

Hansom driver awaits his passengers, circa 1895

moved away when they were twelve, about his dog Roscoe, and about working on his uncle's farm.

"What made you decide to become a doctor?" Nicole asked when he paused for a moment.

"Two people influenced me. There was Andrew Burke, my high school biology teacher. He was one of my favorites. He had such an easy way of talking. He had a quiet but warm sense of humor. More than that though, he was an inspiring role model for me. He was the one who challenged me to seek new horizons and also encouraged me to think about medicine."

"Who was the second person?"

"That was old Doc Flint. When he learned that I was thinking about becoming a doctor, he would sometimes take me along on his rounds throughout the county. Once I assisted him when he operated on a hunting accident victim, and I knew then and there that I wanted to be a doctor and help other people."

"So he must be happy that you became one."

"Yes. He sent me a congratulatory letter when I graduated from medical school. I wanted him to be there, but he was in failing health by then and couldn't travel. I framed that letter, and it sits on my desk."

"That's so nice, Matt."

"So here I am, the doctor I've always wanted to be, and I'm living in New York City, the place where I've always wanted to live. I'm really fortunate that I am living out all my goals."

These were not things he planned to say, but somehow, he needed to say them. He felt good talking to her. He opened more to her than to anyone else, except for Peg. Matt didn't tell Nicole about her. He wanted to, but he couldn't. Realizing he had been dominating the conversation, he sought to coax some information out of her.

"Well, I've been talking too much about myself. It's your turn to tell me some things."

"You haven't talked too much, Matt. I enjoyed hearing all about you."

"Perhaps, but you'll only make me feel better if you let me hear all about you."

"What would you like to know?"

"Anything. Everything."

"Oh, I couldn't tell you everything. A girl needs to leave a little mystery about herself."

Chuckling, Matt replied, "Then just let me know a few things."

"Well, let's see. You can tell by my last name that my father was French, but my mother is English. I'm Catholic. I grew up and went to school here in the city."

"What was your favorite subject?"

"I liked all my subjects, but I was really good in math and science, so I guess I'll pick them."

"Is that why you decided to become a nurse?"

"I guess so. I didn't have someone to inspire me like you. I didn't want to be a teacher, and I wasn't ready to get married. I like helping people, and since I was good in science, it seemed the right choice."

"Do you still think it was the right choice?

"Oh yes, definitely. I love what I am doing."

"Where did you train?"

"I went to Bellevue Hospital's nursing school, and after I graduated, I worked there for a few years. Then I took a job at Ellis Island when it opened, and that's about it."

"One more question, is your family still here?"

"My father died two years ago. I live with my mother in an apartment here in Manhattan. My two brothers live nearby, so we all see one another from time to time."

They lapsed into a brief silence as they finished eating, and then Nicole said to him, "Tell me about your wife."

Stunned, Matt lamely replied, "You know about her?"

"I didn't at first, but then I accidentally found out later."

"I wanted to tell you about her, but I just didn't know how."

"It's all right, Matt. I understand. Please, tell me about her."

"Her name is Margaret, but everyone calls her Peg. We got married the summer between college and medical school, six years ago."

"Do you have any children?"

"No. Peg has been in delicate health for quite some time. She was with child two years ago, but she lost it and almost died herself. That's when we learned she couldn't have any more children."

"I'm very sorry, Matt," she said gently, reaching out to touch his hand on the table.

"Yes, so am I," he said with a hint of sadness. Aware of her touch, he changed the subject. "Well, it's been a delightful dinner. Are you ready to go?"

"Yes, I am. I'm glad we had this opportunity to learn a little about each other. Thank you for dinner."

Matt smiled and paid the bill. He escorted Nicole outside, and they took a carriage to her place. He asked the driver to wait and accompanied her inside and up to her floor.

Outside her door, he looked at her, wanting to take her in his arms and kiss her, but he did not. Until now, their dinner together had been an innocent encounter in his mind, but a kiss would change that.

So, after a fleeting pause, he smiled tenderly and said, "I'd better be going. I can't tell you how much I enjoyed this evening with you. Good night."

Nicole looked at him and said softly, "Aren't you going to kiss me?"

Her question eliminated his inhibitions. As he had fantasized, he took her in his arms and kissed her with parted lips. Her lips were as succulent, as soft and tender, as he had imagined. He kissed her again and again. Gently their lips roamed over each other's and pressed together. Their tongues parried, and the moistness of their kisses intoxicated him. He had never been so affected, with each kiss so wonderful that he craved another and another.

When at last they parted, Matt realized that—even though they had only embraced and kissed—his feelings had been unlike any he had ever known.

December 1895

Each person lives two lives, an external one of social interactions and an internal one of self-awareness. The public self—revealed to outsiders, even colleagues—is often a façade masking real thoughts and vulnerabilities of the private self.

Dr. Matthew Stafford was the envy of everyone. Often the topic of conversation at Ellis Island and in New York society, people praised him as handsome, warm, sincere, competent, and as someone with a promising career and a wonderful wife. They did not know his inner torment. Guilt-ridden and frustrated, he felt like two different people. Peg brought love, stability, and many social interactions into his life. When he was with her, he recognized his love and obligations, and he embraced them.

Yet when he was with Nicole at the hospital, he was a different man. Ever since she had given him a glimpse a few weeks ago of sexual excitement and fulfillment he had never before known, her presence delighted him. To coworkers their interactions always appeared professional and friendly. Unknown to the others, however, were Nicole's occasional secret light touches of Matt's hand when he least expected them. Those glancing contacts electrified him, and sometimes he squeezed her hand in response. She would then just smile and move away.

Her sensuality enthralled him. Once, seizing an opportunity when they were alone, he whisked her into an examining room and grabbed both her wrists. Raising her arms above her shoulders, he pressed her against the wall with his body and kissed her passionately.

His unexpected actions, momentarily rendering her helpless, were not unwelcome. In truth, what he was doing excited her. She eagerly kissed him back, and he released his grasp, allowing her to embrace him as he embraced her. Their few clandestine moments ended all too quickly, however, inasmuch as they could not risk being discovered.

Since then, there had been numerous flirtatious moments and fleeting kisses. He relished the physical pleasures that dallying with this beautiful, sensual woman brought him. The experiences were all so wonderful that he didn't want to end them, even though he realized that he must.

Without question, time spent with Nicole was far more exhilarating than time spent with Peg. He realized that part of his feelings were influenced by the thrill of the new and forbidden against the familiar and routine, but he was also certain it was more than that. And so, when he was alone, his emotional tug-of-war anguished him. One woman he had loved enough to marry. He still loved her, but now believed that he was falling in love with Nicole. With her, his sensual nature found expression. With her, his innermost self found release. And with her, he had rediscovered the joy of life.

*   *   *

Nicole Devereaux often reflected on the wisdom and irony of her situation with Matt. Her looks had long attracted men's attention and her friendly manner had often been misinterpreted as an invitation. With a small joke or polite demurral, she would turn aside those unwelcome advances, wary of getting involved because she found most men shallow and selfish. All most people knew were the superficialities of contact with her and, most especially, her beautiful face and beguiling smile.

Her seemingly unapproachable public image hid her sensitive, passionate nature. It was her defense against getting hurt again. Years earlier, she had lost her virginity to a man she cared deeply about. Soon afterward, that relationship ended, and it ended badly. Still believing in herself and possessing a healthy self-esteem, she occasionally took risks in forming new relationships, but she also exercised great care about whom she allowed to get close to her.

Tom Lindstrom had been the best of the lot until she discovered Matt. In their all-too-few moments together, everything about Matt—his face, his body, his scent, his charm—were all sensuous and exciting. She enjoyed his kisses and thrilled in experiencing the sensation of his body pressed against hers. She could also tell by the way he kissed her that Matt was the man she hoped he would be. He kissed her gently, sensitively, and lovingly. She sensed that he would be a generous lover, giving of himself as fully as she wanted to give.

Here was a man, she believed, who could unleash fully all her passion. Yet, she didn't dare let go, because he was married and not hers to have. She knew that their sensual playing, as agreeable as it was, would lead to no good. There were too many negative factors regarding his married reality—the need for secrecy, fear of discovery, conscience, limited opportunities, frustration—that undermined his positive qualities and the chemistry between them.

Time with Matt was pure pleasure and time away from him was torture. She found herself thinking about Matt even when she was with Tom. She felt like a hypocrite, luring Matt away from his wife and deceiving Tom as well. She didn't like such duplicity in herself.

She knew she traveled a dangerous course bound for pain. Their relationship could also jeopardize Matt's career. Things had already gone too far. She resolved to do something about the situation before she became even more entangled in the web of pleasure and pain. She decided that John White's Christmas party for the medical staff would provide the opportunity.

*   *   *

Because Peg didn't feel up to going, Matt went to the party alone. Sipping a cup of hot, spiced wine, he heard his host's voice behind him at the front door.

"Why, Miss Devereaux! What a delightful surprise! I'm so pleased that you came."

Matt turned around, looking across the parlor past the heads of the mingling guests, as John greeted Nicole. He smiled at the unexpected joy of seeing her and walked over. Only then did he realize that she was not alone.

"Dr. White, I'd like you to meet my friend, Thomas Lindstrom," Nicole said, her eyes glancing at Matt.

"A pleasure, Mr. Lindstrom," John replied happily and vigorously shook the man's hand. "So you're the lucky fellow who's captured this young lady's heart."

"I hope I've captured her heart, sir. It's good to meet you."

Matt was silent and immobile. He felt pressure in his temples, took a deep breath and released it slowly as Nicole moved toward him.

"Tom, here's another of my colleagues, Dr. Matthew Stafford. Dr. Stafford, I'd like you to meet Mr. Thomas Lindstrom," said Nicole, introducing the two of them.

"How do you do, Dr. Stafford," said his smiling, unknowing rival, extending his hand.

Masking his envy, Matt looked into the face of this blonde, blue-eyed, good-looking, and well-built man. He played out his role, effectively hiding his agony, returning both the smile and his hand, saying as they shook hands, "Nice to meet you."

"Where is Mrs. Stafford?" Nicole asked, looking directly at Matt.

Her question jolted him into the realization that he was more alone at this moment than he had ever been. His wife's absence deprived him of a social partner while his marital status denied him Nicole's company.

With that flashing thought, he answered, "She's—she's not here. A little under the weather, I'm afraid."

"Oh, I'm so sorry," Nicole replied. "We would so have liked to meet her. Well, give her our best and tell her we wish her a speedy recovery."

Matt smiled and nodded as they walked away to greet others. He felt empty, wishing he could leave. Propriety demanded he stay, however, at least for a little while longer. Though he tried hard not to, throughout the evening his eyes sought out the couple, and he renewed his torment. He didn't want to look again, but he did so repeatedly as the evening progressed. Each glance at their closeness or sounds of their shared laughter was further affirmation that Nicole was not his to have. Whatever fantasies he had previously entertained were shattered by the reality before him.

The evening seemed to drag on interminably. Finally, when he felt enough time had passed to allow for a graceful exit, he did so, saying his goodbyes to all and heading for the hallway to get his coat and hat. As he left, he did not see Nicole's longing gaze or the tear welling in her eye.

January 1896

As usual, the hospital nurses were already caring for their patients when the doctors arrived for morning rounds.

Nicole entered her ward, cheerfully calling out, "Good morning, everyone. We've got a bright sunny day today."

From her right, a dark-haired man in his forties responded, "*Buon giorno, mia bella signorina.* You are the sunshine in this-a room every day! And your hair, she is gold like-a the sun."

"Antonio," she said laughing as she brought him a pill to take, "what a nice compliment."

"It's-a true," added another patient. "You are as beautiful inside as outside. Ask-a anyone here."

"*Grazie*, Paolo, and *grazie*, Antonio," Nicole replied. "Now let's get up, and get ready for the doctor."

"*Si, signorina.* Anything for you," said Antonio.

Nicole went around to each of the patients, dispensing medicines and assisting a few patients out of bed with the help of Pete, her usual aide. Three of the men were too weak to get out of bed, so Nicole propped them up a bit on newly fluffed pillows and provided bedpans. Other patients, more independent, were able to care for themselves before going to the dining room after the doctor saw them.

Nicole knew the doctor on morning rounds today would be Matt. She hadn't seen him since the party, their holiday vacation schedules keeping them apart for two weeks. She looked out the second-story window and saw him arriving.

Matt approached the hospital with mixed emotions. He wanted to see Nicole again and talk about the party, and yet he didn't. He feared that he already knew; she wanted the type of relationship he could not give her. Logically, he knew she was making the right moral and practical choice, but emotionally, he didn't want to let go.

He saw Nicole at the end of the second floor hall. The sight of her buoyed his spirits even as he realized that their conversation might crush him. For the moment, though, he allowed her appearance to provide that brief joy.

"Good morning," Matt said pleasantly as he reached her.

"Good morning, Matt."

"Nicole, we need to talk."

"Yes, I know. Matt, let me explain. We're mixed up in something that just can't be. It's not that I don't like you. In fact, I'm afraid that I like you too much. It scares me how much you affect me."

"Then why—"

"Oh, Matt, you know why. It's not right. It's too risky. It's not fair to your wife or to me. And we work together. I can't separate my personal life as easily from my professional life as you can. I need to show my feelings, not hide them, but I can't express my feelings for you because that would create a scandal and too many problems."

"I realize that."

"But do you understand? I think you're a warm, sensitive man. I could easily fall in love with you, but I can't keep seeing you and risking our jobs and our reputations as well. Do you have any idea how I feel about coming between you and her? And if anyone ever finds out, they'll hate me! I can't do this anymore! We've got to stop this before it goes too far! We can't see each other anymore. I have to live my life without you."

Torn between his feelings for Peg and for Nicole, and despite his strong feelings for Nicole, he knew this was a love that could not be. He was a married man, and that was that. It wasn't fair to Nicole to continue. Ending their relationship would free both of them from guilt and torment, but it would be at a costly price. He couldn't imagine life without her and knew in that instant that he truly loved her.

He searched for the right words to say. All he could think of was, "If only there were the two of us."

Struggling with her emotions, Nicole replied, "Well, there aren't! The only twosome is you and your wife. I can't let this go on any longer. Please don't make it any harder than it already is."

He looked into her eyes and saw the pain. There too he saw his own. It was more than he could bear.

"I'll back off, Nicole. I won't make working here awkward. I hope we can still be friends."

"Oh, Matt, of course, we have to work together, and we'll stay friends, but otherwise I have to invest my personal life in a healthier relationship. I'm already twenty-five years old! Most women my age are married and have children, for God's sake!"

"All right then," he said, putting up a brave front, "I wish you a happy life."

"Oh, Matt," she said, the tears welling up in her eyes, "I truly wish you the same."

He looked at her for an instant, nodded his head, and with a grim smile, slowly turned and walked away.

*   *   *

After morning rounds Matt headed for the main building where he met Ed McSweeney.

"Top o' the morning to ya, Matt."

"Hello, Ed."

"Well, you seem glum today."

"I'm sorry. It's been a difficult morning."

"Something troubling you? Is there anything I can do?"

"No, thanks. I'll be fine."

"All right, but if you need someone just to talk to, or if you need anything, I mean it when I say that I want you to feel free to come to me."

"Thanks, Ed. I'll keep that in mind."

Ed sincerely meant his offer. He felt a connection to Matt in that they were both from Massachusetts and close in age. Despite their differences in education and occupation, their personalities meshed with one another. He watched Matt walk toward his duty station in the Registry Hall where Guenter was waiting.

"Good morning, Dr. Stafford. Good to see you again."

"Good morning, Guenter. I see we've got some nervous people waiting in line for me, so let's get started."

"Yes, Doctor," answered Guenter, and he walked over to the aisle and sent the first immigrant forward.

That day's array of immigrants was another diversified assortment, each with a past and a hope for the future. One of them, a skinny, underfed boy, peered intently at Matt, waiting his turn.

Sam, traveling alone, knew absolutely no one, but it didn't bother him. He had set an independent course for himself ever since running away two years ago at age twelve. He had hated the crowded ghetto slum in Warsaw. Behind him were poverty, oppression, and the yoke of parental authority. Behind him also was a miserable ten-day ocean voyage in steerage and the agony of seasickness. He looked at the doctor who was about to examine him as just one more authority figure to get past before he could be free to achieve his destiny.

Matt looked carefully at this undernourished boy with his deep-set, blue eyes. He was unimpressed. The boy was about five feet ten and still growing. He was not very attractive with his large, slightly pointed ears, a rather determined chin, and a very prominent nose.

As was his custom while examining immigrants, Matt struck up a conversation with the boy. "Are you traveling by yourself?" he asked.

Sam was taken aback. Though his English was limited, he understood the question. He had not expected this inquiry from a doctor. When he looked into Matt's friendly, smiling face, his suspicions vanished. Half returning the smile, he answered, "Yes, I am alone."

"You must have had quite an adventure coming here then."

"My adventure is just beginning," Sam answered.

Matt laughed, delighted at the youth's precocity.

"Well said, young man. Your accent tells me that even though you sailed from England, you're not English. Where are you from originally, Poland or Russia?"

"Poland. Warsaw, actually. You mean you can tell where people come from by their voices?"

Chuckling, Matt replied, "Sometimes. After awhile you can tell by the way people pronounce words."

Sam nodded his head in appreciation as Matt continued his examination. Noting the boy's gauntness, he checked cautiously for tuberculosis.

"Cough, please," he asked, placing the stethoscope on Sam's chest.

"Cough?"

"Yes, cough. I want to hear your lungs better."

Amazed at the doctor's ability to hear inside his body, Sam obliged. When Matt finished, he asked, "Can I hear?"

Smiling, Matt indulged the boy, already satisfied that Sam was only undernourished. Then it was time to move on.

"Good luck," Matt said and turned to the next immigrant. For him the boy was already becoming a faint memory, one of the hundreds he would examine that day. There was no special reason to remember that gangly, homely youth.

Sam now had to wait in a long line until an inspector was free to question him. At last he reached the front of the line, where he stepped forward and faced John Mueller.

"What is your name?"

Sam said his last name in Yiddish.

"How do you spell that?" asked Mueller, scanning the manifest sheet.

Sam attempted to spell it, but got mixed up in his English, Polish, and Yiddish, producing an unintelligible answer.

"Never mind," said Mueller curtly and entered the name as Goldfish on the official documents as the boy's legal name.

With help from an interpreter, Sam answered the other questions and received his landing card. Then he was transported to the Barge Office in lower Manhattan. He had no idea where he was going next.

As always, many kinds of people lurked about the Barge Office, waiting to pounce on the greenhorns. Predators waited to victimize unsuspecting immigrants. Labor agents tried to hire the new arrivals, and others tried to entice the newcomers to take lodgings at various hotels and rooming houses. A smooth-talking labor recruiter, seeking workers for a glove factory, quickly approached Sam. Signing up for three dollars a week, three times the amount he had been making as an office boy in Warsaw, he climbed into the back of a truck with other recruits and headed for the factory town of Gloversville, located forty miles northwest of Albany.

Years later, after investing money in a moving picture called *The Squaw Man*, Sam would move to California and realize his goal of becoming a millionaire, under his legally changed name of Samuel Goldwyn. While he may have been one of Ellis Island's more famous and financially successful "graduates," the struggles of his life in the old country and the travail of the ocean voyage were similar to those of the many other immigrants that Matt and his colleagues processed. Ironically, though Matt elicited these stories from many immigrants, Sam's was one he never heard.

Movie poster for The Squaw Man, *1905*

February 1896

Sitting side-by-side, Matt and Peg held hands in the solarium. Bright sunlight basked the cheery room as the many ferns and potted plants absorbed its nutritional energy. The sunlight also accentuated Peg's pallor, making Matt painfully aware of the disease's progress in her body.

A few weeks ago Peg's health had deteriorated. What at first seemed a persistent cold and cough, turned out to be consumption. After fruitless efforts by Matt and his colleagues, he had reluctantly placed her in this sanitarium. Because his work schedule at Ellis Island had more regular hours than at Presbyterian Hospital, allowing for more quality time to be spent with Peg, he had asked for an indefinite extension of his leave of absence, which an understanding Dr. Jensen had arranged.

"It's so good to feel the warmth of sunshine again."

Matt smiled, "Yes it is. It's been a dreary week."

"It's been a dreary year so far, Matt. Sometimes it seems that winter will never end."

Matt knew her comment went beyond the weather. Her depression was only natural.

"I know it's been hard on you, Peg, but better days are

coming. The warm weather will be here soon, and you'll get to go outside again."

"Matt, am I going to get better?"

"Of course, darling," he replied with a grin, rubbing her arm and hiding the anguish deep within him. "We're doing everything we can to make you well again. And the warm weather will be a big help."

"I just get so afraid sometimes, Matt."

Peg squeezed his hand. Matt wiped the tear away from her face and caressed her cheek, the warmth of his hand and his love soothing her.

"I know," he said quietly and held her in his arms. "Peg, I want you back with me just as much as you do. Together we'll beat this thing."

"I hope you're right."

"I know I'm right."

"Hold me tight, Matt. Let me feel your strength."

He held her in his arms, fighting back the tears. Silently he prayed for her recovery and for strength for himself.

March 1896

Signs of an early spring had come to Ellis Island. In flowerbeds in front of the buildings, the tulips had poked their leaves above the softened, moist earth.

Matt looked at the harbingers. As he smiled at this promise, the words of Tennyson came to mind, "In the spring a young man's fancy lightly turns to thoughts of love." The idea demeaned his mood; melancholy hovered nearby. Neither of the two women he loved could be with him and love him back. Instead, Matt's other love, his work, sustained him. He smiled again when he saw the "Keep off the grass" sign on the lawn near the flowerbeds, thinking that sign pretty much summed up his life at the moment.

He saw Peg regularly and did what he could to comfort her. She continued to be sickly but stable. They would talk and reminisce about life in Massachusetts, and he would tell her stories about the immigrants, as usual. When it was time to end his visit, he'd caress and kiss her, bidding farewell until the next time.

He saw Nicole every day at work. Their encounters were cordial and professional, but a sexual undercurrent percolated despite everything. He still longed for her, but he "kept off the grass." He kept his word and didn't make further attempts to change her mind. She continued to date Tom, and Matt tried to content himself with her presence, her voice, and her warm smile. At least he was near her.

His private life followed a dreary routine. In his quiet, lonely apartment, he would fix dinner and eat in solitude, then came a brandy, and reading until sleep finally came.

His time at Ellis Island was the best part of Matt's day, for it was in his work that he found fulfillment. In his daily experiences with hundreds of newcomers, he did more than just examine the arrivals and treat patients. His multilingual abilities enabled Matt to speak to them, especially those in the hospital where he frequently learned more about them.

And so, he heard their tales of hardship and hope. From them he learned of real suffering and tragedy. He came to admire their tenacity that in turn inspired him to endure his own ordeal.

About midmorning Matt was in the main building examining a middle-aged Croatian man when he heard a woman scream behind him.

"Dr. Stafford, look out!" Guenter shouted.

As Matt started to turn, he felt a pain in his left shoulder. Surprised, he put his left arm up over that shoulder, groping to reach the source. Suddenly light-headed, he dropped to his knees but remained upright.

At the moment of the woman's scream, Guenter had seen the man with a knife poised to strike Matt in the back. Lunging forward, he reached him immediately after the man had stabbed Matt. Guenter grabbed the assailant's wrist and smashed his hand into the railing, knocking the knife onto the floor. He then wheeled him around and slammed his fist into the man's face, knocking him down.

By that time Johann Weppler, another gateman, had joined the fray. He bent the man's right arm up behind his back while

Guenter yanked him up by his collar. Together they led him away to a holding cell.

Meanwhile Herbert Manning, the doctor at the adjacent examining station, rushed to Matt's side.

"Matt, let me see what that madman did to you."

Matt nodded and allowed his colleague to remove his jacket and undershirt. He still felt faint and could feel blood trickling down his back.

By this time Ed McSweeney had reached the scene also and assisted Manning.

"He got you just below the clavicle, Matt, well above your lungs," Manning declared. "You were lucky."

"Who was he?" asked Matt.

"I have no idea," answered Manning, now applying a bandage to the wound and placing Matt's arm in a sling.

"Let's concentrate on you right now. As soon as I finish, we'll get you over to the hospital for a closer look."

Manning completed his ministration and then wrapped a blanket around Matt's naked upper torso. Ed—assisted by Guenter, who had now returned—helped Matt across the hall, down the stairs, and over to the hospital. John White, alerted to the situation, had a wheelchair waiting.

"Congratulations, Matt," he said with ironic humor. "You're the first doctor to be wounded in battle at Ellis Island. Who was the enemy?"

"Damned if I know," said Matt, as Guenter wheeled him behind White, who was leading the way down the corridor.

"He was a Pole," offered Guenter. "He was waiting for examination by Dr. Manning when he suddenly went after you."

"Why me?"

"Couldn't say, Dr. Stafford," Guenter replied. "He made no sense with his gibberish. I think he's insane."

"He would have to be, to do this to a doctor who hadn't

anything to do with him," John said, shaking his head. "Here we are, Matt, your own private room."

"John, I don't need a room. Herb said the wound isn't that serious."

"Why are doctors always the worst patients?" John countered. "Matt, face it. Right now, you can't work, and I'm not sending you home where there's no one to look after you. You're better off here where we can keep an eye on you, at least for twenty-four hours. If there are no complications after that, I'll discharge you. Until then, consider yourself our guest. Now, let's have a look at you and put on a clean bandage."

"All right, John, you win. I'll stay."

"Good man. You don't really have a choice though."

As John examined the wound, Matt said, "I still don't understand what provoked that man into attacking me."

"We may never know, but one thing is certain," said Ed. "We will have him off this island and on a ship back on tomorrow's morning tide, I promise you."

"Ed, I'd rather you not do that, at least not until I see the man myself."

"Matt, what purpose would that serve?"

"Ed, I was the one who was stabbed. Humor me. No one has ever tried to hurt me before. I need to satisfy myself about this. I speak the man's language. Perhaps I can learn something or even help expel the demons in his mind."

"You'll be wasting your time, Doctor."

"Maybe, Guenter, but I need to do this. Ed, please let me talk the man before you do anything."

"All right, Matt. You certainly earned the right to face your attacker. Tomorrow morning, you can see him."

"Thanks, Ed."

"That's enough, everyone," interjected John, finished with applying a new bandage and replacing the sling. "It is time to clear out, and let the man rest. Matt, take these."

"John, I don't need any painkillers."

"Let me be the judge of that. Come on now, take them."

As Matt swallowed the pills with some water, John added, "Good man. Well, we'll leave you now. I'll send the nurse in to help you get undressed. Lie down and get some rest."

Matt instantly had a vision of Nicole removing his clothes. A short time later, when the door opened, he was disappointed to see Amy Whitfield, another attractive young nurse, coming to his assistance.

*   *   *

Time passed slowly for Matt. Around noon, he was sitting up, reading a newspaper, when the door opened. In came Nicole, rushing to his side.

"Matt. Oh, Matt," she said, kissing his cheek. Matt reached up with his right arm and caressed her face, the back of his hand brushing against her blonde hair.

"I'm all right," he said softly.

She sat on the bed alongside him.

"I was so upset when I heard, but I couldn't come over here until now."

"You're here now. That's all that matters."

"Are you sure you'll be all right?"

"Yes. It may be awhile before I regain full use of my left arm and shoulder, but I think there's no permanent damage."

"You could have been killed! I would have been devastated!"

"I wouldn't have liked it much myself."

"Matt, don't joke about it. This was a terrible thing to happen to you. You were so lucky."

"I know. The man upstairs was looking out for me today."

"Well, guess who's looking out for you tonight?"

"Who?" he asked, secretly hoping.

"Me," she answered coquettishly. "Mrs. Froesch is sick, so

I volunteered to work a double shift and take her place. I get to tuck you in for beddy-bye later."

"I'll look forward to that."

"You do that, mister."

The remaining day's activities were normal hospital routine. Dr. White saw his patient again just before dinner. Soon thereafter, Nicole brought Matt his dinner and stayed with him briefly as he ate.

She watched his mouth open to receive each forkful. As his lips closed and moved as he chewed, memories returned of those lips pressed against hers. She remembered his wet lips traveling a slow, sensuous trail along her neck, all the time feeling his warm breath as she delighted in the erotic chills he created in her. No man had ever before so affected her just from kissing.

She recalled the sensation of his male firmness pressed tightly against her and glanced at the cover over his body. She knew he was wearing only a hospital gown underneath. With that thought, she also knew she had better leave and did so.

Nicole checked in on Matt twice more before the promised bedtime tuck to give him his pills. Their exchanges were warm, pleasant, and neutral, despite their mutual but separate awareness of an unspoken sexual longing.

After midnight, most people on Ellis Island were asleep except for a few watchmen and duty nurses at the hospital. In the empty silence on her floor, Nicole completed her medical charts. She put the last of them away and walked down to Matt's room.

She opened the door to his room a little, a sliver of light enabling her to see him asleep. Swept by a wave of tenderness, she closed the door behind her and waited a few moments for her eyes to adjust to the darkness. Then she quietly walked to his bed and gazed on his face.

She had never seen him asleep before. She had watched him awake, his hazel-green eyes looking at her, his face animated in conversation. Here he lay peacefully, his eyes closed in slumber, and so she fondly looked at his sleeping countenance. Alternating feelings of love, lust, and denial coursed through her. At last, she bent over to kiss his forehead before leaving.

Matt, sleeping lightly, felt the sensation and opened his eyes. He reached for her while her face was still close to his. Pulling her to him with his right arm, he kissed her lips softly.

Though surprised, she didn't resist. Instead the kiss unleashed her pent-up passion. She eagerly returned his kiss and its gentle beginning grew into a long, amorous exploration. Hungrily her lips roamed over his, feasting everywhere. Her tongue thrust into his mouth, touching and caressing his tongue, as their lips pressed passionately together.

She snuggled beside him on the bed. He embraced her awkwardly with his one arm. His right hand tenderly caressed her face, head, and back, continually rubbing, stroking, and fondling her, while the delightful sensations of their nonstop kisses drove all caution away.

Swept onward by her emotions, Nicole reached over to complete her embrace. In doing so, her forearm brushed against his erection. That accidental touch heightened her desires even more. As she kept on with their kissing, she reached under the bedding and past his stomach.

Matt felt her hand approaching. When she actually touched him, after first going around and underneath before encircling her hand, he moaned from the sensation.

Stirred by the feel of him yielding slightly to her tightening grasp, she relaxed her grip and moved her hand along its length, caressed his inner thighs, returned to his stiffness, and stroked him longingly, lovingly, passionately.

Her delicate movements brought Matt to the brink.

"Please," he whispered, "I can't take much more."

Nicole slowed her motions and withdrew her hand. She kissed him once more and got off the bed.

"Nicole, what—"

"Shhh. Don't talk."

She removed her undergarments and opened her blouse. Then she pulled back his covers, raised her long skirt, sat astride him, and slowly lowered herself onto him. She moaned as she felt his fullness go deep into her until she completely engulfed him. With a gentle rocking rhythm, she savored the movement and physical ecstasy as she slowly rode him.

Matt kept silent, afraid his words would somehow mar the rapture of the living fantasy. He looked up at the woman now connected to him as she controlled their body motions. Her eyes were closed, her mouth open, and the beauty of her face set in a captivating expression of sexual ecstasy.

Her breasts beneath the cotton chemise heaved from her movements and heavy breathing. Reaching into her opened blouse, he fondled one breast, then the other, pressing gently with his right hand as it enveloped each mound. Lightly tracing his fingers around her nipples, he could feel their hardness.

Low sounds of pleasure escaped from both of them. Next Nicole lay upon him and their rhythm intensified. Matt thrust upward to match her downward moves and soon they climaxed together.

They lay together quietly, basking in the afterglow. All too soon Nicole said, "I'd better be going before the watchman comes by."

She got up and went to the table. Pouring some water from the pitcher into the bowl, she quickly used the washcloth on herself. Then she dampened the end of a towel and returned to Matt. As she cleaned and dried him, he closed his eyes to relish even more the physical sensations of her tender care.

Nicole completed her enjoyable task. After dressing, she returned to Matt and kissed him once more.

"Good night, darling. Sleep well."

"How could I not? You're an angel who just brought me to paradise."

"You weren't the only one in heaven, Matt. Good night." She closed the door behind her, leaving Matt with her lingering scent. Sleep came quickly.

Back at her duty station, Nicole sat at the desk and sighed. Her body still felt wonderful. She smiled as she thought back. As the night wore on, though, her pragmatic side insinuated itself and she reflected on the wisdom of her actions.

Their beautiful lovemaking aside, she realized nothing had changed. He was still married to a sickly woman who might live for years yet or even recover. She still could not see him openly. Any hint of scandal could ruin both their careers. Not only had she failed to control her passion for Matt, she had escalated her involvement.

What now? she thought. *Where do we go from here? I love him, but I can't have him.*

As sobering thoughts of the reality of her situation played on her mind, Nicole recognized she had let her emotions overcome reason. For all the physical bliss of their lovemaking, she had been foolish. Despite her feelings, she had worsened a bad situation. No good could come of this. Somehow she had to extricate herself.

If only tonight hadn't happened, she thought.

*   *   *

Matt held Nicole in his arms. As they lay naked together, he caressed her firm, upright breasts. His hand traveled slowly, tantalizingly, down the length of her body and between her thighs. Feeling her wetness, his fingers probed further into the yielding flesh. Kissing first her lips, he gradually moved downwards, kissing and running his tongue along her neck, then lingering on her breasts.

She was writhing and moaning, with the intensity of her

passion increasing every second. Matt was aware of his effect and he sensed their needs were mutual. He entered her and slowly pushed his pelvis into hers and eased back in continuing, steady rhythmic motions. It was wonderful and he knew he could not last long.

"Matt, time to wake up."

Startled, he opened his eyes to see Nicole, fully clothed, standing alongside his bed. He had been dreaming.

Aware that the covers were not lying flatly, she simply smiled at him and said, "Good morning."

"Nicole, I just had the most wonderful dream."

She again glanced at the covers and gave a knowing smile.

Seeking a neutral exchange, she said, "That's a good way to start the morning. How are you feeling today?"

"Don't you want to hear about my dream?"

"Perhaps later, but right now, I've only a few minutes to wake everyone before I go off duty. You didn't answer my question. How are you feeling?"

"I feel wonderful. Your loving care has made a new man of me."

"What about your wound?"

"I'm a little sore," he answered, raising his left arm about hallway up before the pain stopped him.

"Matt, don't do that! Give it time to heal."

Then, lessening the emotion in her voice, she added, "I'm going to wake the others now before I go home to get some sleep. I'll see you tomorrow."

He returned her smile, waved, watched her leave, and relived the memory of the night. A short time later Amy Whitfield entered with his breakfast tray.

"Good morning, Dr. Stafford. How's my favorite patient?"

He laughed. "Amy, you call everyone your favorite patient."

"And they all are, each one, but you are my extra-favorite patient. You're my first doctor."

He laughed again. "Thanks for making me laugh, Amy. I needed it."

"You're welcome, Doctor. I'll be back later. Enjoy your breakfast."

As Matt finished his breakfast, Herbert Manning came in. "I hope you're feeling better than you look, because you look terrible."

"Thanks for the compliment, Herb."

"Seriously, how are you feeling?"

"As good as can be expected, I guess. I just want to get out of here."

"Can't blame you for that. I don't see why you can't, but you'll have to wait for John to release you. Officially, you're his patient."

"Have you seen him yet?"

"No, but he'll be around soon. It's time for rounds. I'll see you later."

As Manning left, Frank Martiniello arrived.

"*Buon giorno, dottore. Come state?*" [How are you?]

"*Buon giorno, Francesco. Mi sento meglio oggi, grazie.* [I'm feeling better today, thank you.]"

"*Bene! Siete stato fortunato. L'incidente poteva andarvi molto peggio.*"

'Now you're beyond me, Frank. I understood your telling me that I was lucky, but what did you say after that?"

"I said that you were none the worse for the incident. Your Italian is coming along *molto bene.*"

"*Grazie.* Actually, I am a little the worse. I'm sore and don't have full use of my arm and shoulder yet, but it'll come. I appreciate your stopping by."

"It was just for this quick minute. You know us working

119

stiffs. I've got to get to the main building or get docked in pay. You take care, Doctor. See you soon."

"I will. Thanks, Frank."

Shortly after Frank left, Guenter, McSweeney, and Senner stopped by, one by one, to visit briefly and express their concern and wishes for a speedy recovery. At last, Dr. White came.

"How's our wounded doctor?"

"Better, John, but I'm not a very good patient. Can I get out of here?"

"I think so. Let's have a look first."

He removed Matt's bandage, satisfied himself of the wound's healing progress, and applied a fresh dressing.

"It's coming along fine, Matt. It'll heal faster if we keep this area immobile for a while. I want you to keep wearing this sling for at least a few days. After that you'll have to work on slowly regaining full use of your arm. You know, like standing next to a wall and walking your fingers up it, forcing the ligaments to stretch once again."

"Yes, I know. How about pulling my left arm up with my right using a rope and pulley?"

"That works well too. None of this yet, though. Give the wound time to heal. Now I'm discharging you and putting you on medical leave until next Monday. Then we'll station you here on hospital duty only until you're fit enough to conduct medical exams again."

"All right. Before I leave the island though, I want to talk to the man who attacked me."

"Fine. I'll send Miss Whitfield in to help you get dressed, and then you can go over to the detention pen."

A short time later, Matt looked at his attacker in the detention cell. His brown hair was messed, but otherwise, he looked no different than any other new arrival. He wore baggy, coarse woolen trousers, badly scuffed shoes, a white shirt, and dark jacket. The left side of his face was badly bruised and swollen.

Matt attempted to converse with the man in his native Polish, "Why did you stab me?"

The man just looked at him without responding. Matt repeated the question and still got no reply.

"Look, I'm not going to harm you. I just want to understand. Why did you stab me?"

A few seconds elapsed. The man came closer to Matt, stared into his face for a few seconds more, and then finally said in Polish, "I don't know what you're talking about."

"You stabbed me yesterday. There were many witnesses. Just tell me why you did it, and I will leave you alone."

"I don't know what you are talking about," he repeated and walked away.

Matt tried again to communicate but without success. He left the island realizing that he would never learn the reason he was attacked.

April 1896

It was Friday morning, April third. Nicole should have been at work, but she was home.

Her apartment revealed her inclination for neatness. Never was there clutter anywhere, not even on mornings when she left for work. Nor did any handicraft evidence lie about, since she had no interest in such things any more than in cooking, unlike many other women. Instead, she preferred going to the theater and dance performances, the latter continuing a fondness she had developed from taking classes as a child and teenager. Another favorite pastime was reading, and her small bedroom bookcase revealed a preference for histories and biographies.

At the moment, though, she did not want to read or contemplate the theater or dance. Depressed and anxious, she had a terrible headache. She was late, and the early changes in her breasts could only mean one thing.

She felt trapped in a dilemma of her own making. Given Matt's marriage and ailing wife, she decided against telling him. An abortion was definitely out of the question, given her religious beliefs and the real dangers of such a procedure. Yet if she had the baby, both she and the child would be constant objects of shame, scorn, and ridicule. She couldn't let that happen.

As she lay there crying, she realized she had only two options. She could move away and start a new life somewhere, pretending to be a widow. She knew, however, that she could not cut herself off from her family. Also, as a stranger somewhere, it would be a struggle to support herself as a nurse with an infant. She had no desire to live a marginal existence. Her other choice was to marry Tom, and quickly, before he learned she was carrying another man's child. He had been asking her to marry him for months. He wasn't Matt, but he was a decent man and fun. It was really her only choice.

* * *

On Ellis Island a problem was also brewing. Public opinion had turned against the increasing flow of southern and eastern European immigrants. Congress was considering a literacy bill to keep out the illiterate peasants streaming into the United States. Under pressure, Commissioner Senner had ordered more stringent examinations of new arrivals, resulting in a substantial increase in detainees and rejections. Ellis Island was now severely overcrowded, mostly with Italian aliens.

Republican newspapers, in their steady barrage against the Cleveland administration, had recently launched broadside attacks against Senner. Ridiculing his heavy accent, they called him an incompetent political drudge and accused him of poor management for the overcrowded conditions at Ellis Island. Such criticism was effective, for it fired up both friends and relatives of the detainees as well as anti-immigration forces. Ellis Island served nicely as a touchstone for Cleveland's opponents to illustrate their charges of Democratic incompetence.

To counter the vitriolic attacks, Herman Stump converted one of his routine trips from Washington into a highly publicized inspection tour of Ellis Island. On Saturday, April fourth, accompanied by an invited press corps, he asked Senner to show them the island's facilities.

With foreknowledge of Stump's visit and motive, Joseph willingly led them through the processing station's facilities. He too wanted the press to see the congestion and backlog. Their newspaper accounts could help sway public opinion to his side and perhaps even produce more funding for badly needed expansion.

Ed McSweeney accompanied the group. Occasionally he filled in some details, trying to make certain everyone understood that the staff was doing the best job possible under extremely difficult circumstances.

Just in case this visit was a prelude to some head-rolling, Ed wanted to protect himself. He believed that Stump's visit was either an effort to defuse the situation or to find a scapegoat, or both. Ed wanted to ensure that he did not become the sacrificial lamb. So whenever an opportunity came, he offered self-serving remarks to the press to safeguard his position.

"Dis is John Mueller, our chief registry clerk," Senner said, introducing his newly promoted compatriot. "He is very competent man und he vill explain about de problems we have."

"Welcome, gentlemen," John said warmly. "Allow me to try to make sense of this vast array of immigrants you see before us."

Persuasive as ever, John informed and charmed his audience. He apprised them of the questions asked during legal inspection and how increasingly more immigrants must be detained for further inquiry.

The *New York Times* reporter commented, "I still don't understand why there are so many more detainees."

"I'll answer that," said Stump. "The inspection is more rigid, and more of the recent arrivals are undesirables. This is especially true of the Italians. They are coming in record numbers to escape military service in Abyssinia. They leave Italy in droves, escape into France, then sail for here."

"Are you saying, Colonel Stump," followed up a *New York Herald* reporter, "that the inspection is more rigid because there are more Italians arriving?'

"Basically, yes. They have to be examined more carefully than the others, and that takes time. For example, several nights ago eight hundred immigrants were detained on the island all night. Generally, we deport to Europe less than two percent of the immigrants. Now, we are sending back eight to ten percent. We sent four hundred back last week and one hundred just yesterday alone. Most were Italians."

"How do the steamship companies feel about this?"

"As you might expect, they complain. However, they can easily resolve the problem by refusing to bring over persons they think will be rejected. With the exception of the Italians, the aliens immigrating are fine."

Stump's prejudicial remarks went unchallenged because they reflected the prevailing attitude of most Americans, including Senner, McSweeney, Mueller, and the reporters. The country was alarmed by the annual influx of tens of thousands of dark-complexioned Italians.

At the end of the tour, the reporters had a few more questions.

"Colonel Stump, given the situation here, what do you think of the performance of Ellis Island officials?"

Ed listened attentively.

"The officials on Ellis Island are to be commended for their vigilance in processing undesirable immigrants."

Ed breathed a sigh of relief as Stump continued.

"They work overtime and put up with great inconvenience in order to investigate every doubtful case. To expedite the work, we have just detailed three inspectors from interior cities to work here, and we have increased the number of clerks and interpreters."

"Are these permanent or temporary assignments?"

"Probably permanent. However, let me remind you, gentlemen, the problem is not with the number of immigrants. We're actually getting fewer than before. I believe we may have more than a million less immigrants in the nineties than in the eighties. Despite lower numbers, the number of detainees and deportees has escalated far out of proportion."

"Are you doing anything else to ease conditions here?"

"Our most pressing need is more dormitory space. We will shortly issue contracts to put another story on the detention house, and a bridge from the main building to that new floor. We can now accommodate 250 persons overnight, but when that story is added, we can keep 500 persons."

"If you can only accommodate 250 persons overnight, what did you do with the 800 immigrants from several nights ago?"

"We had them sleeping here in the Registry Hall on the floor," Joseph explained. "Then we woke them up in the morning, and after breakfast, we put them in an excluded pen here in the hall."

The reporter persisted, "So even with the additional dormitory floor enabling you to house 500, your facilities will still be inadequate, is that right?"

"At times that will be true, and we will have to do some of the same things we have been doing. We really need Congress to authorize greater funding if Ellis Island is to become an adequate facility."

Later, after the reporters had left, Stump and Senner sat together in Joseph's office, slowly puffing on their cigars. Both were pleased over how the press had reacted, but Joseph wanted to take the opportunity to press a few of his other concerns.

"I really do not like using de excluded pen here on de same floor vere ve process de new arrivals."

126

"What choice do we have, Joseph?"

"I vood like to set up un outdoor detention area. De varmer veather is coming now. On nice days, dey could be outside in de fresh air. Ve could build fence, guard de perimeter, und make de Registry Hall less crowded."

"You think you have adequate manpower for this?"

"*Ja.*"

"All right, go ahead. We need to be a little creative to handle what we're getting. Good thinking, Joseph."

"Tank you. If ve do not do dis, I tink ve are playing mit fire, keeping dose people penned up all day und night in vun place. Und speaking of fire, ven are ve going to get funds to dredge un channel around dis island, so de fireboats can have access?"

"Joseph, this is not the time," Stump replied, trying to avoid an often-heard argument. "It was all we could do to get funds for the dormitory, and we still need more space. Dredging the channel is expensive. It will have to wait."

"I pray to God ve never regret dis delay."

"You worry too much, Joseph," Stump said cavalierly. "Now, is there anything else on your mind before I go?"

"As un matter of fact, yes."

"Ha!" laughed Stump. "I knew I shouldn't have asked. Well, what is it?"

"Dis is not new tought either, Herman. I am fed up mit having so many incompetent political hacks vorking here. Several times I have asked und I have written to have de Immigration Bureau brought under civil service regulations. Dot vay ve vill get good people und keep dem, no matter vaht de election results."

Stump drew the cigar from his lips, saying, "No fan of the spoils system, are you?"

"No, I am not."

"Yet we are the results of political appointments."

"*Ja*, und I may be gone after de next election, de vay tings look right now. I can zee appointments at de top for de managers.

But at de lower levels, dose dealing directly mit de immigrants, ve need people mit temperament und competence to make dem suitable for de vork."

"Well, Joseph, you'll be pleased to know something is in the wind. The president is backing a proposal, and Congress seems supportive, to extend civil service regulations to immigration personnel. It may happen before the end of the year."

"Really? Dot is *wunderbar*. It is really for de best, you know."

"You're probably right, Joseph. Well, I'd better be on my way. Good day."

"Vait. I vill valk you to de dock."

May 1896

As usual, Frank Martiniello got to the Barge Office before 8:40 to hop aboard the ferryboat with other Ellis Island employees. For many, this short trip across the water was a pleasant, relaxing means of commuting to a hectic day's work. However, such was rarely his experience, as the cross-river journey often strained Frank's nerves, thanks to the other passengers. Armed with passes from the steamship office, hundreds of people of many nationalities eagerly converged on the dock, all frantically clamoring to get on the boat to meet their friends or relatives either arriving that day or held as detainees, many of them Italians.

His short, stocky build, dark hair, and dark complexion suggested he was an Italian American. Because his uniform identified him as an Ellis Island employee, his countrymen would frequently seize him by the coat, arm, or even his neck, pleading for his help as they blurted out their problems. Sympathetic to their concerns, aware of their hopeful and desperate entreaties to a fellow Italian, he nonetheless could do nothing. As he tried to explain, some grew even more persistent, causing him sometimes to lose his patience and yell at them to leave him alone.

He didn't like the situation. His inability to help and the anger or dismay of his supplicants brought too much stress. Consequently, he dreaded the boat journey more than his work as an interpreter where the drama actually unfolded.

This morning he was pleasantly surprised when the fifteen-minute ferryboat ride ended with no pleas for help. Relieved, he walked to the main building to which Matt was heading from the hospital. Entering different sides of the building, they would not yet encounter one another.

After securing his lunchbox and having some coffee in the staff room, Frank headed to the high registry desk where he would be working. With his ability to communicate in Italian, German, French, Spanish, and Polish, he now functioned as both primary inspector and interpreter. Recognizing him as a bright, conscientious employee, McSweeney had recommended him for promotion.

Frank walked past the excluded pen, set off to one side by a high iron grille. Inside, he saw about five hundred men, mostly Italian. Unpleasant thoughts that he had on the ferryboat returned. Shaking his head, he dismissed them from his mind and reached his desk.

*   *   *

Matt was still brooding about Nicole. Last month he was dismayed when he learned of her resignation. His attempts to communicate with her by telephone or mail were fruitless. Then her note came. He still carried it with him, and he now took it out, rereading it once again.

April 17, 1896

Dear Matt,
*   Forgive me for leaving so abruptly, but*
I couldn't bear the heartbreak of saying

*goodbye. You are such a wonderful man, and
we had some special times together. Perhaps
under other circumstances our relationship
might have become more, but it wasn't to
be. All we were doing was inflicting torment
on one another. I needed to find happiness
without secrecy or guilt, and I have. You know
I've already left my job. Tomorrow, Tom and
I are getting married, and by the time you
receive this, we will be on our honeymoon.*

   *Please wish us well. I pray that your life
will be a long, happy one, and that Peg gets
better. I shall always remember you most
kindly, and I hope that you will think the same
of me.*

Yours truly, Nicole

Matt sighed, folded and replaced the letter in the envelope, and returned it to his pocket. He went to his work station and began his examinations. The morning proceeded normally for the first two hours and then shouts rang out from the excluded pen.

*   *   *

At that moment, Frank was questioning an Italian woman and her two children. As the noise level increased, he stopped his processing and rushed over to the pen and saw a watchman hurriedly exiting.

"Jim, what's wrong?" Frank asked.

"We need a doctor fast!"

"I'll get one," he answered and ran over to the medical examination area. Reaching Matt's station, he excitedly shouted, "They need a doctor right away in the excluded pen!"

Matt hurried across the Registry Hall, Frank trailing along behind. About a thousand landing immigrants were then being processed on the main floor. Alarmed by the loud uproar coming from the pen, this crowd had become a surging, excited mass. Fortunately, the iron rails keeping different manifest groups apart contained them.

Inside the excluded pen, the detainees were howling and gesturing wildly. Something in the center of the pen had captured their attention, for their backs were all turned toward its entrance. In one corner of the pen were some desks and tables where the watchmen normally worked on their records, but none were there now.

As Matt approached the entrance of the pen, he found the watchmen—men whom he had seen undisturbed by most situations—standing several yards away, except for one other watchman. This one, a man whom Matt knew to be fearless, was hanging on the locked gate, the color drained from his face.

"What's the matter here?" Matt asked him.

"The Italians are killing a Jew!"

Matt was appalled. He had expected some medical problem, not a loss of crowd control.

"Why do you need a doctor to do your work for you?" he complained. "Open the gate, and let me in. By now, the man may actually need a doctor."

Matt went into the pen. The watchmen only followed him with their eyes, none daring to enter. To their amazement, Matt elbowed his way into the crowd. Some of the immigrants recognized him and began to give way.

"*Il medico!*" some shouted to the others, as a path through the noisy throng opened up before him.

At first, all he could make out of the noisy uproar were epithets and cries of "Kill him!" in Italian and Polish. Then an

Italian yelled in Matt's ear, "He's the bastard who has given us all lice!"

When he got deeper into the crowd, Matt found at its center a long-haired, long-whiskered Jewish man wearing a sheepskin-lined, floor-length Russian overcoat. Those nearest this man were excitedly shouting at him and shaking their fists, but taking care to keep back eight or ten feet. The man looked decidedly dejected but not nearly as frightened as the watchmen outside the gate.

Matt walked up to the man, took him by the shoulder, and started toward the gate. The crowd backed away, creating a wider swath through which they walked without further incident. Once outside the gate, Matt instructed a watchman to take him to a medical examining room.

"Fine work, Dr. Stafford," congratulated McSweeney, who had arrived at the scene just after Matt had entered the pen. "You brought an explosive situation to a quick, peaceful end."

"I only did what anyone could have done."

"I didn't see anyone else try," Ed countered. "The point is that you did it."

At that moment Joseph Senner, obviously agitated, joined them, asking, "*Was ist los?*"

"Dr. Stafford," Ed explained, "just single-handedly quelled a disturbance here. The watchmen had left the pen out of fear. Dr. Stafford went right into the middle of that angry mob and immediately took charge."

"Vaht vas de problem?"

"A man with lice," Matt answered. "The others wanted revenge for his contaminating them."

"Vere is he now?" Joseph asked.

"I've sent him to a medical examining room, so I can look him over," replied Matt.

"Gudt vork, Dr. Stafford."

"Thank you, sir. Now, if you'll excuse me, I had better go and take care of that fellow."

Joseph nodded, and Ed smiled in approval, as Matt headed for the examining room.

Matt found the man in good health but infested with lice in his hair, beard, and clothes. He had the man strip, put on a hospital gown, robe, and slippers. Matt then sent him under escort to the hospital to go through the delousing process and have his clothes placed in the steam disinfector.

He then returned to his duty station, as word of his deed spread quickly along the employee grapevine. Later, when he reached the hospital, the chief medical officer and the rest of the staff added their praise. Missing was the one person, more than anyone else, whose words he would have most liked to hear.

June 1896

Overcrowding on the island was worse than ever. Balmier traveling weather coincided with a substantial increase in the numbers of immigrants, in turn generating more detainees and deportees than previously. The entire staff worked longer hours to keep up with the heavier workload, but it was in vain. The processing lines became longer than ever, and the cramped facilities could not accommodate all of the detainees.

Since new dormitory space had not yet been built, Senner was forced to take other steps. Placing additional beds in the sleeping facilities caused severe overcrowding, with little walking space. Because the facility was primarily used for sleeping, however, the congestion was somewhat tolerable. In the daytime, the situation improved, as some detainees left the dormitory to be processed, while employees moved the deportees to the excluded pen.

Long lines in the Registry Hall, however, necessitated relocating the pen. As Senner and Stump had agreed earlier, an outdoor one enclosed by a high wooden fence was constructed alongside the main building. In poor weather, the aliens remained inside their cramped sleeping quarters, but on good days, such as today, they went into this open area to benefit from the fresh air and sunshine.

As guards patrolled the perimeter, several hundred detainees—mostly Italians—stood or sat in the pen. They either sullenly rested against their baggage or restlessly paced about. Frustrated and depressed, their hopes of a new life in America dashed, they grumbled among themselves.

Enrico was twenty and short-tempered. At his parents' urging he had come to America after accidentally killing a man in a fight over a girl. The man's relatives had sworn revenge, and Enrico's parents told him to leave immediately for America to escape this blood feud. America would not accept him, though. His slight limp had been detected, and now he awaited deportation back home to a future that held little promise and much risk.

Nicola stood beside him. He was twenty-nine, married, and the father of two boys and a girl. He found it difficult to eke out even a subsistent existence for his family in the *Mezzogiorno*, the harsh land to the east and south of Rome. At great sacrifice, he had saved a year to raise the passage money to earn enough in America to send for his family. Instead, an immigration doctor rejected him because of his clubfoot. A year's savings, a year's planning, a year's hopes were gone.

Standing with them was Pietro. A widower at thirty-eight, with three daughters left in the care of his sister, he had come to earn money for their dowries to secure a better future for them. With no intent to stay in America, he planned to return to Gioi Cilento where his wife lay buried. When the doctor detected trachoma, however, his dreams for his daughters ended. He would return home empty-handed and poorer than before because of the money spent to come here.

The three men passed the time telling their stories to one another. In the boredom of the morning, they complained about their fate. Their frustrations triggered something within each of them, as their disappointment grew into anger and resentment.

"In the old country," snarled Nicola, "the mark was on my children before they were born. *L'animale!* I had sworn before God that my children would not live as I have lived. I've worked hard all my life! Who are these men to judge me—to say that I am unable to work? I showed them the calluses on my hands to prove I have worked. I can work! Why won't they give me a chance?"

"My friend," said Pietro, "in the old country, the landowners, the schools, the church all ignored us. Why should these authorities be any different?"

"Maybe they will change their minds."

"*Si, e i maiali possono volare* [Yes, and pigs can fly]!" Pietro answered.

"I had heard wonderful things about this country. I thought here we could live like human beings," Nicola replied, shaking his head.

"Like human beings!" shouted Enrico, his loud voice attracting the attention of other Italians nearby. "Here they even cage us up like the animals others have called us!"

"Quiet down in there, you monkey!" shouted one of the guards outside the wooden fence. Timothy Ryan, the Irishman who had shouted, loved to throw his weight around or pick a fight.

Enrico's English was limited, but he had understood.

"*Maledetto bastardo* [God damn bastard]!" he raged. "Who are you to call me a monkey? *Non sono un animale* [I am not an animal]!"

With that he charged the fence, with Nicola, Pietro, and others following him. Enrico tore at the wooden slats, and Ryan smashed his club against Enrico's fingers, causing him to cry out in pain. This ignited a mob frenzy. Dozens of men surged toward the fence, trying to push it over or tear it apart. The fence yielded, and the mob poured through the forced opening.

Whistles blew, and guards, gatemen, and other personnel came running to the area. Some, like Guenter, left the main building to assist.

Before they reached the scene, Enrico led the attack toward the guard who had insulted and hit him. Ryan stood his ground, his club raised over his head, two other guards standing to his right.

"Get back in there, you greaseballs!" Ryan screamed.

The mob charged right into the guards, who became panic-stricken. Frantically, they swung their clubs in a desperate effort to beat back the frenzied mob.

As Enrico reached his tormentor, Ryan hit him in the head with a vicious blow. As Pietro reached out to assist his staggering comrade, Ryan swung his club again, breaking two of Pietro's ribs. As Pietro doubled up in pain, moaning, Ryan swung again, hitting him on the head, knocking him unconscious.

With Ryan's body bent forward from the momentum of this last swing, Nicola threw himself against the guard, hurling the man off balance onto the ground. Ryan was stronger, though, and quickly regained the upper hand by flinging Nicola off him. He hit Nicola with the club against the left side of his face, cracking a tooth. As Ryan raised his club to strike the defenseless man a second time, it was grabbed from his hand from behind. Surprised, he turned around and saw Enrico's blood-streamed face, his hand now holding the club just before it bashed into Ryan's skull with full fury.

Meanwhile, a full-scale riot was underway. The rioters had overpowered the other two guards, punching, kicking, and knocking them unconscious. By now the reinforcements, also armed with billy clubs, had arrived. Taking the offensive, government personnel compelled the mob to retreat.

Snatching broken fence pickets as weapons, the Italians furiously counterattacked. Many simply used their fists. Screams pierced the air as fists and clubs made brutal contact with flesh and bones. Outnumbering the island personnel, the mob forced them to pull back as more fell victim to the onslaught of the surging throng.

At one point, Guenter and three others attempted to repel

the advancing mob. For a few moments, they were successful, as their fierce, rapid swipes at heads and limbs took their toll. As they fought their attackers in front of them, Enrico and some other men broke through the battle line and launched a flanking attack.

Turning to face Enrico, Guenter readied himself to strike. However, another Italian hit him with a piece of fence from behind, followed in quick succession by a second blow to the head, this one from Enrico. Guenter fell to the ground, a pool of blood forming under his head.

The island personnel retreated a few yards and then regrouped. Standing an arm's length apart, they formed a phalanx and steadily advanced on the unorganized rioters. Constantly swinging their clubs, they forced the Italians to retreat.

Spotting Enrico with a guard's club acting as a ringleader, they moved in on him. Enrico furiously lashed out in all directions with his weapon, but the guards relentlessly came after him. He swung in one direction, only to receive a blow from another. Hit repeatedly on the arms, shoulders, back, sides, and head, Enrico dropped his club and fell to his knees. With savage brutality, the guards continued to beat him into unconsciousness.

The guards' ruthlessness intimidated the nearest rioters, and they lost their will to fight. Encircling other combatants, the guards painfully succeeded in overpowering them as well. Soon, guards stopped the bloody rebellion, forced the aliens back into the dormitory, and locked the doors.

At the hospital, Drs. Geddings, Manning, Stafford, and White worked side by side, treating broken bones, bashed skulls, bruised ribs, broken teeth, and numerous other injuries. The three most seriously injured were Enrico, Guenter, and Timothy Ryan. Enrico had a fractured skull, a broken arm, four broken back ribs, a broken nose, and numerous contusions. Both Guenter and Ryan had fractured skulls also.

Guenter was the more seriously injured. He remained unconscious, and the doctors feared for his life. Deciding any movement off the island was too risky, they put him in the room where Matt had once stayed overnight, and they put Ryan in another.

Matt decided to stay on the island overnight and keep vigil over his friend. Amy Whitfield, who had been assisting Matt earlier in his caring for the injured, came into the room with some dinner.

"I thought I'd bring you this before I go home, Dr. Stafford."

"Thank you, Amy."

"Has there been any change?"

"No, he's still in a coma. These next twenty-four hours are critical."

"Poor Guenter. This was a horrible day. I've never seen anything like it. So many people hurt. And so brutally! What makes people do such things?"

"Many things, I guess," Matt answered. "Desperation, mostly, but frustration and anger too, I suppose. And, once it starts, it takes on a life of its own."

"I hope I never see another day like this one. This was such savagery! I hate to see people hurt each other so viciously."

"I know what you mean, Amy. You were a big help today. Thank you for all you did."

"We each did what we had to do, but it was good working beside you, Dr. Stafford. You and I made a darn good team."

Matt gazed at the young, attractive nurse. Her coy, flirtatious look triggered thoughts he didn't want to consider, so he dismissed those enticing thoughts from his mind.

"Yes, we did," he said with a faint smile. "Thanks again for dinner. I'll see you tomorrow."

"Yes, doctor," Amy said, smiling pleasantly to mask her disappointment at his failure to pick up on her cue.

Next day, workmen restored and reinforced the fencing of the excluded pen, and Joseph doubled the number of guards. Fearing another outbreak, he telegraphed Washington for approval to employ armed constables as long as the overcrowding continued. An hour later, Stump cabled back, denying the request. Instead, he informed Joseph that marines stationed at the Brooklyn Navy Yard were now on standby orders, ready to come if future needs ever arose.

That afternoon, Guenter regained consciousness. Relieved, Matt determined that he appeared not to have suffered any permanent damage from his injury. Still, the healing process would take quite some time before he could return to work.

Commissioner Senner sent letters of commendation for valor to Guenter Langer and Timothy Ryan for "brave and heroic actions in defense of comrades and American ideals." By the time the two men returned to work, all their adversaries had long been deported.

Detention pen (in good weather) on roof of main building, 1902

July 1896

McSweeney completed his tour of the island and entered the commissioner's office.

"Dr. Senner, I've just inspected all the facilities, and everything seems in order for Mr. Carlisle's visit," he reported.

"Gudt. The secretary does not come here often, so ve vant to be at our best, especially after last month's riot."

"Well, we're ready for him, sir."

Two hours later, Joseph was much more relaxed. The Secretary of the Treasury and his party had satisfied themselves about the housing and security arrangements, given the continuing overcrowded strain on the island's facilities. Since the riot three weeks earlier, no further disturbances had occurred. Once satisfied, Carlisle had paid greater attention to showing his guests the variety of immigrants being processed in the Registry Hall.

Now they were all concluding their visit in Senner's office, enjoying cigars, cognac, and conversation. Carlisle decided to have some fun at Joseph's expense.

"Tell me, Commissioner," he teased, "what exactly is the official language of Ellis Island? Everyone, including the employees, seems to speak his own language. I scarcely heard English spoken. You could easily forget you're in America."

Unaware he was being baited and sensitive to this oft-repeated criticism, Joseph began a vehement defense of the Americanism and linguistic attainments of his staff.

"Mr. Secretary, notting could be more false! De workers here speak many languages ven dey talk to de immigrants, but dey are all Americans und speak English vell."

As luck would have it, an incident elsewhere on the island had just occurred to cap this exchange.

A resourceful Irish detainee pried a bar off a window on the second-floor detention quarters. His timing was poor, however. As he dropped to the ground, he landed almost on top of Ludwig, a watchman who was passing under the window. Staggering against Ludwig as he landed, the escapee spilled a pail of hot coffee that Ludwig was bringing to his fellow watchmen for their midday meal.

Ludwig collared the man before he was able to run away and marched him back upstairs. Then, after consultation with his colleagues, Ludwig concluded that the attempted escape was an incident of sufficient importance requiring a personal report to the commissioner. Convincing the protective attendant outside Senner's office of the importance of his mission, Ludwig entered Senner's office.

Discussion over the staff's English proficiency was still going on as Ludwig entered. Somewhat rattled at finding himself unexpectedly in this company, Ludwig began in a dialect common in Brooklyn's Williamsburg section, "Herr Commissioner, *er mann hat escabbed dem fenster aus—*"

Gales of laughter interrupted him. In fact, Carlisle and his party laughed so hard that tears came to their eyes.

Disconcerted by the laughter and mistaking Senner's look to indicate rage at the escape, Ludwig added, as soon as he could make himself heard, *"Aber ich hab'ibn ge-kotcht."*

Again raucous laughter erupted. Joseph brusquely waved his hand, dismissing Ludwig. When the confused watchman left, Joseph began a futile attempt to salvage the situation.

"Mr. Secretary, dot man—"

"No need to explain, Commissioner," Carlisle interrupted, still laughing. "We understand. It's time we were leaving. Thank you for your hospitality. I'm sure I speak for my friends when I say we've all enjoyed our visit."

"Yes, indeed," volunteered one of the others.

"That's true, Commissioner," said another, still laughing as he shook Joseph's hand.

Joseph saw the amusement on all their faces. With a tight smile, he maintained his composure as he escorted them to the motor launch. He then returned to his office, still fuming.

*   *   *

The following week brought hot, humid weather to the region. Because of vacation schedules and understaffing, Matt worked a double shift and spent his off-duty hours sleeping on the island. Ellis Island remained his bedrock of strength, as he struggled to keep his personal life on an even keel. Peg's health stayed precariously stable, and he had not seen or heard from Nicole since April.

On this excessively hot, sultry night, Will Gaines—a careful, steadfast watchman—was making his evening rounds on the ground floor of the dormitory building. In the dormitory were about three hundred men, mostly Europeans, and even some from Asia.

Will was a powerful, big hunk of a man. Most noticeable was his neck—thick and long, red and leathery, and crisscrossed with furrows. As he walked through the dormitory, he noticed a man lying on his bed fully dressed, while everyone else was practically seminaked because of the heat. He went closer to investigate.

The man, lying on the upper bunk of the bed, was about on a level with Will's shoulders. As Will approached the bed, the man raised his head to see who was approaching. Quick as a flash, the man kicked Will in the face with both feet, like a vicious mule. Knocked unconscious, Will fell to the floor as the man ran away. One awake immigrant, concerned for Will, immediately summoned help.

As his fellow watchmen picked him up, Will slowly regained his senses. He pointed to the imprint of a hob-nailed shoe heel below the lobe of his left ear, weakly saying that a crazy man had kicked him.

Meanwhile the man had disappeared. A search party formed, and one of the watchmen went to get Matt, as the doctor on call. Before Matt arrived, the search party found the deranged man in a lavatory—naked, lathered with soap, and his body soaked with perspiration. He attacked the watchmen like a cornered animal.

By the time Matt reached the scene, the man was ripping the clothes off two watchmen trying to subdue him. Other watchmen were attempting to control more than a hundred of the man's undressed countrymen, awakened and agitated by the disturbance.

"*Aiuto* [Help]!" he screamed to them, but they only watched the unfolding drama.

As the two embattled watchmen vainly struggled to hold the man, slippery from the soap and perspiration, Matt yelled, "Get him outside! Get him outside!"

The three combatants continued to grapple with one another. Eventually, the two watchmen succeeded in forcing their assailant out the door of the dormitory.

"Throw him on the ground! Get him down in the sand!" Matt shouted to the watchmen.

Again, the watchmen followed Matt's instructions. As the sand clung to the man, the watchmen were able to hold him more effectively. Matt put a straitjacket on him and had him taken to the hospital.

* * *

Next day was Friday, which meant Matt would be seeing Peg for the following two days. Tired from his interrupted sleep, he was less intrigued by the people he was examining.

At one point in his routine examinations in the Registry Hall, Matt realized McSweeney was standing behind him, watching. He nodded a friendly salutation and turned back to face a young Bulgarian woman approaching. It was apparent that she had some eye problem, for she had trouble seeing at a distance.

Matt followed the usual procedure. He took a buttonhook—a small, stiff metal hook with a handle that was normally used for drawing buttons through buttonholes—and placed it against her upper eyelid, so that he could roll the eyelid upward and examine her eye more fully. As he did so, Ed peered over his shoulder, to Matt's uncharacteristic annoyance.

"I think this woman has trachoma," Ed volunteered.

Matt wheeled around and lashed out angrily, "Damn it, Mr. McSweeney, go do your job and allow me to do mine!"

Ed glared at Matt for a brief moment and then walked away.

Matt resumed his examination. He found the woman to have a common abnormal condition of the retina of the eyes: myopia and choroiditis with partial detachment of the retina. She would inevitably become totally blind from the complete detachment of the retina, an event that could occur at any time. He marked her clothing in chalk with an "E," mandating a more detailed examination. In all likelihood, Matt knew, she would be sent back.

The rest of the day was routine, mostly tiresome repetitions of tasks. He couldn't wait to get home.

Finally his day did end, and he entered the silent emptiness of his home. He removed his jacket and tossed it onto a chair. Opening his collar, he turned on a lamp, walked to the liquor cabinet, poured himself a glass of schnapps, and sat in his easy chair.

He reflected on the naked wild man and laughed. Next, he thought of Guenter's near-fatal injuries and his anticipated return to work next week. He recalled his own, now fully healed injury and that fantasy night with Nicole. He thought of Peg, of their past life together, and of seeing her tomorrow. At last fatigue overcame him, and he fell asleep in the chair, the half-empty glass falling from his hand and spilling onto the carpet.

June 1897

Joseph got up from his desk to go home. It had been a busy day, but lately all the days had been busy.

Today had been the first day of operations with all the improvements finally completed on the island. Only yesterday had workers completed laying the cables for telephone and telegraph communication to New York City via Governor's Island. The new dormitory, the additional story on the detention house with its connecting bridge to the main building, was also finished.

Further augmenting the increased efficiency in immigrant processing was the fact that all island personnel were now under civil service regulations and protection. Achievement of civil service classification for his staff was a hollow victory for Senner, however. Washington made a blanket ruling, giving civil service standing without examination to all workers already holding immigration jobs, including McSweeney and Mueller, as well as the incompetent ones he wanted to discharge.

Otherwise, Senner was content. It had taken four years, but the island's facilities now were sufficient to meet present needs. Absorbed in these thoughts as he went downstairs and headed for the door, he was startled by a deep voice.

"Good night, Commissioner."

He looked up into the friendly face of the burly island watchman, one of eight scheduled to be on duty that night.

"Good night, Will," he replied pleasantly and left the building.

Will Gaines looked at the departing figure for a moment, then turned back and smiled.

Headed for a shorter stay home than he yet realized, Joseph looked back as usual at his workplace growing smaller as his boat moved farther away. Turning forward, he relished the thought of enjoying a quiet evening at home with his wife.

As Will continued along to his various checkpoints, he met Matt in the first-floor corridor.

"Hello, Dr. Stafford," Will greeted. "I see you're on the night shift again."

"Hello, Will," Matt responded. "Yes, summer vacation schedules mean double shifts for some of us."

"Yeah," said the watchman, "you'll need a vacation yourself from working so much."

"There's truth in that, Will."

"Dr. Stafford," said Will awkwardly, "I want to express my sympathy on the death of your wife. I read about it in the paper."

"Thank you," Matt replied, fighting the emotions welling up inside.

Peg had taken a turn for the worse a few weeks ago. Matt maintained a bedside vigil during her last few days. He tried to comfort her as best he could, agonizing each time her tormented body, wracked by coughing seizures, coughed up bright red blood. Despite his medical knowledge, he felt frustrated and helpless as he witnessed the ravages of the disease in his wife's body.

At last she went to her rest, quietly in her sleep, as Matt sat by her, holding her hand. When he realized that she died, he cried silently, caressed her face and hair, and then kissed her for the last time.

Peg had been his wife almost all of his adult life. He may not have experienced the passion he had known briefly with Nicole, but he had loved her. Now, ten days later, he had accepted her death with decidedly ambivalent feelings. He felt some relief in the end to her suffering and his anguish, but he also felt guilt over that relief, as well as over his recurring thoughts about Nicole. Both women were now out of his life, yet they remained in his thoughts and memories, even if no longer in his future.

Will looked at Matt and realized the doctor was lost in his grief-stricken thoughts. Sensing his presence was an intrusion, Will mumbled, "Well, anyway, I just wanted to tell you. See you later, Doctor."

"What?" said Matt, coming out of his reverie. "Oh yes, take care, Will."

Matt turned and continued his final rounds. He couldn't tell Will, or anyone really, that he was glad for the extra work. It occupied more of his conscious moments, preventing him from dwelling on the loss of Peg to her Creator and of Nicole to another man. He needed to stay busy to keep from wallowing in self-pity.

By midnight, all was quiet on the island. Three nurses were on duty as fifty-five immigrant patients in the hospital slept. Asleep in another nearby dwelling—the chief medical officer's house—were John White, his family, and their servant. In the dormitories slept 136 immigrants.

Most of the staff—Drs. Geddings and Stafford, two engineers, a pharmacist, four firemen, two laborers, a matron, a cook, eight railroad watchmen in care of the baggage, three restaurant employees, and the ferryboat captain and crew of the *John G. Carlisle*—were also sleeping in their quarters. Besides the nurses, only the eight island watchmen on duty were awake.

Will Gaines left the commissioner's corner office. As he neared the tower nearest the Battery, he glanced at his pocket watch; it was 12:38 am. Then he smelled smoke. Quickly investigating, he saw the tower ablaze.

"Fire! Fire!" he shouted, running to give the alarm.

Even as Will ran downstairs, the flames raced along the walls and floor. He reached the nearest alarm station and triggered the alarm, alerting everyone. Will then reached Superintendent Harry Burke, who took charge of operations.

Almost immediately, the lookout post of the Harbor Police Station at the Battery spotted the fire. Police officials rushed twenty policemen to the island to assist. Within minutes, fireboats and tugboats steamed to Ellis Island, but they were useless. Because the water around the island had never been dredged, they could not get close enough, except next to the ferry. Even there, the thin streams of water did little to contain the raging flames.

Already, the fire was out of control. The conflagration hungrily devoured the large wooden building. A strong breeze whipped the flames, speeding their advancement along the roof and two sides of the building. Burke quickly surmised that fighting the fire was hopeless. Evacuation was his first priority.

As the fire ravenously ate its way through the big structure, Burke led some of his night force into the adjacent dormitory building and aroused its sleeping inhabitants.

"*Veneti subito* [Come quickly]!" he instructed the mostly Italian immigrants. As the frightened people showed early signs of panic and hysteria, immigration personnel quickly quieted them. As each group awakened and dressed, a staff member led or pushed them down to the boat.

At the hospital, Matt—awakened from a troubled sleep— took charge of the evacuation of one floor while Frank Geddings did the same downstairs. Within minutes John White rushed over from his house to help.

Working as a well-disciplined team, the medical personnel methodically removed the patients. Saying nothing to alarm or excite them, they wrapped patients in blankets before assisting them out of the building. Those who could not walk were placed on stretchers, carried out by Ed Brandow and George Emmons, crew members of the *Carlisle* who had come to assist.

Completing their second trip of carrying out bedridden patients, Matt and the others were aghast to see that the long, enclosed passenger shed leading to the ferry slip, built as a protection against the elements, was now ablaze also. The long corridor was serving as an air shaft, sucking the flames down its length and threatening to engulf the dock and ferryboat in the expanding inferno.

Spreading in all directions from the main building, the fire ran along the rain gutters, licking up and down the trellises, and beginning to consume other buildings from the wind-blown flaming embers and intense heat.

John ran back to his house to help his wife and servant remove the furniture and bring it onto the ferryboat. His home was not yet on fire, but it was clearly in danger.

As flames raged through the shed, Matt began shouting to the men nearby, "Knock that shed down! Get something to knock it down!"

Finding lumber left over from the recent construction lying near the dock, Matt and the others each grabbed one of the long boards. Attacking the blazing shed with the boards, they kept pushing on it to force its collapse.

While they were locked in this effort, a tugboat steamed into the ferry slip and its crew threw several grappling hooks onto the ferry. Once the hooks were in place, the tugboat started off, intending to claim the vessel as salvage, even as other panicky fire victims attempted to board. With its mooring ropes now only loosely holding the ferry, the tugboat's power pulled it away.

As the tugboat dragged the *Carlisle* away from the island, its captain angrily ordered the crew to chop the tugboat's lines with fire axes. By the time they accomplished this, the ferry had been dragged about fifty yards from its dock. It now returned to load the remaining people still on the island.

Meanwhile, the men had succeeded in knocking over the shed, thus removing the fire threat to the dock and ferryboat. Racing back to the hospital, they carried the few remaining patients over the hot tin roof of the collapsed shed and to the boat.

Soon, another thirty police officers arrived. All were pressed into action in different parts of the blazing island, now attracting spectators along the Brooklyn, Manhattan, and New Jersey shorelines. The fire lit up the dark sky, offering a spectacle to those watching at a safe distance.

Seventeen minutes after Will reported the fire, the last of the immigrants was aboard the ferry.

"That's everyone from the hospital," Matt informed Superintendent Burke at the gangplank.

"We've got all the detainees too," he replied. "All staff are accounted for, except Dr. White and his family."

"I'll find them," Matt said.

He wheeled around and ran to White's house. White and his servant were struggling to get a large sofa out the door.

"Forget that!" Matt shouted. "There isn't enough time!"

John looked at Matt, torn between leaving his expensive English import behind and his family's safety.

"Come on, John! Now!" Matt demanded.

Grabbing a few lamps, jewelry cases, and boxes they had hurriedly packed with clothes, china, and other possessions, the entire family—adults and children alike—hastened out of the house. Matt scooped up the youngest boy in one arm, held a valise in the other, and led them to the boat. They boarded it, and the *Carlisle* steamed away.

The ferry passengers looked back at the island all afire. Like most other staff, Matt's face and hands were dirty and smudged with soot; his clothes smelled of smoke. He looked about at the people and saw a range of emotions. Some were simply curious, others bewildered. A few were crying, apparently over possessions left behind on the island. A few young men were laughing, enjoying the tragic adventure.

It was now after one o'clock in the morning. The fireboats came into the ferry channel, and the firefighters aimed their hoses wherever they could. Others leapt ashore to aid their comrades who had come earlier. There was little any of them could do. The wooden buildings were too vulnerable.

At an early stage of the fire, authorities had notified Joseph, who was asleep at home. He raced to the pier, watching with alarm as his motor launch headed toward the fiery island. He was about midway there when the roof of the main building collapsed, crashed to the ground, and sent an explosive shower of sparks and burning embers flying high into the air. The wind blew them down everywhere around the still-burning hulk. Fire now spread over the docks, the grounds, and the ferry house. It destroyed the cook-house, residences, and most of the other buildings. Virtually the entire island was now swallowed up in a raging fire completely out of control.

When he saw the sky-filled pyrotechnics caused by the roof's collapse, Joseph was heartsick. His boat came beside a fireboat, and he stepped onto the still-burning, heat-filled island, dreading what he would learn. He hurried to the fire chief overseeing the firemen running lines of hose ashore from the fireboats.

"How many are trapped inside?"

"None, Commissioner."

"Vaht? Are you sure?"

"Yes, sir. Superintendent Burke told me the headcount of evacuees agreed with his tallies of everyone listed as on the island."

"Tank God!" exclaimed Joseph, relieved. "Ve vere lucky."

"Yes, we were. It would have been a mighty different story, though, if the wind had been blowing in the opposite direction."

"Vy is dot?"

"Look over there, Commissioner. You see those boats about three hundred yards away?"

"*Ja*, I zee dem."

"Well, those are government ammunition boats loaded with gunpowder. If the wind carried flaming embers to them, we'd have had one big explosion."

"Gudt God!"

"Count your blessings, Commissioner. No one died, but we won't be able to save much here. Now, if you'll excuse me?"

"Of course."

Joseph watched for hours, as the firemen futilely fought the fire until it had run its course by daybreak. Then he surveyed the wreckage. In the smoking ruins lay the warped and twisted remains of the main building. Smoke and the smell of burned wood assaulted his nostrils.

He discovered that the electric light and steam plant was intact without a mark on it. The chief medical officer's house was standing and could be restored; inside, the English sofa was damaged by smoke and water. The walls of the kitchen and record office were also standing, but all else lay in ruin—a tangle of charcoal, battered and rusted iron, and ashes, from which smoke still lazily rose.

*   *   *

On its arrival at its Manhattan dock, officials kept the *Carlisle* secure until guards and gatemen could escort patients and detainees into the Barge Office. Ed McSweeney was in charge of operations, and still sensitive to previous escapes, he wanted to be absolutely certain that no one would do so this time.

Ed's primary concern was to get everyone situated for the rest of the night in a safe and secure arrangement. Staff members concentrated on their areas of interest. The doctors established a makeshift hospital ward, while others set up places for the detainees to sleep throughout the building. Ed walked about, observing the immigrants huddled together on the first floor. Six Hindu men, wearing bright, colorful robes, loudly wailed over something. When he attempted to quiet them, one pointed to his feet. Looking down, he noticed all were barefoot. Through an exchange of gestures, Ed learned the men were upset over loss of their shoes. He gestured to the men that he would do something about it, and they quieted down.

He came to another man wandering about clad only in his underwear.

"Where are your clothes?"

"Where do you think? Back there."

"Of course. I'll get you something to wear. What is your name?"

"Josef Rozynski."

"All right, Mr. Rozynski. Just stay here. I'll find you some clothes.'

Ed went to the building entrance where aid societies and missionaries had brought surplus clothing. He found a pair of blue overalls, an old coat, and worn carpet slippers for Rozynski and assorted tan footwear for the Hindus. After bringing these items to the grateful recipients, he encountered a young couple sitting forlornly in a corner. The woman's crying drew him to them.

"Can I help you in any way?" he asked.

In a heavy Prussian accent the woman replied tearfully, "Dere is notting you can do. Ve are destroyed."

"I will help you if I can. Just tell me the problem."

The man with her sadly explained, in the same accent, that they were from Leipert, Saxony. Because he was divorced, they could not marry there and had come to the United States with a trousseau and a complete set of items to set up their household in their new country. All had been left behind in the fire. They had nothing left and would even have to postpone their wedding.

"I will help you send a cable to your relatives in Saxony," Ed offered. "Perhaps they can send you some money. In the meantime we'll provide you with food and shelter."

"Tank you, sir," the man replied, disconsolately.

"I'm sorry for your losses. I know many things probably had sentimental value. All I can do is promise you that we will compensate you for them, so you can start over."

"Dot vood be most kind. Tank you again."

The man explained to his fiancée what Ed had said. She forced a little smile and nodded her head in appreciation. Ed moved on, continuing to console people and supervise arrangements.

Joseph returned to the Barge Office to meet with his staff and to set in motion a plan of action. He conferred with Ed for a half hour and next assembled his staff in an upstairs room. With McSweeney at his side, he looked at the attentive faces of his people. Their fresh appearance easily identified the day shift reporting in, unlike the more unkempt, disheveled, unshaven look of the nighttime staff.

"Ladies und gentlemen," he began in an uncharacteristically quiet voice. "I do not have to tell you vaht has happened. Vile almost everyting has been destroyed, I am proud to tell you dot de night crew performed heroically und everyone vas evacuated safely."

A loud cheer rang from the group. Guenter, back at work for the past eight months, patted Matt's arm twice in congratulations. Frank was also standing with them and offered a handshake. Matt smiled at his colleagues.

Pausing a moment to let the cheers die down, Joseph continued, "Dose buildings vill be rebuilt und vun day Ellis Island vill function again. Until den, however, ve vill have to make do mit lesser facilities.

"Ve must get ready immediately to process new immigrants. Today six hundred new immigrants vill arrive in de harbor, und I am told dot seven tousand others are aboard ships now on de high seas und are due to reach New York zumtime dis week.

"Today no new arrivals vill be processed. Dey vill remain on board de ships dot transported dem here. Dose people presently under our care are to be processed today. Ve have to get dem out of here. Mr. McSweeney vill inform you of de precise location of your temporary workstations.

"Tomorrow ve vill set up inspection facilities on de piers. Ve vill arrange for dose who are sick to go to city hospitals. Dose mit contagious diseases or requiring disinfection vill go to quarantine. Dose detained vill be lodged here in de Barge Office. Dis vill get us true de immediate crisis. Ve shall deal mit other contingencies as dey arise. Now, ve have a great deal of vork to do, so let us pitch in und get it done. Tank you."

Joseph strode out of the room as his staff exchanged looks with one another. Matt and the others from the night crew left for home while Ed began to brief the new shift more fully about the day's make-do arrangements.

Downstairs a *New York Tribune* reporter asked Senner, "What caused the fire?"

"I do not know und I am told ve may never know, for all is in ruins."

"What are your thoughts, Commissioner?"

"Ever zince I have been in office," he replied, the gutteral sounds of his German accent seemingly making his words more emphatic, "de fear of fire has haunted me. Now dot it has come und no lives ver lost, I am glad of it. Un row of unsightly, ramshackle tinder boxes has been destroyed, und ven de government rebuilds, it vill be forced to put up decent fireproof structures."

Armed with a provocative quote, the reporter hurried to write his front-page story.

*   *   *

By afternoon, the island had cooled down sufficiently to examine the ruins. By then Herman Stump had arrived by train from Washington to survey the damage firsthand. Although he had had virtually no sleep in more than thirty hours, Joseph went with his superior and a crew to inspect the charred remains.

They were delighted to find that about two thirds of the current files in the records office could be recovered. Although damaged, they were still useful. One irreplaceable loss was the past immigration records. Not only were those of the Barge Office and Ellis Island lost, but so too were those of Castle Garden from 1855 to 1890. These only had been turned over to Ellis Island authorities the year before.

A company employee opened the railroad office safe. Inside were the charred remains of its paper money, and all its silver and gold coins melted into a single alloyed blob of metal. Money exchanger Francis Scully was more fortunate. When he opened his safe, its contents were intact, including more than ten thousand dollars in paper, notes, and coins. He was the only one so fortunate. All other safes had burst open from the heat, resulting in the destruction of all contents.

Returning again to the Barge Office, Joseph and Ed led the superintendent through that facility, explaining how they would convert it to their needs. Until some physical changes could be made within the building, however, they agreed that outdoor processing on the piers would be necessary.

Afterward the three men sat down to plan further arrangements.

"You've done admirably, gentlemen," said Stump. "It looks to me as if you've made the best of a bad situation."

"Tank you, sir, but dese facilities vill not be enough."

"No question about that, Joseph. I want you to find some suitable building nearby and rent it to handle the overflow."

"Mr. Stump," Ed interjected, "we have many immigrants who lost their baggage and belongings, as well as staff whose uniforms and personal effects were destroyed."

"Get written declarations from them of their losses, and we'll reimburse them," Herman answered.

"How vill ve know dot dey are telling de truth?"

"We have no choice but to take them at their word, Joseph."

"*Ja*, zum vill make a profit from dis fire."

"No doubt, but we really have no alternative."

Joseph gave out a small laugh.

"What's so funny?" Herman asked.

"I vas just tinking, Herman. President McKinley vill be replacing us soon. I did not tink ve vood go out in zuch a blaze of glory."

The two men laughed at the macabre joke. Ed also laughed, both at the unexpected humor and because it reminded him that his wish to be rid of Senner would soon come true.

August 1897

In the two months since the fire, immigration officials had completed their adjustments to the loss of their processing station at Ellis Island. At first they had set up temporary outdoor inspection stations on the piers where the ocean vessels docked. Immigrants moved through several roped aisles to awaiting doctors and then onward to the desks of inspectors.

Once partitions had been removed or added as necessary in the Barge Office, the processing was relocated to that large, two-story granite building. In addition, the Customs Service vacated the Barge Office Annex, allowing its use as a dormitory for detainees. Unfortunately, both facilities proved inadequate.

What had once been spread throughout larger facilities on Ellis Island—baggage handling, inspection lines, medical and legal examinations, money-changing counters, railroad ticket agencies, administrative offices, and hearing rooms for boards of inquiry—were now jammed into the cramped quarters of the Barge Office.

What was gained in a shortened workday by elimination of the round-trip, half-hour ferry ride to and from the island was offset by the more difficult working conditions. Immigration personnel grumbled and plodded onward, sustained by the knowledge that Ellis Island would be rebuilt. Congress had just approved a bill authorizing $1.5 million for construction of fireproof buildings of steel, stone, and brick. However, those facilities were at least two years away.

Matt was about to resign. His six-month, temporary assignment at Ellis Island had lasted almost two years because of Peg's illness. When she died, he no longer felt the need to work regular hours. Ellis Island had afforded him the opportunity to be with her more often, but now he could return to a more challenging schedule and resume his medical/surgical practice. He had quietly sounded out his old boss, Richard Jensen, about coming back and was in the process of completing arrangements when the fire had struck. Out of a sense of duty, he had delayed his return to Presbyterian until September to help his colleagues stabilize their situation.

No reasons remained for him to stay on temporary duty with the Marine Hospital Service. With all immigrants requiring hospitalization now sent directly to city hospitals, this was the first time in his career that he wasn't working with patients, and he missed it. Instead, all he had left was the monotonous routine of continuous medical exams, and the allure of immigrant diversity was no longer enough, especially under the present overcrowded conditions.

Moreover, President McKinley's appointment of Thomas Fitchie to replace Joseph Senner as commissioner was also a factor. Like everyone else, he knew it would happen, ever since McKinley's inauguration last March. When he named Terence Powderly of the Knights of Labor as commissioner-general to replace Herman Stump, it was only a matter of time before Joseph would go. Although Matt had never gotten close to the man, he liked Senner and their occasional interactions. Matt didn't relish the thought of working under an inexperienced new man and under such trying circumstances.

Most upsetting, however, was the rumor that John White was leaving. Supposedly, he was about to be transferred to run a US Marine Hospital in Cincinnati. It made sense. With no immigrant hospital, John's abilities were wasted in the Barge Office. Yet it gave Matt a major reason to relinquish his own position. It wasn't just the loss of a boss who was bright, energetic, and blessed with a delightful sense of humor, although that was important, for John's style helped them all through these tough days. It was also that his replacement would be either one of his senior colleagues or an outsider, perhaps even someone from whom Matt would learn little.

He approached John's office, determined to confirm the rumored transfer, prior to submitting his own resignation.

"Matt, come in," John said in his customary warm manner as Matt stood in the doorway. "I was just going to send for you. What can I do for you?"

"Hello, John. Rumor has it that you're being transferred to Cincinnati. Is it true?"

"So the word is out on me, huh? Yes, it's true. It's what I was about to tell you. I'll be leaving in two weeks."

"I'm sorry to hear that, John. It's probably best for you, though. At least you'll be back in a hospital again."

"Perhaps, but I'll miss the East Coast. I'm not certain that I'm cut out for midwestern life."

"You'll do fine. I hear Cincinnati's a good city. John, I've decided to make a change myself."

"Matt, let me say something first. I've recommended that you become the liaison between the Marine Hospital Service and the architectural firm designing the new hospital."

"What?"

"You're the best man for the job."

"The Marine Hospital Service has many career physicians. Surely one of them is better suited for such responsibility."

"With less than one hundred doctors, the service is spread

pretty thin at all our hospitals throughout the country. I was asked to recommend someone here."

"What about Stoner or Geddings? They've been here longer."

"Stoner will be my replacement, and he will be busy enough. Geddings won't do. We need someone else able to concentrate on the new hospital. Since you've worked in a major city hospital, you bring more insights into planning for the needs of the diverse patient population that we get here. This new hospital will be bigger than most city hospitals and most likely a model for the rest of the country. I trust you more than anyone else to make it a good one. Washington agrees that you are uniquely qualified. The job is yours to take."

"John, I don't know what to say."

"Say yes. You won't get a position like this at Presbyterian for many years."

"You knew?"

"I knew Jensen wanted you back. He told me. I can't blame him. You're a fine doctor. So what do you say?"

"How can I refuse? It's a wonderful opportunity. Thank you for your confidence in me."

"It's well placed," said John, smiling. "There is one condition, though. We would need to change your special assignment status with us and make you an officer in the commissioned corps if you are to represent officially the service on this project. Is that all right with you?"

"Well, I already wear the uniform, so we might as well make it official."

"Well then, congratulations, Matt. I'm very pleased. I'll talk to you more about this later. I know you have to do exams now."

"Yes, I do. Thanks again, John. I can't tell you how much this means to me."

Matt was thrilled. The cramped work quarters and a new

commissioner no longer depressed him. He would soon have new challenges and new opportunities. With renewed energy, he approached the male immigrant line awaiting his inspection.

Enthusiastically, he greeted his gateman, "Hello, Guenter!"

"Good morning, Dr. Stafford. You're in a good mood."

"Couldn't be better, Guenter. I haven't felt this good in a long time."

Guenter looked at Matt. He had not seen him this cheerful in a long time.

Near the end of Matt's examinations for the day, a boyish-looking young man approached him. Alejandro Veles was a second-class passenger traveling from Vera Cruz. His small hands showed no deformities. His eyes were clear, intensely returning Matt's gaze into them. The eyelid rollback revealed no disease. Hair and scalp were free of lice and ringworm.

As the immigrant unbuttoned his shirt, Matt placed his stethoscope against the partially exposed chest and discovered the presence of small but definitely rounded breasts. Stunned, he opened the immigrant's shirt further, confirming the reality.

"Guenter," he called, "please take this person to an examining room. Have Mrs. Stucklen conduct a full examination to determine sex."

Guenter looked quizzically at Matt, then at the alien who had rebuttoned the shirt.

Matt offered no further explanation, simply saying, "Guenter, please."

As Guenter complied, Matt, shaking his head, began to inspect the next immigrant.

Elsewhere in the building, Assistant Commissioner Ed McSweeney, Chief Registry Clerk John Mueller, and Inspector Frank Martiniello were discussing the puzzling case of Jose Maria. It had baffled them for days because no one had been able to communicate with him to establish his identity and clear him for landing. Up to now, at least one interpreter was able to speak the language of every immigrant who arrived. This time, every interpreter's efforts met only with Jose Maria replying, "Me no sabe."

Because the mysterious man looked like a mixture of Japanese, Chinese, and Malaysian, Ed had requested the assistance of the Chancellor of the Japanese Consulate. This diplomat had a reputation for speaking and understanding virtually every dialect of the Orient, but he too had failed. Newspapers had printed the story. Many offered suggestions of what to do, one paper even guessed that the man was Burmese. No one, however, could actually determine the man's nationality, and nothing on his person offered any clues. He had $1.50 in German money and a satchel with two envelopes in it. One was covered with Chinese characters that gave a detailed description about a restaurant somewhere. The other was empty, addressed to "Jose Antonio Chins, Rua de Mancel, Rio de Janeiro, Brazil."

As the men discussed the case, Ed said, "Well, we know that the man sailed here from Bremen. No one there knows anything, and no one here has come forward to claim him. Since he is carrying the address of some place in Rio de Janeiro, he must have taken the wrong steamer, coming to New York by mistake."

"You may be right, Mr. McSweeney," replied Mueller, "but what do we do now? The man has no money to book passage to Brazil, and there's no one to contact."

"I'll strike a deal with the steamship company. It will be cheaper for them to take him to Brazil than pay his food and lodging expenses here for an indefinite period."

As they concluded their conference, Matt knocked on the door.

"Gentlemen," Matt began, "forgive the interruption, but I have a case that requires your attention."

"We were just finishing, Dr. Stafford," Ed answered. "Come in, and tell us about it."

After Matt explained the case of Alejandro Veles matron had indeed found to be a woman, Ed instructed her to be brought before them.

With Frank serving as interpreter, Ed began, "We know that you are a woman, not a man. What is your real name?"

The woman glared at the four men, then answered defiantly, "No one has ever questioned my identity before! How dare you? I am Alejandro Veles."

"What is your real name?" Ed insisted.

"Why do you wear men's clothes?" Mueller asked.

"I would rather kill myself than wear women's clothes!" she angrily replied.

"Why is that?" inquired Matt.

"I have always wanted to be a man. It is no fault of mine that I was not born one."

When Frank translated her Spanish into English, the men exchanged astonished looks.

Then the young woman broke down. Sobbing, she pleaded, "I have done harm to no one. Please let me be! Let me enter your country."

"So you speak English!" Ed noted in surprise. "What is your real name?"

Still sobbing, she replied, "I am Alejandra Veles."

"Young woman," said Mueller, "you have broken our immigration laws. You have falsified your name, your sex, and all background information. Do you realize that you can be arrested?"

Matt turned and whispered, "Aren't you being a little rough on her?"

"I know my job, Dr. Stafford," he answered. "It's the only way to cut through their lies."

"I insist you send for my attorney, Ashley Cole," the woman suddenly demanded.

Her request for one of New York's most prominent attorneys dumbfounded the men. How would this alien have such a prestigious personal attorney? Ed had his secretary call Cole's office, and to their further surprise, he agreed to come to the Barge Office at once.

Ashley Cole entered Ed's office about twenty minutes later. A tall, thin, dignified, silver-haired gentleman of sixty with a neatly trimmed beard, he looked the part of a renowned attorney for the rich and influential. When he saw "Alejandra," he smiled and greeted her as she simply nodded her head in acknowledgment.

"Thank you for coming so quickly, Mr. Cole," Ed said, shaking his hand and introducing him to Matt, John, and Frank. "Tell me, who is this woman?"

"First, gentlemen, I must have your solemn word never to reveal her true identity to anyone."

When the men had intriguingly pledged their word, he explained, "Alejandra is the daughter of Sir William Howland, a gentleman of breeding and culture who married a wealthy Spanish woman. The English government sent him to a diplomatic post in the Far East, where Alejandra was born.

"While a little child, for some reason she became unhappy at being a girl and insisted on dressing as a boy. Although her parents did all they could to discipline her, she would tear her dresses to shreds. She defied all control, so they finally allowed her to grow up as a boy.

"At the age of fifteen, she ran away. She came to the United States and worked for two years as a hostler in a New York stable. Then she went to the West Indies, where she was a field supervisor over some men on a sugar cane plantation. No one ever suspected she was a girl. She is returning to New York from there."

"Where do you fit in the picture, Mr. Cole?" Matt inquired.

"Her father, frantic and at his wit's end, engaged me to look after her when she first came to New York. He has provided a liberal fund for her support. I periodically draw from that fund when she requests some money."

"How old is she?" John asked, taking notes.

"She is twenty."

"Mr. Cole," said Ed, "when she came to this country the first time, immigration laws were different. We cannot let her into the country under these circumstances."

"I understand," the attorney replied.

Throughout these exchanges, Alejandra had remained silent, allowing her attorney to speak for her. Cole now turned to her.

"Alejandra," he said, "I have brought some money for you." Handing it to her, he asked, "Is there anything else you want?"

"Yes," she said, "give me two plugs of tobacco and a pipe."

In disbelief, the men watched Cole open his briefcase, take out the requested items, and give them to her.

"Young woman," Ed stated, "we will permit you to leave here if you promise to leave the country at once."

"I will," she agreed.

"I will see to it that she does," Cole promised. "Where would you like to go, Alejandra?"

"England. I think I'll visit my parents," she answered, lighting her pipe.

"England it is, then. Your parents will be happy to see you," Cole said, rising from his chair. Shaking Ed's hand, he said, "Thank you for your understanding and cooperation, Mr. McSweeney. Good day, gentlemen."

Cole shook each one's hand. He then left with Alejandra,

who puffed on her pipe, walked casually past them, and went out the door without ever acknowledging their presence.

"That is one of the strangest cases I've ever encountered," Ed said.

"That's for certain," Frank agreed.

"For me, this entire day has been most incredible," added Matt.

"I'll bet the unexpected treat of seeing her breasts made your day, hey, Dr. Stafford?"

"That's not what I was thinking about, John."

"Really? Well, it would boggle *my* mind. That I know."

Mueller turned and walked out the door as Matt watched, with a look of disgust on his face.

November 1897

"Inspector, please, could we have a word with you?"

Mueller, about to enter the Barge Office, turned to the man who had addressed him. He was well dressed, about forty, and anxious. Beside him was another man, slightly younger, also well dressed, and looking concerned.

"Yes? What is it?" he replied, joining them.

"I'm David Rohrlich and this is my brother William. We have a nephew, Andrew, who arrived here several days ago, but he was sent to the hospital and placed in a ward for contagious diseases. He can't have any visitors, and we can't get any information on his status as an unlanded immigrant. Can you help us?"

"I don't know, sir. I am not with the medical officers."

"You are an inspector, though, and we have heard you are a man of influence. You can contact them. That's more than we can do. Please."

"Well, I don't know—"

"Look, Inspector, let's be frank. I am a man of means. I will make it worth your while to do this for me. Say, twenty dollars?"

"Well—"

"All right, forty dollars," said David Rohrlich, opening his wallet and taking out the money. "Will you do it?"

"I really shouldn't, Mr. Rohrlich, but, well, yes, all right. I will do this for you," John replied, taking the money. "Can you meet me here at twelve fifteen?'

"Yes, of course," the man replied. "We will be here."

John nodded his head and walked away smiling about his easy good fortune.

He was not the only one to discover the advantages of the forced return of immigrant processing to Manhattan. Once again, as in the days before there was an Ellis Island, swindlers robbed immigrants of their money and baggage. Hotel runners waited to take the greenhorns to overpriced rooms. Inside the Barge Office, bribery and corruption among the staff was commonplace, as were carelessness and incompetence in screening the immigrants.

Presumably ruling over these deteriorating conditions was

Waiting outside the Barge Office for newly arrived family or friends

Commissioner Thomas Fitchie, Senner's successor. Although a man of high character, he was an elderly man unfamiliar with immigration. To Ed's delight, he was disinterested in making executive decisions or even in working a full day at the Barge Office, and so Ed assumed the power of running things.

Employees quickly realized that Fitchie was a figurehead; McSweeney was the man in charge. And with McSweeney in charge, corruption flourished among some of the staff.

Mueller, one of the more opportunistic employees, walked into the Barge Office and to the designated medical section.

"Good morning, Dr. Stafford."

"Good morning, Mr. Mueller. What brings you here?"

"An inquiry for a friend. Are you familiar with a teenage boy, Andrew Rohrlich, who arrived a few days ago? He was sent to a city hospital and placed in a ward for contagious diseases."

"Yes, I do, in fact. He was a pleasant young man."

"What's his situation, Doctor?"

"The boy had measles. He's in quarantine right now; the report on him is that he's doing fine. He should be released in about a week."

"Will there be any difficulty in his being admitted?"

"Not for any medical reason. I can't speak for the rest of it."

"I understand. Thanks for the information."

"You're quite welcome," said Matt as John hurried off.

At twelve fifteen, John met the Rohrlich brothers.

"Gentlemen," he began, "I'm afraid I have some bad news for you."

"What? Tell us!" pleaded David Rohrlich.

"Your nephew has several physical problems and is presently in quarantine. The doctors inform me that they plan to deport him."

"Oh no, they can't deport him! Can't you do anything to stop them?"

"Mr. Rohrlich, I am an inspector, not a doctor. I have no power to stop a deportation, if that's their decision."

"Then they haven't made a final decision yet?" asked William.

"No, not yet," John replied.

"Then it might still be possible to change their minds?" asked David. "Could you prevail upon them to let the boy in?"

"Mr. Rohrlich, you credit me with influence I do not possess. No, I cannot influence them, but your money can."

"How?"

"If you will give the doctors a sufficient sum of money, I am certain that when the present symptoms are less severe, they will clear your nephew for entry into the country. I'll serve as your go-between."

"How much money do they want, Inspector?"

"Two hundred dollars."

"Two hundred! That's a lot of money!"

"How much is your nephew worth to you, Mr. Rohrlich? You're asking doctors to violate the law, to risk their jobs and licenses. You're asking them to hospitalize your nephew for another week at government expense, instead of immediately sending him back home."

"But we'll pay for his hospitalization! Tell them that!"

"Don't you understand? He failed his medical exam, and that is now a matter of record! They've got to change records, then justify his hospitalization and release by saying it was measles or something else. You've got to make it worthwhile, if they're to take this considerable risk. If you want your nephew admitted, this is the only way."

"Very well," said David resignedly. "I'll have the money for you tomorrow."

John smiled and said, "As soon as you do, I'll convey it to

the doctors. I guarantee that the boy will be released within a week."

"Thank you, sir. I don't know what we would have done without you."

"Believe me, gentlemen," John responded with a smile, "the pleasure is mine. I really enjoy helping people like you."

February 1898

Matt was deeply absorbed in his review of the architect's plans for the hospital. It was to be constructed on a separate island to be built across the ferry slip from the main island. He and his superiors in the US Marine Hospital Service were determined to make this new hospital one of the best in the nation. Carefully, he checked the blueprint, wanting to ensure that his suggestions had been incorporated in the revisions.

The knock at the door interrupted his concentration.

"Excuse me, Dr. Stafford," said Guenter, "Mr. McSweeney wants you in his office immediately."

"Do you know what it's about, Guenter?"

"He's got a woman and five children in there with some missionary woman. It's a question of their clearance."

"I see. All right, let's go."

Matt left the office with Guenter, the two men chatting briefly during the short walk to McSweeney's office. He knocked and entered the assistant commissioner's office. Smiling and nodding to Ed, he quickly surveyed the people with him—a woman in her late thirties with five solemn children all under ten years of age, a missionary woman, and Ed's secretary.

"Ah, Dr. Stafford, please come in and sit down," Ed said.

"This is Mrs. Stanley, and over here is Mrs. MacHugh and her children. You know Mr. Donnelly, of course. Ladies, this is Dr. Stafford."

"Hello, everyone," greeted Matt as he sat in the remaining chair.

"Mrs. Stanley," Ed began explaining, "learned about the destitution of the MacHugh family and brought their case to my attention. Mrs. Stanley, would you please tell Dr. Stafford what you told me?"

"Yes, of course," the missionary woman replied gently. "Dr. Stafford, this family came to the United States five weeks ago from Scotland. Mr. Sionn MacHugh, the husband of Mrs. MacHugh and father of these poor children, came with them. He was a mechanic, but he was unable to find any steady employment, at least in any work that suited him. The money they had brought with them has been spent in supporting the family since their arrival. A few days ago, Mr. MacHugh left his family in their tenement to look for a job. He never came back. He was a devoted family man and would never have deserted them. We fear he may have been murdered or committed suicide, although we have not been able to determine this."

Matt noted everyone looking even more somber as the story ended. Then he asked, "What is it you want me to do, Mr. McSweeney?"

"It's obvious this family is likely to become permanent public charges, and the law thus requires us to send them back to Scotland at government expense. However, if you would examine them, I was hoping that you might discover some physical or mental condition existing prior to arrival. In that case, we could have the steamship company that brought them pay part of the cost of sending them back."

Ed had a tight relationship with several shipping companies but not with the British lines. In this case, his loyalties were to the government. Moreover, as an Irishman he relished the prospect of sticking it to a British company.

Matt made a superficial inspection of the six people. All looked healthy and well nourished, making him reasonably certain that no diagnostic procedure would reveal any mental or physical defects. Standing behind the family, Matt shook his head, indicating to Ed that his hope was not likely.

"Have you notified the police about the disappearance of your husband, Mrs. MacHugh?" asked Matt, coming around into her field of vision.

"N-no. I had not thought to do so."

Matt found this reply strange, but before he could say anything, John Mueller knocked and entered the office, carrying some papers.

Ed asked immediately, "What did you find out, Mr. Mueller?"

Reading from the registry sheet, John reported, "The MacHugh family arrived from Edinburgh, Scotland, on January 16, sir. Doctors found the children and both adults to be healthy, with no afflictions or problems of any kind. Inspection questions revealed that Mr. MacHugh is a mechanic and his wife keeps house. Their children range in age from three to nine. Mr. MacHugh had no job waiting for him here. The family paid their own passage and had no relatives meet them here. There are no criminal or political problems in their past, no questions of moral turpitude. Mr. MacHugh showed the inspector that he had five hundred dollars on his person. That's about it, sir."

"I see," Ed said. "Thank you, Mr. Mueller. That will be all."

"Yes, sir, glad to be of help. Goodbye, everyone," he said, smiling to one and all before leaving.

Matt was stunned. He thought it highly unlikely that a thrifty Scottish family would spend five hundred dollars in just five weeks. The woman's evident surprise when Mueller gave those details did not escape his notice, and he attempted to catch her off guard.

"When will your husband arrive back in Scotland?"

"What do you mean?" she responded resentfully, as the others looked at him in surprise.

"You know what I mean, Mrs. MacHugh."

When she said nothing further, he added, "You knew what your husband was going to do when he took the remaining $450 and left that morning."

"It was only $425 by then," she quickly countered. Suddenly realizing what she had just admitted, she said nothing further.

Pressing his advantage, Matt continued, "So your husband left that day with all your money, and you knew what he was going to do, didn't you?"

"No, I didn't," she insisted, "but he said that if he couldn't find work, he might try to get a job back as a cattleman."

That reply confirmed Matt's suspicions. The man had most likely signed up to return to Scotland on a cattle steamer as what the sailors called a "stiff" or inexperienced cattle tender. He may not have been able to say goodbye to his family before sailing or perhaps this was their scheme all along to secure free passage back home.

Whatever the reality, immigration officials had no choice. Ed ordered Mrs. MacHugh and her children placed in detention until they could be deported. This meant that they would be transferred to Ellis Island, where an old steamboat, the *Narragansett*, was anchored. Because of severe overcrowding at the Barge Office, the government had secured this vessel and remodeled it for housing detainees.

"That was good work, Matt," complimented Ed when the two men were alone.

"The government still pays their passage. Ed, we really don't know if the man has returned to Scotland."

"No, but we can find out. I'll cable the American consul

there to keep a watch out for his arrival in Edinburgh next week. We'll keep his family on the *Narragansett* until we can confirm his presence there."

"I'm willing to bet he'll arrive," Matt said and left the office.

Later, Matt walked by the detention pen, filled with immigrants awaiting transport to the *Narragansett*. He saw the MacHugh family sitting together, and then he heard them singing softly the refrain, "Rolling home, rolling home, rolling home to bonnie Scotland."

Stopping by them, he motioned to Mrs. MacHugh. When she came over to him, he asked her, "Tell me, Mrs. MacHugh, did you plan all this?"

In her lilting Scottish accent, the woman replied, "Why, Doctor, I don't know what you mean."

"You have my confidence, Mrs. MacHugh. I won't tell anyone. Did you know what would happen to you if your husband disappeared?"

"Well, I'll tell you, but I'll deny it if you say anything. We all knew the government would have to send our family back if my husband took himself out of the way."

"Thank you for being so candid, Mrs. MacHugh. Have a good trip home."

Grinning, she replied, "Thank you, Doctor. Goodbye."

Matt turned and walked away, smiling at the ingenuity of some immigrants in using the system to their advantage, one way or another. He knew he could do nothing to stop the MacHughs. They had been too clever.

*   *   *

That evening, Ed arrived at a Manhattan restaurant for a meeting he requested with some prominent and powerful friends, including Theodore Roosevelt, the former New York City police commissioner and now assistant secretary of the navy. As they knew, he was locked in a battle with Commissioner-General Terence Powderly, his boss in Washington. Ed was not happy with the turmoil swirling around him, and he wanted to discuss the matter with them.

As a former labor leader, Powderly supported organized labor's successful lobbying efforts to pass a law forbidding immigrants from arriving with a job contract. The newly created contract labor inspectors operated independently of McSweeney's authority, even limiting the role of the Board of Special Inquiry. Ed was convinced that bribes were common and deportations of job-seeking immigrants much too excessive.

Ed worked hard to bring these labor inspectors under his authority. Powderly actively opposed him, seeking influential support in his cause. Ed had his own circle of influential friends and succeeded in getting the Treasury Department to institute the necessary reforms, despite Powderly's objections. The number of deportations dropped noticeably afterward.

Powderly made his displeasure clear to Ed. In fact, he threatened to "get" Ed, telling him that his days as an immigration officer were numbered. Furthermore, Ed believed that someone on his staff was currying Powderly's favor because the commissioner-general knew far too many details about problems that were occurring. Not only was Powderly harassing him with demands for written reports on these incidents, but lately, a sudden barrage of newspaper exposés had appeared. These stories about alleged graft and corruption in the Barge Office blamed his administrative incompetence.

Ed had had enough. Tonight he intended to apprise these men of the current situation and to tell them of his new plans. Soon thereafter, in a private dining room, the assembled group of men listened attentively to Ed's comments.

"So, gentlemen," he continued, "for these reasons I have decided to resign my position. I have an attractive job offer, and I think it is in my best interests at this time to accept it."

"Good God, man! You can't resign! You are needed in that position," argued Roosevelt.

"Indeed so," quickly added Jacob Riis. "You would be deserting your post precisely at a time when your services are most needed."

"How so?" Ed asked the celebrated social reformist.

"Everyone knows Fitchie is an old, feeble man, incapable of running the New York immigration station. You're his right-hand man, an experienced administrator. You run the place. We all know that. And with construction on Ellis Island barely begun, the difficulties of running operations at the Barge Office demand an experienced hand at the helm."

"You flatter me, Jacob."

"No, I simply state the facts. You are a competent man who makes the immigration station run smoothly."

"Not if you read the newspapers or listen to Mr. Powderly."

"We pay no attention to either," said banker Joseph Seligman, "and neither should you. You're too strong a man to let those with short-sighted, narrow minds get to you."

Ed, a longtime politician well practiced in the art of expediency, feared possible disclosure of any of his past dealings. If that happened, he knew the support of these men would wither. He thought it might be best to get out before the dam burst.

Not assured by Seligman's words, he replied, "I'm perceptive enough, Joseph, to know I've become a scapegoat, and that the longer I stay, the more likely it is that I will be crucified. No, gentlemen, it is my fervent wish to resign."

"Damn it, Ed!" thundered Roosevelt, banging his fist on the table and bouncing the tableware in the process. "We are not without influence. You can be assured of our continued advice and full support. We will stand by you and not let you be crucified by anyone. You have my word on that!"

"And mine," offered real estate developer Julius Tishman.

"Absolutely!" added Seligman. "We are in your corner. You have nothing to fear from anyone. Fight the good fight. We will protect you."

"Well," Ed began, wavering in his decision, yet still thinking his wisest move would be to step down. "I deeply appreciate your faith in me, but I'm still not certain I should stay."

"Stay, Ed," said Roosevelt, pleading, though in more of a commanding tone. "It's best for the bureau and for you. We will protect your flanks. At least, sleep on it. Don't do anything until you talk to me again. Promise me that."

"All right, TR. I'll think about it."

"Bully!" said Roosevelt, grinning widely.

Next day, Ed sat in his office, rereading the special delivery letter from Roosevelt. In it, Roosevelt—in his characteristic way—reiterated all of the oral assurances everyone had offered the evening before and then added his own commitment to Ed. Ed still thought he should get out, but swayed by the promises given, he decided against resigning.

September 1898

John Mueller looked into the face of the beautiful, twenty-year-old Austro-Hungarian woman, fully taken by her striking blue eyes, succulent lips, and exquisite features. She had made the journey to America alone, and as he had learned, she was to meet distant relatives with whom she would live and keep house.

Her name was Eva, and she radiated sexuality, despite her innocence. John was determined to have her. Although her answers to his routine questioning cleared her entry, he instead had a gateman take her to a nearby empty hearing room. After examining the remaining two immigrants on his manifest sheet, he found the woman's waiting relatives and informed them that she would be detained overnight and that he would arrange for their reunion outside the Barge Office the next day. This plan had worked successfully several times before, and again this time he convinced the girl's disappointed relatives that all would be well the next morning.

Satisfied that part of the plan was properly in place, he entered the room where the bewildered young woman waited. All he had to do now was to get her to the hotel room he always reserved for his trysts.

He sat at the table, facing her, as she anxiously looked at

him. Despite her modest clothing and demeanor, he found her irresistible. Stripping her in his mind, he was certain that she would be a true delight.

He smiled and said in his most pleasant voice, "Hello again, Miss Radics."

Also speaking in German, she said, "Please, sir, I don't understand. Why am I here?"

You'll know soon enough, he thought, but instead said, "Unfortunately, there are several irregularities that oblige me to reject your entry." *Or at least until you provide me with my entry*, he joked to himself.

"Oh, no!" the alarmed woman cried out. "What is wrong?"

Mueller gently touched her clasped hands resting on the table, keeping his hand there only an instant, saying, "I'm sorry to upset you, but the Immigration Bureau is very concerned about unmarried young women entering the country alone, especially someone as beautiful as you."

"I am not alone. My relatives are meeting me, and I shall stay with them," she protested.

"Yes," he said soothingly, "but they are not here. I have checked. I cannot release you from here without an approved sponsor."

"They're not here?" she said apprehensively. "They will come. I know they will. They must come!"

I must cum too, you delightful bitch, he mused.

"Eva, may I call you that? I want to help you. Really, I do. However, you say the people you will live with are distant relatives, people you have never even met. I am not certain we can approve them as your sponsors even if they were here."

"I have their name and address. They will have proper identification."

"Perhaps, but the government is concerned about morals and exploitation. I must report to my superiors that you are a single, unescorted female without close family or work skills to support yourself. Once I report this, I know from experience that they will deport you."

"Please, sir. There is nothing improper here. Don't other young girls come here as I have, to work, as I plan to work, in a house for others? Is there someone else I can speak to?"

"Trust me, Eva. If you speak to others, you will only make matters worse."

"What can I do? Are you certain my relatives aren't here? They will help me."

"I told before. They are not here."

The young woman was on the verge of tears. John knew she was distraught enough to spring his trap.

"I'll tell you what," he began, again touching her hands, but this time leaving his hand there. "You seem like a very proper young woman, and I feel bad that you are caught up in this bureaucratic nightmare. There is a way that I think I can help you."

"Yes, please. How?"

"It's very risky for me. I could lose my job. You must promise to tell no one."

"I promise, sir. If you help me, I will tell no one. I give you my word."

"All right, then. Here is the plan. I will issue you a temporary landing card. It is only good for twenty-four hours. After that, you must have a permanent card or the authorities will come and deport you. Do you understand?"

"Yes, but—?"

"Just listen to me. With the temporary card, you can leave this building and stay somewhere overnight until your relatives come tomorrow. Once you are safely out of here, I will change a few papers and bring you your permanent entry card on my way home from work."

Overwhelmed, the woman's distress was still evident.

"I am a stranger here, and I don't know the language. How will I find a place to stay?"

"Here is the key to a hotel room. My parents are coming to visit, and it will be their room, but they are arriving one day later than planned. It is the hand of God, it is. The Lord is protecting you. He sent me to look out for you. I will instruct the driver where to take you. You'll be safe there."

"My relatives?"

"Give me their name and address. I will find them and arrange for you to meet them tomorrow. Don't worry. I will take care of everything. However, there's one more thing."

"Yes?" she asked apprehensively.

"You must promise me not to say anything, even to your relatives, about any of this. If you do, they will quickly abandon you because they do not really know you, and they will not want to be punished for violating our laws. Then you would be alone in a foreign country without money, shelter, or means of support. You will be destitute, and I will be fired, all for an act of kindness. Promise me you will never tell anyone."

"I promise you. You are too kind. God bless you."

"Then let's get you out of here before someone starts asking questions."

As he escorted her to a side door and carriage, she said, "I don't even know your name."

"It's better for both of us if you don't. Now I'll have the driver take you straight to the hotel. Go directly to your room and don't leave it until I get there with your permanent entry card. I'll arrange for your dinner later. Do you have any questions?"

"No, sir. Thank you again for your kindness."

Once he had seen her onto the carriage, John returned to work, eagerly looking forward to the evening's delights. He went to the Board of Special Inquiry room where he and three other officials were to conduct hearings, take sworn testimony, and help decide questionable cases of admissibility.

In one of these cases, a woman with four young children appeared and gave testimony that the stenographer duly recorded. The woman's husband, an immigrant residing in the country for two years, was then brought into the room. When he entered, the woman and all four children ran to him, throwing their arms about his neck or legs, kissing him, and sobbing. It was an emotional scene, even for the board members.

"Let's give him the 'father test,'" John suggested, anxious for the afternoon's work to end.

With the others agreeing, John asked him the usual series of questions about the family in such cases: date of the marriage, names and ages of the children, their schooling, and residence. The man's answers were identical to the previous answers of the woman.

Passing the test, the man next satisfied the board's concerns about his financial ability to look after his family. John prepared the pass for the man to enable them to leave the building.

"What is your name?" he asked as he began writing.

Hesitating a moment, the man replied, "I told you that before."

"Yes," John answered suspiciously, "but tell us again."

He could not. Apparently overexcited by succeeding in his role playing, he was unable to remember the name he had given when he came into the room.

"You are an imposter!" John shouted. "Tell us who you really are!"

"I am Eliezer Luftig," the man answered contritely.

"Why did you pose as this woman's husband?"

"I was asked to do this as an act of kindness so her husband would not lose a day's pay."

Dismissing the imposter, the board next followed its normal practice in detected cases of impersonation: asking the woman for a physical description of her husband, which the stenographer recorded for future reference. The woman included in her

Immigrant pleads his case before Board of Special Inquiry, circa 1900

description that her husband was blind in his right eye. The board sent her and the children to detention quarters until the woman's real husband appeared.

Later that afternoon Ed congratulated John for unmasking the imposter.

"That was a good piece of work, John," he said, patting him on the back.

"Just luck," John replied with false modesty.

"Not so," Ed countered. "You're a very observant fellow. I'm going to place a letter of commendation in your file."

"Thank you, Ed. That's very kind of you."

After he left, John smiled. *This is certainly my day*, he thought, *and the best is yet to come. Come*, he laughed to himself, *what an appropriate word!* Before heading for his rendezvous, John called Powderly in Washington to give his weekly account of Barge Office difficulties.

With great anticipation, he reached his hotel door and

unlocked it. To his surprise the room was empty. Neither Eva Radics nor her belongings were to be found.

"Where is that bitch?" he said aloud.

Angry, he left the room and took the elevator back down to the lobby. His eyes scanned the area. Numerous people sat in the richly upholstered sofas and chairs. Not seeing her, he walked through the large lobby to the hotel clerk at the registration desk. His feet sank into the deep pile carpeting as he passed people reading, talking, waiting, watching or dozing.

"I'm John Bachteler," he said, "from Room 617. Are there any messages for me?"

The clerk checked and reported, "No, sir."

"That's strange. I was supposed to meet my niece here. Perhaps you saw her? She is a beautiful young woman with blue eyes, brown hair, about five feet, six inches tall. She was wearing a dark blue dress. Her name is Eva Radics."

"I don't recall anyone like that, sir."

"Would someone else have seen her? I'm very concerned."

"Let me check for you, sir."

John roamed through the lobby once more, looking everywhere. He went outside and questioned the doorman, but like the clerk, he had only been on duty for an hour. Eva would have arrived much earlier. He returned to the registration desk where the clerk had now returned.

"No one has seen her, sir. Shall I page her?"

"No, that won't be necessary," he quickly answered, not wanting to attract further attention to himself. "I'm sure she has just been delayed a bit. I'll wait for her upstairs."

"Very good, sir. If I may be of further assistance, please let me know."

The clerk returned to his desk, and John went upstairs. In his room, he waited impatiently, pacing the floor. From time to time he stared at the bed, the scene of many past sexual pleasures. Realizing that somehow this woman had evaded him and would not satisfy his lust tonight, he grew angrier.

"Damn her!" he snarled, throwing his closed fist into his opened left hand. "Why isn't that bitch here? What went wrong?"

He reflected on all aspects of their conversation and his placing her in the carriage with instructions to the driver as to where to take her. Everything had gone smoothly. So where was she? He had taken the paper with her relatives' name and address. Did she have it written elsewhere and gone there directly? Had she gone for a walk?

The minutes slowly ticked by. He waited. He paced again. He opened the door a few times to look down the corridor. He looked again at the unused bed. He punched the palm of his hand a few more times, cursing the woman and wishing his palm were her face as he punched it some more.

Finally, he left the hotel and headed home. He decided to compensate partially for his frustration by taking his wife tonight. It wouldn't be the same, but it would be better than nothing. At least he could pretend in his mind she was someone else.

Next day he was in a sour mood at work, but one incident did amuse him. As he sat on the Board of Special Inquiry again, he witnessed the heartwarming reunion of the family from yesterday. The man then passed the "father test" successfully and apologized for yesterday's deception.

As the gateman was about to take the family away, the stenographer interrupted, saying, "Something's wrong here!"

"What is it?" asked Charles Matieson, one of the board members.

"According to my notes," said the stenographer, "this woman said yesterday that her husband was blind in his right eye. This man has lost his left eye."

Everyone turned and looked at the man. It was indeed his

left eye that was missing. He could not be her husband. No wife would make a mistake like that.

"Sir, you are an imposter," John proclaimed, feeling a strong sense of *déjà vu*. "Tell us at once who you are or it will go hard with you."

"My name is Reuben Tarnikoff."

"How dare you do this, sir? And, how dare you, woman, attempt to deceive the government a second time?"

"Please, gentlemen," pleaded the man. "I beg of you. Please show us your understanding and sympathy. Her poor husband is sick and greatly worried about his family. He is too sick today to come here. Once he is with his family again, no doubt his condition will improve."

"We are impressed," John answered sarcastically, "with the curative powers this family possesses. Nevertheless, until this woman's husband appears in person and satisfies us as to his identity, health, and financial status, we will not clear his family for entry. Is that understood?"

"Yes, sir."

"Then go back to this woman's husband, tell him to come here himself, and to do so right away. Is that clear?"

Two days later John found himself again sitting on the Board of Special Inquiry, again witnessing a touching family reunion of the woman, her four children and her husband, who was clearly blind in his right eye. This time the affectionate greetings improved, as if the previous rehearsals had polished the performance.

As the board put the "father test" questions to the man, he hesitated and incorrectly answered several of them. It was obvious that he also was an imposter. Fed up, the board ceased all further efforts to land the woman and her children and ordered their deportation.

"What do you make of this, John?" asked Matieson. "This has been a bizarre case."

"It's strange, that's for sure," John responded. "Unfortunately, there are many deceitful people in this world. We just have to stay alert, that's all."

"As long as there are people like you, John, we'll keep them honest."

"Thanks for the compliment, Charley," said John, smiling, as he walked away.

April 1899

Days had slipped by into weeks that became months; the seasons had twice changed. During that time, births and immigrant arrivals added new texture to a society approaching the end of a century, even as deaths brought an end to other elements within the American mosaic. A large new structure was taking shape on Ellis Island, signaling another new beginning.

Change seemed to be in the air everywhere except at the Barge Office. Scandals still abounded. Charges of bribery and corruption, brutality and graft, were now a regular feature of the New York papers. The open warfare between Powderly and the Barge Office administration continued. As a labor appointee, however, Powderly did not have any influence with his anti-labor Treasury Department superiors who aligned themselves with Fitchie and McSweeney. Powderly kept up his offensive nonetheless, using information from Mueller to embarrass the New York office whenever he could.

Immigration personnel, toiling under difficult working conditions, hated the notoriety, including Matt. Seeking a respite from the daily turmoil, he had lunch at a nearby restaurant with his old boss, Joseph Senner. Seated at a quiet table, they had just begun their conversation.

"Congratulations on your commission, Matt. How is de hospital coming along?"

"Thank you, sir. I'm excited about the possibilities. We will have 120 beds, making it one of the largest facilities in the city. Tell me, how do you like the newspaper business?"

"It is different from Ellis Island, but gudt," Joseph answered easily, his expression and tone revealing a man at ease with the world.

"If I understand correctly, you're owner, publisher, editor, and writer all rolled into one. Is that right?"

"*Ja.* Ve do not need too many people. De *National Provisioner* is a small paper devoted to de meat industry und allied trades. Ve have a good circulation und advertisers, so mostly my staff is sales, bookkeeping, und printing people, plus vun reporter. Othervise I do de writing, layout, und management."

"It sounds like quite a change, Dr. Senner. You've gone from a lawyer to a commissioner to a newspaper man."

"Vell, yes, but ven I first came to de United States, I vas newspaper man, editor for de *Staats-Zeitung.* Zo, in a vay I have returned to vere I began in dis country."

"Really? I didn't know that."

"*Ja.* Dere are always tings about people ve do not know. Und zumtimes it is better not to know."

Matt laughed.

"You're right about that. How is your family? Do you still live on 123rd Street?"

"*Ja*, ve do. De family is fine, tank you. Our daughter is getting married zoon."

"That's wonderful. Congratulations. You must be very proud."

"*Ja*, he is fine boy. It is good match. Vaht about yourself? I vas sorry to hear ven your vife died."

"Yes, thank you for your kind note. It meant much to me."

"Zo, if I am not too personal, is dere new voman in your life?"

"No," Matt replied uncomfortably. He did not want to tell Senner that he didn't even have a social life. His work consumed his time and energies, and he led a celibate bachelor's existence. Friends had tried to interest him in other women, but his heart still belonged elsewhere. He found little pleasure in the thought of new female companionship.

"It is not gudt to be alone, Mattew. You are still young man. You should have voman. Life is too short und too hard. Find yourself zumvun to love."

"I just haven't found the right person yet, Dr. Senner. Oh, by the way," he added, "yesterday I received a letter from John White."

"How is he? I have not heard about him zince I vas commissioner."

"I think you knew he had been transferred to a marine hospital in Cincinnati."

"*Ja.* I knew dot."

"Turns out he hated it there. He got disgusted with everything and left the Marine Hospital Service."

"Vere did he go?"

"He said he didn't want to go into private practice, so he decided to put his management skills to good use. He's come back east and is now in Massachusetts as manager of the New England Utility Company."

"Dot is quite un change for him."

"Yes, it is, but he sounds contented."

"Speaking of change und being disgusted, Matt, dot is how I feel ven I read dese terrible stories about de New York station. Vaht is going on?"

"I wish I could give you an answer, but I can't. I'm so busy there; it's all I can do to handle my own work. I've talked to George Stoner about it, but he knows as little about the situation as I do. On those few occasions when I'm free, I've walked around the baggage, inspection, and discharge areas, but I couldn't find anything amiss. I'm sure some things go wrong or are wrong, but I don't see them. I know the medical side is as it should be. It's very frustrating though. These stories smear all of us there. I don't like guilt by association."

"Vaht is Fitchie doing about all dis?"

"Fitchie is not like you. He's an old man and more of a figurehead than anything."

"Vaht about McSveeney den?"

"I've talked to him. He's upset about the problem. He's getting a lot of pressure from Washington, I know. He says that he and the chief inspector, John Mueller, can't find anything."

"Mueller? I remember him. He is kind man. He vas *wunderbar* mit de children. Un hard vorker too."

"I don't know him that well. I've asked two colleagues, Frank Martiniello, an interpreter, and a gateman I know well, Guenter Langer, to keep their eyes and ears open and to let me know of any funny business. I swear to God, if I find anyone profiting at the expense of the immigrants, I'll see to it that they're gone in the blink of an eye."

"Gudt for you, Mattew. I tink I remember dese people you talk about, but I am not zure. Ah, here is our lunch," he added, as the waiter arrived with their food.

*   *   *

John Mueller was spending his lunch hour doing business at the bottom of a dark stairway in the Barge Office. It was not going well.

Stanislaus Zawistowski had just refused to give John the money he demanded for approving his entry. Too many people around earlier prevented him from collecting the money in advance, as he usually did. So John arranged to meet the man here to receive his landing card upon payment of the bribe.

"What do you mean, you're not paying me?" John angrily asked him. "If you don't, you're on the next ship back to Poland."

"You don't scare me, you crooked bastard," Stanislaus answered defiantly. "I'm leaving now, and you won't stop me."

His bluff called, John tried to stand his ground.

"I warn you. I'll have you arrested."

"You won't do nothing!" Stanislaus snarled, pulling out a knife and lunging at John.

Quickly reacting, John avoided the thrust and grabbed the attacker's wrist. As they grappled, John brought his knee up swiftly into the man's groin. As the man doubled over in pain, dropping the knife, John quickly picked it up.

"You're through! I'm turning you in, you bastard!" the man said, as he painfully raised his head.

"Wrong!" said John, quickly plunging the knife with an upward thrust into the man just below his rib cage.

"Uhh!" he cried out softly, his hands grabbing the handle. As he collapsed, his hands still around the knife handle, John caught him and dragged his body under the staircase amid the carelessly tossed rubbish. He placed the bent-over body on its side and left hurriedly for his office.

Three days later, a janitor found the body, giving the newspapers rich material for criticizing the Barge Office administration. Editorial writers suggested that if an employee had not murdered the man and hidden his body there, then the delay in discovering the body proved that supervision over the building was clearly deficient. When the death was officially ruled an apparent suicide, the case faded from public view.

June 1899

Mueller sat at his desk, worrying. *I'm making too many mistakes. If I don't rein myself in, they're going to get me.*

He had once again misjudged an immigrant whom he had tried to exploit. This one had been an Italian immigrant in his sixties. As usual, John had screened the manifest sheets from incoming ships to identify those with a significant amount of declared wealth. This businessman from Naples had seemed an ideal target.

Yet when John attempted to coerce the man to avoid detention on the *Narragansett*, painting a bleak picture of the accommodations on the ship, the man said he would endure the place and ask his son living in New York about how to handle John's payment demands.

John had not expected resistance or a son. Legally, there were no grounds for detention, let alone deportation. He also feared the son's questions about his father's detention would unmask his actions. He could not risk releasing the man outright from the Barge Office in fear of what he might say.

Instead, John arranged his transfer to the *Narragansett* on the last boat that evening. Standing next to the man on the poorly lit boat, John had coaxed him to the back on the pretext of a nighttime view of the city lights and pushed him overboard.

That was last night. This morning, John was reviewing his operations. He knew he had to be much more selective in his future choice of victims. The Pole and Italian had been less vulnerable than he had surmised.

A short time later, Ed McSweeney summoned John and Frank to his office.

"Gentlemen, we've got a mystery on our hands. I want you to help me investigate it."

"What's it about?" John asked.

"A man by the name of Riccardo Monti was transferred from the Barge Office to the *Narragansett* last night. He's missing."

"What?" said John in mock surprise.

"We checked him out of here, but he never got there. Either he never got on the boat, or he fell overboard."

"My God!" Frank reacted. "The papers will have a good time with this one."

"Don't I know it," Ed answered angrily. "I want you to get right on this. Let's see if we can find some answers, reduce the possible options of his whereabouts. John, speak to each crewman on the boat, and also check to make certain he's not in detention or at a hospital by mistake. I want you to interview any personnel who dealt with him here, including the gatemen responsible last night for controlling the exits and boat loading. Also, find out if he has any family here.

"Frank, here's the list of people we transferred to the *Narragansett* last night. I want you to go there, and talk to each them. See if any of them know anything.

"Give me your report later today. All right, let's not waste time here. Let's get answers. Be thorough."

Their investigation provided no answers. No one knew anything. John even covered his tracks so successfully that he felt emboldened enough to call Powderly in Washington to report this latest embarrassment for McSweeney. Newspapers again criticized the lax supervision at the Barge Office.

The old man's disappearance remained a mystery for weeks, as no body was found. His son kept up the pressure with authorities, and the Italian Consul lodged a formal complaint. Still, McSweeney could do nothing more. He tightened up the supervision and accountability as best he could, but the chaos and overcrowding at the Barge Office limited his control.

Under such circumstances, John could continue lining his pockets. At first, he laid low for several weeks to allow the renewed control measures to lapse a bit and to build up his confidence again. Soon, he found a promising prospect among the manifest sheets of the new arrivals. A German man, traveling alone, had declared he was carrying two hundred dollars, even though he had been a steerage passenger. John had a particular fondness for such people journeying as economically as possible to keep more money for themselves in America. They were ripe for plucking, and he eagerly sought them out. He vowed, though, he would be careful.

Just before the first batch of immigrants to be processed approached, John distributed the manifest sheets to his staff, instructing one of them to send the designated German immigrant to a hearing room for private interrogation. The registry clerk did not question this, assuming his superior had good reason.

John went to the room, sat behind the table, and awaited his victim. The door opened, and the man, obeying the gesturing arm of Guenter, walked into the room.

Standing up and smiling broadly, John said in fluent German, "Good morning, sir. I am John Mueller. Please sit down."

The man sat at the opposite side of the table as instructed. Guenter left, closing the door behind him.

John looked at his prey, trying to assess him. The man was

thin and small in stature, perhaps five foot seven. He had dark blond hair and a mustache. His light blue eyes peered at John with nervous intensity.

"What is your name," John asked in German, beginning the routine.

"Jacob Wischnitzer," the man answered in a low, tight voice.

"Where do you come from, Mr. Wischnitzer?"

"Braunschweig."

"What are you going to do in this country?"

"I don't know. I am going to look for work."

"You mean you don't have a job? How can you expect to live here?"

"I have some money, and friends here from my town will let me stay with them."

"Our concern, Mr. Wischnitzer, is that you will be able to find work here. We must know you will not become a burden to the American people."

After a moment's hesitation, the man replied, "I have work."

"You have work? How do you know you have work?"

"I have a letter here," he answered, pulling it from his pocket. "They will pay me two dollars a day."

John now had evidence of the man violating the contract labor law and thus grounds for deportation. He had no intention of reporting it, of course, not if he could get what he wanted.

Frowning and slowly shaking his head, John looked down at the letter and then up again at Wischnitzer.

"Is something wrong?" the man asked anxiously.

"I'm afraid so, Mr. Wischnitzer. Your promise of employment is a violation of our immigration laws. We cannot admit immigrants who have promised jobs."

"But a moment ago you said—oh, please," pleaded the upset man. "Don't do this to me. I have nothing for me in Germany.

No family, no job, no property, nothing. Only here can I have a future. You must let me in."

"I'm sorry, Mr. Wischnitzer. As much as it pains me to do this to a fellow countryman, I must report this."

The man began to cry. John watched him for a few seconds and then rose from his chair, walked around the table, and stood behind the sobbing man.

You pathetic fool, he thought, relishing his ability to control and exploit these greenhorns. *Time now to reel in this sucker.*

Placing a hand on the man's shoulder, he said gently,

"Please don't cry, Mr. Wischnitzer. It breaks my heart to see a fellow German in despair. Tell me, have you told anyone else about your job?"

"No. No one, I swear! Only you know. Can you help me? As a fellow German?"

"You touch my heart, Mr. Wischnitzer, but it is very risky for me to help you. I could get into serious trouble."

"Oh, please, sir. I would pay you for your trouble."

"I do not want your money. Helping a fellow German is reward enough, but it will take a significant amount of money nonetheless to get you out of here."

"How much?"

"Well, I must give money to the man who brought you into this room and to the man out there who would issue your pass to leave the building. They both know something is wrong with your credentials, and they will challenge your admission unless I quiet them with some money."

"How much?"

"I think I can arrange things for $150."

"My God! That's almost all the money I have in the world!"

"If I could do it for less, I would, but you are asking them to take a big risk to look the other way. They could lose their jobs. You decide, Mr. Wischnitzer. You may keep your money and go back to Braunschweig, or you may spend your money and enter America. You will be making much more money here. It is your decision."

The man wrung his hands, grimaced, and replied, "I will pay the price. I must enter America."

"Very well then, if you will give me the money, I will make all the necessary arrangements."

"Thank you, sir. I am very grateful to you."

"You are a good man, Mr. Wischnitzer. And, as one of my countrymen, I could not deny you."

John took the man's money, counted it, and turned to leave. Stopping at the door, he turned and said, "Just wait here. I'll arrange everything. Just one thing more though. You must not tell anyone about this arrangement, absolutely no one. If any of this becomes known, I will lose my job for being kind to you. Those men out there will lose their jobs, and you will be deported. Everyone loses. It is important that you understand this. Not a word to anyone, ever. People get rewards for reporting illegal aliens. People you think are your friends will turn you in for the money. If you are careless, you will suffer the consequences. I want you to give me your solemn word that you will never mention this money or our conversation to anyone, ever. Do you swear that?"

"I swear to you on my mother's soul. I will never say a word about this to anyone, ever."

"I believe you, Mr. Wischnitzer. You are a decent, God-fearing man. Wait here now. I will fix things for you. You will be out of here within a few minutes."

John pocketed the money and left the room. He went up to the registry clerk.

"That man, Jacob Wischnitzer, on your registry sheet?"

"Yes, Mr. Mueller?"

"I've completed my interrogation of him. I thought there

was a problem there, but he's all right. I'm clearing him. Give me a landing card for him."

"Yes, sir," answered the clerk, completing the paperwork. "Here's his card."

"Thank you," said John, taking the card and walking back to the room where the immigrant anxiously awaited.

"Everything is arranged," he said, smiling. "Here is your landing card. If you'll come with me, I'll see to it that you can leave the building without further trouble."

"Thank you, thank you,' the relieved man said in appreciation.

"Remember now, only your silence guarantees your staying in this country. Do not hurt me for being kind to you."

"I understand. Thank you again."

He escorted the man to the exit and returned, patting his pocket, pleased with the day's profits. *If I can keep finding these suckers,* he thought, *I'll be a wealthy man one day. And they're so grateful!*

"John, we've just gotten the news on that missing man."

He turned to see Ed McSweeney's grim face.

"What is it?"

"They found his body floating in the harbor. He obviously fell overboard."

"That closes the case then."

"Not for the newspapers," Ed replied. "They'll play this up for all it's worth."

John nodded in agreement and returned to his office. He didn't think any heat generated by the incident would affect him, even if some publicity-seeking politician launched an investigation. *This place is a gold mine,* he thought. *I just have to be careful. I cannot be careless or greedy. Find the right suckers. They will keep showing up as surely as the sun rises and sets.*

October 1899

Matt was on board the *Narragansett* to consult with his colleague Frank Geddings, on ship duty that week, about some new ideas he had for the hospital. Moored near Ellis Island, the old steamer furnished sleeping accommodations for up to eight hundred detainees. There were also quarters for a matron, attendants, nurses, and a physician. As the two men were talking in the hospital, a Russian immigrant entered.

"Yes? What can I do for you?" Dr. Geddings asked.

"Excuse me, doctor," said the man, with only a slight accent. Removing his hat and holding it with both hands, he nervously continued, "My wife and I are worried about our boy."

"Do you want me to examine him?" Geddings asked.

"No, it isn't that. Well—maybe you could, I don't know. You see, doctor, he is twelve years old. He had a fever and the other doctor examined him. He told us the boy had the mumps and sent him to a hospital somewhere in the city. We haven't seen him since. Could you find out how he is doing and when we can see him again?"

Matt looked at the fatherly concern etched in the man's face. He empathized with the man yet envied his having a son to worry about. *Will I ever have a child to worry about?* he wondered.

"You mean you've heard nothing since he was taken to the hospital?" Matt asked.

The man looked at Matt for a moment, prompting Geddings to say, "This is Dr. Stafford, my colleague."

"Hello, sir," the man responded. "No, I have heard nothing."

"What is your name?" Geddings asked, going to the files.

"Isaac Liebowitz. My son's name is Abraham."

As Geddings looked for the file, Matt offered some reassurance, saying, "I'm sure your son is fine. It's probably just a bureaucratic mix-up that caused you not to hear anything."

"It's been a week, doctor. Shouldn't he have been back to us by now?"

"You said your son had mumps?"

"That's what the other doctor said."

"Well, if he has mumps and there are no complications, he would normally be released after two weeks."

"Here we are," said Geddings, opening the folder. "Dr. MacDowell saw the boy. Diagnosed him with mumps and transferred him to Bellevue Hospital."

"Couldn't you find out more for us, doctor? My wife and I are very worried."

"Mr. Liebowitz," said Matt, "I'm leaving here now. The hospital is on my way home. I'll stop by, look in on your son, and send a report to you."

"Thank you, sir. God bless you."

When the man left, Geddings turned to Matt and said, "Matt, I didn't know anything about this."

"I know, Frank. We need to set up a better system. These rotating weekly assignments don't give us any continuity between hospitalized patients and their relatives here. I suggest that you identify how many other people on board also have someone in one of the hospitals. Send that on to Dr. Stoner at the Barge Office. I'll suggest to him that we initiate a better system for continuity of information among us for future hospitalized cases."

An hour later, Matt entered Bellevue. Going to the isolation ward for contagious diseases, he identified himself and asked to see the boy's chart. Everything was normal, verified by Matt's visit with the boy, who was relieved to hear about his parents. Matt noted that most of the swelling of the parotid glands had disappeared. The submaxillary and the sublingual salivary glands appeared normal. He was certain the boy would be released next week.

Returning to the nurses' duty station, Matt sat behind one side of the counter to write his promised report to the boys' parents. When he had finished, he went to slide the chart into its alphabetized slot. As he did, he noted the name on the chart

A doctor climbs aboard an ambulance outside Bellevue Hospital, 1895

below, and his heart leapt. Below the chart of "Liebowitz, Abraham" rested the chart of "Lindstrom, Nicole."

Could it be her? he wondered. Excitedly, he took out the chart, opened the folder, and began to read, barely aware he had sunk down into a nearby chair.

At the top of the page, he read "Last Name: Lindstrom, First Name: Nicole, Maiden Name: Devereaux, Age: 28."

"Good Lord, she's here!" he said aloud, causing the nurse to turn around and look at him.

Oblivious, Matt's eyes raced to the line reading "Diagnosis: Scarlet Fever." He felt an instant twinge in his gut, given the seriousness of the illness. No one knew its cause or its cure. Further complications and death were very real possibilities.

From the chart, he learned that she had been brought in two days ago, complaining of a sore throat, exhaustion, vomiting, and fever. Since then, her temperature had remained between 103° and 104°, and she had frequently been delirious. Sixteen hours later, the rash appeared, first on her neck and chest, and later on the rest of her body. Her pulse rate was consistently high. Notations by nurses indicated great thirst, restlessness, and delirium—all common symptoms in scarlet fever patients.

Matt closed the folder and got up, walking over to the nurse, whose back was now to him.

"This patient, Nicole Lindstrom, is an old friend of mine. I'd like to look in on her."

"Certainly, Doctor, I'll get you a gown and mask."

After putting on the protective garb, he walked into Nicole's room. She was asleep. Her face was blushed, except for a narrow area around the mouth that, by contrast, appeared white. As Matt drew near, he saw small points of redness, closely grouped together.

Using his stethoscope, he listened to her heart. He held her wrist to confirm her high pulse rate. Gently pulling down her jaw and using a tongue depressor, he examined her throat.

Her tongue was still coated, reaffirming the diagnosis that the disease was still in an early stage. Her tonsils were swollen, and he could see the beginnings of dark-red spots in her mouth.

Just then, Nicole opened her glazed-over eyes, as he removed the tongue depressor. She seemed to stare into his face for a moment and closed her eyes again. He looked at her, his eyes misting, his throat dry.

She was now sleeping restlessly, tossing, and turning. Her face and body were moist from the fever, and beads of perspiration marked her brow. He took a wet compress, tenderly wiped her brow, and patted her cheeks and neck. After wetting the compress again, he wiped both her arms and hands. He placed the compress into a bowl on the adjacent table and looked at her.

He still loved her. He had always known that, longing for her every day during the three years of their separation. He had prayed for the day when he would see her again.

Although overjoyed at seeing Nicole again, Matt was also filled with sadness. Once again, as with Peg, he felt helpless. There was nothing more he could do for Nicole than was already being done. He could do nothing to cure her. He knew she might die.

He left the room and sought out Mark Stuart, her physician. His timing was fortunate, for Dr. Stuart had just arrived on the floor.

"This is Dr. Stafford," the nurse said.

Stuart was a short man, about five foot five. The top of his head was bald, with salt-and-pepper hair around the sides and in his neatly trimmed beard. His wire-framed spectacles rested on a slightly bulbous nose. When he smiled, Matt saw an upper front gold tooth.

"Matt," he added, shaking the older man's hand.

"Mark Stuart," he said. "Pleased to make your acquaintance, doctor."

"I'm a very close friend of Mrs. Lindstrom," explained Matt. "I'm very concerned about her."

"Hmm, yes, I understand. I can't give you any prognosis yet. We'll just have to keep her as comfortable as possible and watch her for the next few days. It's too soon to tell yet. Let's hope no complications set in."

"Dr. Stuart, I'm a physician with the New York Immigration Bureau. I have the next several days free. Would you have any objections if I looked after her while I'm free? I won't interfere with your care."

The older doctor noted the intensity in Matt's face and quickly weighed the pros and cons of the request. Brimming with the self-confidence that competency and experience bring, Stuart did not feel threatened.

"I have no objections, Dr. Stafford," he replied. "In fact, it might be good for Mrs. Lindstrom to see a friendly face, since her husband won't be back in the States for two more weeks."

"He's away?"

"Yes, as you know, he's in the freight forwarding business, and he was at his company's branch office in Rotterdam. He left as soon as he learned of his wife's illness, but his ship won't dock for at least another week. Their housekeeper, Miss Reilly, is taking care of the child."

"Their child?" asked Matt, taken back. Although he had occasionally speculated in the past that Nicole might have borne children in the three years since he last he saw her, the revelation nonetheless surprised him.

Dr. Stuart looked at Matt suspiciously but replied matter-of-factly, "Yes, their son, James."

Matt noted Stuart's reaction and quickly added, "I didn't know. I haven't seen either of them since their wedding. I know them from before then."

"Hmmm, I see. Well, Miss Reilly stops by each morning with the boy. A handsome lad."

"I'll look forward to seeing the boy tomorrow then. Thank you, sir, for allowing me to attend to your patient."

"You're welcome, Doctor. Let's go see how she is."

The two men entered Nicole's room where Dr. Stuart made a cursory check, then patted Matt's arm, saying, "We'll just have to hope for the best."

With that, he left. Matt settled into a nearby chair and gazed at Nicole throughout the evening, until he fell asleep around midnight.

Shortly after seven, the various sounds of the hospital activities of the new day awakened him. When the new nurse on duty entered the room, he got up, introduced himself, and then reexamined Nicole. There was little change. Her temperature and pulse rate were still high. Her rash was more pronounced and now spread over her limbs as well. She blushed deeper, except for that small area of pallor about the mouth. Her tongue, now the expected "strawberry tongue" due to its general redness, had swollen papillae extending above its surface.

Nicole opened her eyes and stared into Matt's eyes, peering back above his surgical mask. She did not respond, and he was uncertain if she knew he was there.

"Hello, Nicole. It's me, Matt. I'm here with you now. We're going to beat this thing, so fight it with me."

Nicole, still delirious with fever, looked into his eyes. Arching her eyebrows in recognition, she said, "Matt!"

"Yes, it's Matt. I'll stay here and help you get better."

Then he lifted her head up and helped her drink some water. He knew that he had to get fluids into her. That was one positive thing he knew he could do for her.

Later that morning, the nurse informed him of the housekeeper's arrival, as he had asked. He walked out to meet her and Nicole's child. He saw them at once among others in the hallway.

"Miss Reilly?"

"Yes?"

"I'm Dr. Stafford, an old friend of Mrs. Lindstrom. I'm looking after her, along with Dr. Stuart."

"Good day to ya, Doctor," she said in a thick Irish brogue, "and how is me mistress this mornin'?"

The woman charmed Matt. *How fitting*, he thought, *that Nicole would hire such a woman.*

"As well as we can expect right now," he answered. "We'll have to wait a little longer to see how she does."

He directed his attention to the handsome, brown-haired boy. He was quite the little gentleman, all dressed up in a gray suit, with matching gray knee socks tucked under his knickers, a white shirt, and green ascot. Matt took an instant liking to him.

James looked up at Matt with his big brown eyes and asked, "Is my mommy still sick?"

Matt's heart went out to the boy, and he felt an urge to hug him.

Instead, he stooped to his haunches and said, "James, your mommy is very sick, but I promise you that I will make her better."

"Can I see her?" he asked. His lip quivered.

"No, son, I'm afraid you can't right now, not until she gets a little better. Then you can. I'll make certain of it. All right?"

The boy slowly nodded his head, holding back a sob.

"Good boy," said Matt, slightly tousling James's hair. "She will be very proud of you. Now you go on with Miss Reilly. We'll take good care of her."

"Yes, sir. Thank you."

"Thank ya, Doctor," smiled the housekeeper as she took James' hand and departed with him.

Matt watched them go, reflecting on how taken he was with the boy. *Small wonder*, he thought, *he is, after all, Nicole's son.*

He returned to Nicole's side. The day passed slowly. As was his custom, Dr. Stuart stopped by twice during the day to look in on his patient. With Matt, he would exchange a few friendly, professional remarks and words of encouragement before leaving.

Matt continued to check Nicole's vital signs regularly. He applied wet compresses and watched her tormented body toss in restless sleep. When she seemed awake, he had one-sided conversations with her and gave her water whenever he could. Occasionally the nurse came in to give her a sponge bath or to minister to her bodily needs.

As the day progressed, Nicole's temperature remained high, although her tongue gradually lost its coating, first along its edges, and then inward to its center. However, the papillae were still enlarged, and the deeper red color created the "raspberry tongue" that was normal for this later stage of the disease.

In early evening, Nicole began to cough repeatedly. What alarmed Matt was its congested sound. Quickly, he propped her up, slapping her on the back.

"Spit it out, Nicole! Spit it out!" he cried, placing a small pan under her mouth.

Nicole coughed some more, ejecting a sputum mixture of saliva, mucus, and pus. Matt saw it and experienced a sinking feeling. When her coughing spell ended, Matt placed Nicole back down onto the bed. He took out his stethoscope and listened to her breathing. The quality of her breathing had clearly deteriorated. Her lungs were now filled with fluid.

Matt's worse fears had become reality, for Nicole had developed pneumonia. That, together with the scarlet fever, dropped her chances for survival down to a long-shot possibility at best.

Fighting back tears, Matt ran from the room. At the supply closet, he grabbed two pillows and hurried back to Nicole's bed. He lifted her upper torso forward and placed the pillows behind her. When he laid her back upon the pillows, her body rested at about a forty-five-degree angle.

At least she'll be more comfortable this way, he thought, *and it might help her lungs fight back too.*

Matt knew all he could do now was treat the symptoms, give her fluids, keep her comfortable, and hope for no further complications. There was nothing else he could do.

Yes, there is, he suddenly realized, and he knelt beside Nicole and prayed.

November 1899

Five days had passed since Nicole developed pneumonia, eight days since her admission to the hospital. So far, she was holding on although she remained weak and restless. Her temperature continued to fluctuate between 101° and 104°, while her pulse rate remained irregular and high, usually around 110. Her nostrils were dilated, and her breathing was rapid, audible, labored, and painful. She was also experiencing diarrhea.

Matt stayed close by, doing what little he could. He had been due back at work at the Barge Office two days ago, but he had called in to say that he could not return to work because of a "family emergency."

When Nicole occasionally gasped for air, Matt would bolt to her side and act quickly to assist her by pulling her arms up above her head or sitting her up on the bed and patting her back strongly. When she coughed up the bloody mucus, which was often, he was there for her with a small pan or towel in which to spit, and with a moist cloth to wipe her mouth. He continually tried to cool down her body with wet compresses and make her as comfortable as possible.

In her quieter moments, he let her rest, unless she was conscious, when he would talk to her briefly about his recent experiences at the Immigration Bureau. He really wanted to talk about his feelings for her, but he knew he should not.

It now appeared that the worst of the scarlet fever was over. Her skin was beginning to scale, marking the final stage of the rash before the skin returned to normal. Ordinarily, her temperature would be declining too, but it had not done so because of the pneumonia. This now became the prime concern.

Matt paced constantly. Most people with such a severe case of pneumonia died. Nicole's situation was even more precarious, because her body first had been seriously weakened by the scarlet fever. Even though that disease was now in remission, she was still perilously close to death.

As usual, Dr. Stuart came in to check on Nicole and speak to Matt.

"How's our patient doing today?" he asked Matt softly, so as not to awaken her.

Matt walked over to the door and softly replied, "We're past the worst with the scarlet fever, but I don't know if she can overcome the pneumonia. She's so weak."

"Hmmm, let's have a look."

Dr. Stuart examined Nicole, checking her pupils, pulse, and lungs. He noted her scaling skin and dried lips. He placed the back of his hand on her forehead for a moment. He put his arm around Matt's shoulder and walked him to the door.

"It may be another week before we know if she'll make it. You've done all you could, my boy. It's in God's hands now."

"Yes," Matt answered in a low voice.

Mark Stuart frowned slightly, feeling as helpless as Matt, whom he now patted on the back in a fatherly gesture. Then he quietly left.

Matt sat down in the chair next to the bed. As he looked at the sleeping figure of his beloved Nicole, he relived the wonderful times they shared together: working together at Ellis Island, their dinner and ride home, their first kiss, the stolen moments at work. He recalled their tender embraces and thought again about their lovemaking after he had been stabbed. Then he thought of his pain the night of John White's Christmas party when she was with Tom Lindstrom, the man she married.

Lindstrom! Suddenly, reality crashed in on Matt. He had been deluding himself, forgetting that Nicole had a husband somewhere at sea on his way home to her. He had focused so tightly on Nicole's health that he had ignored the fact that he and Nicole had not been reunited. Even her son had not reminded him of her husband.

Now, though, he realized that if she pulled through, she would still be lost to him, yet that was far less important than her welfare. He wanted her alive, and he wanted her happy. What was most important was her overcoming the pneumonia, and to this effort, he rededicated himself.

Three more days passed uneventfully. Matt continued his vigil. Nicole became troubled by itching skin due to its scaling. To ease this minor distress while she fought off her pneumonia, Matt obtained some olive oil to rub on her skin. As he rubbed the oil onto her arms and back, the sensuality of his hand upon her flesh excited him. Shaking his head, he completed his task, vowing to have the nurse do it in the future. Two days later, Matt placed his stethoscope on Nicole's chest to listen to her breathing.

Could it be? he wondered. *Her lungs sound better!*

He listened again, intently. It seemed so! Her breathing was not as rapid either! He took her wrist, placing his fingers on the pulsating artery.

Good Lord! he thought. *Her pulse rate has dropped!*

It wasn't normal yet, but it had dropped! He felt her forehead. She didn't seem as feverish.

Overcome with relief, Matt began to weep. He sat on the

bed beside her, lowered his mask beneath his chin, and caressed her left cheek with his right hand. Nicole opened her eyes.

"Matt, it really is you!" she murmured weakly. "I thought I was hallucinating, but you have been with me."

As she spoke, Nicole tried to raise herself up. Matt instinctively reached to help. He embraced her. He held her possessively for a minute, and she held him. His tears flowed freely. *She had beaten death!* He was relieved, and the sheer joy of holding her again overwhelmed him.

"I've never left you, even when you've been away from me," he said softly. "I can't begin to tell you how happy I am right now. You gave me quite a scare. You've been very sick, but now I know you're going to be all right."

"Oh, Matt, I want—"

"Shhh, not now," he interrupted, gently breaking their embrace. "There's time enough for talking later. You need rest right now to regain your strength. Take a little water first, and then lie down and close your eyes."

Nicole meekly obeyed and soon fell asleep again. He continued to look at her. A lump filled his throat, as the depth of his feelings again brought tears to his eyes. His prayers had been answered. *She would live!*

*　　　*　　　*

Next day, Nicole was a little better, her temperature slightly lower, and her coughing much improved. Awake, she smiled at Matt when he came back from breakfast and into her room, greeting him, "Good morning, Dr. Stafford."

The formality of the words belied the warmth of their delivery.

"Hello, Nicole. It's good to see you smiling again."

He was pleased both to see her smile and to be with her in her first lucid moments since he had found her here.

"Matt," she said, "thank you for being here when I needed

you. The nurse said you rarely left this room. I'm so grateful for all you did for me."

"Nicole, you don't have to thank me. Seeing you better is all the thanks I need."

"You're quite a man, Dr. Stafford," she said, smiling sadly as she was reminded of reasons she still loved him.

"How is your wife, Matt?"

"She died two years ago."

"I'm so sorry," she said, looking away, conflicted in her emotions.

"I met your son," Matt said, filling the brief silence.

"You did?" she replied, turning back to him.

"Yes, your housekeeper brought him to the hospital. He's a fine-looking boy."

"Is he all right? How did he handle this? I mean, Tom's away, and I've been here all this time."

"Don't worry. He's fine," said Matt, sitting down on her bed. "Miss Reilly strikes me as a wonderful, competent woman who's looked after him very well. The boy has been bravely dealing with your sickness, but he misses you."

Throughout this exchange Nicole had continued to look at Matt. Now tears rolled down her cheeks as he spoke of the boy.

"I didn't mean to upset you."

"I'm not upset, Matt. I miss him too."

"Well, you'll see each other soon. Nicole, that boy is as perfect as his mother."

"Matt, stop. You'll make me blush."

"Your whole body has already been blushing for almost two weeks," he said teasingly.

Nicole laughed.

"It's good to see you laugh again," he said, sincerely. "It's been such a long time since I saw you laugh."

She continued the smile a bit longer, masking her anguish,

as she looked at the man she loved. He did not see through the veneer to know she agonized over being trapped in a web of her own making, one that she could not unravel. Tom was a good husband and father to James, even though his frequent travels left her lonely. She was as good a wife to him as she could be, considering she loved another. That made her realize the bittersweet quality of this time they had together.

"Nicole," Matt said, taking her hand, "I've got to get back to work, now that you're recovering."

"Of course, Matt, I understand. You've been far too generous with your time already."

"I'm glad I could be with you. Nicole, I want you to know that I'll always be here for you, whenever and wherever you need me. Don't ever forget that, and never be afraid to call me."

"I'll remember that, Matt," she said, squeezing his hand slightly. Matt bent over and kissed her cheek.

A knock on the door interrupted them. Matt stood up, as Dr. Stuart entered with Tom, who went directly to Nicole's side.

"How are you, darling?" he asked, sitting beside her and taking her hand, just as Matt had done before. "I was so worried about you."

"I'm better now, Tom."

Matt was anxious to leave. Tom sensed his movement and looked at him.

"Dr. Stafford, thank you for caring for Nicole. Dr. Stuart said you volunteered to assist him. I appreciate that."

"Your wife is an old friend and colleague, Mr. Lindstrom. I was happy to be of service."

"Still, it was jolly good of you. I hope you will have dinner with us one evening when Nicole is up and about."

"You're very kind. Perhaps I shall."

"Here, let me give you my card," he offered, pulling one out of his wallet and giving it to Matt.

Matt looked at the business card giving the company name, Lindstrom Transport International, Tom's name, and the company address on West Thirty-Ninth Street in the Hell's Kitchen section of the city.

"Thank you. Well, I had better get to the Barge Office. Good day, sir. Goodbye, Nicole."

Putting the card into his pocket, Matt left the room with his medical colleague and asked him in the corridor, "Dr. Stuart, why did you knock? You never did before."

"The woman's husband was with me, Matt. Discretion was called for. You're in love with his wife."

"What? No, no, I'm just a good friend."

"You can deny it if you want, but I know better," the older man replied. "I saw how you looked at her, how you cared for her. Only a man in love would act as you did."

"Dr. Stuart, I—"

"Your secret's safe with me, Matt. Tell me, though, what do you do now?"

"I don't know. One thing I do know, though, is that I had better get to the Barge Office where a pile of work waits for me. That's the only certainty in my life right now."

Mark nodded his head and offered a handshake, saying, "You're a good man, Doctor. I wish you well."

"Thank you, Dr. Stuart," Matt answered, as the men shook hands. "Thank you for allowing me to treat your patient."

With that, Matt headed to the cramped Barge Office.

December 1899

After handing his hat and coat to the maid, Matt stepped into the drawing room filled with dozens of partying guests. All were dressed elegantly, befitting their social status as New York's fashionable elite. His eyes darted about, seeking out his hosts, Nicole and Tom Lindstrom.

Almost as if she sensed him, Nicole looked over from the opposite side of the room. Their eyes locked across the crowded room and, in that brief instant, silently communicated. They smiled. She nodded, and he began to work his way through the crowd toward her and Tom.

Nicole had been waiting for him all evening. The steady arrival of other guests earlier had only heightened her anticipation. Ever since Tom had invited Matt, she had been looking forward to seeing him again. He had visited her regularly during her recuperation in the hospital, but this was different. It was a festive New Year's Eve party, and he was coming to her home.

She had fussed over her appearance. Her hair had to be perfect, her dress the most flattering. It had taken several excursions to the shops to find the exquisite dress she was wearing, a rich black satin, with a tiny, woven floral pattern in pink and green. Beneath the V-shaped *décolletage* was a silk-embroidered, cream net blouse with a neck collar and thin black velvet ribbon at its top. The satin had no pleats at the waist, was pointed front and back, and held in position by stitched ties, sewn at intervals to the taffeta underskirt. It was indeed an elegant, flattering evening dress, and when she saw the other women in the popular fashion of either yellow gowns or else bodices and skirts of discordant colors, she knew she had chosen wisely. Her dress set her apart and drew compliments from many. From the moment he had seen her across the room, Matt was struck by Nicole's dazzling beauty. He, too, found her dress flattering to her shapely, petite figure, but he knew he would have been enchanted regardless of the dress.

"Hello, Matt. How wonderful to see you again!"

He kissed her on the cheek. Though it was perfunctory, he still relished that kiss.

"Hello, Nicole. You look absolutely breathtaking."

"Thank you, but anything would be an improvement over what you've been seeing lately."

"It's more than having your health back. You are absolutely stunning. You're a lucky man, Tom," he said, shaking his host's hand.

"I agree, Matt, and welcome. Here, have some champagne," Tom offered, lifting a glass from the tray brought over by a servant. "This is Paul and Dorothy Blackwell, and I believe you know Sarah Klaessig."

"Yes, indeed," replied Matt, kissing her on the cheek and shaking hands with the newly introduced couple.

"We were just talking about our entering a new century in just a few hours," Tom explained.

"Is it really the new century, though?" Sarah asked. "I still think 1900 completes the old century, and the new one will begin next year."

"Some of my colleagues think as you do, Mrs. Klaessig."

"Now, Matt, I've told you before. Please call me Sarah."

"Well, Sarah," replied Matt, "we can just welcome the twentieth century again next year. One thing is certain, however. Tonight we will enter the 1900s, and who knows what lies ahead?"

"Well spoken, Matt," Sarah replied, laughing. "It's an exciting time to be alive. I wonder what the new century will bring? I mean, think of all the marvelous advances we made in the nineteenth century! The telephone, the telegraph, the automobile, the streetcar."

"And the incandescent electric light and those moving pictures," added Dorothy Blackwell. "Have you seen them yet? They're so fascinating!"

"Don't forget the steam locomotive," Paul Blackwell said. "It's been around our whole lives, but it began in this century."

"You're right," said Tom. "Let's see now, I'll add those crystal set radios, vulcanized rubber, and the reaping machine. How about you, Nicole? It's your turn to name something."

Caught up in the game, Nicole smiled and said, "As a former nurse, I'll turn to medicine. Roentgen invented X-rays to see inside your body through a machine."

"I still find that hard to believe," Sarah countered.

"It's true, though," Nicole answered, "and another wonderful discovery was Pasteur's rabies vaccine. No one needs to die a horrible death from animal bites anymore."

"Your turn, Matt," prodded Tom.

"Well, there's the discovery of the existence of germs and antiseptic surgery. We can save so many more lives now."

"All right then," said Tom. "Now let's each of us make a prediction about what the twentieth century will bring."

"People will live even longer," offered Dorothy.

"Everyone will have an automobile," her husband suggested.

"And half the people will go deaf from the noise of all those automobiles," Sarah said, half joking. As they all laughed, she added, "Just think how loud they are! Can you imagine the din in this city if the streets were filled with automobiles?"

"At least, with the horses gone, you won't have to watch where you step every time you cross the street," said Paul, and everyone laughed again.

"Now that we have steel and the elevator, two other nineteenth-century inventions we didn't mention earlier," said Tom, "I'll predict buildings will be built at least three times as high as now."

"My goodness," said Sarah, "I'd be afraid to be that high off the ground or to walk near a building that tall, lest it fall on me."

"I'm sure it would be safe, Sarah," Matt said. "As for me, I'd like to predict we find cures for scarlet fever, pneumonia, smallpox, diphtheria, cholera, and other diseases."

"I hope that prediction comes true, Matt," said Nicole.

"Amen," said Tom. "And your prediction, Nicole?"

"Flying machines."

"What?" said Tom, incredulously.

"Machines that fly you wherever you want to go," she explained.

"Darling," Tom answered in a patronizing tone, "you've been reading Jules Verne too much. We have balloon airships and gliders, but a heavier-than-air flying machine is physically impossible. Many scientists have tried and failed. I mean, look at the automobile. Two strong men can't even lift it. How could a heavy machine fly?"

"You never know, Tom," interjected Matt in Nicole's defense. "We now have that light metal called aluminum. Maybe some new lightweight internal combustion engine will provide enough power for flight."

"I'll believe it when I see it and not before," Tom answered, dismissing the idea with a wave of his hand.

"Just you wait, Mr. Smart Husband," Nicole countered. "One day we'll all fly away in a machine."

"To the miracles of the twentieth century, then," said Tom, raising his glass in a toast.

"To the future, where nothing is impossible," said Matt, looking briefly at Nicole.

All joined in the toast and gradually dispersed among the other party guests. A short time later, Matt encountered a familiar face.

"Dr. Senner, I didn't know you were here. It's good to see you again. Happy New Year!"

Joseph turned and shook Matt's hand.

"Mattew Stafford. *Ja*, Happy New Year. I do not tink you have met my vife. Cordelia, dis is Dr. Mattew Stafford. He is mit de Immigration Bureau."

"How do you do, Dr. Stafford," she said, offering her hand.

Matt looked at the smiling countenance of the woman, whose face suggested a once-youthful beauty. Following the old European tradition, Matt lightly kissed the proffered hand and said, "It is a pleasure to meet you at last, Mrs. Senner."

"Und how are tings at de Barge Office?" Joseph asked.

"Getting more crowded every day, it seems. We have acquired two nearby houses on State Street, one for short-term detainees, and the other as a short-stay hospital facility. This definitely eases many nuisance trips out to the *Narragansett* or to city hospitals."

"I am zure. How are tings going mit de construction on de island?"

"They're pretty much on schedule, but we won't move in until probably November or December. It'll be another year on top of that, though, before the hospital is ready."

"How are you coping mit everyting?"

"It's exhausting, but I'm managing. How is the newspaper business?"

"It could not be better."

"And your daughter and her husband?"

"Gudt. Dey are very gudt. Now I am looking for de day ven dey tell me I vill be grandpapa."

Cordelia Senner smiled brightly. "*Ja*, und me grandmama. I cannot vait."

"Mattew," said Senner, "vaht about you? Are you going to be bachelor de rest of your life? I am vaiting for a vedding invitation."

"Dr. Senner, if that day comes, I promise that you will get an invitation. I suspect, though, you'll be a grandpapa before I am a husband again."

"Do not let life pass you by, Mattew. All vork und no play are not healty. Find de right voman und marry her."

Matt forced a smile.

A few hours later, about half-past ten, Tom came over to Matt and spoke to him privately.

"Matt, would you please go look in on Nicole? She told me that she was feeling a little weak. She's resting in our bedroom upstairs. I'm worried about a relapse and that all this has been perhaps too much for her. Please go see how she is."

"Yes, of course," Matt answered, masking his rising anxiety.

"Don't say anything to the others. I don't want to alarm them. I'll wait down here until you return."

Matt went up the stairs and knocked on the closed bedroom door.

"It's Matt," he announced, as he opened the door. "Tom asked me to look in on you."

Sitting in a chair near her bed, Nicole had nearly fallen asleep when she heard Matt's voice. She was not surprised, since Tom had told her he would send Matt to her.

Without waiting for a reply, Matt entered the room and went to her.

"How are you feeling?" he asked with concern, as he knelt alongside her chair.

"I'm fine, just a little tired, that's all."

He placed the back of his hand against her forehead. Detecting no temperature, he pulled out his pocket watch and took her pulse.

As Matt looked at his watch, measuring the rhythmic arterial surges against the ticking seconds, Nicole looked at him. His touches may have been clinical actions, but for her, they were endearing sensations.

He looked up into her eyes and saw her looking at him. He smiled, and then he placed his fingers about her left eye, the one nearest to him. Gently opening her eyelid further, he moved the table lamp closer and away, watching the dilation of her pupil. He repeated the process with her right eye.

"Everything seems fine, Nicole. Do you have any pains or aches anywhere?"

"No, Matt, I just felt a little weak. That's all. I think I just stayed on my feet too long. I didn't want to spoil the party, so I just came up to rest. I'm sure I'll be all right."

"Perhaps you're right. No sense taking chances though. Why don't you rest a while longer, and then come back down?"

His concern lessening, Matt's attention now expanded to his surroundings. He noticed the opened door to an adjoining room.

"Your son's bedroom?" he guessed, gesturing toward the doorway.

"Yes," she smiled. "James wanted to stay up, but he's been asleep since eight o'clock."

"I don't know if I ever told you, but James is my father's name."

"Yes, I knew that, Matt."

Naming the boy James had been her idea. It was an oblique way of keeping Matt connected to the boy. Tom had agreed, since it had also been his grandfather's first name.

"How are your parents?" she asked.

"They're fine. Enjoying the quiet life in Massachusetts. How is your family?"

"My mother died from influenza last winter."

"I'm sorry to hear that."

"I still miss her," she said with a trace of melancholy. "My brothers and their wives are downstairs somewhere."

"Really? I haven't met them yet, but you have so many people here, it's impossible to meet them all. This is quite a bash."

"Tom likes to do things in a big way," she said, smiling once more.

"Would you mind if I looked in on the boy?" Matt asked, glad to see her spirits lifted again.

"Of course not."

"I'll be right back."

He quietly entered the room and approached the bed. The sight of the tousled head, the innocence, begged a smile and a feeling of tenderness.

Nicole could not resist seeing the scene. She arose and came up behind him, without his awareness. Impulsively she touched his arm. He turned.

The boy, her touch, her presence, her well-being after the earlier scare, all combined to make her even more irresistible at that moment. He took her in his arms and kissed her passionately.

Though unexpected, Nicole eagerly returned the kiss and embrace. Their hands lovingly caressed each other's backs, as their lips hungrily kissed again and again. Their tongues touched, probed, and caressed, circling each other's.

"I love you, Nicole. I love you so much," Matt whispered,

as his mouth sought out her neck. He kissed her behind her ear and along her neck.

"I love you too, Matt. God, how I love you!" she breathily declared before their lips silenced further words.

Continuing their loving caresses for what seemed hours but lasted less than a minute, Nicole felt her passion rising. With that realization, she regained control. Although she continued her kissing embraces, they lessened in intensity.

Matt noted the difference and became alert again to their situation. A moment later, he took her hand, and they walked back to the master bedroom.

"I had better get downstairs," he said, now holding her before him with both hands on her shoulders.

She simply nodded her head in agreement.

"I'll tell Tom that you are fine and will be coming back down in a little while. Is that all right?"

Again, she nodded her head. Matt placed his hand under her chin and raised it so that her eyes met his.

"I will always love you, Nicole, no matter what."

Her eyes growing moist, Nicole told him, "And I will always love you, Matt."

Matt caressed her cheek, smiled, and looked closely into her eyes. She looked back with the same bittersweet intensity.

"Matt," she said, giving voice to her anguish. "I can never leave Tom. I just couldn't do that."

"I know," he said softly, still caressing her face and hair.

They kissed once more, a tender kiss, framed in a most affectionate embrace. Whether or not it was a farewell kiss, neither wished to know. They simply kissed, glorying in the moment before Matt smiled again, kissed his index finger, briefly placed it to her lips, turned, and left.

Echoing his action, Nicole kissed her finger and held her hand out to him, as he looked back before closing the door.

May 1900

The past five months had gone by quickly for Matt. His work, as usual, consumed a great amount of his time and energies. Somehow, he found time for a social life, and he occasionally ran into Nicole and Tom. Their encounters were friendly, but they also stirred hidden longings.

They had not been alone together since New Year's Eve, nor had either spoken of their brief interlude. Each realized their love had to remain where it was, locked away. Without any explicit agreement, they mutually stayed close as friends to keep their relationship alive. Their occasional meetings were joyful, as they submerged their love to get on with their lives. Even so, the love remained, without finding expression.

Today, Matt was renewing his friendship with an old colleague, and he smiled when he spotted him at the restaurant.

"I appreciate your treating me to lunch," Matt said to his old boss after joining him at a table in the Wintergreen Restaurant, one of Manhattan's posh restaurants.

"It is my pleasure, Matt," Joseph Senner replied. "I like you und you keep me connected to Ellis Island. Dot place remains close to my heart."

"You are a connection for me also, Dr. Senner. If not for Sarah Klaessig years ago introducing us, leading in turn to your generous invitation to work at Ellis Island, my life would have taken a much different path. It's curious how unplanned moments can affect us so deeply, often more than our planned actions."

"*Ja*, happenstance is vun of de wonders of life. Speaking of Ellis Island, I do not like vaht is happening right now, especially dis attack by Powderly. He is behind dis investigation, I am certain of it. His cronies on dot committee have no zympathy for de Bureau's leadership. He vants to embarrass de New York office. He tinks if dey trow enough mud, zum of it vill stick."

Matt nodded his head and sipped some ice water from the lead crystal goblet before him.

"I know there are problems at the Barge Office, but I resent their smearing everyone. Dr. Senner, I don't even know if there is corruption. I mean, I read the newspaper stories too, but I don't have any firsthand knowledge. I'm too busy with my own work."

"Vell, I tink vere dere is smoke, dere is fire. Verever you find ships, you find piracy, and ven you zee travelers, you can find extortion und robbery. McSveeney appears before de committee dis afternoon, I understand."

"Yes, that's right."

"He is de vun who should stamp out de problem. He is on de front lines, not Fitchie."

"Yes, Fitchie's not even around half the time. He's not on top of things as you were."

Senner smiled at the compliment.

"I do have one incident to tell you about though. The other day an immigrant attempted to bribe McSweeney, and he smacked the man right in his face. I didn't see it, but we all soon heard about it."

"Ha!" laughed Senner. "More people should respond to bribes dot way."

"You have a point there, sir."

The two men ordered their lunch and continued a pleasant, wide-ranging conversation throughout their meal.

*　　　*　　　*

At two o'clock the committee reconvened and allowed McSweeney to make an opening statement. He used the opportunity to denounce the charges of widespread graft and corruption. He spoke of the dedication and tireless efforts of immigration personnel, that they were understaffed and overworked in an overcrowded facility. That was the problem, not unsubstantiated accusations that the newspapers irresponsibly reported.

When he finished, committee chairman Herbert Brewer replied, "Mr. McSweeney, this committee has heard weeks of sworn testimony from dozens of witnesses about numerous instances of graft and corruption at the Barge Office. Are you now trying to tell us that it is all simply not true?"

Ed glared at his sneering inquisitor. He knew the parade of witnesses before him had been subjected to intimidation and abrasive questioning. Ed knew that the real motive behind this investigation was revenge, and that Powderly was attempting to make good on his threat to destroy him. No doubt the commissioner-general had instructed Brewer to do whatever necessary to make that happen.

Ed would not allow himself to be baited. He knew his best strategy was to control his anger and not let Powderly's puppet frighten him.

"Mr. Chairman," Ed stated calmly, "let me make my position very clear."

"It would be refreshing if you made something clear, Mr. McSweeney," Brewer countered.

Undaunted, Ed continued. "Much of what you have said, indeed, much of the testimony you have heard, relates to acts of exploitation *outside* the Barge Office. They are unfortunate, but beyond my responsibility. We have asked the city to assign more police to that area."

"We also unearthed a great deal of graft and corruption *inside* the Barge Office, Mr. McSweeney."

"Some, Mr. Brewer, not 'a great deal.' Let's not exaggerate. It does appear that a handful of employees may have committed improper acts. If those allegations hold true, we shall take the proper action."

"Mr. McSweeney, you and your staff are supposed to be the guardians, the ones charged with helping these immigrants enter the country. Instead, many are abused and exploited."

"Sir, I cannot allow you to make such sweeping, unsubstantiated accusations."

"Aren't you Mr. Mueller's direct supervisor?"

"Yes, I am."

"And you claim these charges against him were unknown to you?"

"That is correct. I never heard of them before this."

"You never knew that he spoke improperly to women during inspection, even asking them about their sexual activity?"

"This is the first time I have heard about this."

"How could these events have occurred if you were supervising him properly?"

"First of all, Mr. Brewer, no one, not you nor I, can supervise every single employee on a direct, continual basis. It is simply impossible. Secondly these are allegations, not facts. Third, I have only just learned of them."

"How are we able to find such scoundrels, and you cannot, Mr. McSweeney?" Brewster challenged. "Doesn't that say something about your administrative competency?"

"Let us not call anyone a scoundrel, Mr. Brewster, until all the facts are in. As to your question, you and your committee have been focusing on nothing else but locating such people, and you have an investigative staff. Anyone can work wonders with time, staff, and money. No one made any complaints to me. I must deal with the everyday arrival of more immigrants than we are equipped to handle. My staff and I do the very best we can, under the worst of circumstances."

"Mr. McSweeney, these despicable acts of corruption and impropriety occurred on your watch!" thundered the chairman. "All the alibis in the world don't change that! Perhaps you're just not man enough for the job!"

Angry, Ed shot back with his riposte, "Perhaps you should make that comment about not being man enough to the mirror, Mr. Brewer. I'm not the one whose wife has left him."

As several people in the room gasped at McSweeney's reference to that juicy tidbit of Washington gossip, Brewer flew into a rage. Rising from his chair, he shouted, "You slime! I'll break your neck!"

Brewer attempted to come around the table to reach McSweeney, but several men restrained him.

"Let me go!" he screamed. "Let me at that bastard!"

McSweeney stood up but otherwise did not move. Through the din, another committee member banged on the table and shouted, "We are adjourned until nine tomorrow morning!"

Still struggling to free his arms, Brewer shouted, as McSweeney turned his back and started to leave, "It's not over, McSweeney! I'll get you!"

Next day, McSweeney arrived early and sat down at the witness table. The committee members filed in one by one until only Brewer was missing. Finally, he entered and took his seat without looking at his opponent. After looking at his papers for a few minutes, building the tension even more, he raised his eyes and coldly looked at McSweeney.

"Mr. McSweeney," he began, "yesterday, you succeeded in

making a personal insult derail this committee from examining further your incompetence. That will not happen today, I assure you."

"I am as anxious as you to get this farce over with. Go ahead with your witch hunt."

"Enough!" Brewer answered, obviously angry. "Mr. Samuels, you have the floor."

Samuels began the committee's questioning of McSweeney. For three hours they relentlessly interrogated him about his knowledge of the various alleged incidents, his means of supervision and control over his employees, how much authority he delegates, and how such things could occur so frequently. His questioners continually impugned his integrity and his competence. After adjourning for lunch, they returned to question him for another three hours.

Throughout the day, McSweeney kept his composure and even used his Irish wit occasionally to deflate some pompous comment or soften a harsh question.

"Perhaps the demands on you from staff at the various detention and hospital facilities interfere with your ability to function effectively at the Barge Office,' Brewer heckled.

"On the contrary, I thrive on the challenge."

"Do you, Mr. McSweeney? You sound like J. P. Morgan."

"I wish I had his money," Ed quickly responded.

The resultant laughter helped Ed deflect another attack. When the day ended, the combatants had fought to a draw. The committee had no real evidence against him, only testimony about unsavory events occurring while he was in charge. However, while Ed effectively stood his ground, he was unable to dispel the cloud cast over his leadership.

Ed wanted out of this job now more than ever. However, he would never quit while that cloud remained. Right now, he knew he had to use his political connections in Washington to ensure the committee's report—guaranteed to be critical of him—did not jeopardize his position.

Next day, the committee members met to draft their report. They agreed to recommend the dismissal of McSweeney, Mueller, and about a dozen others.

June 1900

At noon outside the Barge Office on this Friday, a boarding-house runner, carrying an infant to make sure the others followed him, led a group of bewildered immigrants to his employer's address. There, they would be persuaded to stay overnight at exorbitant prices.

A few minutes later, another runner—using the more common practice of carrying immigrants' baggage—led a different group to another boarding house.

Inside the Barge Office, a swindler—successfully claiming the baggage checks for some unsuspecting immigrants—quickly left with his prizes. Perhaps he had stolen linens, shawls, pottery, or cookware that he could sell at a good price.

Mueller was equally busy lining his pockets with extra money. He had an arrangement with a New York jobber to provide cheap labor for American farmers. Taking advantage of the ignorance and gullibility of dozens of newly arriving Polish, Hungarian, Danish, and Swedish males traveling alone, he duped them into signing papers promising their labor for a full year at a fraction of what they might earn otherwise.

Presently, he was turning over twenty-two fine prospects, for whom he received ten dollars each. The jobber loaded the men into the awaiting wagons to take them to his office. There, farmers would come in from the countryside to look them over to choose the brawniest and most innocent. They literally would "buy" the men, providing the jobber with a handsome profit and themselves with dependable cheap labor.

Graft and corruption continued as everyday activities at the Barge Office. Last month's investigative committee had accomplished little. When Commissioner-General Terence Powderly received their report, he expunged Mueller's name to protect his informant and then sent the corrected report to his superior, Secretary of the Treasury Lyman Gage. Gage, who had been critical of the hearings, suppressed the report, but first he deleted all charges against McSweeney before filing it away. Only a few low-level employees without friends in high places were dismissed as soothing balm to the press and public.

As Matt sat at his desk catching up on paperwork, one of the New York congressmen he knew called from Washington.

"Matt, what can you tell me about a young boy named Henry Fleetwood? Your medical officers are detaining him."

"I don't recognize the name, sir," Matt answered. "Hold the line a minute, and I'll check."

Matt scanned the medical detention and hospitalization lists, but he did not find the name.

Returning to the telephone, he reported, "I'm sorry, sir, we are not detaining anyone by the name of Fleetwood."

"Damn it! Of course you are, Matt! I've just spoken to his family, and they are very concerned. Obviously, this is yet another mistake up there. I would appreciate your personally looking into this and using your influence to get the boy cleared for entry."

"I'll do what I can, sir. I can't promise you anything about the boy's clearance, but I can try to find out about his situation."

"Get back to me as soon as possible, Matt. I want to give the family some reassurance."

"I'll do my best."

"Thanks, Matt. I'll wait for your call."

Minutes later, James Dunwood, one of the staff doctors, came into Matt's office. He had boarded an arriving ship anchored outside the Narrows to await the incoming tide. On board, he had conducted medical exams of the small number of passengers. Once the ship docked at the pier, he had disembarked and returned to the Barge Office. That was an hour ago.

"Jim, do you know anything about a detained boy named Henry Fleetwood?"

"Sure do. He was on the *Grampian*. I'm holding him up for a closer examination. The boy's deaf and dumb. I think he's probably feeble-minded as well. How did you know his name? I'm only turning my list in now."

Matt laughed. "I've already received a call about him from Congressman Atherton in Washington."

"In Washington! This sets a new record for pressure calls. I didn't even get a chance to turn in my papers."

"The speed of it certainly is impressive, isn't it? I guess the relatives meeting the ship learned what happened and placed a fast call to their congressman."

"Next thing we'll be getting calls while the ship's still at sea."

Matt smiled and said, "I'll inform the congressman that we have made no mistake as he thought, but that he simply was too efficient for us. He wanted me to expedite the boy's clearance, but I'll tell him the boy's status is in the hands of the Board of Special Inquiry."

He placed the call and finished his day's work. Another weekend was at hand, and it included a garden party hosted by Sarah Klaessig. No doubt she would be trying again to match him with yet another woman. Matt held little hope for agreeing with her choice any more than on previous occasions, but she did have enjoyable socials, and this one would help him get through an otherwise empty weekend.

December 1900

To monitor the progress of the construction, Matt had taken the ferry several times to Ellis Island since the rebuilding began. He continued to work with the architects, Boring and Tilton, in designing the hospital to be constructed on the newly built second island across the ferry slip from the main building. The landfill for the hospital island was excavated dirt and rock coming from construction of the city's first subway system.

Matt had waited more than three years to return to work on the island, and today was the day, even though the hospital would not be completely finished for many months. Built at a cost of $1.5 million, the island's new facilities eventually would be a complex of buildings essentially designed to create a self-contained city with a constantly changing population of bewildered and impatient strangers whose greatest desire was to leave it as fast as they could.

As Matt waited on the ferry for the others to board, he saw Mueller talking to a man on the dock. By his uniform Matt correctly assumed that this man was also in the Registry Division, so he paid them no further attention.

"I'm telling ya, McGaffney," Mueller assured the man, "our return to the island doesn't change anything."

"You're certain?"

"Absolutely. I'll still assign ya to board the ships outside the Narrows, so you meet my man on the ship to tell ya who gets the citizen certificates, so they can land at the piers. As long as ya follow my instructions, things will be fine."

McGaffney nodded his head in agreement, as the two men joined the other island employees and guests aboard the ferry.

Just before the boat began its short journey, Matt found two familiar faces, and he smiled at how easily today seemed like old times. Once again he was with Guenter Langer and Frank Martiniello, his daily traveling companions prior to the fire. With Guenter still working as gateman for medical examinees, Matt had seen much of him at the Barge Office, but only rarely did he see the interpreter who had given him Italian lessons a few years back. Here they were together again, and their conversation flowed easily as if their last trip together had only been yesterday.

"Big day, Doctor, no?" asked Frank.

"Big day, yes, Frank. It's been a long wait under trying circumstances."

"*Si,* I am glad to get out of that Barge Office. It was much too small," Frank replied.

"Well, we won't have that problem on the island anymore," said Guenter. "They say it's big enough to handle five thousand immigrants a day and even more in a pinch."

"That should do nicely, given the numbers we've been getting, don't you think, Dr. Stafford?" asked Frank.

"I hope so, Frank, but it's hard to predict the future."

"How do you like your hospital so far?" Frank asked, eager to restore their relationship to its earlier camaraderie.

"I'm very pleased. It will contain everything I asked for. It's going to be a very fine facility."

"Good. That's good," Guenter said. "If I ever need a hospital again, it's good to know there will be a fine one nearby."

"Let's all pray you never need it, Guenter," said Matt, half laughing, half seriously.

"*Buon Dio*! Look at that beautiful building!" Frank exclaimed.

The other two men gazed at the main building as they approached. Situated at the center of the island, near the site of the old structure, the red brick edifice with limestone trim was set back slightly from the water. Standing sixty-two feet high, it was set off by one-hundred-foot, copper-domed observation towers at each corner. A blend of American and French Renaissance styles, it was indeed impressive, almost regal.

Three massive, lateral arches, extending well up into the second story, framed the entrances. Above each perched a concrete American eagle and the American coat of arms, with elaborate cornices farther up. It was 385 feet by 165 feet, larger than a football field. Its attractive design enchanted the viewer, and its sheer size enhanced further its domination of the small island.

Ed McSweeney was on the same boat, and he peered intently at his domain. He was eager to return to the island for several reasons. He liked the sense of defined territory the island provided and, with it, the greater control. Furthermore, vendor kickbacks would restore some of the income he had been denied while at the Barge Office.

"Excuse me, Mr. McSweeney," said the reporter, "I saw you smiling. Are you thinking about your return to Ellis Island?"

Ed turned and recognized Bertram Wilson, the *New York Times* reporter.

"Indeed I am," he answered, still smiling. "This is a wonderful day for all of us."

"What is that other building?" asked Wilson, pointing to the uncompleted structure of red brick with limestone and bluestone trims.

"That's where the kitchen, laundry, and bathhouse will be. It should be finished in a few more months. We'll be able to

Ellis Island main building and transport steamers, circa 1901

Ellis Island hospital under construction, 1900

put two hundred immigrants at a time under the showers. All immigrants will take showers once a day and they will land on American soil clean, if nothing more."

"Imagine that!" said the reporter. "Two hundred people taking a shower at the same time!"

"This will be like a small city, Bert. We'll have a hospital, eating facilities for thousands, dormitories for more than a thousand people, large waiting rooms, a post office, a customs house, a telegraph station, foreign exchange banks, witness rooms, detention pens, courtrooms, and—"

"Slow down a bit, sir," Bert pleaded, as he wrote furiously.

"Ha! I guess I was getting a little too carried away. You know, our return to Ellis Island should eliminate practically all the unpleasant and irritating features of the Barge Office. No longer will boarding-house sharks defraud immigrants. And that crowd of foreigners who besiege us every day at the Battery will be a thing of the past. They have made life hideous with their quarreling or cursing of our staff in a babel of tongues. This is the beginning of a new era, Bert."

"No question about your enthusiasm, Mr. McSweeney. Sounds like you've got quite a place here."

"Wait until you see it all," McSweeney boasted as the ferry reached the dock.

Everyone gathered in front of the main building for the opening ceremony. Treasury Secretary Lyman Gage, up from Washington with a small entourage, proclaimed the rebuilt Ellis Island as "the model immigration station of the world."

After a few brief speeches by several officials, Gage cut the ribbon and the crowd moved into the main building.

"This is the baggage room," said McSweeney, beginning the tour. "The immigrants will check their baggage here before they go upstairs to be processed. When they have been processed, they'll come down here again by a different staircase, claim their belongings, and continue over to your left to the railroad

Ellis Island Baggage Room, early 1900s

waiting room. That's also where all the support activities will be: money exchange, post office, employment information, and aid society booths. You'll see them a bit later. Now, if you'll follow me, we'll go upstairs."

As they came up the stairs, they entered the Registry Hall, by far the largest room. Dividing its two-hundred-foot length was an iron railing network of narrow aisles, through which the immigrants would travel for examination and inspection.

"On this side of the hall, we do the preliminary medical exams," Ed explained. "If we require closer examinations, we have small, separate rooms over here for that purpose."

Ed led the visitors through this area and back out into the great hall.

"On this end we conduct the legal examination at each of these desks."

Noting the high registry desks, where the legal questioning of immigrants would occur, the reporters then followed Ed to the next area.

Registry clerks (behind desks) and an interpreter (seated, center) question new arrivals.

"Over here are the courtrooms for boards of special inquiry. We'll go in this one."

Behind a wooden banister of spindle design was a long wooden table with chairs for the board members and interpreter. Three small reading lamps with green visors over them sat on the table. On the other side of the room were long, wooden, and park-style benches for witnesses and participants.

Moving on, Ed added, "Over here are detention rooms for people who do not clear our processing."

When they reached the third floor, he noted, "As you can see, this observation gallery gives us a view of the activities below. Visitors can watch the inspectors at work with the immigrants, some of whom, by the way, will be arriving shortly. On all four sides on this level are the dormitories, with a total of six hundred iron bunks screened with wire netting."

"Is that a stairway to the roof?" asked a reporter.

"Yes, it is. Each dormitory has one. The building has a flat rooftop. We are thinking of making it a roof garden for the detainees and possibly even putting on concerts or vaudeville shows to entertain them.

"Now, we'll go downstairs, and I'll show you the exit passages. Here on the second floor, this stairway opens before the immigrants as they leave the aisles. You'll see that it is divided into three passages by wire screens. After reclaiming their baggage, those for New York have free access to the covered passage to the New York ferry slip. Those who are to travel by rail are taken back through the building to the railroad ticket offices to get their tickets, have their baggage properly checked, and then go to a landing adjoining the one where they landed, to be transported to the railway terminal in Jersey City. We usher detainees into one of these detention rooms to remain until further disposition is made of them, according to the merits of their cases."

While Ed conducted his public relations tour, Matt and most of the island personnel readied their areas for the first batch of new arrivals. It turned out to be 654 Italians who were steerage passengers on the *Kaiser Wilhelm II*. Later, other steerage passengers from the *Victoria*, the *Umbria*, and the *Vincenzo Florio* also came to the island. By day's end 2,251 immigrants were processed.

*   *   *

Gage, Fitchie, the press, and other visitors were long gone, as were most of the immigrants, by the time Guenter, Frank, and Matt ended their workday and took a ferry back to Manhattan. Matt relished their companionship, realizing it helped fill somewhat that void of a close relationship in his personal life. With them he could relax, engage in small talk, and laugh. Away from the stress of work or from the restrictive social manners dictated by polite society on social occasions (such as the continuous affairs hosted by Sarah Klaessig), they provided him an important emotional outlet.

As the ferryboat neared the dock, hastening his friends' departure, Matt again sensed his impending loneliness.

"How about a beer, men? I'm buying," Matt offered.

"I should be getting home, Doctor," Frank gently demurred.

"Oh, come on, Frank. Just a quick one. It's a special day today. You can spare a few minutes."

"Well, all right, but just one."

"Just one. How about you, Guenter?'

"Ever know a German to refuse a beer? Of course."

Matt laughed. It was more than the comment. He laughed happily because he knew he had the pleasure of his colleagues for a little longer.

A short time later, Matt and Guenter were sitting at a table in a tavern, talking and laughing, each drinking his fourth stein of beer. Frank had left them an hour earlier to get home to his family, leaving his two single friends to continue without him.

When their conversation ebbed, Guenter asked Matt, "You know what we need right now?"

"What's that?"

"We need some women."

Matt laughed.

"Amen to that, Guenter."

"I know where we can find some. Are you with me?"

Matt looked at Guenter, trying to gauge the meaning of his friend's words.

"What are you talking about, Guenter? What kind of women?"

"Willing women. Trust me, you'll be pleased. What do you say? Let's go have an adventure at a sporting house!"

Matt hesitated, quickly considering his options. It was only a brief moment before he agreed. With a mild euphoria instilled in him by the beers, he decided to end the many months of self-denial.

With Guenter as his guide, they walked a few blocks and went up the stairs of a brownstone. Guenter rang the bell, and a woman in her fifties with heavy makeup, wearing a dress with a plunging neckline, answered the door.

"Hello, Guenter!" she warmly greeted. "It's good to see you again. Come in, both of you."

"Thank you, Marta. This is Matt."

"Welcome, Matt," she said, shaking his hand. "Now, let me take your coats. The charge is the usual, Guenter. It's still early, so you'll have a wide choice."

Earlier, Matt had given Guenter the money he requested, which Guenter now gave to Marta. She led them to closed, sliding wooden doors, behind which Matt could hear music from a phonograph. Marta opened the doors for the men to enter.

Inside the large parlor—its Victorian decor dominated by the color red in the carpeting, drapes, and velvet couches—Matt saw eleven women. All were provocatively clothed only in undergarments, their cleavage leaving little to the imagination. Three men were also in the room. One was dancing with one of the women, while another—an elderly man—was sitting with a drink in his hand chatting with a brunette. The third man had apparently just reentered the room, for he was putting on his jacket, saying, "Thanks, darling. See you next time," to another brunette. As he walked past Guenter and Matt, he winked at them and said, "Enjoy yourselves, gentlemen."

Matt gazed about, appraising the women. Two were fairly plain women whom he found unappealing. Another two were a bit too full-figured for his tastes, and he immediately discounted the woman who had just returned with the winking stranger.

Marta poured and offered each of them a brandy. The women, except for the two with the other men, eyed Matt and Guenter, offering suggestive looks, smiles, and poses to accentuate their wares.

"What do we do next?" Matt whispered to Guenter, naïve as he was in the etiquette of a bordello.

"You can pick one and go upstairs with her, or you can talk or dance with a few of them a little bit until you make up your mind. We'll go our separate ways now, and I'll see you at work tomorrow. So, if you'll excuse me, Doc, I'm laying claim to Rosie over there."

Guenter walked over to an attractive redhead, her long tresses extending down to her shoulder blades. He gave her a kiss, which she freely returned. Then, putting his arm around her waist, they walked out of the room through a back passageway.

Matt looked around the room again into the faces of the alluring, expectant women. He was the recipient of winks, puckered kisses, opened mouths with tongues slowly licking lips, and other lewd sights designed to entice him. He saw no point in conversational or dancing auditions. Selecting the most appealing woman in the group, a raven-haired seductress who reminded him neither of Peg nor Nicole, he walked to where she was sitting, smiled, and extended his hand, fingers slightly bent, palm upward.

She smiled back, pleased that this attractive man had chosen her. Taking his hand, she got up, led him out of the room and upstairs to her small but tastefully furnished room, shutting the door behind her. He noticed immediately the double-sized bed. It was covered with only a sheet, with several pillows propped up against the brass headboard.

"I'm Matt," he offered as she turned toward him after shutting the door.

"Hello, Matt," she said in a sultry voice.

"What's your name?"

"Any name you want, darling," she replied, placing her hands by his shoulders under his jacket and effortlessly removing it.

"I want to call you by your name," said Matt, needing to personalize the impending intimacy.

"You can call me Carol," she told him, unbuttoning and removing his shirt, then rubbing her hands over his nipples before kissing him again.

"Is that your name?" he asked when she stopped.

"Does it matter?' she teased, unbuttoning his pants.

"Yes, I need to know your name."

"It's Carol."

She sat him on the bed and, kneeling before him, deftly removed the rest of his clothes. As her gaze slowly traveled up the length of his body, she said breathily, "Don't you look fine! Now, Matt, you sit back up against the pillows, and let me show you what Carol's got for you."

He did as told and watched, as she deliberately, tantalizingly, removed her clothes until she stood naked before him at the foot of the bed. It had been an incredibly long time since he had seen an unclad woman, and he throbbed with anticipation. She took notice and licked her lips, staring intently at him as she slowly crawled onto the bed toward him.

He was hungry for her, and when she reached him, he took her in his arms. All his restraint, all his repressed physical needs were unleashed. Long before he entered her, he kissed her all over her body, his hands freely roaming everywhere, sometimes caressing or fondling, sometimes stroking or rubbing. He had not been with a woman for so long that he intentionally delayed entering her, not wanting it all to end quickly, as he feared it would. Skilled in the art of lovemaking, she brought him sensations that he had forgotten and even some he had never before experienced. He concentrated intensely on his self control, changing what they were doing whenever he approached too soon the threshold of no return.

When it was over, they lay there, exhausted and satisfied. Matt recognized this was the first time in years that he had made love to someone and the first time in his life that he had done so with both partners so uninhibited. Carol had been pleasantly surprised at his ardor and length of foreplay and afterplay. Their coupling was also far more than she expected and she climaxed several times, a distinct rarity for her.

"You're quite something, Matt," she said, admiringly.

Grinning, he replied, "You were quite something yourself, pretty lady."

Their time was up, though, and after they dressed and gently kissed one last time, she said her standard farewell, but with sincerity this time, "I hope you'll come back soon."

He tucked her chin, smiled, and said, "Maybe I will," and kissed her lips.

Later, sitting in his favorite chair at home with a snifter of brandy, he reflected on his night of passion. He had experienced many physical delights and had no regrets, and yet somehow the experience was not enough to fill his emotional void. He realized that he would still sleep alone tonight, and tomorrow he would again wake up alone, just as he had done for several years.

"Still," he said aloud to himself as he walked to the bedroom, "tonight will leave a pleasant memory."

April 1901

"Frank, there's something you've got to see!"

Hearing the excited amusement in Guenter's voice, Frank, who was eating his lunch, looked up.

"What is it?"

"Just come with me and see for yourself. Believe me; it's worth coming to see."

Curious, Frank got up and followed Guenter, whose work assignment this Friday had prevented their eating together as they customarily did.

Guenter led him around to the outside front of the main building. Standing there were more than two hundred Gypsies waiting to enter for processing. They were part of the almost two thousand steerage passengers from the Cunard liner, *Carpathia,* which had arrived from Liverpool.

"*Buon Dio!*"

"Didn't I tell you?" said Guenter, laughing.

"They're dressed in all the colors of the rainbow! I've never seen anything like it."

"Neither have I. I mean, I've seen Gypsies before, but never so many all at once."

"Yes, exactly. Me too. Look at them! They're all in their tribal costumes. They're a dazzlement of gorgeous splendor!"

"They're what?"

"I said they're a dazzlement of gorgeous splendor, Guenter."

"That's pretty fancy talk, Frank."

"Maybe, but just look at the beauty of all those colors!"

"They are a sight. I'll give you that," replied Guenter, "but I'll bet the inspectors won't be impressed by them. Gypsies aren't very popular here."

"Or anywhere, for that matter," added Frank. "Well, time to get back to work. We'll leave them to their fate."

As the men headed back to their stations, Guenter said, "I'm working this weekend, Frank. Are you?"

"As a matter of fact, I am. We're getting to be peas in a pod with our work schedules."

"Speaking of pees," said Guenter, "I've got to—"

An extended family of Hungarian Roma (called "Gypsies")
await deportation, circa 1901

"I know," laughed Frank, "I know. I can read you like a book, my friend."

*   *   *

The Gypsies soon came to Matt's attention when he and the other doctors in the line division found twenty-five cases of measles among their children. When the first few children were taken into quarantine, the adults began protesting. As more cases were detected and more children were led away, the adults raised a clamor.

Within minutes, Stoner, McSweeney, and Mueller were on the scene. Stoner ordered the children sent over to Kingston Avenue Hospital in Brooklyn, which was the only available site to handle so many contagious diseases. He and Ed next spoke to the Gypsy leader, Jose Michel, to explain what they had done and why, so he could quiet down his people.

After that, Ed ordered the Gypsies placed in a detention area.

"Mr. Mueller!" Ed called out.

"Yes, sir?" John responded.

"Get these people processed right away. I want you to identify all their leaders and have them appear before one of the boards."

"The boards, sir? They haven't had their legal examination yet. How do we know a board inquiry is necessary?"

"How do we know?" Ed curtly replied. "They're Gypsies, for God's sake! The last thing we want is two hundred Gypsies entering this country! I want you to stop them."

"All of them?"

"You heard me, Mr. Mueller. Make it happen."

John identified the more distinctive families among the group in addition to that of Jose Michel. One by one, these six families appeared before the Board of Special Inquiry, with Mueller joining it.

In each instance, the Gypsies met all eligibility requirements. In fact, each family had more money in their possession than most immigrants. Moreover, none planned to live in the United States, as all professed to be on their way to settle in Winnipeg, Canada.

After the last family left the hearing room, Robert Haggerty turned to John and asked, "How can we reject them? They satisfy all requirements."

"Mr. McSweeney said he wants them deported."

"They don't even want to live here," Haggerty countered. "They're on their way to Canada."

"How can we be certain of that?" John answered. "They're Gypsies, aren't they? Lying is in their blood. No, we can't take a chance. We have to exclude them as undesirables. It's what Mr. McSweeney wants. Anyone have any objections?"

The board members acquiesced and ordered the deportation of the entire group, once their children recovered. That same day another fifteen Gypsy children were sent to the hospital with measles.

*   *   *

On Saturday, other Gypsies from Long Island and New Jersey came to Ellis Island to visit the detainees. Later, Frank heard loud, pitiful wails throughout the building. Curious, he went to the excluded pen to investigate. The Gypsy women were gathered in corners, sitting on the floor, crying, swaying to and fro, as some of them wailed loudly. Separated from the women by a wire screen, the men were either morose or visibly disturbed about something.

"What's this all about?" Frank asked Guenter, who was serving as a guard in the area.

"How can you tell with Gypsies?" he answered. "Maybe this is their way of dealing with the fact that we're not letting them in."

"Why now? They knew that yesterday."

"I don't know, Frank. If you figure that one out, let me know."

Frank looked at the crying women and agitated men, gathered in groups, for a few more seconds. Still puzzled, he left.

When the nine o'clock curfew came, none of the Gypsies went to bed. All night, the women sat moaning, and the men consulted with one another.

About ten o'clock Matt came by. Also on duty this weekend, he was making his final rounds for the day, to see if any other measles cases had developed.

"Hello, Dr. Stafford," greeted Guenter.

"Good evening, Guenter. Would you unlock the door for me please?"

"Sure thing, Dr. Stafford," he replied and did so.

As Matt entered the pen holding the women and children, Guenter locked the door again and returned to his table about twenty feet away.

Matt looked around the place, as a few women angrily glared at him. He approached a young girl to take her pulse. As he did, he was quickly surrounded by the women, who struck him with everything they had. Some took off their wooden shoes and threw them at him.

Others hurled pans and kettles, some hitting him and others noisily clanging on the floor. The women's fury and the pain from the barrage forced a hasty retreat.

"Let me out!" he cried to Guenter, as the women kept up their attack. They picked up shoes and cookery and repeatedly threw them at him.

Guenter had sprinted toward the door at the first sign of trouble. It all happened in just a few seconds, but the women pelted Matt several times before Guenter could unlock the gate.

As Guenter and two watchmen stepped inside to quiet the women and rescue Matt, the shower of missiles, including heavy-soled shoes, iron kettles, and pans, continued. With fire in their eyes, the women charged at the men, wildly striking out, scratching, clawing, and screaming.

As the island employees tried to defend themselves and subdue the frenzied women, the Gypsy men desperately tried to knock down the wire screen partition to join the fray. Seeing the long knives brandished by a few of the men, the staff was glad for the strength of the partition that separated them.

The women fought on, ferocious and relentless. Soon, others on the night crew, including Frank, were in the detention quarters, battling with the women.

Matt, Guenter, Frank, and the others kept getting hit, kicked, scratched, and bitten. At last the island personnel overpowered the women and restored order.

While the staff contained the women, Matt examined each of the children. Finding one with measles, he started to escort the boy toward the door. The women erupted again and started a rumpus. This time, though, it was short-lived.

All through the night and early morning, whenever a uniformed immigration officer neared the women, they opened fire again. Using whatever weapons were handy, they cursed and threw the objects at the official behind the partition.

At midmorning on Sunday, McSweeney came to the island after learning of the fight the night before. He sent for Matt and Jose Michel, the Gypsy leader, and asked for an explanation.

"The women were simply fighting for the lives of their children," the dark-eyed man responded angrily.

"What do you mean—their lives?" Ed asked. "We're as concerned about your children as you are."

"You lie! We know the truth. Our friends told us what you are doing."

"What are you talking about?" Ed replied. "Your children are being well cared for in the hospital."

"Again you lie! You have a hospital right here on the island, but our children are not there. No, we know. You bastards are drowning our children!"

Ed threw up his hands in total surprise.

"*What?*" he exclaimed.

Jose Michel persisted with his charge.

"You have taken our children away in a boat. Not one of us has seen them since. We have learned from our friends that you have drowned them."

Matt realized that the Gypsies, frequent victims of hatred and persecution in Europe, actually believed the authorities were drowning their children.

"I assure you, Mr. Michel," said Matt, "that nothing of the kind was done. Mr. McSweeney, would it be possible to allow the parents to go to the hospital to visit their children, to prove they are fine and in good care?"

"Of course. Is that agreeable to you, Mr. Michel?"

Jose Michel nodded his head in agreement. When he reported this offer to the other Gypsies, the suggestion had a calming effect.

When Ed learned that more than a hundred wanted to go to the hospital, he withdrew Matt's offer of a parental visit. Instead, he allowed only the parents of the boy just diagnosed with measles last night to visit their son, under the guard of a watchman.

When these parents saw him in a clean white bed, with a nurse standing over him, and all the other children receiving the same treatment, they were pleased. Upon return to the island, they told the others and the troubles ceased.

For many days afterwards, Matt's arms, legs, and back bore testimony to the battering he took from the Gypsy women. The black-and-blue marks left by the pans and kettles thrown at him took a few weeks to fade away. By the time the marks disappeared, so too had the Gypsies. Once their children recovered, authorities deported all of them back to England.

July 1901

Standing apart from the other island employees waiting to board the ferry to work, John Mueller was quietly talking to Kevin McGaffney, one of his inspectors.

"Here are the names of the ones for today," John said, handing over a piece of paper.

"Right. Still two dollars?" McGaffney asked.

"Yeah, cash in hand, as always. Once you have their money, you can give them their citizenship certificates."

"Who's my contact on the *Ingram*?"

"It's the ship's purser, Wesley Randall."

"This is a great scam, John, selling these papers to steerage passengers so they can get right off the ships without going to the island. I gotta hand it to ya."

"Keep your voice down," said John, looking about. "We don't want anyone hearing about this."

McGaffney looked around too and then asked, "John, why don't we charge more? We could make a lot more than we do."

"Don't get greedy, McGaffney. This is a sweet deal that will bring us a lot of money for a long time. It's the best amount we can get from these people."

"I still think—"

"Look, you do it the way I tell you," John snarled, "if you know what's good for you."

"What's good for me is more money," McGaffney said, holding his ground. "Maybe I'll set up my own operation."

"Do anything other than what I tell you to do, and I'll put you in prison for a long time."

"I don't take kindly to threats, John," the man answered, glaring directly into Mueller's eyes. "If I go down, I'll take you down with me, just remember that."

"Will you, now? Don't bet on it. You'd be the one with witnesses against him, not me, so who would believe your word against mine? And I've still got the goods on you for that other stunt you pulled, remember? If it comes to that, I can put you away for a very long time, and you know it."

McGaffney was silenced. He knew Mueller had proof that he had admitted unfit aliens and could use it at any time. All he had to do was claim he'd just discovered it in a review of the records. No one would then believe him about Mueller's role in the fake certificates scam.

"Look," said Mueller, putting his hand on the man's shoulder, "you've done all right so far by listening to me, haven't you?"

"Yeah," McGaffney answered begrudgingly.

"Well, then, just keep doing what I tell you, and you'll keep lining your pockets. What do you say? Let's shake on it. No hard feelings, okay?"

"No hard feelings," McGaffney answered, shaking hands.

As they joined the other employees now boarding the ferry, John resolved to keep a tight rein on his associate.

*   *   *

As the ferry once again began its journey to the island,

Frank suddenly asked his friend, "Guenter, have you ever, when you went home, found any vermin crawling on you?"

"Vermin!" replied Guenter with disgust. "What are you talking about?"

"Vermin," Frank answered resolutely. "You know, lice. Have you ever found any crawling on your clothes or neck?"

"Of course not, I keep myself clean. Why do you ask?"

"Don't get offended. I keep myself clean too, but yesterday when I came home from work and started to play with my son, he found one of them on my collar. It's not the first time either. Sometimes my wife finds one, sometimes one of my kids."

"How many times has it happened?"

"About five or six times now. It's a disgusting part of this job. Why do you think I get them and you don't?"

"I don't know, Frank. You're obviously coming in contact with immigrants carrying them."

"Yes, but you're with them every day too, and you say you've never had any problem."

"That's right. Guess I'm just luckier than you."

"It's not luck," Frank insisted. "It's something else."

"Well, look for a pattern, then. When you find them, is there anything different you do that day?"

"No, it's the same thing, day in, day out."

"When are the times you're close enough to aliens to get their lice? Is it more one time than another?"

"That's it, Guenter. It's at the inquiry hearings with the board. Of course! They've found most of the vermin on my left side, and at the hearings the alien always stands directly to my left when I interpret for him."

"Don't they get deloused at the bathing house?"

"These people are processed and leave the same day they arrive. They don't go to the bath house. Wait until I tell Dr. Stafford. His doctors are missing those lice, and I'm getting them!"

Guenter laughed and then asked, "Where is Dr. Stafford?"

"He probably went in early again," Frank replied. "That man's working too hard."

*   *   *

Matt had indeed gone in early. He wanted to complete a few reports to have enough free time for his special visitors. Tom Lindstrom had called him a few days ago, asking if it were possible to bring Nicole and James to the island for a tour of the place. Matt had quickly agreed. Any opportunity to see Nicole under any circumstances was always desired.

They arrived in late morning as expected; Matt met them at the dock. After a warm exchange of greetings, he led them into the main building and up onto the gallery where they could gaze upon the processing of the many new arrivals.

"Look at all those people!" exclaimed Tom, when he saw all

Processing of immigrants as viewed from
Registry Hall balcony, early 1900s

the aisles filled from end to end, with others waiting at the top of the stairs to make their way into the great hall.

"Yes, we will be dealing with several thousand immigrants today, as we do every day lately. It's a grueling task for the guardians."

"The guardians?"

"It's how many of us, half jokingly and half seriously, refer to ourselves. We are the ones who screen out the criminals, the physically or mentally incompetent, and others who present a problem to society. We protect America from anyone who would be a burden or moral danger. We protect single females from being exploited, ensuring they are in safe hands when they leave here, and we guide all the newcomers through this place to their waiting friends and relatives, or else to the boats and trains that will carry them to their destinations."

"And you do this for so many them," Tom marveled.

"Well, we do our best."

Matt was a thorough tour guide. He explained the different processing steps, pointing out the various stations. He showed them all parts of the main building—the dormitories, examining and inquiry rooms, the baggage and railway waiting rooms, and the area for immigrant aid organizations. Next, he took them outside to enjoy the view of the New York skyline before showing them other facilities and taking them to lunch in the private VIP dining room.

*　　　*　　　*

As they approached the new hospital after lunch, a flood of special memories about the old hospital engulfed Nicole. Ever since Tom had first proposed this visit, she had been ambivalent about returning to the island where she and Matt had fallen in love. Yet Tom had been so insistent on seeing firsthand the beautiful new structures of the controversial immigrant station that she could hardly refuse. Moreover, any outward reluctance would have raised more questions from Tom than she wanted to answer.

In the eighteen months since their New Year's episode, she had encountered Matt about a dozen times at various social events, including two dinner parties at her home at Tom's invitation. At no time were they alone together. She had seen to that. In Matt's absence, she often thought longingly of him, but in his presence she felt uncomfortable, keenly aware about the reality of her situation.

Somehow, she managed to get through lunch with no one wise to her inner torment. Despite the previous social occasions, their lunch marked the first time just the four of them were together. The men in her life sat on either side of her, as young James sat opposite her.

That seating arrangement symbolized to her the soul searching that she continually went through. She was deceiving the man she loved by not telling him about his child, while she was also deceiving the man she married with her love for another, and by letting him think he was James's father. She reminded herself of Walter Scott's lines: "Oh, what a tangled web we weave, when first we practice to deceive!" Still, she felt she had little choice but to continue the charade.

"Let me first show you the Surgeons' House," said Matt as they went through the front porch and into the vestibule. Together they saw the parlor, library, and kitchen before going upstairs. A bathroom and five bedrooms, used by surgeons and assistant surgeons, faced the central hall.

Opening one of the closed doors, Matt said, "This is my room. It's not much, just a place to sleep between shifts."

Nicole peeked in. The room had an institutional feel to it, lacking any personalized hominess.

"Do you spend much time here, Matt?"

"Not really. I only stay here when it's necessary."

As they entered the hospital, Matt declared, "This is my pride and joy. A lot of me went into this hospital."

"Then it must be an excellent hospital, Matt," said Nicole with sincerity.

"Thank you, Nurse," Matt answered with a little laugh. "I think it is, but come see for yourselves."

Matt guided them through the operating rooms, offices, lounges, and wards, greeting many of the patients he encountered. Toward the end of the tour, he heard a near-hysterical voice.

"Dr. Stafford, come quickly!"

Matt turned his attention to the ward nurse; the panic on her face matched her voice.

"What's the matter?"

"It's Mr. Randazzi. He's barricaded himself in the bathroom, and he won't come out! I've been trying to coax him out, but he won't answer me. He's been in there for almost ten minutes, and I just heard a thud. I think he's fallen!"

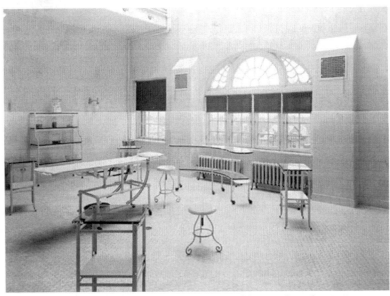

Operating room in the new Ellis Island hospital, early 1900s

"Nicole, Tom, excuse me," said Matt hurriedly before running down the corridor.

As he rushed away, the others followed. Nicole asked the nurse walking quickly beside her, "Has that patient been despondent?"

"Yes, he's become gloomier as his deportation date neared. He told me about his near-starvation life in Italy. He had saved for more than a year for his passage money, hoping he could at last make something of his life here. When the doctors rejected him, he wouldn't talk to any of us."

Ahead, they saw Matt rapping on the bathroom door.

"Mr. Randazzi! It's Dr. Stafford. *È il medico.* Open the door! *Apra il portello!*"

After a few seconds' silence, Matt threw his weight against the door, unsuccessfully.

"Mr. Randazzi, can you hear me? Uh, *potete sentirli?*"

There was only silence.

"Mr. Randazzi, please answer me. Are you all right? *Siete tutto il di destra?*"

With still no answer, Matt resumed his efforts to knock down the door.

"Dr. Stafford, look!" the nurse shouted, pointing to the floor.

Matt looked down. Bright red blood was oozing from beneath the door.

"Damn!" yelled Matt, hurling himself with greater intensity against the door.

By now Tom, Nicole, and James had reached the scene. As Nicole turned James away from the scene, Tom added his strength to Matt's thrusts against the door. After several attempts, they succeeded in breaking it slightly open. As Tom pushed harder against the door, blocked by Antonio Randazzi's body, Matt squeezed himself through the narrow opening and examined the unconscious man.

Randazzi had slit both his wrists and blood was rhythmically spurting out. He had already lost a good amount. Acting swiftly, Matt removed his suspenders and applied tourniquets to both arms. Once they were in place, he struggled to move the heavy man away from the door.

Two attendants arrived, and they carried the man back to his bed.

"Keep those tourniquets tight!" he instructed, and pulled out his stethoscope.

His hands bloodied, Matt listened for a heartbeat from the lifeless form. Hearing none, he moved the instrument to several other locations. A glass to the nostrils revealed no fogging. Another check with the stethoscope reaffirmed what he already knew. Antonio Randazzi had died from loss of blood.

After giving a few instructions to his staff, Matt rejoined his guests in the corridor.

"How is he?" Tom asked.

"He's gone," replied Matt, dejectedly. "Another suicide. He just couldn't face being sent back. What a waste."

"You did all you could, Matt," comforted Nicole.

"I know, but it doesn't make it any easier. These people come here with nothing but a dream. The damn steamship companies shouldn't let them come, but they care only about profits. So the burden of rejecting these people falls on us. They're physically unfit, and we can't let them enter. As a result, we shatter their dreams, destroy their hopes."

Tom reached out and touched Matt's shoulder. Nicole realized that his action was more than a token gesture. Tom was a sharp businessman, but he possessed a compassionate nature, enabling him to identify easily with the feelings of others. Although that talent served him well in his business dealings, its greater value lay in his personal interactions. His sincere expressions of empathy, whenever the occasion required, enhanced further his likeability to everyone, whether they were his employees, social acquaintances, or friends, among whom he now counted Matt.

"Matt," said Tom, "you said 'another suicide.' I take it there had been another?"

"Heh!" Matt laughed cynically. "Death is no stranger to Ellis Island. Over the years we've had more than two hundred deaths, including a few other suicides."

"Really?" said Tom in surprise.

"Yes. Most die from various sicknesses and diseases, but we've also had shootings, stabbings, hangings, jumpings, and drownings."

"I never realized the extent of it," Tom lamely replied.

"We have births here too. Pregnant immigrants are not that common, but each year there can be from five to twelve deliveries here. Nevertheless, deaths far outnumber births, and it is rare not to have bodies lying in our morgue."

"Matt!"

Matt looked at Nicole and then at James, whose mouth had actually dropped open. Instantly Matt regretted his words.

"I'm sorry," he apologized. "I wasn't thinking."

"It's all right, ma," said James. "I think it's neat."

"You do?" Nicole answered.

"Yeah, wait until I tell the guys!"

They all laughed. The tension disappeared. The Lindstroms then said their goodbyes and headed back to Manhattan, leaving Matt to return to his office, sign the death certificate, and look after the living still under his care.

August 1901

The usual seasonal increase in the number of immigrants seeking to make their fortune in "Golden America" continued. And, as usual, some of the staff continued to exploit immigrants.

"Move along, stupid! Don't take all day!" shouted one gateman to a disembarking alien as he stopped to stare at the building before him.

Often with curses, guards pushed the new arrivals into groups corresponding with their tag number on their clothing. At some point, the guards would herd each group of immigrants into the main building, where their fate would be decided.

In the baggage room, the theft of money and belongings had become so blatant that Commissioner Fitchie, at McSweeney's suggestion, requested New York City police officers to guard the stored belongings. Their presence ended that problem, but others persisted.

Unknown to the police, Fitchie, or McSweeney, unscrupulous bankers at the money exchange frequently cheated the immigrants out of much of their money. Bribe-seeking inspectors approached numerous immigrants, demanding payment in return for entry approval. McGaffney, meanwhile, remained busily engaged in selling citizen certificates to shipboard passengers who might otherwise fail their medical or legal inspections if processed regularly.

Despite a warning from Powderly to "keep his nose clean," John Mueller was still at it. Besides his certificate scam with McGaffney, he had found another con game, forcing immigrants into the barbershop where they had to pay for haircuts and shaves. The grateful concessionaire eagerly shared his heavily increased receipts with Mueller.

Meanwhile, Ed had given political patronage contracts to other concessionaires. As long as he got his kickback payments, he looked the other way at the many abuses. These included food stand employees wearing official-looking caps with gold-plated American eagles attached, who compelled immigrants to buy bags of food at inflated prices, as well as the forced labor in the kitchens and dining rooms, where immigrants worked without pay or for a trifle such as a bottle of beer.

Perhaps most notorious was the feeding of immigrants since, unknown to Washington officials, the food served was a far cry

An Ellis Island doctor examines an immigrant's eyes, early 1900s.

from the nutritious meals of past years served by the previous food concessionaires. A typical breakfast saw a long line of immigrants filing into the dining room as a man with filthy hands would fill their hats or handkerchiefs with moldy prunes. Another thrust two pieces of bread into their hands. Each day's breakfast was the same, duplicated again for dinner.

No one did anything about the situation. Matt was insulated from witnessing any wrongdoing. Fitchie cared little about day-to-day operations and was oblivious to it all. McSweeney chose not to act. Innocence, ignorance, isolation, ineptitude, and greed combined to allow the situation to continue unchecked.

On this summer day, thankfully less humid than the previous four days, as Matt was examining a line of immigrants, he heard piercing shrieks of women and children coming from the far end of the Registry Hall. More than one thousand immigrants in the various aisles waited to be processed, and the loud shrieking sparked a panic among them. Fortunately, the division of the floor space by the pipe railings into small enclosures to separate the different manifest groups prevented what could have easily become a stampede.

Before he got there, Mueller stopped him.

"You don't have to bother, Doctor," he said, "It was only a man who fainted. The man's wife and sisters started screaming, and that set off the others."

"How is he? Has he regained consciousness?"

"Yeah, he's all right. I brought him to."

Matt went to the man, now sitting in a chair, still pale with his clothes soaking wet. His left cheek was bruised and his eye was swollen with a puffed eyelid.

"Did he hit his face when he fell?" Matt asked."

"No, that's where the ice hit him."

"Ice hit him? What ice?"

"Look, I found him lying on the floor. Everyone was standing around like a bunch of fools, doing nothing. So I did something. I ran and got the water cooler and threw the cold water in his face, but I forgot about the chunk of ice that was in the cooler."

Matt shook his head and tended to the man. As he placed a piece of the same ice in a cloth to hold against the eye swelling, he was amused by the irony of using ice to tend to the bruise caused by the ice. His assistance completed, Matt returned to his station.

*   *   *

Later that day, Frank worked a few hours overtime, covering for an absent worker. As detainees approached his table, they handed him their meal cards on which he wrote their names. Next, he handed them back and instructed, "Go downstairs." It was a dull, repetitious task, but he could use the extra money, and it would soon be over.

Entering the dining room, the immigrants picked up dirty bowls and approached a helper who dropped a slice of rye bread

Ellis Island dining room, early 1900s

in it. Another ladled a dipper full of prunes over the bread, saying, "Here, now go and eat."

Even as poverty-stricken peasants in their homeland, these detainees seldom had to eat such revolting food before. Here, though, they had no choice, as the food concessionaire offered the cheapest food possible to maximize his profits.

Frank finished his task. On impulse he peeked in the dining hall. He had no motive other than curiosity. Looking in from the doorway, he saw a foul-mouthed Bowery tough, apparently supervising the distribution of the food. Frank was astonished to witness this man dancing on the tables, pouring torrents of obscene abuse on the immigrants.

One old man, a long-bearded Polish Jew whom Frank recognized, simply stopped when he received his bowl of prunes and began shaking his head.

"What the hell are ya waiting for, you goddamned old Jew?" the bully screamed.

When the old man didn't answer, the tough grabbed him by his beard and roughly pulled him past the barrel of prunes, forcing him onto a nearby bench. Then he got back up on the table to shout more invectives at the immigrants.

A German walked over to him to complain. The bully kicked him in the head with his boot, knocking him to the floor. No one said a word. Silently the hungry aliens ate their meager fare. Disgusted, Frank turned and left. *I'd better tell someone about this,* he thought. *Then again, maybe I should keep my mouth shut. I don't want that character to find out that I reported him.*

As he left the island that evening, Frank's conscience wrestled with his fear. He was the last of the day shift employees to depart, leaving behind on the island only the detainees, the night shift, and one other group: the water rats now venturing forth to scavenge among the refuse and filth in the kitchens and dining rooms.

September 1901

Summer had ended. Gone were the steamy, sweltering days and sultry, oppressive nights of August. Yet, even though the weather's heat had abated, another form of heat swirled around Ellis Island.

Just two weeks earlier, on August 20, a new scandal had broken. New York newspapers vied with one another to get more details about the latest case of island fraud. John Mueller's shipboard scam had been exposed, although he himself had not yet been named.

Reporters informed their readers that steerage passengers were landing directly from the steamships, completely bypassing Ellis Island. For an average price of two dollars apiece, split between immigrant boarding inspectors and ships' officers, immigrants—particularly those with physical or health problems—received fake American citizens' certificates, enabling them to land at the piers.

The *New York Times* reported that the practice had apparently gone on for years, with perhaps as many as ten thousand immigrants fraudulently landed. These charges, reminded the *New York Tribune,* were similar to those made last year. Editorial criticism of the island's administration appeared everywhere.

Fitchie directed McSweeney and Registry Division Chief Mueller to conduct an investigation. Mueller was working hard at damage control. McGaffney had been caught, and John was using a carrot-and-stick approach to ensure the man's silence. John was paying for McGaffney's legal counsel and promising to get his charges reduced if he kept silent, but John also renewed his threat to reveal incriminating evidence if he did not. John was certain he had convinced McGaffney that his silence brought a light punishment, but any attempt to incriminate him would result in a far harsher sentence.

*   *   *

Matt was enjoying a week's vacation in upstate New York. He, like thousands of others, had been attracted to the Pan American Exposition in Buffalo. Serving as commissioner-

President William McKinley addresses
an audience at the Pan American Exposition.

general of the exposition was Col. John B. Weber, Senner's predecessor at Ellis Island. He had earned his rank of colonel from his service in the Union army in the Civil War, when he commanded soldiers in the Eighty-Ninth Colored Infantry.

Today was Matt's second day at the exposition, and he was alone, enjoying the many sights and activities, visiting the specially constructed pavilions, and enjoying the foods and exhibits from North and South American countries. Bypassing the concerts and special performances for the time being, he visited the area set up for rides instead, thinking he might try a few just for fun.

Matt approached the Ferris wheel. Introduced to Americans in 1893 at the Columbian Exposition in Chicago, it was still quite a novelty and one of the big hits at this exposition, where many were seeing one for the first time. It was one of the marvels of the age, powered by an electric generator and offering the thrill of ascent and descent unlike any other human experience. Like many others, Matt had never been on a Ferris wheel, and he looked forward to the experience. Expecting a long line, he found exactly that. What he did not expect was Nicole and James.

Matt had seen Tom and Nicole at a few social events since their tour of the island in July, but this was the first time he had seen the five-year-old since then.

"Nicole, hello. I don't believe this!"

She was equally taken aback.

"Matt! What are you doing here?"

"Same as you, I guess. I wanted a ride on the Ferris wheel."

"But, I mean, here in Buffalo! There are thousands of people here! What are the chances of the two of us coming here, to this particular spot on the same day, at the same time?"

He shrugged, obviously happy at his good fortune. "Where's Tom?" he asked.

"Oh, darn it all. We no sooner got here than he was called back to New York because of some big problem with one of the shipments. He said we might as well stay here, so James and I could enjoy the sights."

"Well, I'm about to go on this wonderful Ferris wheel. Why don't the two of you join me? I'd enjoy the company, and you won't have to go to the end of this long line for tickets."

"Mother, please, can we?" pleaded the boy, looking up at this vaguely familiar man talking to his mother.

Hesitating for only a brief moment, Nicole replied, "Yes, that would be nice, Matt. Thank you. James, do you remember Dr. Stafford? You last saw him at Ellis Island. He's a good friend of Daddy's and mine."

"Oh, I remember. How do you do, Dr. Stafford," he said, offering his little hand to Matt.

Matt laughed and shook it.

"What a fine young gentleman. Hello, James. Now, let's get those tickets and have some fun."

Their ride was exhilarating, filled with laughs and squeals of delight. James sat between them, and when they were temporarily stopped at the top, Matt pointed out a few of the other sights.

When the ride ended, Matt was determined not to let this opportunity slip away.

"Nicole, let me take you and James to the other rides and events. Please? It'd mean a lot to me."

Nicole didn't hesitate this time. The thought of James's father sharing this pleasant time with them was decidedly appealing, and in this public arena, she felt it would be safe to be with Matt.

They had an active, exhausting afternoon together. Not a single ride escaped them, nor did any of the exhibits. Matt lavished lots of attention, treats, and prizes on James and won a small doll for Nicole. It was a pleasant, fun-filled time for all.

That evening, they ate dinner at the Canadian Pavilion, watched the illumination of the Electric Tower and evening fireworks, and afterward Matt escorted them back to their hotel.

After ten when they arrived, James had fallen asleep, and Matt carried him up to Nicole's suite. Lavishly furnished, it had two bedrooms adjoining a sitting room. Following Nicole's lead, Matt took the boy into his bedroom and laid him on the bed. He stood back and watched as Nicole undressed her son, put on his pajamas, and covered him up. She looked up then, smiled at Matt, and they went into the next room.

Matt turned and looked into her eyes. The sexual tension, slowly building between them, was now more intense. In that fleeting moment, thoughts and desires raced through them. Both were aware of their repressed passion, but neither dared speak of it.

Then Matt broke the silence.

"I'd better go, Nicole. Good night."

He placed his right hand on her left cheek. His opened lips pressed against hers in what Matt intended as a brief goodnight kiss.

She had longed for his kiss for almost two years, since that unforgettable New Year's Eve. She had tried to put him out of her mind, to forget how sensuous a man he was; he made her feel like no other man, not even Tom, ever did. God help her, right now she wanted him!

As Matt tried to pull away, she held fast to the back of his head. Returning and prolonging their kiss, she held him with closed eyes, and he wrapped his arms around her. They kissed and embraced for another moment, savoring the sensation.

Nicole's eyes fluttered open. She looked into his eyes and then took his hand and led him into her bedroom.

"Nicole, I don't think this—"

She silenced him with a kiss. Pushing the door shut, she kissed him passionately, her hands roaming all over his upper torso. Matt reciprocated her movements. Her impulsiveness conquered his last inhibitions. The fire inside them, smoldering for so long, could no longer be contained.

Matt's hands lovingly caressed her body as he showered her with kisses on her mouth and neck.

Nicole felt an erotic chill from his warm breath on her neck. She kissed him just below the ear, raising goose bumps on his neck. She wanted him so badly that she wanted to drive him past the point of no return. Matt rapidly went past that point.

Denied too long the combination of sexual pleasure and emotional involvement, she was at last alone with the one she loved, and she knew this was to be their time. Locked in each other's embrace, their desires mounted. She pressed herself tightly against his erection. Then she reached down, touching and caressing him.

Matt picked her up and carried her to the bed. He laid her down gently and removed his jacket and tie, tossing them onto a nearby chair, his eyes never leaving her. Nicole got up from the bed, went to Matt, and kissed him again. As she did, she slowly unbuttoned his shirt.

Her own dress, powder-blue cotton, had an ivory silk front bodice. She began undoing the hooks and eyes first of the front bodice and then of the underbodice. Seething with desire, Nicole enjoyed the sensuality of slowly undressing in front of him. She relished his eyes on her as she peeled away her garments.

Matt at first stood transfixed as Nicole revealed herself to him. Then he helped her remove her clothing and she unbuttoned his pants. They continued to undress each other, interrupted only by passionate kisses and embraces. Eventually, they were both naked.

Matt wrapped his muscular arms around Nicole, drawing her closer. Bringing her back to the bed, he sat beside her, and his soft, gentle tongue explored her mouth. First, his tongue moved against hers, and then their tongues danced with each other in sensuous encircling patterns. It was not long before they were lying together on the bed.

Nicole closed her eyes again to heighten her enjoyment of his touch. She marveled at how his delicate touches made her feel. She could sense her moistness between her legs and his effect on the rest of her body as well.

After caressing and fondling her breasts, he let his index finger slowly trace a path around each nipple. He gently ran his finger back and forth across the tip of one nipple and then the other, watching her pink nipples harden, making them even more inviting.

Tempted, he brought his mouth to one. She felt the warm wetness of his mouth's caress and the sensation of his tongue. She opened her eyes and moaned, unable to wait any longer. Moaning again, she reached for him. Matt gently pushed her back, all the while kissing her deeply. His hands drifted down to her stomach, rubbing in slow, circular motions. She writhed in ecstasy, her passion growing even more than she thought possible.

Slowly Matt moved his hands farther down, caressing the silky smoothness of her inner thighs. Then his fingers played with the curly pubic hair. He pressed his fingers into her crevice, touching her and bringing her intense pleasure.

She moaned again. She arched her back as the pressure within her unbelievably built up even more. He brought her from heavy breathing to full arousal to a climax, the most intense of her life, leaving her limp and breathless. When she came, she cried out in rapture, surprising herself. She had never been vocal in lovemaking with Tom.

"Matt," she panted, "come inside me, please," as her body still quivered.

Matt positioned himself above her and slowly thrust forward, delighting in the intoxicating physicality of his motion. Nicole gasped at the sensation. He felt so big, so good inside her.

Matt relished her snugness, wetness, and warmth. He couldn't believe he was in her, her naked breasts pressed against him, her face in ecstasy, her eyes closed and mouth open.

Nicole stroked his shoulders and moved her hands down his back to his backside and cupped his ass.

Following her lead, Matt placed his hands under her.

These actions intensified their sensations and the penetration. Slowly, Matt moved in and out as Nicole thrust her hips toward him. They moved as one, their tempo gradually increasing until, finally, they climaxed almost simultaneously.

He did not pull out immediately. They held each other closely. Then he used his left arm to raise his body weight off her and began lightly caressing her face and body again with his fingers. Nicole let her hands roam over his back. Soon, they embraced again and basked in the afterglow. With her breast pressed against his chest, each could feel the other's heart pounding. Neither wanted the moment to end.

They fell asleep that way, nestled in each other's arms. Just before daybreak, Nicole awakened first. Realizing James might come in the room at any moment, she wakened Matt. He got up and dressed. Kissing her goodbye, he arranged with Nicole to return after breakfast to take James and her back to the exposition. He left, filled with a satisfaction almost alien to him, already looking forward to his return.

Nicole second-guessed the wisdom of her actions, just as she had once done almost six years earlier when Matt had been a patient. This time she did not reproach herself. She was glad for their time together. Where it would all lead she didn't know. For now, here in Buffalo at least, they were together.

*   *   *

Matt returned later, and the three of them revisited the exposition to see the pavilions and exhibits they had missed the day before, and to revisit some of the rides, including the Ferris

Horticulture Building and Temple of Music
where crowd awaits entry, 1901

wheel. The next day was filled with an excursion to Niagara Falls. Both nights, after James had fallen asleep, Matt and Nicole made love.

On Friday they returned to the exposition. In early afternoon, they neared the Temple of Music, knowing that President McKinley would soon be inside at a reception to greet the public. They joined the line that had formed outside the building.

After a short wait, with a much longer line now forming behind them, they heard the cheers and applause from the crowd as the president's carriage drove up to the side entrance of the temple. Shortly thereafter, the doors at the southeast side opened. The public entered and proceeded along an eight-foot aisle formed by a line of soldiers from the Seventy-Third Sea Coast Artillery on either side, interspersed with neatly uniformed guards from the exposition police. They were more than an honor guard, as the president's secretary, George Cortelyou, was worried about McKinley's prolonged two-day appearance. Only last year, an anarchist had killed King Umberto of Italy and another had fired at Edward VII, Prince of Wales. Incredibly, last April an editorial in William Randolph Heart's *Journal*, which continually attacked McKinley as a "puppet" of wealthy industrialists, had asserted, "If bad institutions and bad men can be got rid of only by killing, then the killing must be done." Twice, Cortelyou had attempted to cancel this activity, only to have it reinstated by the president, who so enjoyed handshaking that he had become quite good at it, sometimes handling about forty-five people a minute, as with one swift jerk, he would turn the person to the right, let go, and ready himself for the next one, continuously smiling throughout.

As they awaited their turn, Matt and Nicole saw the president, flanked on either side by Cortelyou and John Milburn, president of the exposition. In front of these two men were Secret Service operatives George Foster and Sam Ireland, who formed a two-foot passageway to scrutinize all who approached.

McKinley, neatly dressed in pin-striped trousers and a dark frock coat, cheerfully greeted the well-wishers who came up to shake his hand, as the organist played a Bach sonata. Milburn acted as host, introducing Buffalo notables to the president as they appeared. About half the greeters were women and children. To every child the president altered his handshaking routine to bend over, warmly shake hands, and say a few kind words.

Their line moved along with little delay. Eventually, only about ten people were ahead of them, and they could see and hear the president's greetings. Matt observed the president and was impressed with his patrician persona. Healthy and fit at age fifty-eight, his gray hair, high forehead, strong chin, and handsome face gave him a distinguished look. He personified the statesman who—with prosperity at home, victory in the war with Spain, and the acquisition of Cuba, Puerto Rico, Guam, the Philippines, and Hawaii—basked in popularity.

Matt, Nicole, and James continued to move forward in line. They saw McKinley warmly greet John Parker, a huge black man. Behind him was a short, dark, heavy man with a thick mustache and piercing black eyes, who immediately raised the suspicions of the Secret Service agents. Agent Foster held his hand on the man until he reached the president and had clasped his hand. Agent Ireland, equally alert to the situation, had readied himself to pounce at the slightest indication of trouble, and when the man held back after shaking hands, he gently but firmly pushed him onward.

Next came a tall, boyish-looking man in his midtwenties. The agents noted that his right hand was wrapped in what appeared to be a bandage, and he carried it uplifted, supported by a sling under his jacket. They assumed that his hand was injured, particularly when he extended his left hand across his right to shake hands with the president. McKinley smiled, bowed, and genially extended his hand for a handshake. The man swiftly brushed aside McKinley's hand and whipped out his right hand that held a small .32 caliber Derringer revolver. Two shots, in rapid succession, rang out.

After the first shot, McKinley quivered and clutched his chest. With the second, he doubled slightly forward and then took a step backward, his face paling.

Foster and Ireland sprang into action, pouncing on top of the shooter. Ireland knocked away his weapon and the two agents were joined by soldiers and exposition police in crushing the assassin to the floor.

Seeing this, McKinley said weakly, "May God forgive him," then turned and, leaning heavily on Milburn and Cortelyou, walked into the passageway leading to the stage and sat down on a small wooden chair.

As this occurred, Foster dragged the shooter to his feet and grabbed him by the throat with his left hand. "You murderer!" he shouted. He punched him in the face so viciously that he was knocked through the guards behind him onto the floor, where soldiers kicked him repeatedly, until Captain Damer of the exposition police drew them back. Police hurried the prisoner out of the open area into a small room, quickly guarded by a detachment of US marines and police, before removing him to a more secure area.

Confusion reigned. A reporter would later state, "Men shouted, women screamed, and children cried." Those nearest the doors fled the building in fear of a stampede, while hundreds of curious onlookers outside struggled blindly forward to see what had happened.

Now in shock and color draining from his face, McKinley sank back in the chair. He made no sound while holding his abdomen with one hand, the other hand fumbling at his breast. He looked up into Milburn's face and called out, "Cortelyou!"

"Here, Mr. President," said the horrified secretary, coming into McKinley's field of vision.

"My wife, be careful, Cortelyou, how you tell her—oh, be careful."

"I will be careful, Mr. President," he said brokenly.

Matt struggled to reach the president.

"I'm a doctor. Let me help!" he cried, and the protective guards let him through.

As Matt reached the wounded man, McKinley, moved by a sharp pain, writhed to his left. Matt hurriedly opened the president's waistcoat and loosened his other garments. He saw a trickle of blood winding its way down the man's chest, spreading its crimson stain over his white linen shirt.

Tearing away McKinley's clothes, Matt looked more closely. He found one bullet wound just below McKinley's right nipple, from which the blood flowed. It seemed a superficial wound, with the ball from the pistol not deeply lodged, it apparently having glanced off a rib. The second wound was in the abdomen, about two inches left of the navel. Its depth and damage could only be determined by surgery. Matt did what he could to bandage the wound.

"We've got to get you to a hospital, Mr. President," said Matt, and McKinley nodded.

Pandemonium still reigned in the building as a force of exposition guards tried to clear the floor. The crush of the crowd was intense, with spectators from the galleries cramming the stairways and those on the floor surging to the dais. Finally, the guards succeeded in dispersing the crowd.

Within minutes, attendants carried McKinley outside to the exposition's electric-powered ambulance. This vehicle was a common public sight, as electric vehicles had been outselling gasoline cars by ten to one for several years, but its gravely injured patient caused the crowd to look on in alarm. The driver immediately turned the switch to power the motor, and the electric ambulance rolled silently forward on its sad and fateful journey to the exposition's emergency hospital, located on the west side of the grounds near the Elmwood Avenue gate.

Leaving the president's care to the medical team awaiting his arrival, Matt rejoined Nicole and James.

"How bad is it, Matt?"

"I'm afraid it's very serious," he answered. "If that shot to his abdomen perforated his stomach, its contents could ooze into his intestines, causing peritonitis. That sort of infection could be fatal."

"Could he survive, though?"

"Well, yes. There are cases of complete recovery after operations for perforated stomachs. The first four days are the critical ones. However, we don't know yet if that's what happened."

"You think it did, though?"

"Given the position of the wound, I'd have to say yes."

McKinley was rushed into the emergency hospital where

physicians Matthew D. Mann, Presley M. Rixey, Eugene Wasdin, and Herman Mynter were waiting. Exposition Medical Director Roswell Park was in Niagara Falls and would arrive later. McKinley remained conscious and alert for the doctors right up to the time of his anesthesia.

Unlike Dr. Park and Matt, who were trained in antiseptic medicine, the others were not. Although he was the chief surgeon during this one-hour operation, Dr. Mann was an obstetrician and gynecologist, with no experience treating gunshot wounds. None of the doctors bothered with disinfection, they did not wear gloves, and they used improperly sanitized probes.

Examining the abdominal wound, they found a small bullet wound in the front wall of the stomach, which they carefully closed with sutures. Carefully turning the stomach to avoid any of its contents spilling into the abdominal cavity, they found a jagged wound over an inch in diameter in the back wall of the stomach. Sewing up this wound in three layers, they next determined the bullet was lodged in the back muscles. Unable to retrieve the bullet from this direction, the surgeons closed the five-inch incision but without first draining the wound, opting to postpone retrieving the bullet until the president's condition improved.

Afterward, an ambulance took the president to the Buffalo home of Exposition President John Milburn for further treatment and recuperation. Isolated in the quiet location of a back bedroom on the second floor, McKinley remained cheerful in conversations with his wife, colleagues, doctors, and nurses.

Back at the hotel, Nicole asked Matt, "Do you think the president will be all right?"

"Well, darling, he's a strong man in almost perfect health. Barring any setback, he could be back to work in the White House in three to four weeks. We'll have to see what happens in the next four or five days."

That evening, after James had fallen asleep, Matt and Nicole lay together in bed, locked in an embrace. It was their last evening in Buffalo; in the morning they would be returning to their separate lives. This thought was in both their minds, a reality they had to face, although neither wanted it to intrude before their lovemaking. Now, afterward, words needed to be said. Nicole broke their silent reverie.

"Matt, we have to talk about us."

"I know."

"Where do we go from here? If I keep seeing you, sooner or later we'll be found out."

Placing her hand on the side of his face and looking into his eyes, she added, "I couldn't involve you in a scandal that would place your job in jeopardy. They'd never let you keep it, once the news was out."

"My job doesn't matter, Nicole. A doctor is always needed. I'd give up this job in an instant for you. Divorce Tom and we'll go somewhere else and start a life together."

"What about James?"

"I would love him and raise him as if he were my own son," answered Matt, unaware of the irony of his words.

His words, though, had a sobering effect on her. Reason regained control over her emotions.

"I know you would, Matt. What I meant was that a divorce would have a harmful effect on James. It would tear him away from Tom, and besides, Tom would never agree to a divorce. And even if he did, he would insist on being able to see the boy regularly. He would insist on my remaining in this area, which means you would also, which means your job options would be limited at best. I'm thinking of you and your career, Matt, but mostly I'm got to think about James."

Matt listened to her words, delivered with increased intensity. Determined, though, not to lose her again, he reassured her, "We'll go slowly. Let's just take it one day at a time and see where it takes us."

"It takes us to living a double life again as hypocrites, just like six years ago," she replied, more in sorrow than in cynicism.

"The only other choices are for us to return to things as they were before we came to Buffalo or else stop seeing each other entirely."

His kindhearted tone, helped by his continuing caresses, calmed her.

"I can't bear the thought of not seeing you again, or of not being with you again like this," she said, hugging him tightly. "Matt, you're so wonderful. What a mess this is," she said, burying her head in his shoulder.

Holding her in his arms, he squeezed gently, feeling the warmth of her naked body alongside his, before he spoke.

"We had this time together, darling. It was very special, more than I dreamed possible. We'll face our tomorrows as we must, and I promise you, we'll be careful."

"Matt, make love to me again. Who knows when our next time together will be?"

*　　*　　*

On Tuesday, September 10, they returned to New York City, clinging to their memories, hoping the future would be kind to them.

President McKinley had passed the danger point, his close friend and advisor, Sen. Mark Hanna, happily reported to the press. Bowel and kidney functions were normal, he said, but vital signs were still abnormal. The president's pulse was usually around 120, respiration at 27, and temperature at 101°. However, he was now eating spoonfuls of pure beef juice. Buoyed by McKinley's recovery and medical reports, his friends began leaving Buffalo.

Life went on, as did the processing at Ellis Island. Everyone's attention, though, was focused on the daily medical reports out of Buffalo. Throngs of New Yorkers hovered at Park Row to read the newspaper bulletin boards, while news vendors hawked their papers, shouting out the latest reports on McKinley's condition.

"The Shooter," as the papers called him, was Leon Czolgosz, a self-professed anarchist from Cleveland. He told police he had become convinced that the American government had to be destroyed, and the best way to accomplish this was by killing the president.

Wednesday, September 11, brought the gratifying news that no blood poisoning had occurred from the bullet still lodged in McKinley's back. He was now breathing normally, and his nourishment increased from one to three teaspoonfuls of the beef juice. He was becoming "more healthy," said his physician.

"The medical reports are very encouraging," McSweeney said to Matt as they dined together on the island.

"Yes, but I'm not convinced," Matt answered.

"Why not?"

"His pulse rate is still high. They must be giving him digitalis or something to bring it down. Why does it stay so high? I worry about his heart. Something's wrong."

*   *   *

McKinley's attending physicians were also worried about the abnormally high pulse. Following normal procedures, they had indeed tried digitalis, but with no effect. Yet, McKinley's good spirits and otherwise good health, combined with his steadily improving appetite and bodily functions, made them optimistic.

On Thursday, McKinley had his first solid food, a breakfast of chicken broth, toast, and coffee. He felt so well after this that he asked for a cigar.

In early afternoon, he began complaining of fatigue. Because he had been buoyant and cheerful previously, his doctors were troubled. His pulse rate at 126 was about fifty beats higher than normal.

His condition steadily worsened. By evening, he was showing signs of intestinal toxemia. The danger of heart failure increased. Doctors gave him oil and calomel to clean out his bowels. Around midnight, he had two bowel movements, giving hope to his concerned physicians.

However, Friday the thirteenth brought misfortune to the Milburn residence and the nation. Shortly after two o'clock, the physicians and nurses detected a weakening of the heart, as McKinley's pulse fluttered and weakened. Doctors immediately administered more digitalis. At nine thirty in the morning, Dr. Mynter gave a hypodermic injection of strychnine.

McKinley opened his eyes and feebly asked, "What is that, Doctor?"

"A heart stimulant," Mynter replied.

"Is the necessity great?" McKinley asked.

"Yes, Mr. President," answered Mynter, "you are a brave and very sick man."

"I realize it," the president said, both resignedly and cheerfully.

Although weak, McKinley remained conscious. A half hour later when nurses sought to readjust his pillows to shut out the light of the window, he protested, "No, I want to see the trees," he murmured. "They are so beautiful."

McKinley's brother Abner, Senator Hanna, and cabinet members quickly made their way to the Milburn residence, most arriving by midmorning. As McKinley's condition deteriorated, doctors administered a saline injection and then gave him oxygen. By six o'clock, it was clear to those at his bedside that the president was dying.

McKinley slipped in and out of consciousness. When conscious, his mind was alert, and he shared poignant moments with various members of his cabinet, whose faces were strained and tearstained. They knew this was their last visit with their chief executive.

At 7:45 pm, McKinley awakened and asked for his wife. She came to him, and everyone left the room except for one of the nurses. For ten minutes, husband and wife spent precious time together.

When she left, McKinley murmured words from the hymn, "Nearer, my God, to Thee." Then he looked at his doctors and nurses, smiled, and said, "Goodbye, all, goodbye. It is God's way. His will be done, not ours."

Minutes later, he lapsed into a coma. For an hour, his wife sat at her husband's bedside, holding his hand. At midnight, she retired to her own bed.

Dr. Rixey, their family physician, maintained his vigil. About two o'clock Saturday morning, he saw death was imminent and summoned the family, except for Mrs. McKinley, whose own frail health was a concern.

As they gathered about the bed, Dr. Rixey bent forward and listened, as the president's fluttering heart stopped. A moment more he listened, and he then straightened up, saying in a choked voice, "The president is dead."

When the papers carried all the details, Matt read them intently. An autopsy revealed that President McKinley had died of gangrene poisoning, not peritonitis. The body had not been able to repair itself. Dead tissue throughout the bullet track—in his stomach, kidney, and pancreas—had gradually rotted.

Surgical or medical treatment could not have saved him, his doctors concluded. The entire track of the bullet was contaminated, leading to unsubstantiated speculation in the press of a poison bullet. Matt dismissed this theory as absurd.

December 1901

Christmas was approaching, and holiday shoppers crowded the sidewalks and stores, seeking gifts for loved ones. The city streets, more congested than ever, were jammed with horse-drawn carriages, motorized cars, teamsters' wagons, and peddlers' carts. Newspaper boys and vendors hawked their wares to the passing throng, their sounds periodically joined by the sounds of the traffic patrolmen's whistles and of tooting car horns.

Away from the din of the bustling crowd, one shopper had taken refuge. After an hour's shopping in which she rapidly bought a half-dozen items, Nicole, as planned, went to Matt's place. With a cover story of a day's shopping trip and lunch with a friend, she would be able to spend about five hours with him without any problems ensuing. She still disliked this duplicity, but her desire to be with Matt overcame whatever reluctance she experienced.

When Tom was in New York, as he was now, she and Matt could only manage to see each other about once every two weeks. In mid-October, however, his trip to Rotterdam to oversee his company's move to a larger office gave them four weeks of frequent times together. Even then, she had to be careful lest she arouse her housekeeper's suspicions. Under the guise of an evening social, luncheon, visit, or charitable work, she arranged to be with Matt secretly at his place, for they dared not risk being seen together in public.

Today, their pattern was the same as before. Almost immediately, they made love, consuming more than a third of their time together. Now sitting up in bed, still naked, they sipped their champagne and ate the sandwiches Matt had prepared earlier. This was when they talked about happenings in each other's lives or other matters of interest, before returning to another round of lovemaking, the second time usually gentler, sometimes sweeter, than the exquisite intensity of the first.

One topic never discussed, by unspoken mutual consent, was their future. In Matt's house, especially in his bedroom, they shared a fantasy world, and neither wanted to say anything to undo the magic of these special times together. By compartmentalizing this part of their lives as separate and distinct from the rest, they heightened even more the pleasures their companionship generated.

They talked, of course, about the outside world, including Nicole's husband and child, but their conversation assumed an objective quality that minimized any negative thoughts about their own future. Whenever such thoughts crept in their minds or the conversation seemed to veer into a negative direction, the affected person would stop it with an intimate touch of the other, thus silencing thought or words with the renewal of physical pleasures.

And so, as they talked this time after eating, Nicole told him, "Tom's planning another New Year's party and plans to invite you."

"Do you think I should be there?"

"Why wouldn't you be? You've been there the last two times."

Unwilling to tell her he felt uneasy about facing the man

whose friendship he was betraying because that would only remind Nicole of her own betrayal, he instead said another truth, "It's different between us now than before. I want to know if you'll be comfortable if I'm there."

Looking at him, her heart and mind battling for dominance, she said, "I want you there. We can handle it. I'd miss you if you weren't there. Besides, Tom would be hurt if you didn't come."

"Speaking of that—"

"Oh, you," she laughed, as they lay down and resumed their lovemaking.

March 1902

Ed walked into the Oval Office to keep his appointment with the president, who had requested the meeting. This would be the first time they would speak directly to one another since Roosevelt had been thrust into the presidency six months earlier.

McSweeney was eager for the meeting. Rumors in political circles and in the newspapers about a thorough housecleaning at Ellis Island were rampant. Roosevelt had always been a strong supporter, and Ed had no reason to believe the president felt differently now. After all, Roosevelt had pledged his complete support, reiterated that support in writing, and had actively been his defender while vice president. Moreover, Ed had powerful allies in political circles in New York, Connecticut, and Massachusetts, as well as among the steamship companies and missionary societies. Protected by civil service, Ed knew the politicians could not remove him from office.

He had reviewed the possible reasons for this meeting. It was no secret the inefficient Fitchie would be replaced next month when his term expired. It could well be, Ed thought, that Roosevelt would ask him to succeed Fitchie as Commissioner for the Port of New York, thereby giving him the position he already fulfilled in all but name.

Another possibility was that the president would offer him a better post in the federal government. He was receptive to this option, since it would be a good career move and take him out of the line of fire from the island's critics.

So, with hopeful anticipation as he was announced, Ed approached the president, who rose from his desk as McSweeney entered the room.

"It's good to see you again, Ed," greeted the president, smiling and vigorously shaking hands.

"Thank you, Mr. President," Ed replied, savoring the warmth of the moment. "May I again offer my congratulations, this time directly, on your becoming president, although it was under such tragic circumstances."

"Yes, thank you," Roosevelt responded, the smile gone now and his face grim. "That was a great loss to our country. McKinley was a good man."

"Indeed he was, sir."

"How is everything in New York?" Roosevelt asked suddenly. "How is your family?"

"Thankfully, all of my family are well, sir. Things are also going better on the island. I think we've succeeded in removing all the personnel involved in that fraudulent landing scheme."

"Ah, yes. I asked you here to talk about Ellis Island."

"Oh? Well, I can assure you, Mr. President, that I have again stepped into the leadership vacuum to correct the situation."

"Ed, the newspapers say the problems of corruption still exist."

"Mr. President, the papers are always attacking us. It helps sell papers. Now, I don't claim the place is free of all scoundrels, but we are making a conscientious effort to root them out."

"I just don't understand why you haven't rooted them out before this."

Ed became defensive. He didn't like the drift of this conversation.

"Mr. President, when you were Police Commissioner of New York City, you didn't know about the policemen taking graft or the abuses in the police station lodging rooms until Jacob Riis brought them to your attention."

"No, I didn't, but when I did, I acted swiftly. I kicked those rascals off the force and shut down the lodging rooms."

"Yes, sir, but you have to admit that didn't end police corruption entirely. All I can say is that we are doing all we can."

"You have a point, Ed. Nevertheless, the Ellis Island administration has been badly compromised by this steady stream of scandals. I can't shut my eyes to it. Everyone I speak to is of one mind on this subject. I must make a complete change of leadership to restore public confidence. As the saying goes, 'A new broom sweeps clean.'"

"What are you saying, Mr. President?" asked McSweeney, now alarmed.

Roosevelt felt uncomfortable, but maintained his resolve, and said with obvious reluctance, "Ed, I am asking for your resignation."

"Resignation?" Ed could not believe his ears.

"Yes, Ed. I think it is for the best."

"Mr. President, I'm shocked! When once I wanted to resign, you were the one who convinced me not to. You said I was needed there, and you pledged your word to support me. Now you say this?"

"Ed, be reasonable," Roosevelt pleaded, clearly not relishing his task. "Things are different now. Too many new scandals have broken out. If I am to restore public confidence, I must make a complete leadership change."

"Mr. President, this is unfair!" Ed indignantly replied. "When I wanted to leave and be rid of the constant character assassinations, you said you would protect me. Now you intend to make me a public victim of those very slanders? I never thought you would break your word."

"Goddamn it, Ed!" Roosevelt roared. "I've got to do this! You are not being singled out. I'm replacing Powderly too, even though most of my advisers have advised me not to."

"Powderly's position is an appointed one, mine is not," Ed answered. "You can't remove me."

"That's why I'm asking for your resignation, Ed. It becomes your action, not mine. You wanted to resign before, as you said. Well, now I'm asking you to do that."

"The difference is that before I would have left on my own terms. This is a forced resignation."

"Call it what you want, Ed, but I want your resignation," Roosevelt said, grim-faced. "If you resign now, you don't leave under a cloud of accusations or singled out for further newspaper attack. You leave with the others and enable your president to install an entirely new team. That's what I want."

"What about a position here in Washington?"

"No. For many reasons, that is not possible."

"Very well, Mr. President," Ed replied stiffly. "You shall have my resignation in the morning. I regret our old friendship has brought us to this moment."

"So do I, Ed, so do I. I believe it is best for everyone. Take my word for it. You will be a happier man when you are away from public criticism. You have many powerful friends and will easily find a better-paying and less-frustrating position."

I took your word once before, you bastard, thought Ed. He realized, though, that Roosevelt was right. Ed knew he would land on his feet.

The two men stiffly shook hands for the last time, each knowing they would never speak to one another again.

*   *   *

Like the train that brought Ed to Washington, another

headed south from New York. Among that train's passengers, one man sat alone, deeply absorbed in thought. Staring vacantly out the window, he half consciously placed his right hand to his white, starched collar, feeling its rounded ends held neatly in place by a gold collar pin under the knot of his tie. Assured it felt right, he lowered his hand.

William Williams was a thirty-nine-year-old, highly respected Wall Street lawyer whose fine clothes marked him as a man of means. His ruggedly handsome face—together with his short, dark hair and fashionable brush mustache—enhanced the image. Slightly short, his fine muscular build correctly suggested a man of athletic ability, which he had put to good use in the recent Spanish-American War, by achieving a commendable record with New York's Squadron A.

Williams had received a surprise summons from the White House. Although he had served as junior counsel for the government during the recent Bering Sea arbitration, he had never met Roosevelt, even though they were both New Yorkers. Satisfied with his law practice, Williams had not angled for any job, nor had he been politically active to earn any patronage rewards. Therefore, the summons was puzzling.

Unknown to him, however, several influential Republican leaders, including Nicholas Murray Butler, acting president of Columbia University, had highly recommended him to be the new Commissioner of Immigration for the Port of New York. They convinced Roosevelt that Williams possessed the administrative skills, integrity, and toughness to deal with the Ellis Island problems.

No sooner had they been introduced than Roosevelt, in his characteristic manner, came directly to the point.

"I've asked you here, Mr. Williams, because I want you to take charge of Ellis Island as my commissioner."

Williams was stunned. He knew, of course, about the scandals. For months now, ever since the news broke that

Roosevelt was replacing Commissioner-General Terence Powderly with another labor union leader, Frank Sargent, the newspapers had been speculating about Roosevelt's search for a successor to Thomas Fitchie. Williams, though, had had no inkling whatsoever that he was even being considered.

"I am honored, sir," he said, after brief pause, "but I have absolutely no experience with immigration."

"You have exactly what I want in a man for that post: competence, determination, and integrity," the president responded in a strong voice.

"Thank you, sir. I'm flattered, but I'm not the man for the job."

"I think you are," Roosevelt replied decisively. "Good heavens, man! I have not chosen you on a whim! You are exactly the kind of man I want there!"

"You're very kind, sir. I—I just don't know."

"You should take the job, Mr. Williams. I assure you, it is the most interesting assignment I could offer you. You know, almost a million immigrants a year are now passing through Ellis Island, and they are being improperly inspected, robbed, and abused."

"Yes, I've read the newspaper accounts," Williams said, still uncertain about the offer.

"It's worse than you think. Much needs to be done, and it won't be easy. This position will be a difficult one. You won't know your friends from your enemies. It would be one of your greatest challenges. You are the very man to take on those scoundrels and rid the island of them."

"Well—"

"Look, don't give me your answer now. Consider it for a few days and then let me know. I know you'll make the right decision."

What is the right decision? he wondered on the train ride back home. His private law practice was lucrative, and he was reluctant to give it up for a position of lesser income and one filled with headaches and controversies. Still, Roosevelt had piqued his interest by presenting the post as challenging.

Once home in his posh bachelor quarters at the upper-crust University Club in New York, Williams studied the immigration laws and learned all he could about Ellis Island. Over lunch at the club, he acquired knowledge about the commissioner's role from a primary source.

"I tink now you know all dot I could tell you," Joseph Senner said, at the end of their lunch as the two men enjoyed their coffee and cigars.

"I'm grateful for all you've told me," Williams replied.

"De most important piece of advice I could give you, Mr. Villiams, is to get out of your office every day und vatch everyting. It is de only vay you vill take back de island from dose crooks. Too many staff are corrupt."

"I think you are right, Dr. Senner."

"Another ting. As bad as it might be in many departments, I can guarantee you dot it vill be *wunderbar* in de medical section. Dey are good people dere."

"That's good to know, but the health service is to be independent of the immigration service from now on."

"Really? Dot is interesting. So vill you take de job?"

"I believe I shall. It's a challenge I want to try."

"Gudt!" exclaimed Joseph, his blue eyes twinkling behind his spectacles. "You und Roosevelt are not of my politics, but I tink he made vise choice in you."

"Well, thank you," said Williams with a laugh.

"I leave you mit dis advice you did not ask me to give: you vill be de number vun guardian of dose immigrants. Be tough, be fair, und never forget dere humanity."

"Sounds like good advice, Dr. Senner. I'll remember it."

April 1902

A death in the family forced McSweeney to leave before his resignation took effect. Concerned that his successor, Joe Murray, would probably occupy his office before he could return, Ed instructed two employees to clean out his office. He told them to box up his belongings and put them in one of the record vaults in the building, where he would sort them out when he returned.

While Ed attended to personal affairs, several powerful friends pressured Roosevelt to keep McSweeney in his position. Charlie Burke, the president's assistant, detected his superior's annoyance and decided to discredit McSweeney. Learning about McSweeney's stored boxes, he instructed the Secret Service to confiscate them and examine their contents.

Agents went to Ellis Island and seized the boxes. They found mostly books, pamphlets, and letters from family members and personal friends. The agents read them all and made copies of parts of a few but found nothing incriminating.

Frustrated, Burke asked the agent in charge reporting to him, "What else was there? There must be something else!"

"Not really, Mr. Burke," the agent replied, "except for two

medical certificates that must have been put in the boxes by mistake."

"Medical certificates?" said Burke, intrigued. "What do you mean, medical certificates?"

"They're not McSweeney's. They're part of the island records. They're of no value to McSweeney. That's why we think they were in his boxes by mistake."

"Mistake or not, they'll do nicely."

"I don't understand, sir."

"You don't have to, Mr. Ross," Burke replied, dismissing the man.

Burke believed he now had an expedient means to discredit McSweeney and undermine his support. Citing an old federal statute making it a punishable offense to sequester a public document, Burke leaked the story to the press. Papers across the country announced that an investigation revealed that Assistant Commissioner Edward McSweeney had secreted public documents, presumably in an effort to cover up official misconduct and would be prosecuted.

Trying to capitalize on the barrage of publicity about McSweeney and the "stolen papers," Burke telephoned Commissioner John Shields of the US Circuit Court for the Southern District of New York.

Shields, sixty-two years old, had been in government service for decades. A dutiful public servant, he enjoyed a well-earned reputation for fairness and integrity. A longtime survivor of Washington's political intrigues, he understood clearly the power that Charlie Burke wielded.

"I want you to hold McSweeney for the federal grand jury in order to secure an indictment," Burke instructed Shields after a brief exchange of perfunctory pleasantries.

"We really don't have any legal cause to move for an indictment."

"Goddamn it, Shields, you have those certificates. They're public records. You know the statute."

"It's a weak case at best, Mr. Burke. I can't in good conscience move for an indictment."

"Look, Shields," Burke answered angrily. "Either you move to indict McSweeney or you no longer have your job. Is that what you want? Do you really want to lose your pension?"

"Mr. Burke, that isn't right! I have always done my job and done it well."

"Then do it well this time, as I tell you, or you won't be doing it any longer," Burke snarled. "I want to hear from you within the week, and I had better like what I hear."

*   *   *

On April twenty-eighth, newly approved by the US Senate as commissioner, William Williams arrived for the first time on Ellis Island. Approaching the main building, he was greeted by an overly friendly staff member determined to get into the new man's good graces.

"Welcome to Ellis Island, Commissioner. I'm John Mueller, chief of the Registry Division."

"Thank you, Mr. Mueller," Williams replied, shaking hands. "It's nice to meet you."

"If I can be of service or answer any questions as you get yourself oriented, please call on me at any time," John offered with a big smile on his face, trying to exude as much warmth as he possibly could.

Appreciative of the warm welcome, Williams replied, "That's very kind of you, Mr. Mueller. I may take you up on your offer, for it will take me awhile to get on top of things here."

"Anytime, sir," said Mueller, still smiling. "Just let me know."

Williams went to his office and spent a few hours looking at correspondence, reports, and information about the passengers scheduled to be processed that day. Then he pulled out a letter from Herbert Parsons, leader of the New York Republican reform faction, one group that had been influential in recommending his appointment. He reread one particular paragraph:

> *The food concessionaire is a front for Charles Hess. He is the former Republican leader of the Twenty-Fifth Assembly District and one of the most unmitigated scoundrels in this city. It is our fervent wish that you will root out the abuses by his people and sever Hess's contract.*

A new group of immigrants was due to arrive at the island momentarily. Williams went outside to watch unobtrusively how they were treated, work his way through the various processing stations, and then go to the main dining room.

He saw the immigrants rudely greeted and hustled into the building. Inside, walking past each of the processing stations, Williams witnessed several other instances of roughshod treatment, and he overheard some coarse remarks from a railroad employee to an immigrant. Angered by all he had seen and heard, Williams turned and left. The dining room would be his last stop before he returned to his office to issue a directive about proper staff behavior. As he passed the Discharging Division, Williams heard a belligerent shout, "Hurry up, stupid!"

He looked over and saw an employee berating two immigrants. They had not moved quickly enough to suit him.

"Didn't you hear me, you moron?" the employee continued. "We haven't all day! Let's move! Now!" he shouted.

The two uncomprehending Armenians silently moved along.

Williams had had enough. He walked over to the man.

"What is your name?"

"Who are you?" he countered.

"I'm Commissioner Williams. What is your name?"

"Sparkling, sir. Nathaniel Sparkling."

"Well, Mr. Sparkling, I find your behavior intolerable. You are never again to address any immigrant in such a rough and unkind manner."

"I'm sorry, sir."

"You have been warned, Mr. Sparkling. I am placing a reprimand in your file. If you behave like this again, you will face a two-week suspension without pay. Do I make myself clear?"

"Yes, sir."

"Then return to your duties in a proper fashion."

Sparkling returned to his post and Williams went on to the main dining room. Nothing he had heard or witnessed so far prepared him sufficiently for what he saw next. The greasy floor was covered with days-old bones and food remnants. He saw immigrants handed dirty bowls to use for their meal and many forced to eat without any utensils.

Williams had seen enough. He tracked down the concessionaire.

"How do you do, Commissioner?" said Rodger Yates, after learning he was facing the new commissioner.

"Seeing the disgusting conditions you permit here, Mr. Yates, I do not do well at all! Nor do these poor wretches forced to eat in this filthy place!"

"Sir, let me explain—"

"Mr. Yates," Williams interrupted, "I have no interest in your explanations. I am only interested in results, and I am warning you now, that if you do not immediately clean up this place and keep it that way, I will not renew your contract when it expires in June. Do I make myself clear?"

"Yes, sir."

"Very well. Good day, sir."

Williams left the main building and went to the hospital

for an unannounced visit. He looked in on several of the wards before George Stoner got word of his presence and caught up with him.

"Commissioner Williams? I'm George Stoner, the chief medical officer."

"Ah, yes, Dr. Stoner," Williams answered, shaking the extended hand. "Dr. Senner has told me some nice things about you and your people."

"That's good to hear. May I show you around the rest of the hospital?"

"Yes, fine. I'm just gathering some first impressions today."

"Of course," answered Stoner as he led him next into the operating room.

Sitting at his desk back in his office, Williams drafted a notice to be posted in all buildings and rooms throughout the island. Mandating that all immigrants be treated with kindness and consideration, he also stated:

> *Swindling immigrants is contemptible business, and whoever does this, under whatever form, should be despised. It is the duty of all government officials to go out of their way to protect immigrants against every kind of imposition. Let everyone at Ellis Island clearly understand that all impositions, whenever detected, will be punished as severely as the law permits.*

*   *   *

Two days later Commissioner Shields telephoned Charlie Burke in the White House. He had agonized over the case all that time, weighing Burke's threat and desire for McSweeney's hide against his legal principles.

311

"What have you got to tell me, Shields?" Burke asked with an air of confidence.

"Mr. Burke, I am an old man preparing to meet my God, and I will not do this immoral deed."

"Shields, have you lost your mind? I'll get rid of you and put someone in your place who will indict McSweeney. What kind of fool are you, to lose your pension like this?"

"Fire me, if you will, Mr. Burke. My conscience is clear, but I promise you this: if you fire me, I will go to the newspapers and tell them the truth about what you wanted me to do. You cannot defend your actions, and the president and public will quickly realize which of us is the one with honor."

Burke slammed down the receiver. His bluff had been called, for he knew he could not pull off Shields's ouster. He would have to find another way to get McSweeney, because he had said he would do so, and Burke always kept his word.

May 1902

It was only his fourth day on the job, but Commissioner Williams, determined to end the abuses at Ellis Island, had zeroed in on his first target.

"You wanted to see me, sir?" asked John Mueller, opening the office door and looking in.

"Yes, Mr. Mueller. Please, come in and sit down."

John obeyed, scrutinizing his new boss who was looking down at some papers on his desk. John was curious as to why he had been summoned and assumed that Williams was taking him up on his earlier offer of assistance.

"Mr. Mueller," Williams began, "I have been studying the manifest sheets of recent months, and I find a rather disturbing pattern."

"Sir?"

"I found several manifest sheets incompletely filled out. Others are improperly prepared, and in several instances the steamship companies did not even give us manifest sheets for their cabin passengers. Are you aware of this?"

Mueller was fully aware of the situation and was its chief beneficiary. The manifest sheets were sent to his office to be used by his inspectors to ask screening questions for landing approval. The improper or missing sheets helped him to fill his pockets and cover his tracks. So he recognized the danger of the question. If he answered no, Williams could accuse him of incompetence by not controlling the functions of his office. If he answered yes, then Williams could question his integrity in overlooking these obvious infractions. That he had taken bribes to ignore the incomplete or missing manifest sheets was obviously not something he wanted revealed.

Thinking fast, he quickly responded. "Yes, of course, I'm familiar with the problem, Mr. Williams. It has long been a sore point with me. Those improper sheets make our job much harder."

"Why didn't you complain about it then?"

"Oh, but I did, sir. I complained several times to Mr. McSweeney about the problem, but he never did anything about it. If you ask me, he had an improper relationship with the steamship companies. As you know, there was quite a scandal about him."

"Yes, I know," replied Williams. "Tell me, did you make your complaints in writing?"

"Yes, sir. Not once, but twice."

"Really? I found nothing from you about this in the files."

"I'm not surprised, Commissioner. It was not the sort of thing Mr. McSweeney would want anyone to find. I'm sure he destroyed my memos. Maybe now with you in charge, we can put an end to this problem."

"Be assured of that, Mr. Mueller," said Williams emphatically. "As of now, this slipshod business ends. I will immediately send out letters informing the shipping companies that the law imposes heavy fines for failure to provide the required manifest information, and that I intend to slap them with a fine each and every time a manifest is carelessly prepared or missing."

"Good for you, Commissioner!" John said with a burst

of energy. "We've needed someone with gumption in charge here."

"Thank you, Mr. Mueller," said Williams, clearly flattered. "I intend to reform this island, and I hope to have your cooperation in that mission."

"You can count on me, Mr. Williams. I have put in many years with the Immigration Bureau, and I am sick about the corruption here. It will be a pleasure to work with you to improve our operation."

Later, John considered his options. If Williams was hell-bent on cleaning out scoundrels, then he better lay low for awhile. Eventually, the man would settle into a routine, and then John could resume his activities. Right now, Williams wanted to make waves to show he was accomplishing something. *So,* John thought, *the best thing to do would be to get on Williams's good side by exposing a few staff members. That way Williams could feel he was making progress, get a little publicity for it, and learn to rely on good old John Mueller, his trusted registry chief.*

*   *   *

When Mueller left, the commissioner returned to the letter he was writing to Thomas Platt. The senator from New York was one of the Republican Party's top leaders, and he had written to Williams, urging a promotion for a gateman to the rank of inspector. Platt was a powerful man, but Williams was intent on keeping Ellis Island independent of all political pressures.

He resumed writing " ... not fitted either by temperament or training." He reread the letter, then added another sentence. "This man's promotion would be detrimental to the best interests of the service to which I must at all times give precedence over any outside suggestions."

With a determined smile, Williams signed the letter.

A few days later, Mueller overheard a German immigrant complaining. He had attempted to purchase some food for his journey from the island, only to have the vendor refuse his money as counterfeit. What irked the immigrant was that the coin he used was his change from sending a telegram to his relatives waiting for him in Indiana.

John seized the moment. Speaking in German, he said to the man, "Come with me, sir. I shall take care of this for you."

He took the man to Williams to recount the story, and then he added, "That young man in the telegraph office has done this before, Mr. Williams. He's one of the ones you've wanted to find out."

Williams, fuming, thanked John and reimbursed the man out of his own pocket. Shortly after the two men left, he summoned the telegraph clerk to his office and confronted him with the complaint.

"I didn't mean any harm, sir," the young man said sheepishly.

"No harm? You cheated that man. This coin is so obviously phony that it could not have escaped your attention."

"I'm sorry, sir. It will never happen again."

"That's truer than you know. I will not tolerate dishonesty and exploitation on this island! Did you think my posted notices were a joke?" he shouted. "You, sir, are going to jail, for I am pressing charges against you. The police are outside my office waiting to take you away. Now get out of my sight!"

A week later, Williams learned from a payroll clerk that one of the registry clerks, a protected civil service worker, had missed four days while on a drunken binge. He seized upon this situation as another means to restore discipline on the island and make an example of the man. Williams pressed charges against the employee, seeking revocation of his civil service status.

Mueller was upset over the charges. This man was one of his key players in many of the scams. Not only would John lose a valuable ally, but Williams's charges would, if allowed to stand, show others that Mueller's position could no longer protect them. John had to squelch this.

"Commissioner," he argued, "the man is a Civil War veteran. He should get special consideration for such a minor infraction."

"No infraction is minor!" thundered Williams, revealing a hot temper easily unleashed when confronted by challenges to his decisions. "Furthermore, this man merits no special consideration. His veteran status only entitled him to special preference in getting a government job, not to special privileges thereafter. He and everyone else who works here will be reliable and responsible workers, or they will find themselves without jobs. Do you understand, Mr. Mueller?"

"Yes, sir," John answered, realizing the futility of further comment.

"One more thing," Williams said as John turned to leave the office. "If you want to remain chief of the Registry Division, you will stop making excuses for the staff and get tougher on any shirkers or rude employees."

"Sir, that's not fair. You know I have brought dishonest personnel to your attention. I thought with this man being a veteran and it not being a case of dishonesty, that this was a special case."

"All right this time, Mr. Mueller. I have heard you and accept your explanation. Now you have heard me, and I trust you will accept my words."

"Yes, sir, I do, indeed."

"Then good day, Mr. Mueller," said Williams, returning to his paperwork.

*　　　*　　　*

As John left the commissioner's office, silently cursing his boss, George Stoner faced his own staff absenteeism from alcohol. Adam Harper, one of the line physicians examining immigrants in the main building, was out again today. Stoner had recently learned that Harper was an alcoholic, and today's absence, preceded by many others, was the final straw. He notified the Public Health Service that the man was hereby terminated, and he wanted a replacement.

Meanwhile, the shortage of doctors and large numbers to be processed meant that Matt would work the line today. Unlike the older doctors who considered working the line a hardship, he really didn't mind. It reminded him of his first years at Ellis Island and the joys he had meeting the many different kinds of people.

About midway through his first group of examinees, Matt inspected a woman who appeared healthy. However, she had a queer look on her face that seemed so unusual that he decided not to clear her. Instead, he turned her aside and had Guenter seat her in a nearby area for temporary detainees. Matt suspected the woman had some sort of mental problem, and he wanted to give her a more thorough check after he finished with this remaining group of immigrants.

The woman, who spoke fluent English, immediately returned to Matt.

"Why did you stop me?" she demanded. "Why can't I go through?"

Matt, in the midst of examining another woman, responded calmly, "Ma'am, I can't speak to you right now. Please go sit down, and I will speak to you later."

Clearly annoyed, the woman returned to her seat. Ten minutes passed, and she got up again, walking over to Matt who was examining still another immigrant.

"This is ridiculous!" she exclaimed. "Why must I wait? Why are you detaining me? There's nothing wrong with me!"

"I am busy right now, ma'am," Matt snapped, not looking at her. "Go back and sit down! We will discuss this later."

With his back to the woman, Matt resumed his examination of the immigrant at his station.

The woman, unsatisfied, tapped his shoulder and said, "I am prepared to meet the charges now."

Something in her voice alerted Matt, causing him to turn around slowly. As he did, he saw that she held a .38 caliber revolver in her right hand. The trigger was cocked and pointing at his stomach.

With flashes of McKinley's assassination running through his mind, Matt tried to keep his composure. In a soothing tone, he said, "Nothing would give me greater pleasure, ma'am. I'll suspend my work here, so we can talk the matter over together. Let's sit over there, shall we?"

The woman nodded her head and, pointing the revolver into Matt's side, began walking with him to a nearby bench. Guenter saw the problem and took a few steps toward them, but Matt shook him off. Guenter told another gateman, and the two of them stood nearby, watching intently, ready to act when needed. Matt and the woman sat on the bench; all the while, she kept the revolver fixed on Matt's midsection.

"Now I want you to tell me why you have stopped me," she demanded.

"When I looked at you, I could see that you were very troubled," Matt said gently.

"What business is that of yours?"

"I'm a doctor," he answered soothingly. "I thought I could help."

"If you want to help, leave me alone and let me go."

"You speak English very well," said Matt, deliberately changing the subject. "You have no accent. Where did you learn to speak English so well?"

"Why shouldn't I?" she said curtly. "I was born in this country."

"You're an American?" Matt responded with surprise. "Then what are you doing here?"

"I was on holiday abroad. I am returning from Europe."

"You don't understand," said Matt. "If you are an American, you shouldn't even be here on Ellis Island. Somehow, you got yourself mixed in with aliens coming to this country."

"That's why I want you to let me go!" she insisted.

"Of course," Matt replied softly. "This is no place for you. If you'll just give me your revolver, I'll get you out of here immediately."

The woman studied Matt. Then, with his promise of prompt release, she handed him the weapon. Matt then signaled Guenter and the other gateman hovering nearby, and they led her away.

Matt returned to examining the immigrants. About thirty minutes later, Guenter returned.

"Dr. Stafford," he said, coming up to Matt's side, "guess what the matron found on that crazy American woman?"

Matt turned to him and replied, "What?"

"Besides the revolver, she was carrying a dagger with an eight-inch blade and a point like a needle!"

"Really?"

"Yes," Guenter answered. "Can you imagine if she had pulled out the knife instead of the gun? She might've stabbed you when she first came up behind you!"

"Maybe, but one stabbing is enough for me," said Matt. "Where is she now?"

"Dr. Stoner is about to have the matron take her on a cutter over to Bellevue for a psychiatric examination."

"Good. There's no doubt in my mind that she's a very disturbed woman."

"You were lucky, Dr. Stafford. Tonight I'll treat for the beers."

"You've got a deal, Guenter, but no other stops afterward, if you get my meaning."

Matt had not been to the bordello since Buffalo, although he did return a few times before that. He and Guenter had not gone again together since that first time more than a year ago.

"Oh no, Dr. Stafford," Guenter replied, laughing. "I don't do that anymore. I've got a girlfriend now."

"Good for you, Guenter. All right, then, we'll have a few beers later."

"Yes, sir," said Guenter brightly.

Matt returned to his duties, looking forward to sharing some beers and conversation with his friend, but not as much as he looked forward to his day off tomorrow with Nicole.

June 1902

Commissioner Williams, now in office for two months, was preparing the annual report for the fiscal year. He planned to announce that all past immigration records had been broken, and a rising tide of immigrants at Ellis Island was creating a serious strain on the island's limited resources, once thought to be sufficient for all future immigration.

He also made his move against the concessionaires. Fed up with their arrogance and exploitation of immigrants, he informed the baggage, food, and money-changing vendors that their contracts would not be renewed at the end of the month. He requested bids from other firms and had already selected those who seemed to offer the best service. He looked forward to a much better situation.

One area of improvement already producing positive results was in the respectful treatment of immigrants. His daily tours, a suggestion from Senner, ensured that humane processing was now the norm. The change was apparent everywhere.

Williams's emphasis coincided nicely with Mueller's *modus operandi*. His successes over the years partly resulted from his ingratiating charm and feigned kindness to his targeted victims. Feeling secure in his developing alliance with the new commissioner, John resumed his domination of the Board of Special Inquiry, influencing decisions regarding questionable cases in return for handsome rewards from concerned relatives.

Presently, John's attentions were on the pretty young girl sitting opposite him in one of the hearing rooms. She was twenty-one, traveling alone, and vulnerable.

Beginning the ploy that so often resulted in sexual adventures with intimidated young females, he smiled at her and said, "I'm afraid, Miss Steinholz, there are a few irregularities in your papers. Perhaps, though, we can work something out. Let us see."

*   *   *

During lunch hour, Matt was eating outside with Guenter and Frank near the sea wall, where they could enjoy the almost perfect June day and occasionally gaze at the harbor activity or New York City skyline. Matt treasured these special opportunities for friendly conversation, especially now when Nicole was vacationing overseas with James and Tom.

"How did your morning go, Frank?" he asked.

"It was wonderful, Dr. Stafford. I got to be a witness at another wedding. It's one of the things I like best about this job."

Guenter looked at Frank with a sly smile.

"How many times have you done this?" asked Matt. "Seems like you always are."

"More than a hundred times now, I think," Frank replied. "You know the Immigration Bureau. They won't let a single woman leave with her fiancé unless they have a civil ceremony in our chapel first."

"Yes, I know," Guenter answered. "They are so afraid her morals will be compromised, they want a ceremony here even if their wedding is planned for the same day."

"It's called 'moral turpitude,' fellas," said Matt. "The government wants to prevent women coming here as prostitutes. That's why they make certain everything is nice and legal before the couple leaves the island."

"Well, I don't care about the reason," Frank said. "I just get a lot of pleasure watching these loving couples take their vows at the beginning point of their lives in America."

Matt smiled but kept silent. Frank's comment endeared the man even more to him. It reminded him of his own feelings about interacting with the immigrants from his first day on the island and ever since. He had not lost his enthusiasm about meeting them, despite all the problems and pressures since that first day.

"Speaking of couples taking their vows," said Guenter, "by coincidence I have some news to tell."

"Guenter, don't tell me you—"

"Yes, Matt, I'm getting married."

"*Buon Dio!*" exclaimed Frank in surprise. "It's about time!"

"Congratulations, Guenter! That's wonderful!" added Matt, smiling happily.

"So tell us all about it," Frank implored.

"Well, her name is Marie-Helene."

"That doesn't sound German," said Frank.

"Why would you think she'd be German?"

"Because you are!" answered Frank.

"Well, she's not German. She's French Canadian. Her family moved from Quebec to Lowell, Massachusetts, where she was raised, and she came to New York about a year ago."

"How old is she?" probed Frank.

"She's twenty-four and she's beautiful, with blue eyes and black hair, to answer your next question."

"Where'd you meet her?"

"At a dance social last October."

"Oh, I thought you might have met her at the kissing post when you were assigned to work there."

"Very funny, Frank."

"What and where is the kissing post?" asked Matt.

"It's in the west wing by that partition for the detainees. It's the first place immigrants get to reunite with their loved ones here in America."

"Oh, I know where you mean," said Matt.

"You should go there sometime, Matt," Frank commented. "I can't begin to tell you how many times I have seen friends, sweethearts, husbands, wives, parents, and children shriek, embrace one another, kiss, and shed tears of joy. I often get a lump in my throat and all teary-eyed when I observe those moments."

"I will definitely have a look," said Matt.

"Good. Maybe then the magic of the kissing post will rub off on you," Frank responded. "You're about to be the only bachelor among the three of us. Your turn is next."

"We'll see," said Matt, grinning, as he envisioned Nicole marching down the church aisle as he waited for her at the altar.

*   *   *

Less pleasant thoughts were in the mind of New York Governor Benjamin Odell. He was outraged at Williams's severance of the contracts of the concessionaires. So too were several congressmen and political bosses, some of whom were financial backers of the concessionaires and shared in the profits. Whatever their motives, all protested loudly to the president and demanded that Roosevelt overrule Williams. In response, the president summoned Williams to the White House.

"You certainly have stirred up a hornets' nest, Mr. Williams," Roosevelt said in a gruff voice.

"So I understand, sir," he simply replied.

"Virtually every New York politician is pressuring me to rescind your recommendations on replacing the concessionaires."

"Is that what you intend to do, Mr. President?"

Roosevelt paused before answering, looking directly at Williams and trying to size up the man.

"Mr. Williams, I want you to explain why you believe these actions are necessary."

"Mr. President, when you offered me this post, you said the immigrants were being improperly inspected, robbed, and abused. You asked me to meet that challenge and clean up the place."

"Yes, and that's indeed what I want you to do."

"You also said you'd stand by me when I ruffled some feathers."

"So I did, but the concessionaires? How are they a part of the problem? If I support you on this, I need something to say to quiet your critics."

For an hour, the two men talked privately, with Williams detailing the many abuses. Because of the extensive fraud at the money exchange, with immigrants often cheated out of as much as 75 percent of their savings, Williams asked the president for authority to terminate this vendor's contract even before it expired, saying he wanted to make an example of him. The others could wait until the end of the month to be replaced.

Williams also made clear to Roosevelt that he would resign his position if he did not have a free hand to eliminate corruption, no matter whose toes got stepped on.

Roosevelt was convinced. He pledged his full support and later informed the New York congressional delegation that he intended to back Williams all the way. To Governor Odell he wrote, "The management of the Ellis Island business has been rotten in the past, and Williams has got to make a thorough sweeping out."

Charlie Burke, upon learning of Roosevelt's commitment to cleaning up Ellis Island, thought the timing was right to settle an old debt.

"Mr. President," Burke began, "your actions in this matter are commendable, but there's an unfinished piece of business that could undermine all you are doing in standing up to the New York delegation."

"What's that, Charlie?" asked Roosevelt, aware that Burke's political astuteness had served him well thus far.

"It's the McSweeney case, sir. There was all that publicity about wrongdoing on his part, and since then the government has taken no action. There are rumors of a White House cover-up. Some of your enemies are calling you a hypocrite and that you protect your friends no matter what they do."

"What?" Roosevelt roared.

"This could hit you with both barrels, sir. Public opinion could turn against you, and the New York delegation would also believe you were double dealing them."

"Damnation! I won't have it, Charlie! What do you suggest?"

After conferring with his attorney general, Philander Knox, Roosevelt's office announced to the press that he had directed the prosecution of Edward McSweeney on charges of abstracting and unlawfully withdrawing public records and documents. The US Attorney of the Southern District of New York, Henry Burnett, who had gained fame years earlier as the prosecutor of Abraham Lincoln's assassins, would be the government's prosecutor of McSweeney.

July 1902

"Gentlemen," said the commissioner to the men seated at the table with him, "I invited you here as my way of thanking you for the dedicated service you render. Although the Public Health Service is now independent of the Immigration Bureau, I want us nonetheless to remain closely bonded to one another, as we all work together in dealing with the immigrants."

The physicians and Williams were seated in a private dining area of the restaurant, having lunch. Williams had arranged the luncheon meeting partly to seek a closer bonding with the key personnel in the newly named Public Health Service and partly to ferret out any information from them that he could about his operation.

According to protocol, Williams, as commissioner, sat next to Stoner, the chief medical officer. As their time together neared its end, Williams complimented Stoner on the fine assistance he had with the men under his supervision.

"Thank you, Mr. Williams," replied Stoner, "but I would imagine you are equally fortunate."

"I wish I were," he candidly replied, "but I'm not. It's no secret that my assistant isn't worth a damn."

"I'm sorry to hear that. You don't think Joe Murray is pulling his weight?'

"He's a complete incompetent. He doesn't do half of what he should. I think he should move his office to the island's barber shop, since he spends so much time there every day."

"I'm sorry to hear that," said Stoner sympathetically. He and his medical team had virtually no interaction with Murray and had no firm opinion about him one way or the other. "Can you get rid of him?"

"Not easily. He's an old crony of the president, and he's protected by civil service. Oh, let's not talk about him anymore. It'll only give me indigestion. How are things over in that new hospital of yours?"

"Real fine. My only concern is that we can't handle patients with contagious diseases, and if the number of immigrants keeps growing the way it has, we won't even be able to handle normal cases."

"I know. The numbers are incredible. We are processing far more than anyone expected. We need to expand our facilities before we are overwhelmed."

Sitting alongside Stoner, Matt had been a quiet listener to this conversation, and he decided to speak up.

"Commissioner," began Matt, "there's something that I'd like to talk to you about."

"What is it, Dr. Stafford?"

"Well, maybe it's nothing, but given the scandals and what you've uncovered so far, I think I should tell you about it."

"All right, you have my attention. Tell me."

"A few weeks ago, I was examining immigrants on the line since I was needed there, as I often am these days. Anyway, there was this boy whose eyes had such a vacant stare that I thought he was dull witted, and so I marked him for further examination. When he was later given the usual jigsaw puzzle to solve that we require of all such suspected cases, he couldn't do it. He couldn't answer the basic questions in logic either, so we ruled him mentally incapacitated and planned to have him deported."

"Obviously something happened," said Williams, "or you would not be telling this story."

"That's right," Matt answered. "Next morning, I caught up on my paperwork and wrote up the boy's chart. When I went to put my report in his file for the hearing board, I discovered that the board had already admitted him. I was stunned to hear they had acted so fast and without our documentation."

"Have you ever known a board to act without such a report before?"

"No, I haven't."

"Did you speak to anyone about it?"

"Well, I asked John Mueller."

"What did he say?"

"He said we've been getting so many immigrants that some slip-ups are inevitable. He said he'd check on it."

"Did he?"

"Yes, he did. He said it was as he suspected, that it was a slip-up and a case where the board's efficiency outstripped my own."

"I see. Tell me the boy's name," Williams requested, not pleased with what he'd heard.

Afterward, Williams returned to the main building and began to check the admission records personally. He looked at numerous manifest sheets, discharge sheets, and transcriptions of hearings conducted by the Board of Special Inquiry. The more he looked, the more irregularities he found. He was stunned at his discoveries. Suddenly, Allan Robinson, his secretary, interrupted.

"Excuse me, Commissioner, there are two people waiting to see you. They insist upon talking to you at once."

"Do you know what it is about?"

"They wish to make a complaint about someone."

Williams got up and went to his office. He spoke with his visitors for almost an hour, his secretary recording everyone's comments. Then he spoke with them further, while their remarks were being typed, after which he asked for their signatures. After they left, he sent for Mueller.

"Hello, Commissioner," said the cheerful registry chief as he entered the office.

"Sit down, Mr. Mueller," Williams replied quietly. "I have some questions to ask you."

"Sir?"

"You know Allan Robinson, my secretary?"

"Yes, sir. Hello, Mr. Robinson."

Robinson nodded his head as Williams continued. "I have asked Mr. Robinson to record this conversation. Do you have any objections?"

Mueller realized something was in the wind. Instantly on his guard, he faked a casual attitude.

"Not at all, Mr. Williams. How can I help you?"

"Do you know Morten Knudsen?"

"The name does not sound familiar, sir," John replied, his mind racing to connect the name with any incident.

"He came through on June 18, a dull-witted boy who the doctor classified as mentally incapacitated. He was nonetheless admitted by the Board of Special Inquiry, in a decision directed by you."

"Directed by me? No, sir, that's not possible. The board is an independent tribunal."

Williams persisted. "The transcript shows one board member saying to the others that you wanted the boy admitted."

"There's something wrong here, sir. The transcript doesn't tell everything."

"Since when don't transcripts tell everything, Mr. Mueller?"

"Look, Commissioner. I remember this case now. There was a little political pressure here, and I mentioned something about that to Mr. Haggerty, but I assure you, I did not direct them to do anything."

"Let's leave that for moment," Williams said, readying his second salvo. "I found several manifest sheets in which you marked 'hold' against the names of immigrants, all of whom, by the way, are shown on the manifests as carrying considerable sums of money. You had these people brought to you personally for inspection."

"Yes, there were a few like that, Commissioner," John answered, his pulse racing. "I did that as special favors to some congressmen. You know, the royal treatment for VIPs."

"VIPs in steerage?"

"Not in that sense, Commissioner. I mean they were aliens some politicians wanted processed carefully."

"I would hope all arrivals are processed carefully, Mr. Mueller. I will want the names of those politicians from you, so I can check your story. I have also found instances of your personally examining detained immigrants and then discharging them, bypassing the Board of Special Inquiry."

"Commissioner," John laughed nervously, "what are you accusing me of? Those were cases that didn't need to go before the board. I never bypassed or dictated to any board. All I did was my job, something others before you have praised me for doing."

Unimpressed, Williams continued. "At best, Mr. Mueller, these were inappropriate actions. The resulting power of blackmail from your interference with normal processing can be readily seen."

"Commissioner, I assure you—"

"I don't want your assurances, Mr. Mueller," interrupted Williams. "Tell me, is the name Mildred Steinholz familiar to you?"

A chill coursed through him, but John held his ground, answering, "I don't recall the name, Mr. Williams."

"Well, let me refresh your memory. She is one of those immigrants you recently examined for entry."

"Are you certain?" John asked, his agile mind racing ahead for a means to escape the enclosing trap.

"Absolutely certain," Williams insisted.

"I still don't recall the name," John said and paused for effect. "Oh, wait a minute. Yes, now I remember her. Yes, I did examine someone by that name."

"Why?"

"I don't understand."

"Why did you, the chief clerk of the Registry Division, examine her?"

"As I recall, we were heavily backed up that day. I stepped in to assist."

"So," Williams countered, "you examined other immigrants as well that day?"

"Well, no," John admitted, realizing the commissioner knew otherwise.

"Why not? Why just this one female?"

"I had planned to do others, but I was called away."

"Why was that?"

"I don't recall just now, but it was a problem brought to my attention by one of my inspectors. Commissioner, with the heavy number of immigrants coming, day in and day out, and with so many demands on me, it's hard to remember the specifics of one particular day."

"Perhaps you can recall the specifics as to why you examined Miss Steinholz in a private room instead of out in the hall with your clerks," Williams said sternly.

John had not expected this. How did Williams know? She obviously made a complaint. *Little bitch*, he thought. Quickly, he came up with an answer.

"Sir, it was very crowded and noisy in the Registry Hall. No space was available. I admit that I used my rank to conduct the interview in a less hectic atmosphere."

"Why did you select this particular young woman? Her name is in the middle of the manifest sheet!"

"She was next in line. I didn't seek her out, although I must say, she was a good looker."

"Well, Mr. Mueller, I have a signed statement from this 'good looker,' as you call her, that you attempted sexual blackmail against her."

"What?" John uttered, stunned at the gravity of the charge.

"You propositioned her. You told her she would not be admitted. You demanded her sexual favors in return for clearance to land."

"Mr. Williams, that is an outright lie! I am a family man. I would never do such a thing!"

"Then why would she make such a serious charge?"

"I don't know, sir. Perhaps she misinterpreted something I said."

"Not likely, Mr. Mueller. The two of you spoke in German, and she understood you clearly."

"Mr. Williams," John protested, desperately trying to save himself, "does this woman claim we were actually intimate?"

"No, she does not."

Recovering his composure, John then asked, "And the records show that I admitted her, don't they?"

"Yes."

"Well, that proves the lie right there," John replied, more self-assured. "I examined her, found everything in order, and simply admitted her."

"She claims you admitted her on the condition that she meet you that evening in a hotel."

"Oh, that is utter nonsense, Mr. Williams. What hold could

I have on her once she was released? Besides, think of the long hours we all work here. After a hard day's work, all I want to do is go home, enjoy my wife's dinner, and relax."

"Perhaps, Mr. Mueller. Or perhaps you left the island early that day. We can check on that, and we can check if you made any arrangements at the hotel where you tried to send Miss Steinholz."

"Go ahead, Commissioner. I'm certain you will find no connection. I have had no dealings with whatever hotel that is. It is that immigrant woman's word against mine. I have many years of faithful service with the Immigration Bureau. My proven performance has been rewarded several times with promotions right up to my present rank."

"Mr. Mueller, my concern is with these serious charges against you and the many irregularities that I have found, all of which involve you."

"Commissioner, I am innocent of any wrongdoing. These things are lies, misunderstandings, and normal processing taken out of context to look improper. I assure you, sir, nothing is improper."

"Well, Mr. Mueller," Williams replied, "it appears that either you are an innocent man who is the victim of some combination of misunderstandings and remarkable coincidences, or else you are a first-class scoundrel. I want you to take a two-week vacation, effective immediately. My secretary, Mr. Robinson, will temporarily take over your duties. While you are away, we will conduct a full investigation. You will have a hearing and an opportunity to answer all charges. Good day."

"Mr. Williams, I—"

"Good day, sir!"

Curtly dismissed, John headed for the records office. Systematically he went through the files, destroying as many incriminating records as he could find. Then he went to his own office and did the same. Satisfied that he had eliminated any evidence that could substantiate any charges against him, he left the island, convinced he would be reinstated.

"Allegations are one thing," he said aloud to himself, "but proof is another. It's now that woman's word against mine. I'm protected by civil service, and they can't dismiss me without cause. Williams will soon discover that he cannot get rid of me. I'll be back, Williams. Count on it."

September 1902

The leaves had not yet assumed their brilliantly colored mantles of autumn, even though the new season had officially begun. Green hues still dominated the landscape, today complemented by a bright blue sky and darker blue river gently flowing by Ellis Island.

On the island, government employees were abuzz about John Mueller, who clearly had underestimated Commissioner Williams. Just prior to the end of his two-week vacation, John received notice that he was suspended without pay, pending an investigation of his official conduct.

Even though John destroyed many incriminating records, Williams filed eighteen charges against him, including the destruction or mutilation of official files. In addition, the commissioner charged Mueller with "indignities perpetrated against women, favoritism in assignments given inspectors, permitting immigrants to be forced into working for the former restaurant concessionaire, accepting wines and other gifts from the steamship companies, and interference in virtually every branch of the Immigration Service."

John fought back, steadfastly maintaining his innocence. He answered all the charges in detail, claiming he was not responsible for some of the alleged violations while denying others outright. However, when he sensed things were not going well for him, he offered to resign in return for the suppression of all charges and the expunging of his record except for his commendations.

Williams refused, and in Washington, Commissioner-General Frank Sargent heartily supported him. In a letter released to the press, Sargent wrote to Williams, "I do not believe in allowing rascals to go out of the service by resignation with letters of endorsement of good character and faithful service, when we know them to be unprincipled scoundrels."

Emboldened, Williams then announced he had dismissed Mueller from the Immigration Service, and was turning all evidence over to the Manhattan district attorney for grand jury action. In his statement to the press, Williams declared his full intention to root out all corruption, brutality, and incompetence on the island. To make his point, he announced the suspension of two inspectors and charged them with threatening deportation unless immigrants paid them bribes.

Meanwhile, across the river in the federal building in lower Manhattan, Edward McSweeney appeared before US Commissioner John Shields to answer charges pressed against him by the US government.

Ed had come down from his home in Boston with a retinue of supporters, including Col. William A. Gaston, the unsuccessful Massachusetts gubernatorial candidate, for whom Ed now worked as private secretary.

Henry Burnett stood up to read the charges. An imposing courtroom figure, his reputation as a formidable opponent preceded him. Since mustering out of the army with the rank of a brevet brigadier general, Burnett had such a brilliant career as a trial lawyer that *Bench and Bar of New York* called him "the peer of the greatest advocate of the age." Now he was the district attorney of the Southern District of New York, appointed in 1898 by President McKinley, with whom he had been on especially close terms.

With understandable trepidation, McSweeney listened to the words of his prosecutor.

"This complaint," began Burnett, "charges Edward McSweeney with embezzling the following papers just before Stepping down as Assistant Commissioner of Immigration for the Port of New York:

1. A letter from the Austro-Hungarian Consul to Commissioner Fitchie, dated October 23, 1901;

2. An affidavit of Rebecca Cohn, dated June 17, 1897;

3. Letters from T. V. Powderly, US Commissioner-General to Commissioner of Immigration Thomas Fitchie, dated May 20, 1900;

4. An affidavit of Mary Maroney, dated February 20, 1899;

5. A receipt for five pounds sterling, signed by E. P. Johnson, surgeon;

6. Sworn testimony in certain immigrant cases;

7. Correspondence between the Acting Secretary of the Treasury and the Commissioner of Immigration at New York;

8. Papers containing the answer of August W. Bostram to charges made against him by the Commissioner of Immigration at New York;

9. A similar answer of Inspector A. A. Wimmer to charges;

10. Several department reports.

"These charges are detailed in the papers previously provided to defense counsel and the US commissioner. However, they are not all the charges we plan to bring against the defendant."

"Commissioner Shields?"

"Yes, Mr. Rose?"

Abram J. Rose, McSweeney's lawyer, rose from his seat. His deep baritone voice, thick silver hair, and handsome appearance gave him a charismatic presence in the hearing room.

"In all my years as an attorney, I have never dealt with a case as flimsy as this one. These charges are so trivial that I am astounded that everyone's time is being wasted here. The ten counts refer to inconsequential papers of no value to my client, or to the government, for that matter. I move for dismissal of all charges."

"General Burnett?" the commissioner said simply.

"Commissioner, the government does not consider these charges to be trivial, and since no evidence has yet been presented, there is no basis for requesting a dismissal. In fact, we plan to amend the complaint to add further charges. For that reason, the government requests a continuance of this case."

"Mr. Shields, I must strenuously object to this motion," Abram Rose countered. "Mr. McSweeney has come down to New York specifically to answer these ridiculous charges. He has rightly expected an immediate hearing. Requesting an adjournment now is unfair. If the government is not ready to try this case, it should have said so before inconveniencing everyone else here present."

"Mr. Shields," began Burnett courteously, "there were hundreds of papers to examine. We have only just discovered several other papers we wish to add to the list of embezzled government documents."

"You should have completed your work before filing the charges," Rose admonished his adversary.

"Would you prefer we presently deal with only these charges, and then have your client answer the other charges at a later date?" countered Burnett. "I think it would be in everyone's best interests if we adjourned."

"How much time do you need, General Burnett?" asked Commissioner Shields.

"Two weeks."

"What do you say, Mr. Rose?" Shields asked.

Rose quietly consulted with Ed and responded, "All right, we'll consent to an adjournment until one week after I have received the amended complaint."

"I will set bail at $1,500," said Shields, "and we stand adjourned until October 2."

After posting bail, Ed and his companions left the building. Outside, reporters clamored for comments.

"Mr. McSweeney, what do you have to say about this?"

"What's your side of the story?"

"Are you guilty?"

Rose seized the opportunity to secure some favorable press for his client.

"Mr. McSweeney is not worried about the charges against him. They are of the most trivial nature. The papers on which the complaint is based were contained in boxes that clerks packed for Mr. McSweeney, boxes he had not yet sent for after going to Boston. Mr. McSweeney never removed these boxes from Ellis Island. Secret Service investigators removed the boxes and opened them. They found the papers in question along with private papers, such as a letter from Mr. McSweeney's wife."

"Why were the documents with his private papers?"

"They were put there by accident," Rose answered, "by clerks who packed the boxes. What is important to note here is that the papers were never out of the actual physical possession of the government at any time. No jury would ever convict my client of theft, since no theft ever occurred."

"Are those papers of any value?" a reporter asked Rose.

"Not by the wildest stretch of the imagination could those old letters and affidavits specified in the complaint have been of any use to my client. If he had really wanted them, and if they had been of any value to him that he was willing to steal government property to have them, it seems obvious he would have just removed them directly, inside his coat pocket. This case is a sham, a political vendetta."

"Whose vendetta, Mr. Rose?"

"I leave that for you to find out, gentlemen. Good day."

With that, Rose ushered Ed away from the reporters and into their waiting vehicle.

*   *   *

Their lovemaking ended, Tom watched Nicole get up from the bed and go into the bathroom. Hearing the water running in the sink, he followed her, and through the partly opened door, he saw her wiping her eyes with a face cloth.

Silently, he returned to the bed, and when she rejoined him, he asked, "Nicole, what's wrong?"

Instantly on her guard, she answered with her own question, "Why do you think there's something wrong?"

Looking at her in the darkness, searching for the right words, he replied simply, "You know there is. You hardly ever want to make love anymore, and when we do, your heart doesn't seem to be in it."

"I—I don't know what to say," she replied truthfully, torn between telling him everything or nothing.

"Look, I've been away for three weeks. This is my first night back. I thought you would've missed me enough so that tonight would be special between us. Instead, it didn't even seem like you got any pleasure out of it at all."

"No," she lied, "it was fine. Some times are just quieter, that's all."

"I know you well enough," he countered, "to know it's more than that and that this isn't the first time."

"I'm sorry, Tom," she began, struggling for the right approach to take. "Maybe part of the problem is that you are away so often and for so long."

"What does that mean?"

"I don't know. I guess I have a hard time adjusting. We're not newlyweds anymore. I'm not an electric light that you can suddenly turn on after I've been off for so long."

"I thought that absence makes the heart grow fonder."

"Oh, Tom, give me more time. It'll be different next time, you'll see."

"All right, darling. Next time, I'll try to find the right switch to turn you on."

She forced a laugh, kissed him on the forehead, and turned away from him.

They both lay there in silence, thoughts racing through their minds.

Lying on his back, staring at the ceiling, as his wife lay on her side with her back to him, Tom replayed their conversation in his mind. Not only was he dissatisfied with what she had said, he also became more suspicious as he dwelled on her passionless intimacy. He decided that tomorrow he would hire a private detective to get the real answers.

October 2, 1902

"Mr. Fitchie," began Abram Rose, "can you offer any explanation as to the presence of government papers among Mr. McSweeney's personal papers."

"Yes, I believe I can," answered the ex-commissioner, the first defense witness called in McSweeney's trial after the government had rested its case.

"Please tell us," Rose prompted.

"When I assumed my duties in 1897, we were at the Barge Office. When it became necessary to move back to Ellis Island, there was a general mix-up of papers."

"You are saying that both personal and government papers were packed together when your department relocated to Ellis Island?"

"Yes."

"Why?"

"It was a matter of expediency. We simply packed whatever we could into the boxes. We were also behind in our filing. You'll note all of the papers in question predate our relocation."

"Mr. Fitchie, were you aware at the time that this mixing of government and personal papers had occurred?"

"Of course I was. We simply threw everything together to get the job done, with the intent of straightening out everything later."

"Why didn't things get straightened out later?"

"I'm not sure. You know how we say the road to hell is paved with good intentions. I suspect we just got caught up in everyday work that we put it off and then forgot about it. Immigration kept increasing and so did the paperwork. We never had enough hours in the day to keep even, let alone go back to refile, even if we had remembered."

Fitchie proved to be a strong defense witness, but Abram Rose had yet another.

"What is your full name, sir?" he asked.

"John William Steele."

"What is your connection to Edward McSweeney?"

"I was a clerk in his office when he was the assistant commissioner."

"Do you have any knowledge about the packing of government papers among Mr. McSweeney's personal effects?"

"Yes, I do."

"Please tell us what you know."

"Mr. McSweeney told me to pack his personal papers in the five empty wooden boxes in his office. I was to nail up the boxes and forward them to his Boston address. I emptied all the drawers of his desk into the boxes, and also the file cases that were marked 'personal.' Before I could ship the boxes, Secret Service agents came and confiscated them."

"So the boxes never left government possession? They were in your possession until the agents took them, is that right?"

"Yes, sir, that's correct."

"Did Mr. McSweeney supervise your packing?"

"No, he did not."

"So he had no knowledge of what you put into the boxes?"

"No, he couldn't have."

"Did you realize you were putting government papers in the boxes?"

"No."

"Didn't you read them to be sure?"

"There were thousands of papers. I just packed them all into the boxes. I just assumed they were all his personal effects."

Since Rose earlier had the Secret Service agents admit no government papers were in the folders marked "personal" when they examined the contents of the seized boxes, he had fully demonstrated that McSweeney had not engineered any theft. He next played his last ace.

He had Ed testify. Ed was a calm, self-assured defendant. After he corroborated both Fitchie's and Steele's testimony, Rose asked him, "Of what value could those papers be to you or anyone else?"

"None of these papers can be of any possible advantage to me or anyone else. They are old records and useless. They are not worth stealing. No one could find any use for them whatsoever. It is beyond ridiculous to be accused of stealing absolutely worthless pieces of paper."

When testimony concluded, Commissioner Shields held off announcing his decision on whether or not to move for an indictment. He had already decided to absolve McSweeney of any wrongdoing, but not to announce that yet. Since he had sixty days to make his recommendation, he would wait.

12:30 PM

Matt hungrily kissed her, and Nicole responded with equal fervor. Each time for them was like the first time, each lovemaking session as passionate and rewarding as the one before. Matt couldn't wait until they got into the bedroom.

There, in the parlor, he began undressing her as he continued to kiss and caress her. As her dress fell to the floor, he picked her up and carried her into the bedroom.

Outside, Dennis Cahill, a retired police sergeant and now private detective, chuckled and put away his spyglass. He had followed Nicole to Matt's place, watching from across the street as she entered the building. Pleased that two weeks of tailing her had finally yielded results, he figured, rightly, that it would be awhile before his subject would leave. Meanwhile, he kept an eye out for the postman, planning to extract nonchalantly any information he could about who lived there.

A couple of hours later, Matt and Nicole, their desires temporarily abated, were in the midst of their normal in-between talking time. She told him of her conversation with Tom when he questioned her lack of passion.

"Matt," she said, looking directly into his eyes, "I've thought of nothing else ever since. I absolutely cannot go on like this any longer. I'm going to tell Tom everything."

"When?"

"Tonight. He's working late tonight. I'll go there so there's no chance of James hearing anything. I wanted to talk to you first, though, to be certain this is still what you want me to do."

"Of course it is," Matt quickly answered, a joyous excitement filling him. "I'll go with you."

"I don't think that's a good idea, Matt. Your being there would probably make things worse."

"You shouldn't have to face him alone. He thinks I'm his friend. I should stand before him like a man, not hide like some skulking dog. Let's try to talk things through reasonably like adults, for everyone's sake, particularly James. Besides, you shouldn't travel down to that area alone after dark."

"All right, Matt. We'll do this together." Hugging him, she

added, "Oh, Matt, this is going to be the most difficult night of my life."

"That's also why I want to be there with you."

He embraced and caressed her, then kissed her, tenderly at first, then more passionately as she willingly returned his loving. Despite the uneasy evening they knew they must face, these moments at least were theirs, away from all of life's cares, and they made the most of them.

4:30 PM

Cahill had followed Nicole back home. From a talkative postman he had learned Matt's name and position. Eager to make his report and collect his money, he telephoned Tom.

"I've got that information you wanted, Mr. Lindstrom."

"Yes?"

"Yes, sir. When would you like me to stop by and give you my report?"

"I'm pretty busy right now. How about if you come here at seven thirty?"

"That's fine. I'll see you then. Goodbye, sir."

Tom hung up the phone, feeling a mixture of sadness and anger. Though not surprised, he was hurt and uncertain how he would react once he learned the details.

5:30 PM

"What's yer hurry, Johnny boy?"

Mueller looked at the Irish tough who had just grabbed him and yanked him into an alleyway. He knew that the man and his rough-looking companion were collectors for O'Bannion.

John's gambling losses had put him three hundred dollars into debt to O'Bannion. With his income cut off from his many Ellis Island enterprises, John had no way of paying him. He had not saved any of his previous "earnings," content instead to spend it on himself and others for drink, whores, and gambling.

"Look, Tim, I'm on my way to close a big deal. Should bring me a big bundle of change."

"Will it now, me boy? Well, that's good. That's good. 'Cause ya see, Mr. O'Bannion's getting mighty anxious about that money ya owe him, be jasus, seeing as how ya been fired and facing that trial real soon on yer conduct."

"O'Bannion's got nothing to worry about. I told you I'm about to close a big deal, and I gotta get there now. O'Bannion wouldn't like it if you caused me to blow it."

"No, we wouldn't want that to happen, now would we? So ya be on yer way now, ya hear? But before ya go, Mr. O'Bannion wants me to give ya this reminder about prompt payment."

He threw his fist fiercely into Mueller's stomach, doubling him over. John cried out in pain.

"Just a minor preview, Johnny boy, if ya don't have Mr. O'Bannion's money by Friday."

Holding his stomach, John looked up at the departing men. Then he slowly headed to the saloon where he was to meet Kevin McGaffney.

Joining him at a back table, John ordered a boilermaker. He threw the shot of whiskey down his throat and washed it down with the beer chaser.

McGaffney studied John's actions before asking, "Anything wrong? Ya look upset."

"Nothing I can't handle. Tell me, did you find out when he'll have the money there?"

"Yeah, he'll get the money delivered in an hour as usual. Then he'll make out his payroll, putting the bills in each guy's envelope, before putting them all in the safe. He always does this between seven and eight. If we get to him sometime after seven, when it's dark enough, that money's ours."

"Are you sure of the amount?"

"John, it's like I told ya. It's around seven hundred smackeroos. That's what he needs to make that big a payroll."

"Are you sure that he's always alone when he does this?"

"John, he's been alone each time the last three weeks. I've seen him through the back window. I'm telling ya, this will be a piece a cake."

"All right, then," said Mueller, knowing this was his only means of getting O'Bannion off his back. "In two hours we'll both be a lot richer than we are now."

7:00 PM

"Come in, Dr. Stafford," said the smiling Irish housekeeper. "Mrs. Lindstrom will be right down."

"Thank you, Miss Reilly. It's good to see you again."

"Thank you, sir."

Nicole descended the stairway, radiant as ever, this time in a dark green, S-curve dress in the art nouveau fashion of the times.

"Hello, Matt," she said, greeting him. "I'll be just a moment."

"Hello, Nicole," he replied, delighting in her appearance, as he watched her strategically place the hatpin to hold her wide-brimmed hat with its plumed feathers. Taking the proffered coat from Miss Reilly, he helped Nicole put it on and guided her to the front door.

Saying their goodbyes to the housekeeper, they walked to the waiting cab to take them to Tom's office and to a difficult but necessary encounter.

7:25 PM

In his company office near the docks, Tom was seated at his desk, finishing his final task of the day when the gunmen broke in through the back door.

"Don't move. Don't talk. Don't do nothing," McGaffney demanded, pointing his gun right at Tom.

Tom froze. He looked at the two men, each with drawn guns and wearing caps and bandannas covering their faces below their eyes. Mueller threw the money and envelopes into a brown bag.

"Now just sit there, quiet-like, for five minutes," he instructed, "if ya know what's good for ya."

As the men turned and hurried to the door, Tom reached into his desk for his revolver, quickly aimed, and fired twice.

His first shot hit McGaffney in the head, killing him instantly. His second shot missed Mueller. Tom fired again, hitting him in the fleshy part of his side, right below the rib cage, just as he wheeled around. Before Tom could shoot again, John fired his weapon. Tom felt the searing pain in his chest but managed to fire again, hitting his target in the leg before falling across his desk.

Mueller ran as best he could out the back door, leaving a trail of blood as he tried to escape with the money.

Cahill heard the shots as he approached. With his gun drawn, he ran into the office within seconds after Mueller ran out. Seeing the opened back door, he gave chase down the alley toward the street.

Closing in on the limping man, Cahill shouted, "Stop or I'll shoot!"

Mueller was not about to surrender. Knowing he could not outrun his pursuer, he wheeled around and fired.

Two shots rang out almost simultaneously. Mueller's shot was wild, but Cahill's found its mark, hitting Mueller in the heart. After ascertaining he had gotten his man, Cahill grabbed the bag and ran down the street back to the office, entering the front door.

Matt and Nicole arrived in time to see him run into the building. Concerned, they followed him. Matt, ahead of Nicole, rushed into the building and through the reception area and clerical office. He stopped at the back office doorway when he saw the dead man. Then he looked into the office and saw Cahill attempting to lift Tom off the desk.

As Matt rushed over to assist, Nicole was right behind him.

"Tom!" she screamed when she saw him, and she ran to his side.

They laid him on his back. Nicole bundled her coat, put it under his head, and held his hand. Matt tore open Tom's shirt to examine his wound, instantly realizing its seriousness. Cahill sprang to the telephone to get help.

"They've killed me," Tom said softly.

"Easy, Tom, you'll be all right. We'll get an ambulance."

"No, too late for that. Cahill!"

"Here, sir," he replied coming into Tom's view.

"Where's that report?"

"Right here, sir," Cahill answered, pulling it out of his inside pocket.

"Burn it, right now."

"Mr. Lindstrom!" Cahill protested.

Forcing his head up a little, Tom insisted, "Do it!"

Puzzled, Matt and Nicole watched Cahill strike a match, light the envelope, and hold it aloft to allow the flames to grow before placing it on the floor to be consumed fully.

Satisfied, Tom reclined into Nicole's arms and looked up into her tear-streaked eyes, saying, "I love you. I want you to be happy."

Weeping, she could only utter, "Oh, Tom," her grief preventing further words.

Turning slightly, he weakly said, "Matt, I owe this man some money. See that he gets it."

"I will," Matt agreed, puzzled.

His voice growing weaker, Tom gasped, "Look after Nicole and James for me."

"Of course," Matt answered, realizing those were the last words Tom would ever hear.

Nicole sobbed, still holding Tom in her arms. Neither of them moved for a few moments. Then Matt gently laid Tom's body completely onto the floor, helped her up, and led her into the next room while Cahill called the police. When they arrived, Cahill quietly greeted his old colleagues and explained what had happened.

After Tom's body was removed and they received clearance to leave, Matt secured a carriage and helped Nicole into it. Turning to Cahill who followed them out, he asked, "How much did Tom owe you?"

"Fifty dollars."

Matt took out his wallet and paid him.

"Thank you, sir."

"You're welcome. We're thankful you were here to get Tom's murderer. By the way, what was in that report that Tom had you burn?"

Cahill looked at Matt for a brief moment before answering, "It was just business. It's not important now."

Matt looked at him quizzically, nodded, shook his hand, and climbed into the carriage.

About the Author

Vincent N. Parrillo is a professor of sociology at William Paterson University of New Jersey. An internationally recognized expert on immigration, he is the executive producer, writer, and narrator of the award-winning PBS television documentary, *Ellis Island: Gateway to America* (1991). He is also the author of numerous articles and textbooks on immigration and diversity.

Author's Note

Matt Stafford, Nicole Devereaux, Guenter Langer, Frank Martiniello, John Mueller, and Kevin McGaffney are fictionalized composites of actual employees at Ellis Island in those times. The other main characters are real-life people. Although some liberties were taken for dramatic purposes, all the events described in this historical novel relating to the employees and immigrants at the Barge Office and Ellis Island are authentic. Often, however, the minor characters experiencing those events have pseudonyms. The primary sources for these occurrences were drawn from the pages of the *Brooklyn Eagle,* the *New York Times*, and the reminiscences of Ellis Island employees Frank Martoccia and Victor Safford.